The Things We Save

DATE DUE			
GAYLORD			PRINTED IN U.S.A.

ISBN: 1463696248
ISBN-13: 978-1463696245

LCCN: 2011914171

39905002768856

Grateful acknowledgement is paid for permission to reprint excerpts from the following
copyrighted works:
"Family Affair" by Sylvester Stewart. ©1971, 1991 Warner-Tamerlane Publishing
Corporation. Rights controlled by Mijac Music/Sony Music Corporation. All rights
reserved. Used by permission.
"Magic Carpet Ride" by John Kay and Rushton Moreve. ©1968, 1996 Universal Music
Publishing. All rights reserved. Used by permission.

For my father and my brother

ACKNOWLEDGMENTS

Many thanks to my family, Lar, Cecily and Simone, for their love and support, and for being the type of people who like to sleep-in, providing me with quiet mornings. Hugs and kisses to my first readers, Debi Workman and Sallee Brossard for saying the two things any writer wants to hear: "you made pictures in my head" and "that character was so real." Thank you to those mentors who encouraged me along the way, including Molly Ramanujan Daniels, who taught me the importance of the object.

And a very special thank you to anyone who ever told me "No."

CHAPTER 1

Everyone has a box. Oh, don't bother to deny it. You have one, you know it. It might be an old-fashioned steamer trunk made of wood, strapped with worn leather bands and framed with embossed metal corners. It might be a hyper-feminine heart-shaped box, lined in velvet or satin, girlish in pink or flaming in scarlet. Maybe it's a banker's box with an orderly progression of beige manila file folders. Or an ornately carved Chinese box with its surprising secret of a box within a box within a box—the opening of all those lids leading to … what?

That depends on who you are. For just as we all have boxes, same but different, what's inside them varies with the owner. One woman's treasure is another woman's trash. My artifacts, your detritus. My talisman, your fetish. Relics, debris, mementos, sediments, keepsakes, crumbs. And maybe it's not even the things themselves that are important—but how they got there, who they belonged to, why they were saved instead of discarded, why they were put in the box.

Because that's the story, isn't it? The story where you are the hero, on your hero's journey, answering the call to adventure, encountering your mentor, crossing the threshold to the other world where you'll be tested and forge alliances and make enemies and face the ultimate ordeal. It's the story where you

1

seize the elixir or the jewel or the ring and flee down the road, pursued by the furies, which you will vanquish. Or perhaps not. But you *will* return to your world, transformed, with the treasure in hand, older, wiser, a survivor.

And you'll place the object in your box. And set off on the next big adventure, for we are all Scheherazade, with tales to fill a thousand and one nights, warding off the sword with the cliff-hanger.

At some point, you'll stop adding things to the box, thinking that particular tale is at an end. And you'll tuck it away in a closet or up in the attic or down in the basement. And you'll forget about it... well, not really forget. You'll just move it out of your working memory, to free up space. But then one day you'll come across it, maybe when you're spring cleaning, or gathering items to drop off at the Recycling Extravaganza, or searching for that black cape that has attired many a Halloween trick-or-treater, from Dracula to Darth Vader. And when you open the box, the present-day world will fall away, and it will be just you and the things you saved, and the story.

This is what it means to be haunted.

The call came on a Tuesday evening in early May. The lilacs on the bush outside the back door were already withering, their sweet perfume decaying into a musky, earthier odor just this side of rot, the purple blossoms bruised and wilting, melting at the touch of my hand. Through the screendoor I saw Tally lunge for the telephone with the lithe grace and awkward anticipation of a sixteen year old in love. Her initial tone was low, expectant, almost sultry. Then her voice changed to the higher pitch of a child talking to an adult.

She murmured into the phone, turning every now and then to gaze over her shoulder in the direction of the screendoor and me. Then she held out the receiver and said loudly, to no one in particular, "It's Grandpa Joe."

So of course Aaron had to take it. He rose from the armchair he claims as his own when he's in residence, put his journal down on the end table with a weary sigh and glanced through the window as he made his way to the telephone.

I stepped down off the patio and moved to the stone bench under the maple tree, the better to watch him through the sunporch window, to interpret the tone and import of the conversation through his body language, because when he talked to my father he never talked loud enough for me to hear, as if to punish me for the great sin of refusing to talk to him myself.

He's a big man, tall, broad-shouldered and just starting to go a little soft around the middle as he moves into his 50s. When I first met him, he was lanky, raw-boned, just starting to fill out again after his tour in Vietnam and the aftermath years. Strong-jawed. That Dutch Vanderhout blood.His blonde hair was already streaked with gray then. Now it's gold and silver white. My old man.

Listening intently, the receiver pressed to his ear, his shoulders fell into a slump, as some aspect of the conversation deflated him. He sat down at the secretary and ran the fingers of his free hand through his hair. He glanced over at the patio where he thought I'd be, then passed his hand over his eyes. Taking up a pen, he scribbled on the pad of notepaper that rests by the phone. I could picture his small, tight vowels and consonants starkly black against the white page.

He hung up and sat for a moment, big hands on his knees, before he rose with the notepad and walked to the screendoor. He's still lovely to watch in motion: walking, running, playing tennis or softball. He moved deliberately, yet gracefully, like a big Clydesdale, stepping down off the patio, striding across the grass, sitting down on the bench beside me.

"I hate this bench. No back." He stretched, and then leaned forward, elbows on the worn, dusty-blue knees of his jeans, tapping his forehead with the bound edge of the pad.

"Claire …that was your dad."

I tilted my chin a degree in acknowledgement.

"Your Grandma Sophia died sometime yesterday."

Aaron never was one to sugar-coat anything.

And, of course, it was really no shock. She was old, terribly old, hovering in frailty throughout her nineties. It was more of a surprise that the call hadn't come sooner.

He ran a hand up and down my back and let it rest around my waist.

"I'm sorry, babe." He rested his chin against my head for a moment. "Joe said she just died in her sleep. He talked to her the day before about groceries, went over this morning to drop them off and found her. Thought she was sleeping." I felt his lips brush my forehead, soft and fleeting as errant petals. "He's going to set the wake for Friday and the funeral Saturday."

Once again I nodded with the merest tilt of my chin.

"I'll book us some plane tickets." He stood and looked down at me for a moment. "I guess it's time you went home."

He turned and strode back toward the house, all fluid bigness, his shoulders straight and square again, his hand combing again through that white gold mane.

"We could drive." I flung the words at his retreating back.

He stopped, turned and threw me his offhand grin. "Pro-cras-ti-nation. Pro-cras-ti-nation. It's letting me wait. It's keeping me sa-a-a-a-fe," he sang to the tune of an old Carly Simon hit. He saluted me. "Nice try. We fly."

"Hotel. Not his house."

He winked. "Baby steps for my baby."

"You're a lousy singer, farm boy."

The tears didn't come as I had hoped they would, not even later, when the arrangements had been made, for bereavement fares and hotel suites and pet sitters and the holding of keys and pick-up of mail and newspapers; and after seminars had been re-arranged and graduate student consultations postponed; when all the piles of things that we call our lives had been filed into temporary holding bins and the house was dark and the bed was soft and the complacent, fat tabby was nestled in the crook of my legs and the nervous, skinny calico was tucked against Aaron's feet. When it was quiet but for the whispery stirring of infant leaves and the sweet and sad breathings of the flute next door, then I wanted to cry; I yearned for the hot, salt-water kisses, the trembling, achy, convulsive body caught in a heaved breath, and the smothering comfort of a face pressed into a pillow to keep the quiet. But I didn't. I couldn't. I hadn't in a very long while.

Another small piece of the fabric of my early life gone, ripped away. *Why cry over it?* What little was left was so frayed and faded the pattern was almost indistinguishable. It was so ugly I had tried to throw it away years ago, and told myself I didn't care, because the square of fabric upon which I now stitched was a stronger cloth that I had wove all by myself. It was Aaron and Tally who had rescued that old fabric from the scrap heap, who held out a hope the fibers might somehow be repaired. So I had locked it away in the dim attic of memory. Now, awake in the night, I clung to that fabric even as it unraveled in my fingers, even as I wondered: *Why am I doing this? I don't want to do this.*

But I could shed no more tears.

The flight from St. Louis to Chicago takes less than an hour on a good day with a tail wind. You're up, sip your soft drink, and you're down. It can take longer to get out of O'Hare and down to the Loop if the traffic on the Kennedy Expressway is especially bad. We crawled along in the rental car, marveling at the difference between rush hour in St. Louis and rush hour in Chicago, strangers returning to a strange land, expatriates come again to the homeland, twenty years later, bug-eyed at the changes. The river of cars flowed slowly toward the delta of sky-scrapers, the Sears Tower, the John Hancock, the Emerald City skyline of my childhood, but there were considerably more towers looming now, nameless ones, crowding together, bumping shoulders.

"I think we're in Oz now," I murmured.

Tally cracked away at her gum, its strawberry essence filling the little sedan. "Surrender Dorothy," she drawled, leaning forward, her chin resting on my seat back.

Aaron grinned. "When we get to the Loop, it's okay to gawk and crane your neck to see the building tops. We're rubes, you know."

5

She was trying hard not to be impressed. "No gawking," she sniffed. "It's 1999, not 1899, and we're not country bumpkins visiting the big city."

But at the hotel she was disappointed that we weren't boarded on the lake side, sounding ever so much like Miss Lucy Honeychurch in her quest for a room with a view.

"I would have liked to see a Lake Michigan sunrise," she grumbled, her forehead pressed to the pane that offered only buildings and grids of streets stretching west into the early twilight.

"When do you ever get up to see the sunrise?" I mocked.

"I'm up every day. You know, like, for school."

"The times when I'm over, it seems like you spend more time admiring yourself in the mirror than any sunrise."

"You're not always there, are you?"

That left me with my mouth open but temporarily without words to fill the gap. Aaron glowered. It was sore spot with him, and she knew it. It used to bother her more—why her mother and father weren't married—the convoluted explanations she'd have to give to playmates and teachers: *no, they're not divorced, they just never got married; no, they don't live together, but she stays over a lot and we sometimes stay over there.* Realizing that it bothered him, too, perhaps even more so, she lately had begun to wield it as a weapon.

My aim was true on the mirror issue. She did spend a lot of time at her toilette. But then, why not? She is her father softened and molded into a feminine form, tall, a golden Palomino of a girl; Thalia, the grace of Good Cheer.

Finally Aaron choked out a retort. "Name me the last time you saw a St. Louis sunrise. Hey, you want to see a real sunrise, you come out with me to Cahokia. Now there's a sunrise."

A sigh of exaggerated weariness. "That's so like a dad."

"I am a dad."

"Are we going to see Grandpa Joe tonight?"

"Tomorrow," I said quickly. "At the wake."

"But—"

Her father headed her off at the pass. "Tomorrow," he reiterated, steering her out of our room and into hers, handing her the hotel's restaurant and nightlife guide in its blue leatherette binder. "For tonight, investigate dinner. Find someplace we'll all like."

His hands on my shoulders felt like anchors, holding me in place. "Almost home."

Through the window, car lights glowed, turn signals winked red under the topaz shimmer of streetlights. Concrete heaved, asphalt flowed, glass and steel flashed neon. And underneath the colors and hard surfaces there was a low, constant thrum, the electric life of a city: cell phones, beepers, Palm Pilots, laptops. People talking and showers spraying and toilets flushing and horns beeping and whistles blowing and elevators whirring—and under that cacophony, below it all, the lapping, liquid, inexorable, hungry, yearning siren song of the water.

"My home is 300 miles away."

It drew me in the morning, called impatiently to me as I laced up my running shoes, pushed me through the revolving door of the hotel into the brisk air, pulled me along the concrete and through the early rush hour jostle of taxi cabs and pedestrians with bleary eyes and resolute mouths, into and out of the flatulence of articulated buses inching along the pavement like monstrous irradiated caterpillars. When the streets ended and the grassy sprawl of Grant Park began, I could see it just beyond, a dark, roiling green-gray mass beneath the breathier, misty gray of the clouds. Crossing Lake Shore Drive, I saw it in all its sullen glory and felt the ancient chill in the northeast winds that came tearing down the length of it from those northern locales with exotic names: Manistique, Muskegon, Munising. I should have gone north to spite the wind while I was still fresh but I turned south instead, some vestigial homing instinct setting my course. The wind pushed me along past the sailboats and cigarette boats and miniature yachts that shifted and sighed as waves swept through the harbor.

Things had changed. The Drive, which in my childhood had split in two and wound east and west around the white limestone shoulders of the Field Museum, had been moved to the west. A wide green lawn stretched where the concrete and asphalt had once lay and I marveled at man's ingenuity and nature's triumph. The Shedd Aquarium sported a curved wall of glass on the lakeside like a sheath of funky, ultracool, wraparound sunglasses. Swinging back around and heading north, I could see Navy Pier jutting out into the lake, looking alive and faintly garish, with an enormous Ferris wheel rising up and anchoring its horizontal span like a captain's wheel on a quarterdeck. Staring into the visage of the Loop, at its bared, jagged teeth of steel and glass, took my breath away as much as the force of the wind in my face.

My city was gone. And some other thing had risen in its place. Oh, it was breathtaking, the towers defiant under the leaden clouds, but also breath taking, leaving no space to breathe amid the looming surge of concrete as immovable as some neighborhood bully. The lake roiled, the buildings leaned in and then it began to rain. And the city hissed.

The funeral home squatted on a corner of the Southeast Side facing a vacant stretch of dirt and rubble slowly being reclaimed by urban vegetation: trees of heaven and thorny spurge, wide swaths of dandelions in full yellow glory. The Skyway rose beyond like the skeleton of some giant amusement park roller coaster. Conveniently, a tavern crouched on the opposite corner, belching its peculiar odors, promising relief for those who like to drown their sorrows after—or during—an evening spent across the street.

The parlor was the same—blessedly, cursedly—it hadn't changed in nearly 30 years. Oh, the carpet was different, but it was still the same worn beige, the traffic patterns of mourners clearly embedded in the industrial strength fibers, a runway down the center between rows of brown vinyl-padded folding chairs, a taxi area in front where the caskets rest, permanent indentations marking the placement of the kneelers. The sofas and armchairs were different but the same, blue and beige now, striped and solid, instead of the rose tones of before, but still faded and bearing the same, minute, tell-tale stains, brown spots of spilled coffee, yellow blooms of sweat, a purple blotch—spillage from a child's juice cup? The walls were different but the same, a dingy off-white. The crack that had fascinated me long ago had been plastered over but a new one had taken its place.

Even the casket at the far end of the room seemed familiar, the gleaming gray surface begging to be caressed, yet forbidding, too, in its highly polished silence.

And then there was my father, who should have looked familiar above all else, comfortable as an old shoe, inviting as a well-worn easy chair, but who instead was foreign territory, standing in his charcoal-gray suit that looked a little too big, the shoulders drooping a tell-tale fraction of an inch, the sleeves hanging a little too far below the wrists, the cuffed pants covering a bit too much area of shoe.

"That's not his suit," I whispered to Aaron as we paused at the entrance to the room.

He was bent over the condolence book, adding our names. He had pressed me to call my father when we got into Chicago, just to chat, but I'd resisted. So now his hand was on the small of my back, propelling me forward, guiding me as if in a dance down that center aisle past the three or four other mourners who had already arrived, viewed, condoled and staked out their territory for the rest of the late afternoon and evening. Aaron's hand gently compelled me onward, and then brought me to rest in front of the man in someone else's suit who was, indeed, my father.

He turned his head from the condolence of an elderly couple who leaned heavily on their matching canes and smiled. It was the same smile that had thrilled me as a child when he flashed it my way, bestowing it like a king's largesse. And then I was a child again—and I hated that feeling—and it seemed to go on forever, the smile and the thrill and the resentment all tangled up in the two feet of air between us.

Aaron broke the spell, extending first his right hand and then wrapping his left arm around my father's shoulder, shaking hands and pressing the flesh in a perfect man-hug.

"Joe, good to see you, though I'm sorry it's under these circumstances. You look good."

"Well, old man, you look older," came my father's reply.

They grinned like old friends, these two men who had only seen each other thrice in a span of 20 years, their communication limited to scattered phone calls at birthdays and holidays.

Then my father looked past me to Tally, hovering behind, the nervous child undermining the fledgling woman.

"There she is, and more beautiful than her pictures." He folded her in a tentative embrace but she was surprisingly willing to hug back, giving him a glancing kiss on the cheek as well, quickly wiping away the little pink smudge that her lip gloss left on his pale skin.

What is up with that?

I had sent no recent photographs. Lord knows what went on under their roof, ten blocks from my own. I made a mental note to conduct an interrogation later.

He turned his focus on me and the space between us felt impenetrable, more lead than air. But there was Aaron's hand again, the steady pressure, the irresistible force that moved its object. The hug and brush of lips against cheek were over in a matter of seconds on my part, but my father lingered in that moment, his hand replacing Aaron's on my back, pressing me against his chest until there was nothing to do but surrender my face to the soft fold of his lapel and feel the rapid thrum of his heart in my ear and through my cheek.

"Claire," was all he said.

If he wanted to say more, he didn't and I didn't let him, for at the first sign of release, the first lessening of pressure from his hand, I eased away and made my way up to the casket. The brown velveteen on the kneeler was faded and splotched, having absorbed from the tears and sweat of countless mourners. The scent of death was strong, but it wasn't the rank odor of decay, just the peculiar sweetness of institutionalized flowers: the forced freshness of gladiolus and bridled spice of carnations; that concentrated floral essence found only in the coolers of florists' shops and surrounding the dead in funeral parlors.

She was ancient, Grandma Sophie, but then she always had been, to me. She looked the same as I remembered, hair floss white, but still in the braids she always wore wrapped neatly around her head, her face a cosmetologist's nightmare of folds, lines and creases, her hands in repose all airy bones and transparent, paper-thin skin peppered with fawn-colored age spots, weighted down with the black globes of her rosary beads and the rococo silver crucifix that rested on her ridged, yellow thumbnail.

Sophia was baptized Zofia in 1903 in Poland and lived by that name until an immigration official changed it to the more conventional spelling. In the heyday of immigration, Greek, Italian, Polish, Irish, German, they were all the same. Come to the New World, change your fortune, change your name, marry, live, give birth, raise your family, grow old, die, and be surrounded by all the blooming artificiality we can muster.

"One more year, one more year and you could have bragged that you stood in two centuries, Grandma. I should have brought you crushed lilacs and lilies-of-the-valley." I bent to kiss her powdered cheek with a pinch of trepidation, for fear she would crumble into dust.

After we paid our respects, we sat on the sofa against the wall, rather than in the folding chairs. It afforded a view of the entire room and the trickle of mourners in and up to the casket. They wore faces vaguely familiar and undeniably strange. I could also watch my father as he ran through his lines and blocking in the one act called "The Mother's Wake."

If Aaron is a draft horse, my father is a Mustang, all tight, wiry energy, supple-muscled, compact of bone and movement, flaring, glaring, charming-turn-on-a-dime-mean and vice versa. Black mane graying to distinction. Pockmarked cheeks under intense brown eyes that always, even in the midst of a smile, seem on the verge of a glare. Shifty-skinned, snapping at flies and fools. A stranger would never guess he was seventy-five. Sixty-five, maybe—and only because of the furrows that fanned out from the corners of his eyes and settled around his mouth like parentheses, and the skin that drooped under his eyes, the baggage of his life and the force of gravity weighing his flesh down. But not sapping his energy. The years hadn't granted him repose: his fingers were still in his pockets, jangling his keys and change, his eyes were still scanning the perimeter of the room, making note of the available exits.

But he went through his paces like a show pony or a glad-handing politician, grippin' and grinnin', good ol' jocular Joe. *No tears, folks, 96 for Christ's sake, a good life, a full life, yes, and how are you doin', Mrs. Piskorowski, nice of you to come, is this the little Tiffany that used to visit her grandma next door, well, I'll be damned, you're getting married now?*

And so on. But I knew he hated it and would have rather been in the back of the room against the wall or in the corner, or, better still, across the street in the dark refuge of the tavern with one beer in his belly and another on the way. The oversized suit and the actor's mask couldn't hide that from me.

The dinner hour came. Tally's adolescent metabolism required a meal and her adolescent temperament craved relief from the tedium of meeting and greeting a parade of blood relations that for all intents hadn't existed the day before and would vanish again, like Brigadoon, in the span of 48 hours. She and Aaron left to find the kind of solace only fast food, familiar, fat-laden and salty, can provide.

Then it was me and the room, same but different, the faint hiss of polyester, the scent of the gladiolus, this time less sympathy, more reproach from the eyes of the women, curiosity mingled with disdain. The old men looked resigned, slack-faced, flesh delicate as parchment or the outer skin of onions, goggle-eyed behind their thick-lensed glasses. The younger ones, my age or less, cousins perhaps, looked Target fashionable, the women's hair still frozen in spiral perms a decade after they went out of fashion, the men in business casual instead of suits, clad in their nervous tics, hands running through hair, inside shirt collars, fingers drumming on knees, twisting wrists to check the time without any pretense of stealth, gauging how many more minutes until they could blow this popsicle stand. I didn't know them.

Two faces struck me. One smirked above a decent, navy-blue suit and red-striped tie, eyes shifting under a slick of neatly trimmed brown hair. The other face looked as pliable as clay, grayish flesh molded over hollows and jutting bones, unreadable, except for the startling curve of pink-tinged lower lip. When our eyes met, the lip trembled slightly, threatening some revelation, until big front teeth closed down over it, and a big-boned hand swept down over the face and kneaded it back into expressionless submission.

When I rose, it was ostensibly to visit the powder room, to splash water on my face and wrists. I paused in the foyer that connected the two parlor rooms. The other was unoccupied, as it had been 30 years before. So I stepped in.

CHAPTER 2

The day my brother Joey—Joseph Matthew Sokol, Jr., Joe Jr., little Joe—drowned was blue-sky bright, polka-dotted with cotton balls clouds, just-out-of-school giddy. The summer lay before us like an empty canvas. We were the artists brimming with ideas, setting out brushes and paint pots. The lake was our muse.

We were drawn to water like baby leatherback turtles, instinctively, as if our lives depended on it. Every summer weekend we would pester Marjorie, our older sister, to take us to Calumet Park and usually she'd happily oblige, enjoying the chance to sport her black two-piece bathing suit and rub on the cocoa butter, to recline on her big blue and white striped towel and lazily tune back and forth from WLS to WCFL on her silver transistor radio. She baked in the heat as the Lovin' Spoonful ground out "Summer in the City" and all our necks got dirty and gritty. She called us water sprites for we came alive in the lake like nowhere else. The minute our feet touched the sand we launched into a sprint to the shore—and not just for respite from the blistering heat under our toes. We tore off our clothes along the way, leaving a trail of T-shirts and shorts for her to retrieve as she made her way at a more sedate pace. My brother was a plunger, dashing straight through the baby waves that lapped at the beach and flopping face and belly into the water's enveloping cold. I was considerably more diffident. Once I reached the water's edge, I slowed and let only the tips of my toes breach the waves. Cold—toes, feet, ankles. Colder—calves, knees, thighs. Coldest—a shivery embrace around my waist, gooseflesh raising the hairs on my arms. Inevitably, Joey would tackle me from behind with a roar and I would be in over my head, resurfacing with a gasp of chilly delight. After that, we were in for the day, one minute thrashing arms and legs in our efforts to subdue the water, the next floating calmly at one with it.

Only the rest breaks prescribed by our mother and strictly enforced by our sister could tear us away from that cold caress and back to the hot, hard shore. We'd make a half-hearted effort to build a sandcastle but we'd find ourselves inching away from the roughness and graininess and stickiness of the sand back to the smooth, wet, sapphire satin.

The lake called. It murmured. It said, "come away." And we answered joyously, "yes."

But Marjorie was eleven years older than Joey and eighteen years older than me and as the 60's shuddered to a close, one week before Neil Armstrong walked on the moon, she walked down the aisle of Immaculate Conception Church to marry a junior-level auto and casualty underwriter. She'd met her groom at a 'singles' bar called Butch McGuire's, a fact which left our Temperance League-eligible mother with a pinched twist to her lips as if she'd accidentally bitten into the pith of the grapefruit she ate for breakfast. Sandy-haired, Brill-creamed, fondue-eating, martini-swilling, up-and-comer Rich whisked his new Mrs. Olmstead off to the home office in Hartford, Connecticut. She willingly left her beach weekends and, for the most part, us behind.

Mom wasn't a beachgoer. I'm not sure she even owned a swimsuit. Ever. She never voiced any particular objections to the beach. It just seemed there was always something else to do: laundry, dusting, ironing, gardening, running errands and doing yard work for her mother-in-law. She was always in motion, like a hummingbird, but without the jewel-toned plumage. The exposed leisure of the beach did not suit her.

My father worked at the steel mill. There were many at the time, but everyone knew which one you meant when you said "the mill"—U.S. Steel's hulking South Works on the shores of the lake. He took us to White Sox baseball games with the box seat tickets he occasionally received as a perk in his position as a turn foreman. He bought us salt-and-butter-soaked popcorn to munch and icy Coke in big, red and white striped waxed cups to wash it down and vanilla ice cream rippled with fudge that we'd eat with flat wooden spoons, while he contented himself with beer and peanuts. He'd let Joey keep score, but watch over his shoulder the whole time. He'd shuffle his feet and tap his heels restlessly until after his second beer, anticipating his third, when he'd finally be able to sit back in the hard seats and semi-relax. He didn't go to the beach either.

So the summer of 1970 didn't bode well for beach-going, especially for me. Joey had older friends with drivers' licenses and parents who trusted them with the family car. He, having just turned sixteen, had a learner's permit and was taking driver's ed over the summer. And it definitely was no longer cool to be seen at the beach with your eight-year-old pest of a sister.

I wore my ratty royal blue swimsuit from the previous summer under my shorts and T-shirt when the boys swung by to pick him up that day. The straps bit into my shoulders, the elastic around the leg openings nipped my skin. But discomfort was a small price to pay for the tiny possibility that he would defy all teenage conventions, give me that look that said "just between you and me, I tolerate you" and, with an exasperated show of helplessness, shrug me into joining them.

I sat on the front stoop drawing figure eights in white chalk, which metamorphosed into butterflies, occasionally glancing at the sand pail and shovel I'd stashed under the evergreen tree near the sidewalk. My beach towel was rolled up and secreted in the bucket for a quick getaway. But when the boys came rolling up to the curb in an old chocolate-colored Rambler, Creedence Clearwater Revival wah-wahing through the open windows, and Joe Jr. strolled out the door, his own towel casually slung over his left shoulder, walking a new walk he'd adopted of late, a loose, rolling gate, strutting arrogance and immortality, I knew it wasn't going to be.

But nothing ventured, nothing gained. "Can I go, too?"

He shook his head. "Sorry, kiddo. If it was Cal Park, maybe. But we're going to the Dunes. Be gone all day."

They were wailing *"Green River"* all out of tune as he folded his lean frame into the front seat. I doubted he would compromise his cool to even say goodbye, but as he slammed the car door and the Rambler jerked away, I saw his hand out the window rise and fall. Maybe his companions thought he was just thumping to the beat, but I knew different.

Later it was all confusion and rush: a phone call, panicky tears, frantic gestures.

"In the water? What?"

"What hospital?"

From upstairs in my bedroom, I heard the front door slam shut and the semi-hysterical catch in my mother's voice. From my window I was watching the fireflies rise from the lawn, winking merrily against the gloomy, bluish face of twilight.

He should have been home for supper long ago. His mashed potatoes were cold gray mounds, his charred piece of round steak was dotted with congealed fat, his green beans were limp alien limbs sodden in gravy that had oozed over from the meat.

I crept down the stairs and sat hidden on the step just above the place where solid wall met open banister, my usual eavesdropping post. My father must have taken the phone.

"We're on our way—take us about an hour."

I heard the click of the receiver.

"Sonovabitch, sonovabitch..."A litany, a mantra. "Sonovabitch. Call up Dodie, maybe she can take Claire for the night. Sonovabitch!"

"No, she can come with—"

"Mary, he's dead. Jesus, whaddya think—they're gonna let a little girl—sonovabitch!"

A teary, panicked anger clutched my father's voice, constricting him, making him sound as if he would vomit and choke at once.

I heard the whirring of the rotary dial. "Shit, I'll call her myself, if you can't bring yourself—"

"You bastard!"

"Hello, Dodie? It's Joe."

"You goddamn sonovabitch. You told him he could go—when I said no."

That last was a fiery whisper. My mother's red, tear-streaked face appeared around the banister at the bottom of the stairs. She still had a yellow dishtowel draped over her shoulder, slung there haphazardly when she'd left her chore to answer the telephone in the front hall. She drew it off her shoulder and swiped her face quickly. She didn't look surprised to see me.

"Your brother was in an accident. Daddy and I've got to go to the hospital." She paused, breathing in a shuddery sigh. She dried and re-dried her hands on the towel, hands that weren't wet in the first place; standing there, drying and drying, her skin reddening under the rough wiping.

"You can stay at Aunt Dodie's."

"I don't wanna."

My father's face appeared, hovering over the round top of the lowest baluster, a talking human head on a wooden chess piece body.

"Get your PJs and a change of clothes. You're spending the night at Aunt Dodie's." A clipped, martial control had replaced the choky emotion in his voice.

"Joey's dead?" The words came from somewhere inside, half a question and half not.

My father's head snapped back as if the words had hit him out of the blue like an uppercut to the jaw.

"Something happened at the Dunes," my mother snapped. The towel finally hung limp in her hand. "Get your pajamas and toothbrush. Here, I'll help you." She slung the towel back over her shoulder and hurried up the stairs, her hand covering her face as she passed.

My father stared at me for a moment, uncustomarily still.

"Did he drown?"

He blinked and turned away. "Get your stuff. We've got to go."

No tears. There was no time for tears. And no sad explanation to bring them forth, as of yet. At Aunt Dodie's house it was even possible to forget that anything had happened. She was my father's youngest sister with an auto mechanic husband. Uncle Bob was a bantamweight cock-of-the-walk with strawberry blonde hair and a speckled face out of whose mouths spewed all sorts of words that I never heard at home. Not the usual foul language—I heard plenty of that—but nasty ways of referring to people of different color and custom: wop, spic, nigger, chink, gook; the guttural, barnyard squawks of the bigot. They had five children. The three oldest, teenaged stair-step kids, two boys and a girl, all named for saints, cast sympathetic and oddly awed looks at me before retreating to their rooms. Dougie, ten months older than me, was engrossed in a re-run of Hogan's Heroes. Linda, ten months younger than me, grasped my hand and led me away from the significant whispers of the adults.

In her room, she revealed the newest addition to her Barbie's wardrobe: a glamorous gown of white and gold lame, complete with a fur-cuffed evening coat, a velvet handbag, gloves, hankie, pearl necklace and earrings, and a fur headband. We dressed and undressed her clique of dolls: two Barbies, a Midge, a Stacy, a Ken, and played out the rituals and scenarios of dating that we imagined, in chic ensembles. Poor Ken did double and triple duty in the escort department. Dougie leered from the doorway and hooted derisively until his mother sent him to the room he shared with his brothers. Later, after I had held my pee until the fiery pain of denial seared my privates and I was forced to finally stumble off to use the bathroom down the hall, he was waiting. He knew the steps to his bullying dance so well. He was the Fred Astaire of the full body block and the arm dodge, the sidestep, the shuffle-and-lean and the *sotto voce* taunt.

"Beg me, beg me to use it. You're about to bust your bladder so beg."

Finally the eldest McConnell boy leaned his blonde head out his bedroom door and muttered, "Knock it off, shit-for-brains, before Dad hears you."

But rescue came too late: the warm liquid was coursing down my legs and onto the avocado-colored carpet and I just stood there and let it flow, relief and shame and anger and defiance freezing my limbs and setting my jaw.

The fleeting look in Dougie's eyes, as he stared into mine, was one of pure terror, before he remembered who and what he was and commenced his hyena-like laughter. What did he see on my face, in my eyes? Aunt Dodie swooped in, her drab, ashy hair feathering wildly around her head, escaping its lacquer cage, tsking and cawing like a flustered hen as her talons stripped me of my clothes and deposited me into a hastily drawn bath. While I sat there amidst the foam, fuming, plotting revenge, I could hear her on the other side of the bathroom door, scrubbing the carpet.

Then it was bedtime. Linda and I brushed our teeth side by side in the green and pink-tiled bathroom, spitting in unison into the white sink, washing our mouths out with water sipped from Dixie cups. As we lay in her pink-and-white bed in her pink-and-white room, she recited prayers on her white plastic-beaded rosary. Aunt Dodie's was a very Catholic house: church on Sunday, fish on Friday, parochial school, catechism, confirmation. I didn't have the prayers memorized like Linda, though it seemed as if I should, so I mumbled and slurred, repeating phrases that I knew—*our Father, who art in heaven, hallowed be thy name, hail Mary, grace*—hoping that, as Linda got caught up in the mantra, she wouldn't notice my ignorance.

From the kitchen, the clatter of pans and the whir of an electric mixer blended with the murmur of the Hail Mary. Aunt Dodie was baking a cake.

Black, navy blue, charcoal gray, the occasional brown, the three-piece suit, the shirtdress, the A-line, the polyester pantsuit, the jumper with white blouse, the black wingtips, the black pumps, the navy flats, a few brown loafers. Blue and gray striped ties, solid blue clip-on ties, genuine white cotton handkerchiefs peeking out of breast pockets. Aftershave, perfume, an underlying odor of sweat, of bodies dressed too warmly for a hot summer day, chewing gum both minty and fruity, the sweet, sticky scent of hard candy, the nostril-flaring, mouth-puckering smell of lemon drops. That first afternoon at the wake was an assault to already my shell-shocked senses. My father moved restlessly among the crowd of mourners, rarely pausing for more than a moment, and even when he did, never truly joining a conversation. His head might nod, his lips might move, but his eyes were always seemingly fixed on some object that lurked on his own private horizon, keeping his back to the casket. My mother sat in the third row of folding chairs, right smack in the middle, enclosed by a barrier of chairs to the front, back and sides, with Marjorie and her husband guarding her flanks. Mourners offering their condolences faced a labyrinthine journey. Her gaze rarely wavered from that which rested before her.

He looked like a wax dummy lying there in the steel gray casket, pan-caked and powdered, blushed and hair-sprayed. Only his lips had a natural liverish hue. His hands were hard and cold in the place where I touched them with one trembling finger. This was not my brother; this was some strange, graven image that the undertakers had placed before us; an idol to which we could genuflect; some mannequin wearing my brother's brown Nehru jacket.

As well as my beach buddy, he'd been my ally in the war against our mother. We could fight like Kilkenny cats between ourselves, from the tips of our nails to the end of our tails, but when the time came to fight the good fight, we put aside our differences and pledged a truce, pooling our resources to vanquish the greater enemy. Joey was wise in the ways of the battlefield. I had been his standard bearer, the little drummer girl, not quite ready for serious combat, but always prepared to come to my man's defense.

Making war was a way of life for my brother. His toy soldiers, little green plastic GIs barely three inches tall, molded in action poses, wearing fatigues and helmets, brandishing rifles, bayonets and hand grenades, conducted surprise raids upon the particleboard walls of my red-brick Colonial dollhouse. Soldiers climbed in through windows, rappelled down from the green faux slate roof to crash through the front door, and crept around the back to pillage the garden and kidnap the children at play. One ambush had led to the trial of the kindly father of the doll family, Mr. Willoughby, before a military tribunal for treason, desertion and various other war crimes. It seems he had burned his draft card and avoided military service by escaping to Canada. My brother didn't have an entirely original imagination; he adapted his stories from the headlines he read in the newspaper, the snippets of news he heard on his transistor radio between Beatles and Rolling Stones songs, the flashes of horrifying information that came from the glowing eye of the television set; and the volcanic and profane tirades that erupted from our father, a decorated World War II veteran, in the face of film clips of long-haired young men with raised fists chanting anti-war slogans on his very own lakefront, in his very own city, in front of his very own, much beloved mayor.

Mr. Willoughby never stood a chance. After barely a minute's deliberation among the three officers, the word came: *"Guilty."* The sentence: execution. But the firing squad and the gallows weren't brutal enough for the likes of a lily-livered draft dodger. He was beheaded. Literally. His little plastic head, with its goofy, sweet grin, sky-blue eyes and jet-black, molded and thus always perfectly combed hair, was severed from his fully pose-able body with a Swiss Army knife. Crying hysterically as my little hands worked feverishly to put him back together, I invoked the spirit of Florence Nightingale to empower me with the healing arts.

Mother, hearing the uproar, had climbed the steep staircase to our bedrooms and loomed in the doorway, disapproval narrowing her eyes before she had even heard a word of accusation or denial, a cry of protest or, my brother's specialty, the rambling filibuster of explanation. These, properly delivered, occasionally bought time before punishment, a cooling-down period, and were designed to lull the lawgiver into handing down probation. Not this day. My brother received a sharp blow to his cheek. I saw the angry red color heightened in relief against the canvas of his pale face before he ran from the playroom and took refuge in the bathroom. Mother sighed, holding out her hand. Mr. Willoughby and his head looked particularly small and fragile in her callused palm. She shook her head, sad, angry, impatient at having to interrupt her housework to referee her children's battles and play nurse to a doll. She made an effort to repair Mr. Willoughby, making a tiny cast out of brown modeling clay, wrapping it around the severed portion of his neck, but, in the end, it just didn't look right—Mr. Willoughby in a permanent neck brace. The clay kept falling off as it hardened. From that day forward, he had been confined to the dollhouse attic, where he lay bedridden, reduced to watching the fabulous activities of his family, but never allowed to participate.

My brother never apologized, but somehow, in the way of siblings, we achieved a rapprochement through peace offerings: a stick of Bazooka bubblegum, half of a Snickers bar, the loan of a prized Lone Ranger comic book. And my mother had her own way of bringing us together. Her wrath touched all, without discrimination. To defeat her—wily enemy that she was: punisher of children, chief critic, deliverer of pious sermons and numbing jeremiads—required the mutual cooperation of united forces that would rival NATO.

But now he was gone, his body replaced by a painted figurine, hard and cold as ceramic, as useless in battle as the Terracotta Army. My instinct was to flee, but I was too proud to run away. I walked instead, casually weaving through the thick crowd of mourners, winding my way through the colors, the fabrics, the odors.

Accidental drowning. Tragedy. So young. Such a waste. Do you think he was drunk? Drugs?

Whispered words, hushed sentences, sympathetic murmurs, regretful sighs scented the air of the funeral parlor like some mournful perfume, wafting and waning between clusters of aunts and uncles, cousins and family friends, the dirge-like odor stronger among the women and weaker among the men, who were already moving on from lamentation and speculation to talk of baseball, team stats and the White Sox road trip.

Away from the casket and its floral plume, the sharp, oppressive reek of cigarette smoke and the faintly rank smell of too many bodies pressed together on the first really hot day of the summer narrowed the room, made the ceiling seem too low. It continued to shrink as candy and sympathy pressed from my dowdy aunts and great-aunts in their decades-old dresses, who slipped Root Beer Barrels and Tootsie Rolls into my hands with gentle squeezes, as if indeed just a spoonful of sugar would help this particular medicine go down easier.

The parlor next door was empty. And huge. Maybe too huge.

I squeezed under the end table next to a sofa at the far end of the room. It was a tight fit sitting cross-legged, my navy cotton dress hiked over my knees, candy cradled in my lap. My head bumped against the underside. The pain felt good. I pressed harder. The pain shot, then throbbed; was acute, then chronic. Momentarily, the pain was all that existed, blocking out everything else. How long and hard could I press before my skull would burst from the throbbing of flesh and bone grinding against unyielding oak? However, it eventually became routine, manageable pain, and the murmurings and images from the wake drifted in again like smoke through an open window. I spied the festering scab on my knee, the remnant of accidental contact with the sidewalk a few days before. It was perfect: a hard, brown-red shell encasing a yellow, watery layer of pus. My nail scraped it gently, then, when it resisted, more urgently. The crust broke with a feeling similar to a sigh and oozed infection, then bright red blood, which trickled down my leg and dripped off to blossom into a tiny, perfect plum-colored rose on the gold carpet. But the suits and the sympathetic looks and, above all, the waxwork figure in its bower of flowers still loomed. I squeezed my eyes shut, pressed my head up harder, and dug a fingernail into the wound, biting down hard on my lip. Voices drifted in and then the whisper of shoes scuffling over carpet.

"I saw her come in here," a boy's voice asserted with whiny certainty.

"She musta went out again, cuz she's not here now." A girl's sneering reply—my cousins, Dougie and Linda. I shrank into myself, held the breath in my mouth and nostrils. I'd had enough of her Barbie dolls and of his brutal idiocy. Their feet shuffled by my hiding place, his encased in black dress shoes, hers in patent Mary Janes.

"Little chickenshit, 'fraid of a dead body." He said it a little too loudly, as if trying to provoke me out of wherever I was skulking. I let the bait pass.

"Come on, let's go get some candy from Uncle Jimmie. He has Necco wafers—I saw." The room was empty again. I closed my eyes and focused on the pain my jagged fingernail could inflict upon an open, bloody sore.

Blood on a gold carpet. My brother and I had spilled enough of it, together and apart. Keeping it a secret from our mother sealed the bond, made it a true blood oath.

Playing football in the square box that was our living room— or "front room" as it was known in our house—was forbidden. But during football season, in the waning light of a November afternoon, when the first flurries of snow flung themselves kamikaze-like against the panes of the picture window and the wind tortured the bare branches of the lilac against the corner of the house, after a day spent watching men pile onto one another with ruthless abandon and fling the ball like a grenade at a moving target, my brother could not resist. He inevitably called for a game. As the most immediately available opponent, I was drafted.

"Okay, I'm Johnny Unitas. No, maybe, Dick Butkus—or maybe Gale Sayers." Joey reeled off the names of his current football heroes, rambling through the play rosters without regard for team or position. "Who you gonna be?"

Dumb silence. My seven year old mind could not register a single player's name. In the space of time it took me to answer, Joey would have rattled off six or seven more names.

He snapped his fingers in my face. "Come on, come on. Okay, look, you can be—"

"Jack Concannon!" I shouted the first name that came to my tongue, a name dredged up from the swamp of memory, a name I had once seen on the back page of the newspaper under the Sports section banner headline.

"He's a quarterback, dummy, but I've got the ball so you have to be on defense. Be someone else."

"I'm being him or I'm not playing." A pout and crossed arms.

"Okay, fine, Jack Concannon. Okay, so it's first down and ten. I've got the ball. I'm gonna run it through and you try to block me." He crouched down in the three-point stance.

"23, 32, 57, hut, hut, hike," he yipped in staccato rhythm. He was center, quarterback, and running back at once. He shifted the imaginary football under his arm and made his move up the field, all sixteen feet of it.

I leaped in front of him just as he made it to the blonde-wood Danish style coffee table. The effort earned me a solid blow to the nose from his forearm and we both went crashing down to the recently-purchased gold carpet, a tangle of arms, legs and laughter.

"First down!"

"I got you before you made it," I whined, putting tentative fingers up to my nose.

The blow had really jarred me and when I pulled my hand away, feeling an unusual wetness, I saw the crimson stigmata on my palm. My impulse was to shriek, but then I heard my mother's voice ringing from above.

"What's going on down there? What was that crash?" Standing at the top of the stairs, she wasn't able to see the disarray.

I stared at my brother, clutching my nose, picturing what my mother would do if she found out we had been engaging yet again in illicit acts of violence and mayhem. My brother's eyes were wide with his own unique expression of fear: the alarm of the instigator apprehended, the culprit caught red-handed. Literally. My blood stained his wrist.

Looking down, we saw its telltale scarlet droplets marring the field of gold.

"The bathroom," he whispered with a fierce gesture toward the central hall, just steps away.

My mother's shoes clicked and creaked on the wooden stairs, the drumbeat of the enemy army on the march.

"Nothing, Mom. I just bumped into the table," he shouted as he hustled me through the bathroom door and shut it behind me. While he staved off the attack on the front line, it was my duty to stanch the bleeding, clean up the evidence and, if the battle should be lost, remain mum when the inquisition of the prisoners began.

Name, rank and serial number. Divulge nothing else or be guilty of treason.

I stepped up onto the side of the porcelain bathtub, leaning over to take a peek in the medicine chest mirror. The blood was not gushing as I had feared. It was just a thin trickle, a little red Chaplinesque mustache growing over my upper lip. Hopping down from my perch, I grabbed some toilet paper to suppress the flow. Holding the wadded paper against my nostrils, I let my body slide down the wall until I was squatting on the black-and-white tiled floor, hunched in the corner between the icy side of the tub and the metal grate of the heat register, alone in my cell, praying for the end of the war and my liberation.

Outside the door I heard the first shot of the battle fired.

"What were you doing? Where's your sister? What did you do to her?" Three rapid-fire missiles, bam, bam, bam. Could he possibly fend off such an unremitting attack, deflect the blows, escape unscathed?

"Nothing! We weren't doing nothing. She's in the bathroom. You know she has a bladder the size of a peanut."

An agile parry to her rapier thrust, with a sideswipe of humor. He alone, it seemed, could make her laugh—or what passed for a laugh with her—and that ability often helped to extricate him from sticky situations, but this time I had little hope that it would bring a truce. We had been warned. Numerous times. And with that ammunition, she was too strong, too quick. She'd draw blood soon. I saw the doorknob turn. Thank the gods of war that I'd had the presence of mind to turn the lock. But that would only temporarily thwart her attack.

"Open this door now, Claire! Do you hear me? And you," this addressed to my brother, "don't you go anywhere. Stand right there."

My time was up. I could no longer postpone the inevitable. I couldn't desert, couldn't flee to Canada, couldn't demonstrate with raised fist and sing clever, passionate anti-war protest songs with Country Joe and the Fish at Woodstock. No, I was dug into my foxhole and it was time to engage the enemy.

I crumpled up the soaked toilet paper. It resembled a red paper rose in my hand. I shoved it into the pocket of my corduroys and took a last quick glance in the mirror. My nose was red, bruised-looking. It would not pass inspection.

The metal latch clicked as I opened the door. With head held high and a steady chin, I faced my personal Torquemada. I would go to my death, I silently vowed, before I would reveal anything.

The Grand Inquisitor stood in the middle of our little square hall, her dark hair askew, dark eyes fixed, hands on her hips, a dust cloth hanging from her tightly closed fist. Would she use that as a blindfold when she hauled us off for our execution?

"What happened to your nose?"

"It was bleeding."

"Why was it bleeding?"

A shrug, a sideways glance.

"Your nose just doesn't start bleeding without a good reason." Stating the obvious was one of her prime methods of mental torture.

"Got bumped."

"On what?"

I chewed on the soft inner flesh of my cheek, but stood tall, the steadfast tin soldier balanced precariously on one leg.

"Not sure."

"You're not sure?" This was her equivalent of the Chinese water torture, the persistent questions and repetitions which were as exhausting and maddening as the drip, drip, drip of water on the forehead.

I shook my head. A comic German-accented voice from some television show kept echoing in my brain: "I know notheenk! I have seen notheenk!"

"He hit you in the nose. Tell the truth."

A direct hit! She had pulled out the heavy artillery and yet, if I kept my soldier's wits about me, though armed only with a popgun, I might still prevail. And tell the truth at the same time.

"No. It was an accident."

Oh no! The millisecond the words spilled from my mouth I regretted them, yearned to catch them and stuff them back before they hit the floor. That was a slip, a critical false step. From the gleam that lit my mother's eyes, I realized that I had blundered into a landmine and killed off half of my forces, giving the enemy an opening in my flank. The resignation I saw in my brother's eyes told me that all was lost.

"Football again, wasn't it?" Her triumphant voice was a dagger aimed at our hearts. "Well, wasn't it?"

Joey hung his head, his wound gushing, a beaten man, a betrayed man. Yet no dishonorable, opportunistic words of denial or counter-accusation polluted his lips. He would fall on his sword before he would allow the massacre of innocents.

"That's it. I've had it with you. I told you no football in the house. You're grounded for the week and no watching football either. I don't care if it's the Bears versus the Packers, you're not watching. Get upstairs." She swung a last blow, this time an actual slap with the back of her hand. Amazingly, she missed. Wonder of wonders, was it intentional? Something seemed to hang on the corners of her lips, pulling them up and then tugging them back down. Something was at war within her, battling over the composure of her face. Did she really want to smile at this dark-haired adversary who had sprung from her body, this wiry, brown-eyed boy now taller than she, who still bowed to her will? This boy-man who looked so much like the other man in her life? Of course, he had made a retreat quick enough to avoid the blow, the mark of common sense in any solder. There is no dishonor in retiring the field when the battle is lost. Better to save one's resources, bind up one's wounds, and live to fight again. It was the loss of one battle, not the war. But had she also pulled her punch this time?

She brought ice, shoved me down on the edge of the tub, tilted my head back with a jerk and pressed the cube against my nose. No gentle succor was offered to this prisoner of war—only the barest humanitarian aid.

"You should know better. Why do you let him get you into trouble—playing those rough games. And in the house!"

I sat in silence, while my nose grew numb and my neck started to ache, a cry of protest coming from my vertebrae, but not my lips.

That night, as we lay in our beds at the opposite ends of the upstairs hall, I heard the creak of linoleum and the soft padding of my brother's bare feet coming closer, closer. In the light cast from the streetlamp in front of our house, I saw the outline of Joey's head craned around the door.

"She can never beat us, kiddo. Not if we stick together. Did you see how she missed when she tried to hit me—I think she missed on purpose. Sometimes I can wrap her around my little finger. Guess what? She's so dumb. She told me I couldn't *watch* any football. But she didn't say anything about listening to it on my radio." He brandished his black transistor. Its silver antenna caught the light and glinted like the steel blade of a fine saber. He flashed a victory sign.

"Peace, babe."

We were comrades still, brother and sister in arms.

But now he'd left me to fight on alone.

"Whatcha doin'?"

My eyes popped open at the intrusion. My brother's face was before me, much younger, baby-faced, but his face nonetheless, those vivid brown eyes barely a foot from mine. Alive, not dead.

"I said, whatcha doin'?"

Then my brother was gone and it was just a boy with curly hair that was struggling to overthrow its smothering layer of

30

Brylcreem. He crouched in front of the table, everything about him seeming slightly off-center. I reached out to straighten his blue clip-on tie, leaving a curl of blood on his white shirt collar.

"Just sittin' here."

"Can I have some of your candy?"

I took a bulls-eye and a lemon drop from the stash on my lap and held out my hand. He took them, his fingers hot and moist against my cold palm.

"You're bleeding. Does it hurt?"

I shrugged, then nodded.

He sucked on the lemon drop. "Will you come out?"

I shook my head.

"Can I come in?"

Another shake.

"Why not?" His voice had a slight accent, a twang, a hint of somewhere else.

"No room," I croaked.

"Yes, there is – if you scoot back." He scuttled in on the side of the table as I shrank away. We sat cross-legged, knee to knee, nose to nose.

"Do you like science fiction stories?" His breath was candy perfume that I inhaled as I shook my head.

He waited for a more detailed reply, then, in the silence, threw out another question.

"Well, what *do* you like?"

"To read?"

He nodded, bumping his head. "Oww."

"Fairy tales."

"Really? I'll tell you a secret." He leaned even closer, his pink cherub lips almost brushing my ear. "I like 'em, too. My mama reads them to me at bedtime. But don't tell my dad cuz he thinks they're for girls—or sissies." That breath was warm on my cheek.

He drew back and smiled conspiratorially. "I'm Jamie, Jamie Sokol."

"I'm Claire Sokol."

His eyes widened, then blinked. "You're cousin Claire. That's your brother in there."

I shook my head fiercely.

"Yes, it is. That's Cousin Joey. Daddy said he drowned."

"That's not my brother. That's just a—just a ..."

Jamie reached out and laid his hand over mine, gently easing my finger away from the sore on my knee. "I know. It's just his body. He's somewhere else now."

He fumbled in his pants pocket, pulling out a crinkled tissue. "I didn't use it—it just got wrinkly from bein' in my pocket." He pressed it against my knee. "Mama might have a band-aid."

We sat in silence for a moment. I dabbed the tissue against my knee, leaving little white specks of lint to mix with the blood and plasma pooling to form a new scab.

"What's your favorite story?" he finally asked.

I thought a moment, lowering my head to relieve the pressure on my skull. "Hansel and Gretel."

"Hey, I like that one, too. What's your favorite part?"

"When they stick together and they're smart and they beat the witch."

"Yeah, she gets cooked in her own oven. But they shoulda never believed her in the first place. A candy house? They shoulda known she was a witch from the start."

"I think the mother *is* the witch."

"No!"

"Yeah, cuz she's dead when they finally find their way back home. So's the witch."

Jamie pondered. "I guess it's possible. Cuz that mama was really wicked, leaving her children to die in the woods."

"I don't get why the father went along with it."

"Me neither."

We lapsed into silence again. He bit down on the sliver that was left of his lemon drop. "How about music? Who do ya like?"

"Lotsa people."

"Jamie? You in here?" It was a woman's voice, a slurry of softness lilting amidst the vowels and consonants.

Then behind Jamie I saw a pair of navy slingbacks and slender ankles and the faint sheen on pantyhose on white skin.

"Jamie, what are you doin' under there?" The twang drew out "what" to two syllables and dropped the "r" in "under." Then the speaker was on her hands and knees and a pretty, pink-lipped, pink-cheeked, mascara-ed and powdered face appeared.

"You need to come on out of there." She gasped when she saw me, just a short intake of breath and a blink of those black-lashed blue eyes.

"Come on out, now."

Jamie backed out, ducking his head low, but I stayed put.

"You must be Claire. Ah'm your Uncle Jimmie's wife, Patrice. But you can call me by my nickname, Peach. Aunt Peach to you. Pleased to meet you and come on, you need to come out. Look at your knee. I believe I've got a Band-Aid for that, hon."

That was the first time that I ever remember being called by a term of endearment. My mother was strictly utilitarian: you had a name, and you were called and referred to by that name. My father didn't go in for sweet nothings, either. But as I later learned, Jamie's mother used an entire lexicon of these terms, as if she'd memorized a thesaurus of love talk: *sweetie, pie,* (and the compound form of those), *sugar, doll, darlin', honey child.* For now, just the abbreviated *"hon"* was enough to seduce me into crawling forward to meet her outstretched hand.

Her skin was powder soft and dry.

"I'll bet that hurts."

I shrugged.

"How did you scrape it?"

"She was pickin' at it."

She turned to Jamie and a whiff of something reminiscent of rose petals and orange peel floated along the curve of her body in space. "It's not polite to tell what somebody else doesn't want to reveal." She turned back to me, a slender blue column in her sleeveless sheath; a taper candle lit by a head of blonde hair sleekly pulled back into a chignon. "Let's get you that Band-Aid."

In the ladies' room, she daubed my knee gently with a moistened paper towel, then took a bandage from her navy clutch and expertly applied it to my wound.

"All better?" "Bettah" to my ears.

I shrugged.

"Well, you know what they say about time and wounds. But I know some heal faster than others." She crouched in front of me, her face so close to mine that I might have drowned in the pools of her eyes. "Sugar, it's time you got back to the wake."

Jamie and I sat on the nubby brown sofa for the rest of the evening, reviewing Beverly Cleary books and TV shows, comparing the merits of the Jackson Five and the Osmond Brothers, marveling at the fact that we were born just two months apart. I was a June baby, my ninth birthday just a week away; he would celebrate his in late August. When Peach passed by and smiled at us, I whispered, "Your mom's pretty."

"Yeah."

"She paints her fingernails."

He leaned closer, whispering. "And her toes." Then he looked at me. "And she irons her hair. It wants to be wavy like mine, but she tames it." He must have noticed the astonishment on my face. "Doesn't your mama?"

I shook my head. "Her hair is stick straight. She pins it at night so it'll be wavy in the morning."

He considered this for a moment, then shrugged. "Tant pis."

"Tawn pee?"

"Tant pis. It's French. It means 'too bad.' My mama talks French sometimes."

"Really?"

He nodded and took a Tootsie Roll from our horde on the end table, as if it was no big deal, as if everyone's mother walked around a funeral parlor casually tossing off French phrases in a Southern accent, high heels and a sleek dress that skimmed her knees, with her hair pulled back like a movie star.

"She says no woman is ever happy with the hair she has. She always wants someone else's."

"Does she wear sunglasses, too?"

He stared at me as if he couldn't believe I had asked such an idiotic question.

That was Jamie. And that was Aunt Peach.

CHAPTER 3

The memory was so vivid that I reached down to touch my knee. But instead of the rubbery roughness of the bandage, I felt the silkiness of my pantyhose over hard, round bone.

"So you finally decided to show up at a Sokol funeral. Of course, it would have been pretty bad if you missed this one, considering."

It was the smirk in the navy blue suit gloating over me, wafting a subtle cologne and broad condescension. *Who? Who is this man? I know—wait, wait, don't tell me—it's on the very tip—*

"Dougie—Dougie McConnell. How are you?"

He stared at my extended hand for a split-second longer than politeness should allow, then grasped it briefly. His hand was too warm, too moist, belying the calm in the cut of his suit. He ran a finger around the inside of his shirt collar.

"It's Douglas now, by the way."

I smiled. "Of course. We are all grown up now."

The talk was small for a few minutes. He was in sales—*why was I not surprised?*—for some kind of manufacturer of PVC pipe and related products. Divorced—*again, no surprise*. Two kids, a boy and a girl who lived with the ex. He was taking classes at Governor's State, going for an MBA. That did register mild astonishment—the fact that he had even completed a bachelor's degree—until he admitted that it had taken him nearly ten years, bouncing from community college to community college, from Prairie State to Triton, from major to major, before finally eking out a diploma from the Purdue -Calumet Extension. It was typical catching-up with old relations bullshit, but there was a history here and the soft hand of contempt drew its finger across my lips so they curled just *ever so,* and pressed my head back with a gentle caress so that I was—at the end of his spiel—staring down my nose at him, just as I had done countless times in my youth.

Maybe he noticed because he shifted his stance from neutral to alpha and suddenly, unexpectedly, went for the jugular.

"So you're here—haven't seen you at one of these family things for years—but hey, some things never change. You're still in the other room."

Keep it light. Self-deprecate. "Well, if you can't stand the heat ..."

"Get away from the corpse."

As vulgar as ever.

"That your husband and daughter? Strong resemblance between 'em."

I nodded without thinking, my eyes scanning for an escape mechanism.

"Nice of him to come along. Amicable divorce?"

"I'm not divorced."

"You're not wearing a wedding ring. What's up with that?"

"You don't miss a trick." I sighed. *How to get out of this conversation?* "We never married."

"Shacked up? At your age? That's setting an example for your daughter. Shit, I may have divorced the bitch, but at least I married her first. Marriage thing just too scary?"

Why am I still in this conversation?

"Yo, is you his baby mama?"

Jive-ass. Time to go.

"It's been a pleasure, Dougie." Emphasizing the diminutive. "As always."

I walked toward the door but he sidled along beside me, buzzing in my ear, a persistent mosquito returning after every fruitless swat.

"Oh come on, admit it. You were always gutless at rock bottom—about everything."

"And you always tried your best to exploit that." *Why am I answering?*

"Gutless—but you always thought you were better than the rest of us."

"I can't imagine why I would have felt that way." *Just stop answering!*

Crazily, inexplicably, instead of retreating to the ladies' room where he could not follow, or to the parlor room where my grandmother was laid out, where there was safety in sheer numbers, I walked to the front door of the funeral home and out into the cool lavender twilight of the early evening.

He followed me like a wasp in autumn, hovering, circling, insistent, hot-tongued.

"Where the hell do you think you're going?"

Don't swat—it just makes them angry. I bit down on my lip to keep a retort inside my mouth.

"Running away? You were always good at that."

Let it land and then it will take flight again when it sees that there is nothing to feed on.

"You're crazy, like always. One crazy broad…"

By the calculations of my cobwebbed memory, it was about four or five blocks to the beach at Calumet Park. Down one or two long city block, turn east, walk a few half blocks, turn left, then another long block or two. The mental map formed slowly, imperfectly. *Whatever!* Go east at the corner and at some point, I knew I would bump into Lake Michigan.

The human wasp was relentless, but quieter now, only occasionally dive-bombing my head with an angry buzz.

"Used to be it took the two of you together to go up against me—now it's just you left. You don't stand a chance in hell."

My god, he never grew up. He never grew up. Oh, his outer shell had expanded and his hairline had receded an inch or so and his skin had roughened, but inside was still the shrunken heart that was two times too small and the shriveled soul that had blocked the path of a little girl who had to pee bad.

Don't provoke a frenzied insect.

"Let it go, Doug. My God, grow up. This is so childish."

The sting seemed off-hand at first.

"What's your—man—gonna think?"

We passed a block of frame two-storied houses in silence. An overgrown lilac bush intruded onto the sidewalk, its blossoms just opening in the late Northern spring. The heavy scent enticed. I broke off a cluster and pressed them purple-sweet to my nose. The wasp hovered and stared. I imagined myself superreflected in his eight million eyes.

"What's he gonna think, you walkin' out?" he repeated. "Or don't you give a shit? What's your dad gonna think? Shit, we know you don't care about his ass."

"Vulgar, as always." This time the thought popped out of my mouth.

I could see the edge of the park up ahead, the oval cinder track where I used to run and the line of trees that marked the cement walkway that bordered the beach.

I slowed my pace now, no need to hurry, the bug was not going away, so best to just ignore it. *Wait him out; he'll tire of the chase.* I breathed in the wind blowing off the lake, savoring its undertones of fish and factory.

"Or is he used to it by now? Does he know what you do with your cousins?"

That one left a welt.

He trailed me across the wide swath of grass, silent, perhaps waiting for another retort to feed upon. At the sand I slipped off my shoes and picked my way closer to the water, tiptoeing around cigarette butts and fast food wrappers. One black sock and limp gray briefs, sand-streaked and sun-bleached, lay half buried, mournful remnants of some past revelry. The sand felt strange under my nylon-encased feet, hard-packed, unyielding. To the water's edge I bobbed and weaved, with my bête noire following behind more slowly, sand seeping into his black wingtips with every shifting step.

"I'm bettin' he don't. Not something you'd tell him."

I stopped on the wet sand just beyond the reach of the waves and felt the cold begin to seep through skin and muscle, into bone and marrow.

"Doug, can't you just let it be? What do you want from me after all these years?"

Try some sugar to pacify the winged fiend.

"What do I want? Nothin'." He moved in closer, his voice a sibilant whine in my ear. "Except maybe to take one more good look at a cold-hearted bitch who'd fuck a boy up and then not have the guts to show her face at his funeral."

The cold tongue of the lake licked at my ankles. It was jolting, raising prickles on my arms and legs.

The wasp had spent its last sting. I turned to him even as I stepped further into the mouth of the water.

"You can't hurt me with this, Doug. It's been twenty years—you can't. But if you must know, if it'll satisfy some bizarre itch you've had all this time—Jamie was buried before I even got the news that he was dead."

He just stared.

I thought he didn't quite comprehend. "My dad was on a bender—drunk for days—he never even called. I found out when I called Jamie's house looking for him because he—" *Too much information.* "I called and they told me about the crash and they'd already taken him down to Georgia and had his funeral—and he was gone."

His eyes narrowed, deepening the beginnings of wrinkles around his eyes. He still didn't seem to understand.

"I didn't know," I repeated, stretching out the syllables of the words, bitch that I am, talking down to him, affirming his opinion of me. Then I turned and started to walk down the shore.

His hot grip on my arm jerked me to a stop.

"What the fuck are you talkin' about? Crash? What crash?"

Confused, malevolent, his mouth was an ugly purple gash in the chill of the deepening twilight. Was he maybe semi-drunk? I breathed deeply but could not detect the odor of alcohol, just the smell of the dead white-bellied alewives that floated in and out with the waves.

"Jamie's crash. The car crash. How he died." Then my patience, fear-driven, fled. "Just get the fuck away from me." I wrenched my arm away.

"How—he—died."

I should have walked on but the history between us stopped me, made me face him again, toe to toe, vulgarity to vulgarity. "Yes, you fucking imbecile. How—he—died!"

"He didn't crash his car, you stupid bitch. He fucking drowned. What the fuck—are you telling me you didn't know? He walked into this fucking lake and drowned!"

I'd forgotten the pull of water, its gravity, its enveloping nature. I'd forgotten the shock of its cold, the pain that shoots up from the base of the spine, tensing arms and legs and neck. I'd forgotten the numb warmth that follows immersion as outer and inner temperature seem to adjust; the cycle of shock, pain and adjustment as you press further on from the shore, deeper into the body of the lake, a cycle remembered from my childhood: first the calves, then the knees, then the thighs submerge. Then hips, then waist, then the small of the back, especially sensitive and vulnerable. Even at the height of the summer, when the lake water is at its warmest, maybe 76 or 78 degrees, only the hardiest of souls will go further.

But *they* did, the boys, and so I did, then, and now. When the lake's icy liquid caress curved around my ribcage, I could see flowers floating in the water around me, tiny violets, miniature pink roses, dipping and bobbing in a wide, undulating circle of blue.

Strange and apropos.

In the deep blue gloom, water and sky melded, melting into one liquid moment with a white arm outstretched. *I am here. If you are, come to me.* Muffled cries from somewhere. But here was only a quiet, fluid seduction. *I am here. If you won't come to me, I will come to you.*

Frozen. Unable. The glowing hand fluttered, then rested on a watery cradle, rocking to and fro, rising and falling.

I am here.

Boys floating, shimmery smiles rippling over the stark, blue-whiteness of their skin, purple-lipped. The cold was gone, the barrier of skin gone, sensationless, senseless. Their arms were around me, but I felt nothing. Come away, baby-child, come away. Blue-white boy whispered, throbbed. Over, under and around. Come away. Outside, inside, blue velvet steel. White-blue boy, stiff as silk, slipped around, selkie-swift, eel-like. I'd forgotten the pull of water. Come away.

A solid embrace abruptly broke the water's hold. Come away.

I am here.

"Come away, Claire. Claire." The voice was urgent, real, tangible, uttering terse syllables that begged to hold and be held.

I turned my head. The clay-faced man with the trembling lower lip was waist deep in the water, his white dress shirt luminescent, wet, stuck to his stomach and billowing from his back. He was pale-faced except for two berry-red splotches of exertion staining his cheeks, his eyes the color of November, his lips, plump red grapes. His hands gripped my shoulders and slowly turned me around, guiding me back to shore.

"Flowers for dead boys." The voice was strange, not my own, something guttural choked through the clench and chatter of teeth. I reached out to pluck one, but it ducked just beyond my fingers.

"Come away," was all he said.

It wasn't until we had reached the sand that I realized the flowers, the little violet and rose tributes surrounding me had only been the floating fabric of my dress.

"Do you remember me?" He guided me over the sand, his arm, all bone and sinew, bent awkwardly around my shoulder, his hand goosefleshed and tense against the skin of my upper arm.

In that instant the name was on my tongue. "Strawboy."

His hand relaxed momentarily, fingers curling. "Nobody's called me that since—in years. Remember my real name?"

"That was your real name," I stuttered through chattering teeth.

He snorted. "Yeah, but to the rest of the world I'm—"

"Kevin. Kevin Straszewski."

The sopping fabric of my dress clung to my thighs. I stopped to gather it in my fists and wring it out. The wind gusting up off the lake felt like a bully's shove on my back as I shuddered and stumbled over the parking lot curb.

"Damn, now's the time I wish I wore a jacket—cuz I could have done the gentlemanly thing and put it over your shoulders."

We scuttled across the asphalt, pushed on by the wind, squelching water and sand.

"You still live around here?" *Ask a question to avoid having to answer one.*

"I'm in my folks' place. My old man passed a few years back, my ma last fall."

"I'm sorry."

"Thanks. So it's just me there."

"Not married?"

"Divorced."

"Oh—sorry. Children?"

"A boy. She's got him—down in Florida. She was always a beach baby. Met her at the beach."

A sputtering laugh spewed out of me, followed by a gasp. His hand tensed again, fingers gripping into my arm, surprising heat searing through skin to the muscle.

"I'm sorry. I'm not laughing at you. I just—it's just so—I mean, god, here I am, there I was, in the water and you—and now here we are—having this perfectly normal conversation, walking along Avenue O or N—or whatever the fucking alphabet letter it is, except we're dripping wet—and I was waist deep in the lake … and now we've got to go back to—oh god, I am so stupid—and sorry—and—"

"Claire."

He planted himself in front of me, gripping both my arms. I couldn't really see his expression in the gloom, but there was a weariness in his voice.

"Claire…" He faltered and let whatever it was go.

"I need to get back. God, I need to figure out what to say. Jesus!"

42

"You were walking on the beach and slipped and ..."

"I don't lie—not to them."

"That your husband and daughter?"

"My daughter—and ..." *Just let it go.*

"Man, your cousin Dougie always was an asshole, wasn't he?"

A graceful pivot, thank you. A grimace stretched my lips in a sickly little twist. "Yeah."

"Well, next time he pisses you off, maybe just throw some sand in his face, huh?"

Nothing was said about anything by anyone. If the residents who happened to be outside at that moment when the dusk became the dark, patting soil over the last impatiens hastily tucked into a flowerbed or bent over the open hood of a car, adding wiper fluid, noticed the dripping strangers walking their streets they made no audible remark. Kevin, after silently ushering me to the rental car, ducked into the funeral home and reappeared minutes later with Aaron and Tally. The darkness provided me with blessed cover. Tally, upon seeing me hunched against the passenger side door, blurted out an accusatory "where'd you go?" only to be cut off instantaneously by Aaron's gruff "a walk, get in, your mother's tired."

When she saw the state of my dress at the hotel, she opened her mouth to speak again, but Aaron's quick frown and the snap of his jaw from side to side made her reconsider. Even the hotel concierge said nothing as the three of us, one still purple-pale and damp, two tight-lipped and wide-eyed, crossed the lobby to the elevators. However, I saw his mouth open just like Tally's and Aaron motion with his palm as if to suppress any sound from escaping.

In the morning, Tally asked for no explanation; maybe he'd given her a private one while I stood under a torrential hot shower, trying to shake the chill that had seeped under my skin. She merely took a muffin from the room service basket and nibbled fitfully, like a skittish rabbit, while Aaron flipped rapidly through cable television stations.

At the funeral, attention was directed solely to the business at hand, commending Sophia Elizabieta Sokol's spirit into the hands of her Lord and entrusting her body to the earth. My father, red-eyed and wild-maned, as if he hadn't slept, held me close again, close enough for me to smell a metallic odor under the scent of his aftershave. Fear, maybe. Shame? Was he aware of last night's indiscretion? My shoulders and arms were rigid under his hands, but the strong crest of his shoulder and the soft fabric of his suit lured my cheek to bend to him again, if only for a moment.

With Aaron at my side, Dougie stayed away, like a vampire kept at bay by the crucifix around a vulnerable neck. But I was bloodless at that point. He couldn't have sucked a drop of anything from me. On the short ride to the church, I stared out the window at the normalcy of a Saturday morning along the avenue, at an old man in sagging gray workpants who doffed his White Sox cap and held it over his heart as the funeral cortege rumbled past.

Even the rendition of Amazing Grace, unusual in a Catholic service, left me dry-eyed.

At my insistence, we skipped the luncheon under the guise of an inflexible flight schedule and needy graduate students. My father clasped Aaron's hand in both of his, hugged Tally close, ran his thumb across my cheek. Then we were gone, riding silently from car to plane to car, leaving home, going home, quiet, still and dry.

CHAPTER 4

It was easy to avoid talking about the elephant in the room at home. There were other issues to use as diversions, as long as I was willing to play the bitch, which was never very tough.

On the topic of Tally's choice of summer job:

"I can't believe you'd rather deal with a bunch of homesick, hormonal middle schoolers than do the internship at Cahokia."

"Mom, that's Dad. He likes playing in the dirt, not me."

"You think won't be getting your hands dirty at sleepaway camp? That's all it is—dirt and mosquitoes. What about the job at the Arch? You'd be indoors—"

"In a climate-controlled environment – doing what? Cataloging old stuff that someone else found in the dirt."

"Artifacts are not 'old stuff'—"

"Whatever. You guys like that. Dad digs, finds stuff. That's his thing. You clean it up and file it away. That's your thing. But that's you. I—me—Tally—want to work with kids. Look, I've accepted and I'm leaving in 2 weeks. Deal."

Later, alone with Aaron:

"We hardly discussed the camp job and suddenly it's set in stone."

"We discussed it."

"Where was I when this alleged discussion took place?"

His face squinched up, as if he suddenly had an itch in a place he was unable to politely scratch. "Guess you weren't there." If *he* enjoyed playing the bastard, he could have added, *"and that's the price you pay for wanting to live the way that we do,"* but he just shrugged. "Look, she's got to make up her own mind about these things. Chick's gonna fly the coop sometime."

I nodded crossly, half wishing to command him to take the chick and go home to his own coop. "Sure as rain's gonna fall, farm boy."

Aaron didn't really dig in the dirt very much anymore. He left that to the grad students and PhD candidates out to make names for themselves scouring the earth for new finds, sifting and brushing and painstakingly chipping away for ancient bones, primitive tools and the fossil coprolites that might provide some revelation, some missing piece of the anthropological puzzle. He preferred to teach undergrads. Oh, he might occasionally supervise a summer jaunt to a dig site, but he concentrated on the Midwest and the Cahokia Mounds just across the Mississippi in Illinois. He focused on the Mound Builders, the Native American tribes who thrived along the river valleys during the Woodland Period from about 1000 BC to about 1600 AD.

He grew up on a Missouri farm in the southeast portion of the state which is riddled with caves. He's another Tom Sawyer who got lost in a cavern overnight, as a scrawny ten year old. When he grew too big and tall for caving, he switched to digging, searching for arrowheads, pottery. Where other boys might hitchhike to St. Louis for a wild time of bar hopping, he'd make pilgrimages to Cahokia, the granddaddy of mounds, the highest man-made mound known.

The first time he brought me to its top, he pointed out the Arch, a gleaming silver parabola off to the west, and then made me lie down and stare up at the sky.

"Closer to heaven," he had whispered.

He is the reason that I get paid to do what I have done since childhood. Tally was correct in her simplistic teenage way: Aaron did the digging and I did the clean up and the filing. Curating is my specialty: collecting and caring for objects. I store. We truly are the descendants of the hunter/gatherers.

When we first met at the University of Chicago, he was working on his dissertation and supervising biology lab sections. I was in the first quarter of my first year on campus, a clumsy girl who dropped test tubes and beakers. He was remote, pre-occupied. I was giddy, silly and, suddenly, unscientific. When we met again, the following spring after the cataclysm, he was still remote and preoccupied, but so was I, the giddiness replaced by pale skin and jutting, aching bones, the vitality buried under a layer of oversized sweatshirts and chopped, disheveled hair.

Now on a Monday morning after my lunatic moment, he knew it was best to let this new site lay undisturbed at present. He would dig later.

My ten-by-ten office at the museum under the Arch was a cluttered, dark little cavern filled with piles: piles of archeological journals, research briefs, and educational philosophy texts; a stack of brochures from other museums across the country, a folder of crinkled papers from the museum suggestion box, a batch of government funding application guides. A few years back I had been coaxed out the archives and into the public area of the museum. *You are so good at organizing this, that and the other, and so good at explaining the significance of these objects – you must use those talents for the public benefit; you must not hide your light under all these 'things'.* Translated that means I was tasked with designing educational programs for schoolchildren to enhance their visits to the museum. I am good at my job. Damn good, some say.

But my mind wouldn't focus on the educational and entertainment needs of the children of St. Louis that morning. It kept drifting away to a chilly beach at twilight and a brutal purple gash and things previously unfathomable that had been said and now had to be fathomed and reckoned with. For awhile, everything was just—fuck. *Fuck Dougie, fuck Dad, fuck family, fuck 'em all. Fuck the lake, fuck Chicago, fuck love, fuck lies, fuck life. This is why I left.* A white-hot fever steam obscured everything and left me lost and groping. Only gradually did it begin to dissipate, like fog under the sun. *Well, he was lying, he was simply lying, like he always did when we were kids…*

Lies, all lies. Bastard boy and man.

And yet … and yet—why? Why? Why lie? Did he really still hate me so very much, twenty years down the line, just because Jamie and I ran away from him at every chance? *He was a frickin' bully!* Just because we didn't let him join our society of two? *He was a frickin' bully!* Just because I laughed at him once when he tried to …?

No, do not go there. Because that way lies something close to madness…

Lies, all lies, same as it ever was. But was there was genuine confusion on his face? Or was it just the dim light playing tricks? Was he really taken aback or just pausing to plot his next move in that moment when his jaw fell open and he seemed to be gasping for breath … or words. How the purple of his lips had deepened in the chill of the breeze off the lake. Was it possible?

No.

Lies, fucking lies. And it will always be that way, from his cradle to his grave.

Stop! Enough!

I tried to work, but words and sentences disintegrated into meaningless jumbles of letters and fragments. Nonsense. As were my thoughts. I tend to obsess, to pick at past events like hang-nails, running a mental thumb back and forth over the sore spot until it stings, looking for—I don't know what. Shoulda-woulda-coulda—as if I could change the outcome by replaying it in my head. I couldn't let this particular wound alone, rubbing it over and over, worrying it, until, like the hangnail on my middle finger, it was raw and bled anew.

I went home at five, having achieved nothing: the program draft lay untouched, my finger and head ached and the past was not changed.

Heat comes early to eastern Missouri. The streets shimmer and people sweat; it slows down the flow of the Mississippi and the pace of life. St. Louis is enough of a Southern town to make adjustments when the mercury reaches a certain Fahrenheit. I grew up without air conditioning in Chicago—I know hot and sticky. But up there the pace never seemed to slow for the weather—it went on, full steam ahead, and if you can't stand the heat, you know what to do. However, in St. Louis, the proper response to 90° and high humidity is—at least from Aaron's point of view—iced tea or lemonade in the shade of the maple tree, where the temperature is a good five degrees cooler thanks to its canopy of spreading branches and wide, glossy leaves. He grew up down here, he knows.

He is a master of the art of stillness. He can settle his frame into an Adirondack chair and abandon himself to repose. In that sweet lull the only movements his body makes are the rise and fall of his chest to breathe or his hand and arm to lift a sweating glass of tea to his lips. Even with all the meditation techniques known to man, I am not able to achieve such quietude. Some part of my body is always moving; a foot jiggling, a finger drumming, a knee bouncing, a heel tapping. My mind racing. Aaron has tried for years to counsel me on how to let go, to just breathe and be, but it's no good. Ohm does not lead me to Shanti.

We sat under the tree every evening after dinner for a week. The semester was at an end so it was crazy time for Aaron, slogging through final papers and determining grades, but he shucked that weight when he sat down in his green wooden chair. He may have wanted to talk about Chicago, but he probably sensed that I still didn't. So we sat and sipped iced tea, letting the water droplets from our tumblers trickle down our arms.

Tally joined us for awhile on Friday night when she took a break from studying for her own finals the following week. Even with the heat, she was chattery and high-strung, hopping from topic to topic and from emotion to emotion like the flashy cardinal flitting from branch to branch in the maple. *She couldn't wait to get finals over with and get to camp. Thank God she was going because her best friend Erika was spending the summer at music camp. Perish the thought of moping around here alone. Well, not alone. Jason Pellier was bugging her again to hang out. Does that mean it was a date or not? Guys were so obtuse. What to do about Jason?* But before we could formulate the beginnings of a plan to determine Jason's sincerity, she was off on another tangent, raising the temperature under the maple by the sheer force of her personality. It was almost a relief when Erika appeared around the corner of the house to collect her for a trip to Ted Drewes for a frozen custard.

"Who the hell is Jason Pellier?" I asked as they skittered out of the yard.

"A likeable boy. Tall, a bit androgynous, if you ask me. Wears his hair a bit long for my taste. Large ears. But I like the fact that they aren't pierced. Don't know about other body parts."

"Hmm."

"I especially the fact that he lives three doors down—and I know his parents."

"That's not a guarantee of safety."

"Safety? Who said anything about safety? There is no safety in affairs of the heart. But proximity—now that helps."

"This 'hanging out.' Could be friends, could be something else. Sounds dicey. And I'm surprised she hasn't said anything to me before."

We sat for a moment in the relative silence of the evening, listening to the first stirrings of crickets and the faint shouts from a game of tag somewhere down the block.

"Why would she?"

"Hmm?"

"Why would she say something to you?"

I rolled my eyes. "Because we talk about these things."

"When you say 'we' do you mean you and Tally or mothers and daughters in general?"

"Jesus, are you parsing my sentences now, Professor?"

"I'm just trying to figure out what you're saying because as far as I can tell, you're the master of incommunicado, the sorceress of secrets, and she's your apprentice."

I felt an inner heat bloom across my face. "What's that supposed to mean?"

Aaron stood up and, balancing his drink in one hand, slowly dragged his chair so that it was directly opposite mine. He sat back down and drummed his fingers on my knee. His own pale face was tinged pink across his cheekbones. "It means that I'm pretty frustrated sitting here not knowing why some guy you knew back in high school had to fish you out of Lake Michigan last Friday night."

"I don't even know—so how can I tell you?" I ran my glass across my cheek and forehead to cool the burn.

"You don't know why you walked into the lake?"

"No." Drops of water slid lazily down over my eyebrows and pooled in the corners of my eyes. "I was talking with my idiot of a cousin and the next thing I knew I'm in the water and ..." I trailed off lamely.

"What were you talking about?"

Evasion came easily, the words slip-sliding out of my mouth without forethought, by instinct. "Ancient history."

He gripped my knees, his large hands covering my kneecaps, his fingers fiery over my already too-hot skin, as if he could squeeze the truth out of me that way. "Not good enough."

I ran the glass over my other cheek and then my lips. It no longer offered relief, was tepid from its journey across my flesh. I spilled the dregs of the tea and ice in the grass. *Placate: to soothe or mollify, especially by concessions: Appease.* Words, I've always been good at words, as good as I am at curating. *Hard blue eyes, staring, glaring, hard blue eyes that I want to soften, so I'll say some words, obfuscate, obliviate, obscure, anything but what I really don't want to say, because that's already been archived and I won't retrieve it, not even for him.*

"Dougie has been driving me crazy for years."

His fingers pressed even harder, bone against unrelenting bone. "You haven't seen him in years."

"Once an asshole, always an asshole."

"That doesn't explain why you would deliberately walk into fifty degree water—"

I wrenched his hands from my knees and stood abruptly, accidentally knocking his glass off the arm of his chair. Ice and tea puddled at his sandaled foot momentarily, before the thirsty earth swallowed them.

"This is my dirt and maybe I just don't want to dig in it right now, farm boy."

He will quit me some day. The thought trailed me as I slammed through the back screen door. One day I'll just go too far, or the cumulative effect of all the years will simply break that camel's back. *One day I will walk away and he won't come after me. And then what would I do?*

It was a cold week in the house. They didn't come for dinner, what with one cramming for finals, the other claiming a heavy workload. I struggled over the program draft, holed up in my office, staring at the computer screen as the text dissolved into the screensaver, the one Tally had designed on her last visit: revolving red words "Wuv U."

On Friday when noon rolled around, my stomach was growling and, craving red meat, I went in search of it. After the midday heat, fast food paradise was a strange mix of frigid over-conditioned air and vaporous grill heat. The antiseptic smell of cleaning solution mingled with the savory aroma of frying meat. The lines were long. It was the height of the lunch rush and everyone in downtown St. Louis appeared to have had the same need for a junk food fix. So we waited and shuffled, paused, then shuffled again, like junkies in a methadone clinic, hanging for our maintenance dose, until at last we stood before the counter and recited our orders to semi-frazzled cashiers who barely managed the cheery smile of greeting required by the franchise.

"Can I take your order? And is this for here or to go?" He was young, the look of a rising senior upon his chin, mixed with blonde whiskers that he had missed with his razor. A red and yellow pimple fulminated at the corner of his lip.

"To go. A number six with a Coke."

"Would you like to up-size that?"

"No, thanks."

He pressed the keypad and turned to get my drink, all herky-jerky motion of fingers, elbows and lanky arms. No grace of movement, no elegance of carriage, but he got the job done in good time, presenting my drink and the paper sack with my burger and fries with another smile.

"That's $4.65, ma'am."

I handed him a ten. He punched in the numbers, the register drawer popped open and he bent his head to concentrate on making correct change. When he looked back up and extended his hand, Jamie was smiling at me. He held out a five dollar bill and two coins, ready to place them in my hand.

"Five and thirty-five cents is your change."

Jamie was smiling at me, his pink lips stretched wide across his face, his brown eyes narrowed ever so slightly in that conspiratorial way he had.

Lush-lipped boy, fringed and wavy, caramel-colored hair falling, you'd never get away with that here, you'd be pony-tailed or braided ... Why are you smiling at me, while a flower of ice blooms in my belly and grows like a vine through my chest, the tendrils curling around my organs with a cold-handed grip, until it reaches my throat and twines its wintery stem around, tighter and tighter, colder and colder ...

"Oops, sorry about that," the boy said as the quarter and the dime bounced off the counter onto the gray tiled floor with a glacial jingle. The paper bill floated down lazily to rest on my shoe.

"Sorry, ma'am," he said again, but he was already looking past me to his next customer, and anyway, Jamie was gone and the teenager was back.

I threw the paper sack in the garbage can, appetite gone. The heat outside felt good. It dried the sweat over my lip and the clamminess on my palms. It seared through the thin cotton of my blouse like a pair of hands resting on my shoulders and back, propelling me gently onward across the crowded plaza, under the gleaming Arch, where the earliest of the summer tourists craned their necks back and their heads up, shielding their squinting eyes against the blinding corona of sun on steel. The heat guided me down the steps that bordered the east end of the plaza until I reached the small bronze plaque that commemorates the level to which the Mississippi rose after the Great Flood of 1993. With an insistent pressure, it persuaded me to sit upon that step and caressed my cheek and chin while I watched the river meander and wink under the white glare of noon. After a while I moved down one step, and then another, and another, inching cautiously like a toddler going bottom-first down a flight of stairs, my purse scraping and bumping along beside me.

I'd be under water now, I thought. If it was 1993, I'd be submerged and the dirty floodwater teeming with bacteria would be in my mouth and up my nose and cars and broken twigs would be tangling in my hair and I'd be coursing downstream, moved by a forced outside of myself, no control, swept along with the rest of the debris.

When my imagination found me at the very end of the Mississippi, where the river mouth opened and spat me into the salted sea, home was the only alternative. But when I arrived, the stolid old Tudor with its muddy-red brick and green-gray slate looked dour, not welcoming. Even the cats barely acknowledged my entrance. They were stretched out on the red-gray Mexican tile in the dim foyer, the coolest place in the house. The calico opened one jade eye, and then closed it again. The tabby shifted only slightly in her stupor.

The clocks kept me company in the still of the house that afternoon. The dark cherry mantel clock that squatted over the green marble fireplace place in the living room announced the hour in its sonorous Westminster chime. The oak schoolhouse clock in the kitchen clicked a soothing rhythm as its bronze pendulum swung to and fro. In the foyer, the little golden bird flitted in and out of its house in the hickory cuckoo clock every hour on the hour, chirruping tunelessly but merrily. They were asynchronous by design, set that way by my hand to the melody of an old Chicago song, the lyrics running through my head— *Does anyone really know what time it is?*—all telling different times so that the first three or four minutes of every hour were enlivened by their music. Then silence ruled again.

The jewel-like Waterford crystal clock on the secretary in the study was mute, but winked soothingly in a rainbow of color as the late afternoon sun shone through its prism-like facets. I visited them all, pacing from room to room, from the front of the house to the back, pausing only to press my over-heated forehead against the smooth, cool, white wood of a doorframe or to lower my burning cheek to the cold, hard red granite of the kitchen counter.

My friends, in turn, announced two o'clock, then three. When the mantle clock chimed the next quarter hour, I was standing at the picture window in the living room, bumping my knees, first right, then left, right, then left, against the edge of the oak coffee table, wincing a little at the jagged notes of pain that played behind my kneecaps and at the sudden, gurgling roar of a lawnmower that had been jerked to life. Across the street, the undergrad who cut the grass for the elderly widow strode back and forth across the lawn, guiding the mower through its paces, cutting narrow swaths of richly-hued turf, trailing a lighter shade of green in its wake. The boy, of medium height and build, paused a moment. His short dark hair glistened as he ran a hand quickly over his head. Taking the edge of his T-shirt in his hands, he humped his back slightly and pulled the shirt up and over his head, exposing his pale back and chest, which clashed with the already toffee-colored skin on his arms and neck, the classic farmer tan. He tossed the shirt casually over the iron porch railing and turned back to his work. For a moment before bending to pull the cord to re-start the mower, he stood in repose, his face turned up to the sun, a smile of contentment easing across his lips.

And it was Jamie's smile, on Jamie's face, the hair no longer dark brown and cropped, but taffy-colored and ripple-waved.

Sugar-lipped boy, reaching skyward, but to the moon not the sun, limber as a cat stretching from humpbacked to belly-flat, muscles crawling under skin soft as velvet, beaded with dew, why are you smiling across the faded gray asphalt and the half-mown lawn, while the heat sears my cheeks and forehead and drives the sweat in rivulets down the middle of my back and between my breasts, while my mouth and throat are strangely dry, parched, my tongue a wad of cotton against my teeth ...

Then he bent to pull the cord. When the mower jolted back to noisy life, Jamie was gone and it was the college boy who diligently pushed the mower across the lawn, through the heat, under the afternoon sun.

At a certain impressionable age, my friends and I would pull the shades in our bedrooms and hunker down cross-legged on the floor, be it Yvette's plush carpet or Brenda's smooth wood or my clammy tile. We would tell ghost stories in the middle of a summer afternoon, our voices murmuring under the Valkyrie hum of cicadas in the trees outside. Yvette, black-haired and black-eyed, whispered tales from the heat of the south that her *abuela* from Mexico had told her, the legend of *La Llorona*, the Weeping Woman, from the days of the conquistadores; La Llorona who roamed the rivers and creeks, wearing a white gown, wailing into the night and searching for children to drag, screaming to a watery grave. Brenda, with dark skin and darker hair blossoming in a loose 'fro, told the tale of the Headless Horseman, and the slave stories her grandmother had handed down from her mother before her, ghost stories told in the dark thirty, the half hour after sunset when the gloom settles on your shoulders like a shawl. I regaled them with the story of Resurrection Mary, a homegrown ghost, who hitchhiked along Archer Avenue in her lovely lace dress, on her way home from a dance, asking hapless drivers who picked her up to stop at Resurrection Cemetery, only to vanish, leaving behind just a cold breath of air.

In the heady atmosphere of rooms perfumed by the scents of Double Bubble gum and Love's Baby Soft cologne filched from older sisters, we clapped hands and singsonged the gruesome rhyme that immortalized the Fall River legend:

> *"Lizzie Borden took an axe, gave her mother 40 whacks;*
> *when she saw what she had done, she gave her father 41!"*

We knew by heart the mystical instructions to conjure the ghost of Mary Warner, rumored to be an infamous child murderess: stand in front of a mirror, turn around three times, close your eyes and thrice invoke her name. *"Come forward, Mary Warner."* If you were so brave as to attempt this, when you opened your eyes you would see her in the mirror behind you. No one ever speculated what would happen next. Depending upon the level of sophistication that we were pretending to at the moment, we scoffed. But none of us ever dared to actually perform the ritual, because we could never be absolutely, positively sure that it was just a silly story meant to ensnare and entrance gullible, wide-eyed young girls.

So why was I now standing in front of the oval mirror that hung over my dresser, tracing the ellipse of its beveled edge with a trembling finger? I saw the material form of my life within that ellipse: the forged iron bed with its plain horizontal and vertical bars, strong and delicate at once, the double wedding ring quilt spread across it, hand-made by Aaron's mother and aunts, a gift for an event that never happened, its once vibrant leaf-green and crisp white fabric faded from time and use; the bow front cherry nightstands that flanked the bed, one a pristine surface, the other stacked with books and journals, the gilded edge and gold ribbon of a bookmark protruding from the topmost volume. There was the earth-toned braided rug spread over the wooden floor and the white wicker hamper. The mirror reflected the running shoes resting in the corner, the hiking boots overturned just behind the open closet door, the pink satin slippers peeking around the edge of the heavy armoire, looking silly and inconsequential beside its plain and simple, Amish-made bulk, a relic of a trip to the Ohio River Valley mounds.

But I wanted the mirror to reflect something else; desired that other reflection, yet feared it too. So when I spoke the words, invoked the conjure, uttered the name, it was in a strange voice that I didn't recognize as my own, a voice quavering with longing and repulsion. *"Come forward, James Joseph Sokol."* Three times the words rose to my lips and I spat them out into the room, into the heat, to bounce off the smooth surface of the mirror and reverberate off the four corners of the earth and beyond, to the netherworld.

Nothing changed the reflection in the mirror; nothing replaced the view of the bed, the hamper, the shoes.

I closed my eyes, and slowly turned three times, feeling the buzz of disorientation in my head and invoked the incantation again. This time the yearning overcame the repulsion. *If you would come to me unbidden, then why not when I ask? If you would come to me in the form of others, then why not as yourself? Corporeal flesh or intangible spirit, I care not. Whether I might touch your cheek and feel solid bone and pliant skin or whether my fingers would slip through the chill fog of a ghostlier corpus, I care not. Only come.*

And when I opened my eyes, he was there, in the mirror, filling the space in the doorway with the lanky awkwardness of youth, his hair pulled back off his face and caught in a white band he'd borrowed from me long ago.

And I was there with him, all pony-tailed energy and t-shirted impudence, bumping up against his arm with a proprietary air and a secret-keeping smile bending my lips.

"Jamie?" I reached out a finger and touched his image in the mirror, half-expecting to feel the warmth of his skin, or the soft fabric of his shirt, instead of the cool, impervious surface of the glass. "Jamie?"

I was caught up in the reflection of the mirror, wanting to turn, afraid to turn, longing to embrace the flesh and bone that occupied the doorway and filled it with a living presence, yet afraid that if I made a move, whether sudden or slow, the vision would vanish like a startled deer turning tail from a highway and leaping back into the dark, obstructed wood.

When I finally did turn and advance toward the object of my desire with an extended hand and the name of past affection on my lips, it was only to shut the bedroom door against the corporeal reality of a young man who smiled quizzically as he tucked a strand of black hair behind his large ear and of my daughter who could only gape and stutter "Mom?" as if she too had seen a ghost—or felt the chilly breath of its miasma on her neck.

CHAPTER 5

In the bottom drawer of the dresser, underneath a layer of neatly folded sweaters that I never wear, yet always neglect to give away to the fall clothing drives, sat a box. It was the kind that department stores used to provide for gift-giving when I was a child: a large, deep, sturdy rectangle with strong, reinforced corners, not the collapsible kind of today; a box made of heavy-duty cardboard, its cover wrapped in a gleaming, white, laminated paper embossed with the Marshall Field's name and famous clock. It was a relic of the days when salesclerks would take the time to fold your gift purchase—perhaps a shirt and sweater for dad or a peignoir set for mom—with impeccable care, and then place it lovingly in the box lined with two or three layers of tissue paper. They would gently enclose it in the crackling, opaque whiteness, tuck the gift receipt into its own genteel little envelope attached to the inside of the cover, and then seal it with the smile of a co-conspirator and a reassuring "I'm sure he (or she) will love it."

As old as it was, the box was in remarkably good shape, with just a few creases along the cover and a small dent in one of the short sides. But then I was not in the habit of handling it very often. Probably the last time I'd lifted the sweaters to remove the box from its shelter was ten years before, after an awkward visit from my father, who had been passing through St. Louis on his way to see his sister at her retirement community down in Phoenix. He had wanted to see his granddaughter. Aaron gave his consent and I sat stone-faced and silent while their conversation moved forward haphazardly, in a series of reckless spurts and abrupt halts, like the progress of a traveler on a footbridge riddled with broken boards and gaps. Afterwards, after enduring seven-year-old Tally's look of confused reproach and the disapproval in Aaron's raised eyebrows, I'd sought affirmation for my behavior in the box.

Now I sat on the floor and ran a hand over its gleaming lid before lifting it off. Instead of rustling tissue paper, the frayed, drab white fabric of a t-shirt washed and worn a few too many times concealed its contents. Folding back the soft cotton, I saw the remnants of a life lived, gathered and sorted and tucked into little piles of once upon a times. In one corner sat a stack of letters and postcards held safe within a beige rubber band, the cancelled postage on the envelopes revealing a progression of commemorative stamps and postal increases. In another corner, a cache of photographs bulged from a wrinkled envelope, the face of an androgynous girl with a too-strong jaw line and too much lipstick grinning above the edge. In the corner nearest my right knee nestled a small square jewelry case covered in red velvet; in the corner on the left rested a tiny cobalt-blue perfume bottle shaped like a scallop, which held a fine gray powder. In the middle of the box rose a stack of old 45 rpm records, lounging in their worn dust jackets. I picked them up one by one, blew off the tiny specks of dust, hanging them over my thumb, like we used to, reading the titles and hearing the music rattle and reverb in my head. *Magic Carpet Ride* by Steppenwolf, *We Can Work It Out* by the Beatles (flipside with *Day Tripper*), *Lola* by the Kinks, *Hot Fun in the Summertime* and *Family Affair* ... as Sly and the Family Stone began to play ...

> *One child grows up to be*
> *Somebody that just loves to learn*
> *And another child grows up to be*
> *Somebody you'd just love to burn ...*

The somber, funky rhythm thrummed from somewhere out of the past as I spotted the tiny body of a doll cradling its severed head within its bendy, twisty rubber arms. Here was the luckless Mr. Willoughby, patriarch, prisoner, victim. My finger rubbed the bit of brown modeling clay still clinging to his neck; rock hard from years without the warm touch of skin. It would never be pliable again.

Much later, when the sunlight that angled through the windows had the mellow glow of the hour or two before sunset, I heard the click of the doorknob, the tread of soft-soled shoes across the floor, the crick of knees that bent to stoop behind me, and the warmth and pressure of a large hand on my shoulder.

We were silent together for a few moments, regarding the detritus spread out before us and the dingy, threadbare t-shirt that drooped across my knees.

"Do you believe in ghosts?" I finally asked.

Aaron eased himself down behind me, his legs and arms spread around me so I could lean back into the solidity of his chest and rest my head against his neck, where his 5 o'clock whiskers felt wonderfully, sandpapery real.

"No, I don't," he answered after a pause. "But what I believe doesn't matter." He fondled an edge of the t-shirt between his thumb and forefinger. "So I'm asking you again—what did you talk about with your cousin Doug?"

In the moment before I answered, I swear I felt the icy water nip at my toes. Reflexively, I drew my legs away, up into my chest.

"Dead boys."

"Your brother."

"And my cousin Jamie. Joey and Jamie."

"Why did that upset you enough to make you walk into the water?"

"I just needed to get away from him."

"That's not what I asked."

"You should have been a lawyer," I said abruptly, leaning forward to pull away.

"Not so fast," he muttered, holding me tight, his breath hot in my ear. A trickle of sweat from his temple melded with my own.

"I need to know—you need to tell me."

Let it go. Let it go. It's a clenching and an unclenching, a muscle tightening to expand, like a contraction in the midst of labor, the rising of pain, of tension, then a slight falling off, as the womb dilates.

"It was something he said. About a boy."

"Which boy?" *Aaron coaching, coaxing, drawing it out, like when Tally was born, gripping my hand and my arm, so I could focus on something other than the pain. But they never really worked, those Lamaze techniques, never took the focus off the pain. Better to just get it over with.*

"Jamie." *Trying still to hold it in, sucking it in, rather than blowing it out.*

"What did he say?"

If I say it, if I repeat the words—will it make them true? It's a lie—I'm sure—but if I say them—if they come out of my own mouth—will that make me believe it? If I believe it, will it be true?

"He said ... he said Jamie drowned."

Aaron shifted and his fingers stuttered on my arms. "You once told me he died in a car crash."

Aah, it is at its peak, the wave of pain, there's the breach and the tear, only a little more, just one more ... "He said there was no crash." The inner grip that clenched my chest as tightly as Aaron's hand made me breathless and my voice a mere hiccup. "He said Jamie drowned in Lake Michigan. Just walked into the lake and drowned. Like maybe on purpose."

It was out, the pain and tension suddenly replaced with an enormous sense of sighing deflation, like the split-second after birth, with the baby pulled free, the sudden emptiness a relief to a womb asked to contain the uncontainable.

Aaron ran his hands down my arms until they came to rest over my own, still clasping my knees. He rubbed my white-boned knuckles. "Do you believe him?"

The easy pressure of his fingers persuaded my own to loosen their grip. My feet skidded back along the floor and once again, I leaned back into Aaron's comfort.

"I don't know what I believe. I don't know what I want to believe." I shook my head. There was the pain and tension again, the clutching and the release, not so strong this time, a lesser contraction to push out the afterbirth, to deliver the next truth. "What I really want is—I want to believe he's still alive. Impossible as that is. And a part of me wants to be with him. Even if that meant going into that water."

For as long as I had gone without tears, I always thought that when they finally returned, it would be with a mighty gush, the kind of heart-aching, gut-wrenching deluge that chokes the throat and nose and blinds the eyes. I anticipated a wailing, keening, rocking sort of cry that rends a hole in the soul and belly until it diminishes to a shuddering, convulsive denouement, leaving only a jumble of tissues and red, swollen eyes to mingle with relief and despair. That was not how it happened. The tears came slowly, quietly, without drama. At first they were barely indistinguishable from the beads of sweat that inched down my forehead. Saltwater and saltwater. But when my eyes brimmed and my vision blurred, I knew. And when they finally overflowed and meandered down my cheekbones and around the flare of my nose, pooling in the curve of my upper lip, I felt they would flow forever.

The light and color leached out of the room, leaving shades of gray. Tally knocked timidly on the door inquiring about dinner and was sent away to forage for herself. Aaron flipped through the stack of records and chuckled his approval, humming a bar now and then, or murmuring a lyric in my ear in his wonderful baritone.

"'I met her in a club down in old Soho ...'"

"Ray Davies you're not."

"'But I know what I am and I'm glad I'm a man ...'"

His voice trailed off as he came to a disk held together by a yellowed strip of adhesive tape which crackled a threat as he ran a finger over it. "Didja wear this one out? Or did someone have a powerful dislike for the Stones?"

Did he notice the breath stutter in and out of my nose and throat? "Played that one time too many, I guess."

"Wore out its welcome?"

"You could say that."

I felt the gentle pressure of his chin against my skull. "What would *you* say?"

When I didn't answer, he ground the hard bone down upon me like he was tightening a vise, obdurate, perverse. I sank down his chest to relieve the pressure. "My mother broke it."

"Just snapped it in two?"

My reply was the merest shrug.

"Why would she do that?"

"Not a big fan of Mick and Keith. Or maybe the sitar drove her to it. As I recall, she couldn't stand Ravi Shankar either."

"Umm–hmm," he mumbled noncommittally as he replaced the 45s in the box. His hand was a shadow as it hovered there for a moment, then rose. Something hung from his fingers, silhouetted against the last light, semi-coiled like a snake.

He shifted behind me as he reached for something above on the dresser with his left hand. I could have told him to stop, could have taken the thing from him with a laugh or snatched it away in anger, but to do so required effort, a strength that I no longer possessed. Far easier to simply recline against a shifting yet solid form and let things happen.

With a sharp scratch, a match flared between Aaron's thumb and forefinger. He touched it to the black wick of the lavender-studded candle resting on its base and shook it out with a snap of his wrist. The smell of sulfur billowed and ebbed as the flame flickered once, then burned tall and true. The light it threw was just strong enough to illuminate the box and the braid that hung from Aaron's hand.

"This can't be your hair. It's way too light."

The braid was shorter than I remembered, and narrower, too, secured at both ends by white elastic bands. Recalcitrant strands escaped here and there ... disobedient as always.

Yet the color was exactly as I recalled: a dirty blonde, a mellow twist of toffee with glints of gold and strands of sun-bleached white mixed in. When I took it and laid it across my palm, the texture was familiar, wiry and soft at once, hair with a mind of its own.

It had always resisted a braid—from the first time I'd ever struggled to divide it into three sections and plait them together under the furtive, curious stares of the other freshmen in the high school cafeteria.

"They're all looking ..."

"So? Let'em look. I don't give a shit. What I don't want is to get singed again with a Bunsen burner."

I would rather have curled it into little ringlets around my fingers ...

"Earth to Claire. Whose hair?"

"Jamie's."

He must have suspected because he didn't skip a beat. "So he did the hippie thing?"

I smiled, wiping my eyes with the back of my hand. The braid left a soft trail across my cheek. "Not really. All the guys had long hair in the seventies. You too, as I recall. His was just a bit longer than the average dude."

"So, why'd he cut it off? And why do you have it?" Aaron's voice was gentle, playful as he took the braid back and held it nearer to the candlelight. "I'm thinking Rapunzel in reverse."

"He got fed up with getting grief from his father so he asked me to cut it. I braided it and I cut the braid off—and I kept it."

"I can't stand it anymore. Just cut it! Just cut it the fuck off." His *cheeks were the mottled red and white color of confusion and frustration and the cut on the corner of his lip, black with dried blood, gaped and oozed a fresh, vibrant scarlet as he spoke.*

"Let's go in and—"

"No, just get the damn scissors. I'll wait out here. I don't want to be in anyone's house right now—I'll just start tearing up the place." He shut his *eyes and leaned his head back against the headrest and exhaled a long, slow breath, as if to expel all the oxygen, or life itself from his lungs.*

"I'll be back in a minute."

"Very Elizabethan of you." Aaron rubbed his rough cheek against my temple.

"Actually, I think the practice of hair keepsakes started a bit later—you know, Alexander Pope, *The Rape of the Lock*. We're talking powdered wigs, men in lace, the age of fops."

"Well, if you want to get technical, truth be told, it's been around for centuries, millennia. We found evidence of it in the mounds, at the burial sites."

I swept my hand over the box now full of light and shadow. "So when the archeologists of the future find my artifacts what will they say?"

"The archeologists or the artifacts?"

"Both."

"The questions are always the same: why is it there and what does it signify?" He turned the braid over in the candlelight and then placed it carefully, almost reverently back in the box beside the old 45s. "You might consider leaving a testament to make the job of deciphering the meaning a bit easier. As a tribute to my own struggles in the field."

"He was the most beautiful boy I ever knew." The words felt both strange and natural leaving my mouth. They hung there in the air around us for a moment until Aaron drummed his fingers on my kneecaps.

"Ah, but you didn't know *me* as a boy," he said lightly. Nonetheless, I could hear the last word catch just a bit at the back of his throat, emotions snagging like a jagged fingernail on delicate fabric.

"And I never knew him as a man."

His fingers skipped a beat on my knees, then came to rest.

"I cut that braid on the last night I ever spent with him."

His fingers again pressed into my skin.

"I think you want to tell me the story."

"No," I shook my head vigorously, bumping up against his jaw.

We were silent for a time again, the quiet punctuated by the faraway sounds of a motorcycle revving and the shattered-glass giggles of adolescent girls, followed by the fluctuating tones of teen-aged boys, low and rumbling at first, cracking into a higher pitch. Then came the hissing hum of the air conditioner shuddering to life. Tally had succumbed.

"We should close the windows," I said, but made no effort to stand.

Aaron eased himself up and held out his hands. I let him pull me up. We crossed to the windows and pushed down the sashes, meeting at the middle one. We left it open for a minute, listening to the wistful notes from my neighbor's flute drift over the fence.

"Tell me the story."

"No, but I'll tell you another. Once upon a time there was a girl who saw dead boys as if they were living, smiled at them, danced with them, made love to them. Then she met someone who eventually made the dead boys go away. And they stayed away for a long time. But today one of them came back."

CHAPTER 6

Two things amaze me about Aaron on a dig: his incredible patience and the delicacy with which his big-boned hands wield the instruments of archeology: the picks and scrapers so like those in a dentist's tray, the brushes large and small used to gently sweep away layer after layer of soil until the treasure is revealed and released. He thought nothing of spending three weeks on three square feet of ground, chipping and brushing, chipping and brushing, heedless to the wicked heat and merciless sun that always burned the thin strip on the back of his neck just above the collar of his shirt where he never did remember to rub sun block.

So, when he first tried to brush it all away in one broad stroke, playing it lightly as we stood as the kitchen counter, he with his tuna sandwich, the cats begging tidbits at his feet, and I with my bowl of mint chip ice cream, so coldly comforting, I was surprised.

"You know, when someone—man or woman—teetering on the edge of forty starts noticing younger men or women everywhere, they usually call it a mid-life crisis," he said, tossing flakes of fish down to his furry supplicants.

"As opposed to what?"

He looked at me, and then looked down again at the cats, who were kneading his golden-haired shins. "Ghosts."

In bed, in the middle of a sleepless night, when the red numbers on our respective clocks glowed 2:59 (mine) and 3:01 (his), he rose up on his elbow and exhaled a long breath. "You've been through a helluva lot in the past few weeks. Grandmother passed, saw your dad for the first time in years, went back to the scene of some traumatic events, your cousin tells you—"

"A lie," I interjected.

"The point is this: some heavy shit's been coming down, as we used to say in country. And when the heavy shit came down in Nam, guys would be shell-shocked, like you are now. We'd see two common reactions: total numbness or gradual freak-out, seeing and hearing things that weren't there."

"Freak-out—that's a comforting way to put it, farm boy. Or what's the trendy label? Post-traumatic stress disorder? Is that easier for you to swallow than saying that your lover is having a fucking nervous breakdown?"

The tears didn't want to stop now. They kept welling up and receding at regular intervals, my own personal tide, following the moon of my mood.

A different man would have hastened to reassure, stumbling over "of course not" and "don't say that" in the midst of an unnecessary apology—or struck back in his own angry helplessness—but Aaron, settling back on his heels and surveying the land to be dug, just laid back down and fumbled for my hand. He held it until sleep finally came somewhere on the dark side of dawn.

When Tally knocked briskly enough to wake us, the clocks read 10:45 and 10:47. She opened the bedroom door slowly, cautiously peering around the edge. Her face was like a talking book, telling a tale of confusion mixed with fear, spiced with a hint of the impatience and resentment that arises with the adolescent realization that one is no longer the hot, burning center of the parental universe.

She was all legs and arms in her khaki shorts and white tank top, brushing her hair with quick strokes. "Jason and I are going to Union Station. I need to get some sandals before I leave for camp. Then we might stop at the zoo."

"You're going shopping together?" Aaron croaked, his arm slung across his eyes.

"Yeah, so?"

"Shoe shopping?"

"What are you implying?"

"I'm not implying anything."

"You've got a tone in your voice."

"Would-you-pre-fer-me-to-talk-like-this?" Aaron's voice took on a robotic monotone.

Tally rolled her eyes. "Don't quit your day job, Mr. Comedy. Anyway, I don't know when we'll be back." She turned on her heel and set off down the hall.

"Bring us some fudge!" Aaron called to the clatter of her clogs on the stairs. He rolled over and tapped his finger on my lips. "That's what you need, some chocolate."

"Do you think she knows her mother's going crazy?"

"Her mother's not going crazy. If she thinks anything, it's that you're entering some pre-pre-pre-menopausal phase, a period which will require infinite patience on her part to get through."

"What the hell? Why do you say that?"

"Because yesterday when I walked in the front door, she pounced on me and said she thought you were either suffering from a fever or had some kind of hot flash because when she and Jason, yes, that Jason, stopped by your room to chat, you looked 'kinda strange'—her exact words—and—"

"And I called Jason 'Jamie' and—Jesus Christ! Am I now to be psychoanalyzed by a pair of teenagers?"

"No, they were just concerned about you—as children will be. Her first suggestion was that we turn on the air conditioning to help relieve your condition! Let her be concerned. It's good for her to think about someone besides herself."

"And what's good for me?" Not waiting to hear his reply, I grabbed my robe and went off to shower, turning my face to the hard spray, letting it wash away the next tide of tears.

Later that day Aaron began to wield a more subtle brush. In the heat of mid-afternoon we took a break from mulching the flower beds and sat back to watch giant cumulonimbus clouds rising and expanding with awesome speed, a white foam wake generated by some enormous silent explosion. They flattened and spread out at the tops, like colossal anvils from which the gods would strike sparks of lightening.

"Thunderheads. Look at the size of that one, it's up thirty, forty thousand feet and growing!" Aaron ran a finger under the rim of his baseball cap. "A storm'll either cool things off or just make it muggier." He winked at me slyly. "That's this farm boy's opinion and you can take it to the bank," he added, letting just the tail end of his Missoura drawl out of the barn as he pre-empted the put-down he knew would be idling on the tip of my tongue.

I rolled back onto the grass, my legs and feet in the shade of the maple, the rest of my body splayed in the bare bulb brightness of the sun. The world through my sunglasses looked liquid and runny from the sweat that had pooled on the lenses. *Melting away, it's all melting away.* And still the clouds grew.

"When I was a little girl, I used to sit on the front stoop or up in the cherry tree in the backyard and watch the clouds form. I'd try to gauge how long it would take before the storm hit: one hour, two. I got pretty good at it. If my mom had done laundry and hung the clothes out on the line to dry, she'd come running out of the house, hurrying to bring it all in before the rain came. And I'd say, 'don't worry, you've got a whole 'nother hour of drying time—'"

"You said 'nother'?" Aaron mocked.

I stuck out my tongue at him. "She never believed me. She'd go on pulling the sheets and towels off the clothesline and hanging the things that were still damp in the basement."

Aaron eased himself back onto the grass next to me, pulling the brim of his cap well down over his eyes. "Ah, Chicago's weather Cassandra."

"Oh, after a while she started to see that my predictions were accurate."

"And she'd leave the clothes out to dry longer?"

I dried my sunglasses on the tail of my shirt, shutting my eyes tight against the furious glare. "Nah, she still took them in too early. She would just lament later that she could have left them hanging."

Aaron nudged my calf with his knee. "Sounds like you missed your calling." His voice slipped into the sonorous tones of a radio announcer. "And now, with today's forecast, here's Accu-weather staff meteorologist Claire Sokol."

"Nope, wasn't meant to be. Cuz when the storms did hit, I'd be hiding in the closet with my hands over my ears. To me, every green-tinged sky foreshadowed a tornado and I was forever trying to remember which corner of the basement we should crouch in when the time came."

"Root cellars—them's the best places."

"Well, what can I say? We didn't have any root cellars on the South Side of Chicago in 1969."

"Where the hell did you store the taters?"

"In the cupboard, like everyone else who didn't live in Bum-fuck, Egypt. Anyway, I got over my astraphobia."

"Came out of the closet, did you? And just how did you over-come your fear? Woke up one summer morning and said enough's enough?"

There he goes again with his digging. The memory of Aaron's criticism echoed in my head: *master of incommunicado, sorceress of secrets.* I felt the silken bristle of the brush pass over me and I let another layer of clay dust fall away.

"My father found me in my closet during one particularly bad storm. I was nine. It was the summer my brother died, not long after, late July maybe. The weather had been miserable, even for Chicago, unbearably humid. Everyone was looking forward to a good storm to cool things off. But when it finally hit in the late afternoon, it was very violent. And I huddled down in my closet, as usual. I could hear my mother, running from room to room, slamming the windows shut against the wind and the rain. I could see the flashes of lightning under the closet door, and the thunder seemed to come right on top of it. Awful, shattering cracks, like the earth was splitting open." My hands clenched around tufts of hot, moist grass.

"Being in the closet wasn't really helping, the booms were so incredibly loud. I even took hold of two of my dresses and pressed the fabric over my ears to try to stifle the sound. It was so stuffy in there, with the clothes and my old toys and shoes and my smelly winter boots, I could hardly breathe. Maybe I was holding my breath, too. Then the door opened. I remember I screamed a little because my dad looked so large and dark against the light and I thought he had come to drag me out. But he just pushed the boots aside, squeezed down next to me and put his arm around my shoulder. Every time the lightning flashed he'd hug me tight to him. He smelled a little of aftershave, left over from the morning, and spearmint, from the gum he chewed to help him quit smoking, and deodorant. It was a good odor, a mannish odor, eau de dad. He sang to me, Stormy Weather, corny as it sounds. Low, under his breath, so only I could hear."

"He told me to count in between the flash and the boom. At first I couldn't count at all, they were so close. Then, slowly, I began to count to two, then three, and finally to seven and eight. And the storm had passed and just rain was left. He helped me get up and walked me to my brother's room at the back of the house. He opened the window and we pressed our faces to the wet screen, and the air was so fresh and clean-smelling. Off to the east we could see the lightning flash behind the clouds like some kind of beacon, signaling a message we couldn't decode. He said, 'Look at it, it's gorgeous. It's a beautiful, true thing. Powerful and true. Yes, sometimes it kills. But it's so beautiful. Respect it, but don't fear it. Never be afraid of truth and beauty. There's too little of them in this world.' After that, if he was home during a storm, we'd sit on the sofa and watch it out the front window together, until ..."

Until what? Was there a moment fixed in time when I had stopped needing or wanting his comfort in a storm, a *that was then, this is now* instant? It didn't feel that way.

"Until?"

Of course, he couldn't let it lay, but had to poke it, dig at it, work at it with the brush some more. I sat up quickly, pulling the damp, clinging shirt away from my back, and dusting off stray blades of grass, brushing aside his question as well. "Until I got too old—and put away childish things."

Aaron tilted his cap back from his face and squinted up at me. "He has a touch of the poet, your father."

"And all the problems that come with it."

"For now we are *determined* to see through a glass, darkly."

"I see what's there."

He hunched himself up on his elbows and shook his head. "You see what you want to see and conveniently ignore the rest. *For now I know in part; but then shall I know even as also I am known.* "

"Since when did you start quoting the Bible?"

A big grin split his face; he took off his cap and shook his head, droplets of sweat flying off his hair before he slicked it back with his hand. "I'm an old Bible thumper from 'way back. My great grand-daddy on my mother's side rode the revival circuit." He doffed the cap with a flourish.

"Jesus."

Arching his eyebrows, he set the hat squarely back on his head. "Your own personal Jesus. You know how it ends: *'and now abideth faith, hope, charity, these three: but the greatest of all these is charity.'* "

"Preacherman." I stood up, grabbed a handful of soft, soggy brown mulch and sprinkled it over him like holy water. Then I turned on my heel and headed up the patio steps. "Stick to singing."

"The only boy who could ever reach me was the son of a ..." he crooned softly.

"On second thought, don't. You're no Dusty Springfield."

The second call came on a Tuesday evening, exactly four weeks after the first. The peonies were in full bloom; their heavy, overripe heads drooped at the ends of their stems, with petals of fuchsia, pink and white as lush and layered as Elizabethan ruffs surrounding the tiny, flame-like stamens in the center. I brought them inside to perfume the house with their sugar-sweet fragrance, despite the risk of ants who unwittingly hitched a ride in with them. Whenever those brave scouts ventured out from between the satin folds of the petals to make the long march down the stems and the glass vase to the table, they were squashed on sight by napkin, newspaper or finger, whichever was handy.

Aaron had just killed one with his dinner napkin when the telephone rang. He glanced at it.

"It's the dinner hour. Let the machine pick up."

But after my clipped message, when my father's voice blared through the speaker, he looked over at me with raised eyebrows. I rolled my eyes, mouthed "twice in one month" and shook my head quickly. Damn if he didn't pick it up.

"Joe, how the hell are you?" After listening a moment, his lips tightened and his broad face collapsed into furrows and creases.

"Man, that's tough. How did it happen?" He nodded gravely.

I scraped the remnants of dinner off the plates into the garbage. Tally nudged me. "Go talk to him. I'll do that," she hissed.

I shot her a look. "He hasn't asked to talk to me."

"He will."

I shrugged, feeling a twinge of irresponsibility immediately afterwards. *Some role model I am ...*

She glared. "Sometimes you are a word that rhymes with—"

"Don't even say it."

She shoved a plate into a slot in the dishwasher savagely, then brushed past me with reddened cheeks, hiding her eyes with her hand. The screen door clattered. Through the kitchen window, I saw her stomp over to one of the Adirondacks, the one Aaron frequented. She turned it away from the house and flopped down, hidden but for the fall of blonde hair which she tossed over its back, its white gold in high contrast to the deep green of the wood.

Yes, I am a bitch too often. But it wasn't always so. I have been many things, shown many faces, just like you, my golden girl. Sugar-tipped, lace-lipped, honey-talking, broad and narrow of mind and body, strong-limbed, soft-fleshed, bend-me, shape-me girl, silk-smooth and rough-edged, knife-tongued, oozing acid, or mouthing velvet and casual balm.

"Claire."

I turned from the window to see Aaron holding out the telephone receiver, a look in his eye that told me he would accept no excuses; that he would stand there all evening, if necessary. So I crossed the twenty feet or so that separated us with the quick step of the terminally exasperated, my black flip-flops clopping a resentful tattoo against the bottoms of my heels. When I reached for the telephone, though, he refused to hand it to me, holding it just out of reach above my head, while he brought his index finger to my pursed lips and drew them gently into a semblance of a smile. Only then did he hand me the phone, but instead of retreating to a discreet distance to eavesdrop, he leaned against the wall beside me, arms folded across his chest, head back, eyes fixed on some point in the distance, like some proud stallion keeping watch over his mares.

I stared at him for a moment, then, when he didn't take the hint, I jerked my thumb toward the door. He cocked his head and raised an eyebrow, but spared me the verbal admonishment, sauntering off to join Tally outside under the maple. I deliberately turned my back to the bow window, breathing deeply before I spoke.

"Hello ..."

"Clairey Jo, I'll bet you didn't think you'd be hearing from me so soon." His voice, usually broad and forceful, sounded a little pinched, but it could have just been the long distance connection, and my own startled reaction to hearing him use an old childhood nickname that would have been less out of place if I'd found it nestled underneath the old 45s in my relic box. Someone else had been delving into the past.

"No, I didn't. What's up?" I had to bite my lip to keep myself from adding "another dead relative?" *Now is the time for the velvet glove, not the jagged fingernail.*

"Well, I do feel kind of embarrassed about this—"

"Embarrassed? You? Never!"

"I know you're mocking me, Claire." He sounded bemused, or maybe just tired.

Two paths presented themselves: one would lead to a place we had been before, and the other was a road not taken in a long while. The former I could walk blindfolded, I knew its dust, stones and curves so well; the latter was much more uncertain, formidable in its unfamiliarity. I had trod it long ago; it was the path of my childhood. It was overgrown now; the landscape of passing time had swallowed up the once-beaten track and if I was to go this way, I would have to blaze the trail again.

I leaned forward, butting my forehead lightly against the wall, blowing the air slowly and thoroughly out of my lungs.

"Claire? Still there?"

I spun around and leaned back, thumping the back of my head now. Through the window I could see Aaron on the stone bench, leaning forward, listening to Tally, engaged in some deep conversation. My head throbbed from the battering. I stopped and stood motionless. Aaron took one of Tally's hands in his.

"Yes, I'm here."

"The reason I called, besides the pleasure of hearing your voice—you know, I think that's what got me through Ma's wake, knowing I'd get to hear your voice—even just a little—but anyway, enough of my b.s., I know that's what you're saying to yourself."

"You're a master of it. You make it—a pleasure to listen to."

"Ha! Now who's bullshitting who? Reminds me of that old joke. Man's daughter comes home after being off at the university for ten years, bringing all her degrees with her. The father looks at a diploma and asks, *'okay, so what does this B.S. mean?'* Daughter says *'bullshit.' 'All right,'* says the dad, *'how about this M.S. What's that?' 'More shit.' 'And what about this PhD?'* Daughter smiles, *'Piled higher and deeper.'"* He chuckled, but again he sounded constrained and tight, as if his chest were held in some kind of vise.

"Aaron always likes that one," he said in a bit of a wheeze. "Probably tell it to him every time we talk. But hell, that ain't so very often, so what the hey."

"Your voice sounds kind of funny. Like you can't catch your breath. Are you okay?"

A moment of silence on his end. "Is that a note of concern or just my old man's ears playing tricks on me?"

Don't succumb to his charm. That would lead to somewhere that I didn't want to go. I felt the pull of the more familiar path, the ease at which my feet could negotiate it. "I'm just asking if there's anything wrong."

"Well, since you asked—I'm not one hundred percent here. I was doing some clean up at your grandma's house—Christ, the woman, may she rest in peace, was a packrat—and I wound up breaking a coupla ribs." He tossed it off so cavalierly, at first it didn't quite register in my brain.

"What?"

"We don't have to get into the nitty-gritty. The upshot of it is my ribs are busted."

"What happened?"

He sighed. I pictured him rolling his eyes and rubbing the back of his neck in embarrassment. "I was carrying some boxes up from the basement, missed a step, fell down and boom sha-ka-laka—cracked a coupla ribs. Happy now that your old man's admitted he's a klutz?"

"When did this happen?"

"Aaah, Friday."

"How long did you wait before you went to the doctor?"

"Aaah, yesterday."

"You spent the whole weekend with fractured ribs before seeking medical attention?"

"Didn't know they were broke."

"You must have been in pain."

"Yeah, but it wasn't that bad."

"Talk about bullshit."

78

"Yeah." Another tight chuckle. "Well, I'm not in too much pain now. Doc's got me good and doped up. Tylenol with codeine," he added with a wink in his voice.

"You do know that you're not supposed to mix that stuff with alcohol?"

Long silence. He cleared his throat with a little half-hurt, half-guilty cough. "You jumped to that assumption awful quick."

"Unlike some, I learn from history."

"Maybe I do, too."

"I'll believe that when I see it." I said it under my breath, but just loud enough, I thought, for him to hear.

He must have, because he sighed. "Well, maybe you'll get your chance. That's why I'm calling. I was wondering if you could come up and help me out for a few weeks. I need to get your grandma's house cleared out. I'd like to get it on the market by fall, and these busted ribs are gonna slow me down." He paused, waiting for a reply. When none was forthcoming, he continued, "I'd call Marjorie, but sounds like she's taking some class this summer, for her realtor's license. Hell, I couldn't even get ahold of her before the funeral—turns out she was off with Rich in Mexico on some insurance conference that they turned into a vacation. And then people wonder why their rates are so high—these idiots going off on their junkets—spending the money outside this country, too. Sunning herself in Cancun while we were putting her grandmother in the ground." A hint of bitterness flavored his voice. He breathed in sharply, like a verbal straightening of his shoulders. "So, anyway, can you spare some time, if not for me, then for the memory of your grandma?"

The movie trailer that played in my head whenever I thought about my upcoming vacation had definitely not included a scene of my father and me emptying musty-smelling closets, sorting through worn housecoats and packing Reader's Digest Condensed Novels into boxes in the dark cluttered rooms that made up my grandma's old frame house. Projected in the dim theatre of my mind had been gardening tableaux and lingering close-ups of my face bent in rapture over a variety of books, and a winsome vignette of Aaron and me hiking the back trails of

Cahokia and picnicking on Monk's Mound as the rays of a dying sun burnished the Gateway Arch to a coppery sheen. Not a single shot of me, my father and a Salvation Army worker loading up a truck with semi-usable donations had ever been conceived, much less filmed for the script unimaginatively titled "My Summer Vacation."

"Claire?"

The paths were again before me. To take the familiar one all I needed to do was say 'no.' Wouldn't even need an excuse. Say 'no' and 'goodbye' and be done with it, leaving it up to him, as usual, to maintain the tenuous connection between us. Estrangement required no effort on my part. It was second nature. Outside, Aaron was leaning forward, grasping Tally's hands in his, his eyes earnest, his lips moving slowly, as if speaking with great effort or import.

"I know you're busy—but I just thought—"

How unlike him to not even try to hide his feelings. I cut off his crestfallen voice. "I can't give you an answer this very minute. I've got to check out some dates first but—I'm not saying no—okay? I'll get back to you in a day or so. How long will it take you to heal?"

The little grin eased back into his voice. "Six to eight weeks. I'm supposed to avoid strenuous activity. But that's not bad for an old workhorse, eh?"

"So no lifting or moving furniture."

"No." He paused. "Damn. Do you think Aaron might be able to come for a weekend, too?"

"I didn't say *I* was coming. I said *maybe.*"

"With you, if it ain't an outright no, things are looking up. So lemme get cuttin' while I'm ahead. You'll call me tomorrow?"

His voice was full of something. Hope? Anticipation? Relief? All those mixed together? Its presumption made me grit my teeth and press my back against the wall.

"I'll call you when I have an answer. Look, take care. Take it easy."

"I'm feeling better just hearing your voice, Clairey Jo. You're a regular Florence Nightingale. Call me."

Was that an order or a plea? Or just the request of an old man in pain?

"I will." I hung up first, letting the receiver go like a burden from my hand.

That evening, I washed the dishes by hand, finding the heavy warm water and the feathery suds soothing. The sheer repetition of the act, the soaping of the dishes in one sink, the rinsing in the other, the stacking in the drying rack, left my mind free to go elsewhere. It meandered down highways that began in a hilly country of bluffs and ridges which eventually bottomed out into acres of farmland, where corn grew with precision in an endless green geometry of vertical, horizontal and diagonal lines. Further on, the cornfields bumped up against newly-sodded sub-divisions that grew tract houses sheathed in pastel vinyl and sprouted spindly trees surrounded by perfect circles of blonde mulch, trees that offered no protection from the leering summer sun, where the morose, unnatural quiet along the winding cul de sacs was punctuated occasionally by the snarls of gas-powered lawnmowers and overlain by the constant, artificial murmur of air conditioners.

My mind pressed on to the urban expressway, clogged with traffic and fumes, then curved along a cloverleaf exit, under concrete columns and spans, onto a busy street where lurching articulated buses belched fumes and the broken glass of liquor bottles glinted in the sun, like diamonds and emeralds under the soles of pedestrians' shoes. It reached a quieter side street and strolled down its steep hill. The cars were older here; no SUVs or minivans, no Toyotas or Hondas had ever laid tire on this asphalt. In front of a red-brick American Foursquare sat a powder blue Ford with four doors, bench seats and chrome bumpers, only slightly scratched. Down the gangway, my mind trod softly, stopping beneath a window on the first floor. It was too high to see through while standing on the ground, but if one were able to float up and hover, like a balloon tethered to the wrist of a child at a fair, then the woman and the child would come into view. They are both small and dark-haired, standing at the kitchen sink, sleeveless in the summer heat. The woman's arms look strong but the muscles are not well-defined by today's standards; they seem overlaid with a layer of soft, pendulous flesh, the biceps plump like ripe plums. The girl's arms are twigs, their long slender line disturbed only by knobby elbows and bony wrists. They are washing dishes, the mother dipping plates in and out of a big pot and scrubbing with a frayed terrycloth rag, then handing them to the girl, who rinses them under the faucet. The woman's lips are pursed, her eyebrows drawn together, a deep furrow in between. No ease of repetition, no grace in the pleasure of small moments guides her movements; there is a tension in every turn of her wrist, as if she has been expecting all along that the tall glass will slip from the girl's hands and shatter in the sink. Minor pandemonium breaks loose: the scolding voice, the haphazard grab, the jerked hand, the dripping blood, the burbling cry. A man steps into the kitchen, adds an expletive to the bedlam, grabs a dishtowel and wraps it around the girl's hand which now holds a scarlet blossom. He takes the girl by her uninjured hand and leads her out of the kitchen. A light goes on in the next window over. To float there would be useless; the windowpane is made of frosted glass for privacy. Behind it is the bathroom.

But my mind knows the tiny black and white tiles of the floor intimately, as well as the porcelain sink perched on chrome legs and the small medicine cabinet behind the mirrored door from which the man takes the metal box of bandages. He applies three of the largest size to the oozing wound at the base of the girl's thumb and a kiss to her forehead. He hands her toilet paper with which to blow her nose and wipe her eyes. He sits on the edge of the tub with her on his lap, rocking gently, until the tinkling sounds of clean-up and resentment coming from the kitchen cease.

I don't know how long I might have stood there at my own kitchen sink with my hands in the dishpan, swaying ever so slightly back and forth. Until the water grew tepid and the suds dissolved? Until the skin of my fingers wrinkled like bleached raisins and my nails grew soft, white and fragile? Or until my mind could remember the precise smell of my father's neck, producing a sensation as exact and redolent as opening a bottle marked "his essence," holding it under my nose and breathing deeply.

"So when are you leaving?" Aaron's question brought my hands up out of the water with a jerk. He was leaning against the counter, thumbs hooked in the pockets of his denim shorts, looking immovable, a human monolith.

"I didn't agree to go help him. I said—well, I didn't even say 'maybe.' I said I had to see about it. Which is true. I can't just drop everything and rush up there at the drop of a hat. Or the crack of a rib, as it were." The words spilled out of me, water to wear down the stone, as if a torrent would do more good than a trickle.

"What 'things?' You're on vacation in two days. We made no official plans. You need to throw some clothes in a suitcase, get your butt in your car and drive up there."

I fished around the bottom of the dishpan for the last of the knives and forks, digging my heels into the hooked rug under my feet. If my irresistible force proves resistible, then I can play the immovable object. "I think this is my decision to make."

Aaron blew the breath from his mouth and slammed a hand down on the counter. "Damn it, but you're too stubborn for your own good." He ran his hands through his hair and clenched, pulling at the roots. "I've dragged you around the country to digs here and there for twenty years. And you always said you loved it. Couldn't wait to go. But, Christ, sometimes I wish I were in some other profession—psychologist, psychiatrist, what-the-fuck-ever—because it's time you started digging in your own backyard, so that maybe, just maybe, you can bury your dead boys once and for all." He stopped short, like a runaway mount brought to heel by the bit and the reins, crumbling in on himself a little, one arm and hand clenched across his stomach, the other supporting his bent head, as if in pain.

Whatever animus was governing my tongue—skittish filly or obstinate mule—he should have known better. He should have known not to cram me at the highest fence. Or so I told myself as I let fly with my heels.

"Spare me your down-home, corn-fed clichés, farm boy. But thanks for finally admitting you think I need therapy. Somehow I don't think a visit to my father would help. And can we please skip the drama? Christ, it's not like he's dying."

I couldn't decide whether the fact that Aaron had been putting up with my verbal nips and kicks for twenty years without flinching or retaliating made him more of a man or less than one as I turned back to empty the dishpan.

He grabbed me from behind, spinning me around so fast the soap bubbles flew from my hands and sprayed the floor, and then lifted me roughly by the waist and sat me down hard on the counter. My head snapped back against the cabinet with a crack that opened my eyes wide. Hands corralling me on either side, he leaned and loomed into my face, so close I could breathe in the acidic scent of his anger.

"Don't you dare be flippant about a man who is in pain and needs your help. Your father—he's your father, for Christ's sake. You owe him—and you owe yourself. He's getting old. Yeah, okay, so it's not like he's dying—but he's getting old, the days aren't going to stretch on forever. And if you never make your peace with him, it will eat you away inside. It's eating you now! When was the last time you ever really grabbed a piece of your life and sank your teeth into it? You hold everything at arm's length. This 'no ties' bullshit. Whatever he did, you've got to forgive and let it go. And if that's farm-boy philosophy, well, it's a damn sight better than what you picked up in the city."

My bottom was soaked now from the dishwater on the counter, the back of my head throbbed from the slam to the cabinet door, but with his face so close that I needed only to lean in an inch to make contact, I found myself intoxicated by the smell of him, the rooted in the earth sweat smell, the fruity odor of the Shiraz wine from dinner, the aroma of warm skin that was his and his alone. Twenty years of smelling him and I still wanted to bury my face in the space between his neck and his collarbone and inhale him like incense. Sinking my hands into his hair, I drew him closer until my nose rested against that smooth place where an artery throbbed and I could breathe him.

"I've never pressed you to tell me what he did. Twenty some years and I've let you hold it to yourself. But now I think I was wrong to do that. Maybe you should tell me. It might help you to…" He moved his hands from the counter to my back. "Claire, just—" his mouth was against my ear, "did he—" He couldn't seem to get the words out. "Did he abuse you? I mean, sexual abuse?"

The laugh burst out and would have thrown me back into the cabinet again, had it not been for his restraining hands. The red blooms of embarrassment across his cheeks made me laugh again. Then I shook my head and tried to pull his neck back to me, but he resisted.

"Claire—"

"No, it wasn't that—he never—no."

"Look, I'm sorry I—"

"No, it's okay. Never mind."

"Okay. I'm sorry, look I—"

"Just forget it."

"No, I mean, okay, yes, but that doesn't change the fact that you've got to go to him. You've got to make things right—whatever he did, you don't want to tell me, fine, but I can't—do this anymore. You've got to make it up with him because I can't be your daddy—or your brother anymore."

"Fine, I will." I said it just to shut him up. I opened my legs and in a quick, spidery move, wrapped them around his hips. "I'll go." I pulled him to me, wrapping my arms securely around his neck, and nestling my head back into that place where I could breathe him again and taste him this time as well. Salty sweet and lemon sour, velvety warm. When smell and taste were not enough, I ran my hand up under his shirt. The skin of his back was nectarine smooth and peach fuzz soft, pebbly along his spine.

"And I can't do this anymore, whatever this is we are doing, you here, me here and there, when the whim strikes you one way or the other. We need to be together, permanent. I need to be here, all the time. We need to be married."

"I believe that's eight."

"What?"

"Eight. The eighth time you've asked me to marry you."

Perhaps not knowing how to respond, or perhaps afraid to, he simply let me have my way with him, absorb him, as I had foreseen, foregoing the hard way for the easier path, going the way of all flesh until the creak and clatter of the screen door broke my fever trance.

"Aren't you guys a little old for a kitchen counter thing?" Tally's voice dripped with the acid of teenage scorn.

Aaron had the comeback. "Why don't you go hang out at the mall for an hour?" He dug his hand into his back pocket for his wallet. "Take a twenty and go to town. Better yet, take my Visa."

"As a matter of fact, I was just stopping in to let you know I'm going over to Jason's."

"Who's there?"

"Don't worry, Dad. His father's home—so we won't be hooking up in his kitchen—or anywhere else." She rolled her eyes in lurid mock delight.

"Home by eleven. I'll be there, waiting."

"Are you sure that gives you enough time?" Then she dashed out the door with another creak and slam.

"I really need to fix that screen door," Aaron sighed. He hooked a finger in my belt loop. "But not just this minute."

CHAPTER 7

Once I made the decision to go, the attitude was "don't let the door hit you in the ass on the way out."

"Why do I get the feeling I'm getting the bum's rush?"

"Because you are," Aaron replied as he sat on the bed watching me fold clothes and stack them neatly beside the open suitcase. "Okay, so at what point do you actually start packing?"

"What does it look like I'm doing?"

"I mean, when do you actually put the clothes *into* the suitcase?"

"When I'm damn good and ready." But I took a pile of shorts and dropped them in.

"Come on, get your head around this. You're going to have a lovely drive. You'll relax, enjoy the scenery—"

"It's corn and soybean fields."

"Ah, but that vista can spark some of the most profound insights, my dear. I found God while traversing the gently rolling farmland of Iowa. The sky never looked so big but when it curved like a gigantic blue bowl over the green and gold fields." He closed his eyes and smiled at whatever memory he was conjuring. "You might say I was lost and *God found me*."

"I've heard of stranger places in which to find God. But I'm not expecting any major revelations on I-55 just outside

Bloomington-Normal. No Our Lady of the Rest Station phe-
nomenon."

"That's my point. Things happen when you least expect them
to. We've all got a particular hole to fill. That day, mine just happened to be the famous god-shaped one. And why are you taking
that?"

"What?"

"Your laptop. I doubt you're going to find much use for it."

"I'll take what I please—and thank you for your advice."

The laptop went into the trunk of the blue Accord along with
the suitcase. As I took a last minute look around the bathroom
for any essentials I might have forgotten to pack, Tally stepped
into the doorway.

"I'll make the ultimate sacrifice by letting you take this with
you." She held up her Sony Walkman.

"A nice parting gift—because you can't be without your
tunes," Aaron squawked.

"Well, it's just a loan," Tally hastened to say. "But Dad's
right. You can't be without your tunes."

"What? You think your grandpa doesn't have all the techno-
logical necessities for life in the Twenty-first Century? Like a
radio? I mean, it is 1999."

Tally rolled her eyes. "Mom, I'm not sure he has all the necessities to live in the Twentieth Century—which is so close to
being totally over. But don't tell him I said that, okay?"

Aaron appeared and rested his chin on her shoulder, holding
out a black CD travel case, soft-sided and zippered, like an old-
fashioned autograph book. It was filled with an eclectic collection of music, running the gamut from Debussy to Sinatra,
Dolly to Madonna, Puccini to Prince.

"Another fine parting gift."

"I'm overwhelmed. What's next, the Nu-Mode hosiery?"

Hugs and kisses at the door, then again at the car.

"Give Grandpa a kiss from me."

Aaron whispered "Be sweet," in my ear.

"As if I could be anything but," I retorted. When I climbed in and turned to place the CD case on the seat beside me, I found something big and white was already riding shotgun—the Marshall Field's box.

"Thought you might want to take that with," said Aaron, resting his arms on the open window.

"You mean you thought it would be a good idea if I did."

He kissed me, soft and long, his lips hovering just beyond mine afterwards. "Be sweet," he said again.

"I don't want to do this."

Another kiss and a grin. "Never can say good-bye, no-no-no-no, I never can say goodbye..." he sang in an uneasy falsetto.

Then it was time to start the engine, for he would never let me stay.

"Be sweet," he said for a third time as I backed out of the driveway onto the sun-baked pavement of a Missouri summer morning.

You can make the trip from St. Louis to Chicago in about 5 hours, if you're motivated—or "motor-vated" as Aaron likes to quip. It's a straight shot up I-55, a concrete and asphalt trail through back of beyond counties with slightly exotic names like Macoupin and Sangamon. It passes the gas-food-lodging signs that mark the exits to towns that cross-country tourists would never dream of visiting. They only pause there momentarily, like migratory birds, perching on the perimeters to fill up at the gas station or the fast food emporium or to rest their heads on the sanitized pillows of the chain motels that cluster along the frontage roads. The interstate passes towns that have histories; towns that might fascinate if one were willing to linger and look with more than a passing, dismissive glance; towns with names like Funks Grove and Towanda and Chenoa.

Time was, before the interstate system made it possible to drive from one coast to the other without stopping unless compelled by the pressing needs of one's bladder or stomach, the road that most people took between the big cities that anchored the fertile stretch of soil between Lake Michigan and the Mississippi River did meander through those towns, obeying speed limits and traffic signals, causing out-of-town cars to stop at State and Main same as the locals, giving the driver and passengers the opportunity to admire the Corinthian pillars of the City Hall, enticing them to take their ease at The Old Log Cabin Inn or the Pig-Hip Restaurant or the Ariston Cafe, providing the opportunity for interactions of a little more depth than *"You want fries with that?"* That road turned mere tourists into travelers; perhaps it even fostered an appreciation for the mellower pace of life less confined by concrete and steel and for that particular rich smell of farm air in August, a scent that makes the nostrils flare to breathe in more of its full-blown, ripe pungency.

I traveled Route 66, the mother road, from Chicago to Flagstaff, Arizona on a family trip to the Grand Canyon. August, 1969. My sister had gotten married the month before so it was just my brother and me in the backseat of the powder blue Ford. Joey spent most of the 310 miles from Chicago to St. Louis splayed out across the bench seat with the earphones of his radio plugged in, nursing the ankle he'd twisted recklessly sliding into home in a pick-up softball game with his buddies the day before.

"How the hell is he s'posed to hike around all these National Parks with a sprained ankle? What are we gonna do—see 'em all from the inside of the car?" From my perch at the top of the stairs, I heard my father grumble petulantly as he prepared to drive to his sister's to drop off the key to the front door and give explicit instructions on how to feed the cats and clean up the litter box and where to put the mail.

My mother's retort sounded just as petulant. "We could just stay home."

The bang of the screen door was his only audible reply.

So Joey got into the car the next morning with a big, tan Ace bandage wrapped around his left ankle. It bulged like a fungus out of the top of his battered Converse All-Stars. As we tooled south, my dad cursed under his breath as the car radio lost a station signal and he would scramble the dial to find another. The easy listening and country music stations my mother preferred didn't have the power to broadcast over the long haul.

90

My brother kept his transistor tuned to the Big 89 WLS. Its 50,000 watts drove a steady stream of hits and the voice of Larry Lujack through the air and kept my brother's head bobbing. It was my first long-distance road trip and I was too fascinated by the view out the window to complain about being forced to listen to Montovani and Engelbert Humperdinck, until Joey thrust one of his plugs into my right ear and a gruff, but sensual voice growled in my head, imploring me to come along with him on a magic carpet ride.

The invitation proved irresistible. That trip was when I really felt the power of music, rock music, its unifying force, its tribal nature. While my mother and father bickered in the front seat over everything from the quality of the meat loaf at the last roadside diner to whether women had smaller bladders because they damned sure needed to stop more often, my brother dragged me into the crook of his arm and let me tune out and turn on alongside him with a drug so powerful it could stop time. Or rather, it gave time its rhythm and pace and taught us that pure bliss could be found in three minutes of jangling guitars, thrumming bass and heartbeat drums.

The Who were as awe-inspiring as the flaming orange and soothing purple striated vista of the Painted Desert; the voice of Jim Morrison made me swoon as much as the throat-catching drop-off at the edge of the Bright Angel Trail along the South Rim of the Grand Canyon. We passed the time in Yellowstone waiting for Old Faithful to spout listening to a station out of Jackson, Wyoming that introduced us, between bouts of static, to Johnny Cash, Loretta Lynn and Merle Haggard. The gorgeous white gush of steam and spray made our jaws drop and let loose with a collective "awwww" but no more so than one particular song's metaphor just slightly beyond our inexperienced youthful comprehension—equating love with a burning ring of fire.

On the way home, on the last leg of our western odyssey, somewhere on the border of Iowa and Illinois, with my mother refusing to sleep in another motel, with a whole state left to cross until we reached our own beds, with our parents having reached a cold and silent truce born of exhaustion—physical, mental and emotional—my brother and I lay in the backseat and stared up at the night sky through the curve of the rear window. It was alive, pulsing with more stars than I had ever seen before. It was the blackest black off-setting the mistiest white and for the first time I understood why it was called the Milky Way and that there were indeed more constellations in the northern sky than just the Big and Little Dippers.

My brother sang in a hush so that only I could hear. *"On a cloud of sound I drift in the night, any place it goes is right. Goes far, flies near, to the stars, away from here ..."*

He was with me on my trip up the mother road's replacement, I-55. I engaged in a sporadic, one-sided conversation with him, which some might call an internal monologue, except that—psychiatric implications of this admission be damned—I heard him occasionally answer me back. Or was it just me writing his dialogue in my head? Here's the problem: I was talking to him as a thirty eight year old woman would talk to her older brother—but he was answering me as a sixteen year old—as I remembered him, as I knew him. Try as I might I could not bring him forward in time, could not advance him into his mid-forties. My mind was unable to morph him like a computer program could: by broadening the width of his brow or lengthening his jaw line or transforming the sweep of dark hair over his forehead into a middle-aged receding hairline. The image frozen in my mind was the face of a high school sophomore undecided between a grin and a glare and a voice that wavered from sweetness to sarcasm.

I stopped in Springfield to pay my respects to Abraham Lincoln and rub the hawk beak of a nose jutting forth from the bronze bust outside his tomb. A dark and weathered patina aged the rest of his face but Old Abe's nose was beacon bright from the caressing hands of visitors seeking—luck? Wisdom? A cute photo opportunity? Arched on my toes, I could just barely brush a finger across the broad tip as I asked the Great Emancipator to help me keep the better angels perched on my shoulders.

A stretch of the legs in Funk's Grove netted me a pint of the local maple syrup. I lunched in Bloomington at an Illinois State University campus deli that Aaron had recommended, lingering over the grilled chicken sandwich with a side of coleslaw, dulcet and pungent. I marveled at the cleanliness of a rest stop outside of Pontiac, pausing to admire the feathery yellow coreopsis and spiky purple meadow sage that softened the corner of the squat brick building. At each stop, my brother's voice urged me to "get moving, kiddo."

I-55 to I-80 to I-94. The mathematics of going home. North, east, north. Through the suburbs of my youth: Lansing, South Holland, Dolton, Calumet City, and over the vast iron span above the Little Calumet River, one of the bridges that spawned childhood nightmares. Oh the remembered terror of sitting up in bed in the middle of the night, clutching and gasping at the vision of our car reaching the apex of a slowly opening span and then falling away to nothing. Too many bridges to cross on the south side of Chicago: the 95th Street Bridge, the 100th Street Bridge, the 106th Street Bridge, opening and closing over the Calumet River where barges slouched under the weight of coal and foreign flags fluttered off the masts of freighters docked in the slips, flags of exotic colors, greens, oranges, golds; flags that let a child believe that the place she was from was important. Had to be! The world came to the south side of Chicago, to load and unload at the place where the water and the railroads met and entwined like mating snakes, soft and hard, yielding and unbending at once.

Steel was still king then and the south side blasted it, molded it, forged it, fired it, enthroned it. It fed us, clothed us, sheltered us. It built houses and churches and schools. It formed the skeletons of the buildings that stood tall on the shores of Lake Michigan, impervious to the buffeting of wind, rain, snow and heat. We breathed it, touched it, smelled it, tasted it. It coursed round our bodies with our blood, from the heart to the extremities and back again; it settled in our guts and rode the electric impulses up and down our spines. It was an essential ingredient in the recipe of who we were.

I am made of nails,
of dictionaries and rosaries.
I am made of cherry trees with wormy fruit and peonies laden with ants,
of evergreens that grew with me and leggy spider plants.
I am made of metal lawn chairs that burned my thighs,
of concrete stoops that scraped my knees,
of iron railings with peeling paint that taught my fingers to twirl.
I am made of brick and frame houses that passed
from white families to black,
of U.S. Steel and Republic Steel and Inland Steel,
of dirt-paved alleys and Frank's corner grocery
where kids stole penny candy from a crabby Greek.
I am made of train whistles in the night
and the orange glow from coke ovens that obscured the stars.

The street was not the one I had pictured just days before. Late model cars hugged the curbs. The row of petite arbor vitae that had, in my childhood, lined the side yard of the old frame house at the top of the hill like feathery green pipe cleaners, now loomed in one solid dark mass that hid the attic windows. The elms that had arched from both sides of the street, branches straining to meet like lovers' fingers, were gone without a trace, the places where their roots had spread and their trunks had risen long covered over by creeping bent or Kentucky blue grass. In front of my father's house, the cherry tree was gone and the elm looked sickly, its dying branches languishing with a spotty growth of leaves. Of the two evergreens that had stood sentinel on either side of the walk that led to the concrete stoop, only the one on the left had survived. But it was enormous, its perfectly conical, Christmas tree top soaring past the roof.

My father's house is made of bricks, like my own, bricks the color of dried blood. There is a slight variation in color between the lower and upper stories, the line of demarcation between the original house that my parents bought after my dad returned from his stint in the Army during World War II and the one they created by expanding the attic into a full second floor when I was a baby. Growing up sharing cramped bedrooms and a single bathroom with numerous siblings, my father had vowed that his own children would each have a bedroom, as well as an up-to-date hall bath with modern conveniences: a showerhead over the tub, sliding doors to enclose it, a medicine cabinet with—by God—a fluorescent light fixture and a vanity!

I am made of asbestos tile floors,
Pink, speckled, marbled, flecked
Which lie cold under your feet on a winter's morning.
I am made of summers without central air,
When the heat rises and fills a room
With the restless sighs of burning skin on damp sheets

Instead of the four-door, powder blue Ford of my child-hood—he was always a Ford man, except for a brief fling with Chevy in the mid-70s—a two-door, midnight blue Ford, an early 90's Taurus, sat out front, still in fine shape, but in need of a wax job. When I parked the car and climbed out, he was waiting at the door, his figure blurred by the gray screen and distorted by the slanted glass of the open jalousie louvers. I popped the trunk to get my suitcase and he came out, easing himself down the steps, his hand coasting along the top of the railing. He looked even thinner than at the funeral, except for his torso, where some kind of corset-like strap bulged under his white cotton t-shirt. His jeans hung low on his hips, but he wasn't making a fashion statement with his pair of faded Wranglers. He looked a little older, too, his face as pinched as his voice has been on the telephone.

"I'll get 'em." I waved him to stop, but he kept coming until he was standing in the street beside me, slipping his arm around my shoulder with a familiarity that rankled, even as, from a small, cobwebbed corner of my heart, the long-suppressed voice of a dutiful daughter reminded me: *"he's in pain."*

"Be sweet," Aaron had whispered as his lips brushed my ear.

"I thought you'd be here awhile ago. Traffic bad?" He took hold of my suitcase. I brushed his hand away and gave him the laptop instead.

"Bad compared to St. Louis."

"Anything else?" He pointed to the box on the passenger's seat.

"I can get that."

He gestured to the case he held as we climbed the steps. "What's this?"

"Laptop."

He grinned and chuckled. "Here's my chance to get some computer education. I feel like such a bumpkin—especially with this whole Y2K baloney everyone's talking about. Something about computers not understanding the rollover from 1999 to 2000. Somebody forgot to allow for extra digits? Sounds goofy to me but then I don't know squat about these things, other than to look up books at the library."

I was struggling to reconcile the incongruous sounds of my father chatting me up with the term "Y2K" and mental images of him puttering around the public library, checking out books—I didn't remember him doing that when I was child—when he opened the screen door and gave an awkward little flourish with his free arm. "Welcome home."

I might have been walking into the house 10 years ago, or 20, or even 30. It might have been mid-afternoon on the day my brother was laid in a rectangular gash in the earth, the end of an exhausting odyssey from home to funeral parlor to church to cemetery to luncheon and finally home again. It might have been that moment when I timidly stepped over a threshold made strange by the lack of something, and when the first thing my mother did was shut the blinds against a sun that was too bright for that sort of day.

It *could* have been that day—there was the sofa where I had curled up and its arm into which I had pressed my face, the place where his head had rested, the place where I had breathed deeply of his scent that lingered still: Brylcreem and Prell and Skinbracer after his still-infrequent shaves. But the slipcover was different now, a drab beige having replaced the more vibrant blue floral of my youth.

It *could* have been that day—the same brown and white metal vertical blinds covered the picture window and the old blonde upright piano still flanked the wall near the staircase and the black rotary-dial telephone still sat on the Danish Modern end table in the entry alcove, a location that discouraged long conversations due to its lack of proximity to a chair. Only a teenager in love would be willing to put up with the discomfort of sitting on the hardwood floor, back against the wall, feet pressed against the front door, in order to chat for hours at a time as the winter draft blew in through the narrow gap between the door and the jamb.

As I climbed the stairs to the second floor, it *could* have been that day—the cuckoo clock still hung at the curve and the door at the top of the landing still opened onto the four little prints of "Birds of the Midwest" in their faux-bamboo frames: cardinal, sparrow, chickadee and bluejay perched in various poses of avian cheer.

If I was eight as I climbed the stairs, I was sixteen when I entered my old bedroom where faded purple lilacs bloomed on the bedspread and hung down from the arching canopy. The sheer fabric felt as inconsequential as smoke beneath my fingers. There was the dresser and the mirror in which I had primped. The cotton, lace-edged runner, bright white when I had first embroidered it with pansies, now aged to a soft ivory, still protected its surface. The cork bulletin board where I had displayed those items of significance that could be shared with other eyes still hung on the wall. It was barren now, a brown canvas empty but for a row of silver tacks that stood at attention as if waiting to be pressed into service. Below it sat the old pine desk with its worn, green felt blotter and the straight-backed chair with its cracked vinyl seat pad. My fingers traced the glyphs that, years ago, they had carved into the soft wood with the point of a dried-up pen. The marks had stood out like bright scars on the dark surface, but the years and dust and the oily residue of a liquid scratch cover that my mother had employed in an attempt to hide them had effaced their jagged edges. A stranger might barely notice them.

"Doin' the white glove test?"

"Barely any dust. You must be a good housekeeper."

"For an old man, you mean. I admit I have some help in that department. One of the ladies from up the block comes over twice a month and does some cleaning for me." He shrugged a little sheepishly. "She offered. I accepted. We set terms. Plus she talks a blue streak. Kinda nice to hear someone else's voice in the house—other than my own, or the idiots on the radio or TV."

"Talk to yourself much?"

"Yep, but I don't answer—yet." He gestured toward the stairs. "Hungry? I got some chicken legs frying."

I am made of babushkas,
of Zofia and Elizabieta,
of three Josephs and two Marys.
I am made of kielbasa, golubke and czarnina,
of honey-sweet kifles and potica,
of fish on Friday nights.

He cooked before it was fashionable for men to do so, at least non-professionally. He made his own breakfast and had a menu of specialties, taking over the kitchen to prepare a meal about once a week. His culinary repertoire featured nothing out of the ordinary; he stuck with staples such as spaghetti with marinara sauce and chili con carne made with hamburger and mildly-spiced beans. The most exotic dish he ever prepared was beef chop suey. His real talent lay as a short-order cook: fried egg sandwiches with sliced franks or bacon; beans and franks in a sauce swimming with chopped onions, served up with hot, buttered toast; grilled cheese sandwiches crisp on the outside and gooey in the middle. But his piece de resistance was the meal he prepared every Christmas Eve. Of course, it wasn't just the meal then, it was the event, the whole shebang, as he liked to say. It was a tradition, perhaps *the* tradition of our family.

We opened our gifts on Christmas Eve. The four of us would dress up in our finest and drive to Midnight Mass. My father stayed home. He was resolutely unchurched. The few times I had observed him inside a church—at funerals and weddings—he looked nervous, like he feared the structure would collapse. He'd pull at his shirt collar, clear his throat and rattle the keys and change in his pants pockets, as if to ward off evil spirits, in the way of whistling past a graveyard.

At age seven, I decided to break with this tradition. All of my friends opened their presents on Christmas morning. I construed that this was the normal way of doing things. I wanted to be like them. Normal.

It had nothing to do with Santa Claus. He was no longer a factor—if he ever had been. My mother, the heroine of famous Depression-era Christmases at which an orange or a bit of chocolate or a new pair of shoes was the ultimate gift, did not believe in Santa Claus. The idea that children were allowed, even encouraged, to believe that someone other than their hardworking parents provided all those toys and clothes under the tree and stuffed the chocolate goodies in the stockings was anathema to her. As for my father, he didn't do delayed gratification. He just couldn't wait for Santa.

I *wanted* the extra few hours of anticipation, the thrill of waking up to the realization that the glorious day had finally arrived. I *wanted* the joy of throwing back the covers, of sitting bolt upright in bed, of bounding down the stairs. I desired the pounding of the heart that preceded the peek around that corner where the banister met the wall and the ultimate sight of the splendor of Christmas morning: the gilded packages wrapped in red and silver and gold artfully arranged under the tree; the larger, unwrapped toys sitting off to the side—perhaps the life-sized walking doll leaning against the stereo cabinet, looking oh so elegant in her dress with black velvet bodice and white satin skirt, a red silk rose pinned at her waist.

I felt cheated out of that, cheated out of all those wonderful, cheek-flushing, palm-sweating emotions. And so I rebelled.

I dressed as usual for church that evening in a dress of red corduroy, and put on my best shoes, the Mary Janes that pinched the sides of my little toes and made me hesitate ever so slightly when I walked.

Other preparations also went on as usual: my father had purchased fresh polish sausage from the butcher down on Commercial Avenue, near the steel mill, and he had stopped at a grocery store for sauerkraut and rye bread. These victuals would grace the table of our traditional Christmas Eve dinner—to be served after Mass. Was this a tradition my father clung to from his own childhood? Did he create it himself? It was never explained—it just *was*.

My father cooked while the rest of the family attended church. While we sang carols and listened to the choir fill the church with a magnificent blend of voices— *"Gloria in Excelsis Deo"*—my father would be listening to the water boil. He would turn down the knob on the stove, lowering the blue gas flames so that the pot full of gray links would hold at a rippling simmer. While we listened to the familiar tale of Joseph and Mary's trek to Bethlehem, of their refusal at the inn, of their taking shelter at the stable, my father would be opening cans of sauerkraut and adding their contents to the pot, stirring with a slotted spoon to mix the meat and shredded cabbage. While we marveled at the story of Jesus' birth, of the seraphim and cherubim and holy host who appeared to the shepherds tending their flocks in the cold hills, of the star that miraculously appeared in the sky to guide the three kings bearing their precious gifts of gold, frankincense and myrrh, my father would be slicing rye bread, eating the brown crusty heel of the loaf, taking that as his pay, his reward for his hard work. While we waited in the long lines for communion, to partake of the tasteless wafer that was our salvation, my father would be waiting, too: for the time to pass, for the flavors to blend, for the sausage to be thoroughly cooked.

When Mass was concluded and the priest bade us go in peace, we drove home in my sister's maroon Rambler. It was then that I began my assault on the status quo.

Walking through the front door, I refused to let the smells of the food lull me into submission. They were usually happy smells; smells I associated with happy times: past Christmases, family weddings, birthdays, christenings. But this night I hardened my heart against them. This night they were the smells of tyranny, of the enemy to be vanquished.

Stepping further into the living room, pushed on by my mother, who was just behind me, I could see the gifts piled under and around the Christmas tree. They covered the table upon which the Scotch pine sat in its bucket of sand, its branches drooping under the weight of the lights, ornaments and fistfuls of tinsel. They spread across the carpet to the stereo cabinet and even reached the slip-covered sofa. They were just waiting, begging even, to be opened. Somewhere between stirring and slicing, my father had laid them out. They were the lure, the bait, but I would not fall into the trap.

Making a loud pretense of yawning, I headed for the stairs. "I think I'm going to bed."

No one spoke—the look they gave in unison sufficed.

My father leaned in the doorway, observing, jangling the change in his pocket. "Going to bed? It's time to open your presents," he finally said.

"I think I'd rather wait until tomorrow."

Silence. Just silence. No gasps, no shocked murmurs. Just simple silence. Only a lilt in the background, the sound of *Oh Holy Night* floating in from the radio in the kitchen.

"Tomorrow? You want to wait until tomorrow?" The foreman in him felt the managerial need to confirm my intentions.

"I'm tired."

Seeing my affirmative nod, the foreman also felt the need to crush my insubordination. "You're tired? Too tired to open presents? That's bullcrap if I ever heard it. No child is ever too tired to open presents. You wait until tomorrow and I'm gonna take every single one of these presents back to the stores. Tonight."

The long, heavy sigh. The rolling of eyes. "The stores are closed. You can't take them back."

"Try me."

My father still leaned in the doorway, with impassive eyes, a stoic set to his jaw. He carried the metallic, smoky odor of the mill on his person, even after changing out of his work clothes. His hand shifted in his pocket, the pennies, nickels and dimes tumbling through his fingers. We stared at each other, measuring the resolve in the eyes and posture of our adversary, asking ourselves why here? Why now? Why was this so important? He blinked and shifted his position, swaying to the other side of the doorway. It was only the slump of his shoulders, the way his eyes remained closed just a split second longer than necessary that gave it away.

He needs this more than me.

The standoff lasted for another moment before I shrugged my shoulders in classic capitulation. "Oh, okay, I'll open them," I said, inwardly cursing my weakness, my lack of resolve. Another rebel without a cause. A rebel without a Santa Claus.

My father watched from the doorway as we tore into our presents, I with no less gusto than Joey, Marjorie with the sedate calm of a twenty-something who already knows the long flat rectangular box holds a pair of leather gloves and the bulkier square one a winter hat. Then he retreated into the kitchen and sat back down in his chair at the green Formica table. But he heard everything, every ooh and aah, every exclamation of joy: the affirmations of his children's love.

I remember just one gift from that year: a revolving fashion show stage with little dolls dressed like models. You could stick their feet onto tiny prongs that jutted up from the plastic surface of the stage, turn the power on and they would strut their stuff on the catwalk with a robotic flare. That sticks in my mind, small dolls wearing outlandish, spangled ball gowns and tiny bathing suits and modish pant suits moving in a circle, around and around and around again, on their merry-go-round without horses.

By the next Christmas my sister had escaped the asylum. By the Christmas after that, my brother was dead. And I had learned to hide a package or two that I could discover and unwrap the following morning, much to my feigned surprise.

I am made of "believe you me" and "qw=dot,"
of "holy Toledo" and "holy cow"
of "father, son and the holy ghost."
I am made of midnight mass and Lenten ash.

I stared at my father in the doorway now, marveling at the way his face showed too much of his eagerness, unlike that Christmas of long ago. *He's losing his touch.*

"I'm not really hungry. I stopped for a late lunch."

He nodded, a quick dip of his chin, looking a little lost for a moment, unsure of his footing. Then he changed leads quickly, the Mustang in him recovering from the bobble. "Well, then, maybe you could just keep an old man company." He flashed me *his* smile, and yet now it seemed less like largesse and more like the offering of a supplicant.

"I'll get settled in here, unpack. Then I'll join you."

"Okay, I'll leave you to it," his voice at once business-like. But he didn't; he lingered in the doorway, hands in his pockets, rolling those coins. *Jingly-jangly man—what are you warding off now?*

Turning away, I opened my suitcase. Beneath the buzz of the zipper, the jingling died away, replaced by the sighing regret of the stairs under his feet.

As I had dawdled in packing, I dawdled in unpacking: lifting one pair of shorts out at a time, placing them carefully in the drawer of my old dresser; slipping the arms of hangers slowly into the necks and sleeves of T-shirts, hooking them over the wooden rod in the closet. An old pair of platform shoes, white sandals with three-inch thick cork soles, relics of my 70's adolescence, hunkered on the closet floor, like faithful dogs waiting all this time for me to take them out for a teetering walk around the block.

The things that some people save... My relic box resting on the bed was a cold white reproach to my mockery. I stuck my tongue out at it.

Some things are worth saving while others—a glance back at the shoes—*are not.*

When I finally made my way down the stairs, one grudging, thumping footfall after another, my father had finished eating and was washing dishes, so I sauntered off to send an e-mail to Aaron, in which I would reassure him that I had arrived safely and was behaving myself. Lugging my laptop and its cable around the house like a high-tech albatross, I discovered that these late 20th Century accoutrements were absolutely useless in a house outfitted with wiring from the Cold War era—the early Cold War era, circa the JFK-Nikita Khrushchev standoff. There wasn't a single, plug-in telephone outlet in the entire house.

Did you really think that he would have a phone jack with Internet access?

My father watched my fruitless search with a mixture of amusement and chagrin on his face. When I finally plopped on the sofa, only to be rudely pinched by a spring coil from under the worn cushion, he smiled and jerked his head in the direction of the front door.

"There's always the old-fashioned way."

"Pony Express?"

"I was thinking more along the lines of Ma Bell." He headed back into the kitchen.

"There is no more Ma Bell, you know," I called after him. "The government broke her monopoly up years ago."

"Monopoly? Sure I'll play a game of Monopoly. But ain't it kinda boring with just two people? Rummy might be better."

"You're a hoot and a half—NOT," I muttered, rummaging through my purse. My cell phone was not in its usual pocket. And it wasn't buried under wallet and change purse and checkbook and the tin of breath mints. I sighed. I could go upstairs and rifle through the suitcase, but I knew it wasn't there and a picture formed of it resting on my desk in St. Louis, cradled in its charger, doing me not a damn bit of good. Well, a telephone was one piece of technology that my father's house actually did possess, even if it was a hard-wired landline. I found it in the entry alcove. *As always.* The front door was open and along with the breeze, sounds of early summer in the city came in through the screen: car doors slamming, engines revving, adults and children laughing, the feathery rustling of pliant green leaves bursting with sugar-life.

Making a connection on the rotary antique required waiting through eleven eternities as my finger spun the dial to the right and it circled back to its original position with a soft purr. Aaron's message cut in on the fourth ring.

"Eating fast food already?" I chided. "Hi, it's me. In Chicago. In one piece. Being sweet. Won't be sending e-mail any time soon. This place is probably less technologically advanced than Cahokia at its lowest ebb. My father's house, I mean. I hear Chicago itself is pretty up-to-date. And don't bother calling my cell phone. In the bum's rush, I forgot it. This is what it means to be almost incommunicado. Love you. Bye."

For whatever reason sleep did not come that night—the wayward feathers that poked through the ticking of my lumpy old pillow, pricking my cheeks like taunting pins; the glare of the streetlight that penetrated the tattered shade and stretched out across the mattress like an unwelcome bedmate; the whispers and sighs of restless ghosts—real or imagined—who paced the floors; the tender hiss of a poet's words from the spirit who inclined its pearl-like cheek against the post at the foot of the bed—"*come away, o human child, for the world's more full of weeping than you can understand*"—its failure to arrive left me bleary-eyed and sour-mouthed at one o'clock in the morning, unease mingling with sweat on my forehead. Even a trip to the outlandish bathroom, with its embracing bosom of pink—pink tiles on the walls, pink sink, pink tub, pink toilet—failed to lift my spirits. If my mother had chosen the décor for its reputed mood-enhancing qualities, she had sadly miscalculated. In the bleakness of this sleepless night—*nuit blanche*, I heard Aunt Peach slur from somewhere in the walls—all that livid pink—*madder scarlet,* she whispered again—just gave me the puke-inducing sensation of being swathed in Pepto-Bismol. For the second time that night I stuck out my tongue, this time at my puffy image, skin gray as old dough, reflected in the medicine chest mirror.

Regressing, are we?

It was true. I felt myself, like Alice down the rabbit hole, growing smaller and smaller, and younger and younger, curiouser and curiouser, until the face that stared back at me had skin blessed with the unlined perfection of a doll and wide brown eyes of immaculate perception and unguarded spontaneity, over which stretched the ragged, untamed eyebrows of a child, nimble as caterpillars.

It was that incarnation of me who walked to the door of my brother's bedroom, trepidation hanging on my feet like ankle weights. It was that little me who leaned against the door jamb and willed trembling fingers to inch up the wall like a spider's legs until they found the light switch. I squinted at the painful first flash from the ceiling fixture until my eyes adjusted to the glare of the bulb under its milky, dish-shaped cover. How could I not be nine years old because it was still 1970 in that room. There was the bed, more stream-lined Danish Modern, all straight lines and angles, topped with the olive drab comforter. There were the desk and chair, twins to my own, and the bachelor's chest, matching the bed in its severe, simple serviceability, nary a feminine curve in sight. The green and beige plaid curtains were drawn across the windows. To block out what? The sun? The view? Time passing?

On the dresser, the phonograph rested in its brown tweed case, looking more like a compact, hard-bodied overnight bag than a record player. The leather binding along the edges was still butter smooth, the fabric cover nubbly-rough. Only a faint residue of powdery dust came away on my fingers.

The things some people save ...

Inside the case the turntable squatted, its black arm resting on its cradle, as if calmly waiting for the next groove to fill with its diamond-tipped stylus, unaware that it was no longer a vital part of a young man's life, as essential as any of the five senses. Once, not a day passed when its needle did not trace the patterns of sounds etched in black vinyl, following the spiral path laid down from outer edge to inner label, like a pilgrim walking the stones of a prayer labyrinth, on a journey of meaning, one laid in notes and rests, sharps and flats, guitar strings and drum skins, and murmurs and wails.

"You're obsolete, old pal," I whispered as I ran a finger around the edge of the turntable. "Not a lot of vinyl left. It's all going digital. Binary code. Laser beams. Photodiodes. Compact discs. MP3s. Don't ask. I can't explain."

The player sat there, mute, insensate. Yet, to my amazement, when I plugged it in and released the arm from its grip, the machine spun to life. I put the adapter down over the spindle and retrieved my 45s from the relic box. If cognizant, the phonograph might have thought that it was just like old times, perhaps a summer night in 1969 or '70, except that the fingers that caressed the volume knob turned it down instead of up. The amplifier and speaker, if capable of thought, would have recognized that the listener had crossed the Continental Divide of music appreciation, migrating from the territory where louder always equals better into the land of nuance and shading.

I played my music full blast when I was eight going on nine, but not because I equated decibels with quality. It was the aural equivalent of pressing my head against the table at the funeral parlor; it was a giant wall of sound to crouch behind, built to shut out thoughts I didn't want to entertain and words I didn't want to hear. There are only so many tears one can shed before the well of sorrow dries up, leaving the cracked, bitter dust of resignation. How many times could I cry hysterically in the bathroom, my arms thrown around the sink, fingernails clawing for purchase and slipping over its smooth, uncaring surface, my head bumping up against the aloof porcelain with each heaving, mucous-laden sob: *"Why'd it have to be him? Why'd it have to be him?"*

Did I mean to leave the door unlocked or was the foresight to turn the latch washed away in the emotional riptide? Who knows? But my father's arms always found their way around me. The first time he faced the volcano that was my grief, he panicked. He paced in a cramped circle over the tile, a skittish horse in a too-small stall, tugging his hands through his uncharacteristically unkempt hair, pounding them open-palmed on the sides of his thighs, the fabric of his workpants softening the slap to a muffled "thwuk." *"Would you rather it was me?"* he kept muttering, his voice a hyperventilated wheeze, until I shook my head, grinding my brow into the cold edge of the washstand as my hands gripped its steel legs. *No, no, no, I don't want it to be anyone!*

107

His foreman's mind went to work immediately following that debacle, thinking, always thinking, formulating a contingency plan, plotting a disaster route, because the next time I erupted, he was calm in the face of the lava flow of tears, recrimination and self-abuse, quietly but firmly gathering me into his arms as he sat on the edge of the tub, folding me into the space between his knees and his chin, not rocking, not swaying, for once just sitting, as his body absorbed the tremors of my own and radiated nothing in return but encompassing acceptance.

Yet in the face of my mother's behavior in the weeks and months after my brother's death, my father appeared permanently clueless, unable to figure out an approach. Sometimes it seemed as if he didn't even care to make an attempt. For her response to the disequilibrium that oscillated through the house was entirely different from mine. If I was a volcano spewing molten rock and steam, my mother was a glacier, her initial cool, imperturbable calm in burying her only son slowly spreading out to encase her daily life in a layer of ice.

They'd always been bickerers, petulant and petty, running hot and cold. How many times had I lain in bed, a pillow squashed over my ears to hush their cacophonous squabbling? They were not particularly unique or clever in their quarrels; they argued over all the usual topics that men and women, husbands and wives, argue over: his improvidence, her frugality *("If it wasn't for me, you'd piss away your entire paycheck!" "You keep your pocketbook closed tighter than your knees!")*; his drinking habits, her temperance *("If it wasn't for me, you'd drink up your entire paycheck!" "You used to enjoy tipping one or two on a Saturday night, before you entered your own little mental convent!" "Well, when you promised to take me places, I didn't think you meant the Do Drop Inn!")*; his taste for a well-turned calf, her jealousy *("That little bitch would just want you for your paycheck!" "So what you're saying is my life would be no different than it is now!")* In these moments our house resembled nothing so much as a barnyard: stallion and mare stomping and screaming; two mules braying; rooster and hen squawking. Sometimes my mother was a fly buzzing around my sire's head, harassing with a taunting insistence while he snapped at her with strong but futile teeth;

sometimes she was a rattlesnake, her staccato accusations a warning of a more deadly possibility which froze him in his path. Yet, after these skirmishes, calm would descend upon the land; the livestock would resume their wary co-existence.

After Joey was gone and the space that he filled was left gaping, hollow and dull, like a ring missing one of its gemstones, the hot-blooded bickering ceased, and a frigid formality set in, polite and contemptuous, an emotional Ice Age that froze us in our tracks, stuck somewhere between grief and resolution.

I'd been playing the music way too loud that night. I knew that. But my nine year old ears and feet, hands and fingers, and most of all, my nine year old brain and heart, needed that sheer volume to ward off the miserable thoughts and feelings that came creeping along at ten o'clock at night, oozing malaise like a slug oozes slime. The music was my circle of fire to keep the critters that bled black despair at bay. In the middle of the heat of the music and the heat of the summer night, one fluid, the other stagnant, I simmered in a brew of sweat and vibration.

But it was too loud. Sitting cross-legged on the hard tile of my brother's bedroom, drumming my fingers on my knees, with my back to the door, I didn't hear my father enter; didn't hear his feet creak across the floor or even the words he spoke, until, out of the corner of my eye, I saw his fingers twisting the volume knob on the record player to the left.

"Hey," I exclaimed, springing up and reaching to turn the knob back to the right. His hand grasped mine in mid-air.

He shook his head. "This is loud enough."

I shook my head in response. Then the song was over. We listened to the swoop and click of the phonograph arm as it lifted automatically, the cluck of the spindle as it released another 45, and the soft thwack as the record hit the small stack of vinyl already on the turntable. The music burst out of the groove like a racehorse exploding from a starting gate: staccato drums, thrumming guitars, the electro-shock vibrato of a sitar. And the voice—nasal, guttural, raw, numb.

My father's hand dropped to his side. Mine continued on its path to the volume knob, where I turned it back to its original place. He shook his head again. I turned it back down one number, then two. Then I sank back to the floor, pulling my knees up to my chest, wondering how Mick and Keith, years and miles away from me, could understand so perfectly how I lived and ached at that moment, wanting to paint my own world black.

We played it three times in a row, my father joining me on the floor, leaning back against the bed, elbows resting on his knees. His bony fingers first massaged his temples where a vein pulsed blue-green and then dug into his black hair where shafts of silvery white glinted. He closed his eyes the third time through, and so did I. We didn't see or hear her come in, didn't even feel the air current waft as she cut through it, couldn't even smell the odor of sweat and dish soap and disapproval. All we heard was the lurching slash of the stylus across the defenseless vinyl, like a brutal jagged knife ripping into a priceless canvas, a sound with all the finality of a rifle shot or the thud of a clod of soil as it hits a casket at the bottom of a grave.

She didn't scream, shout or even raise her voice, merely lifted the record off the turntable and cracked it in two with one swift twist of her strong, red-knuckled hands. Only the label resisted and held the two pieces of black vinyl together, though now they hung limp and useless, like the broken wings of a crow... or a blackbird stopped from singing in the dead of night.

"I told you not to play this crap that loud."

Her voice was as smooth and opaque as an ice-covered pond. She dropped the broken record into the little plastic wastebasket that hugged the side of the desk, where its fall was cushioned by layers of wadded up tissue that had accumulated there. After she left, we sat there in silence, my father's hands—hands that had always looked so capable, fingernails so clean—hanging impotently off his knees, and his jaw, which had always seemed so strong and set, a magnet for my child's hands whether clean-shaven or black-stubbled, now drooping and soft-edged.

I believe it was the first time I ever saw him cry. I couldn't even be sure it was a tear that ran down the valley between his nose and his cheek and not just another bead of sweat brought on by the heat of that August night. But his eyes seemed to swim in their sockets and his hand trembled faintly as he brought it to his face. No shock, no shame on my part; it didn't strike me as unmanly. It was enough that he was awake; it was enough to know he felt … something.

When I pulled the record out of the waste can, cradling it in my hands as one might cradle an injured sparrow, he mumbled that he would buy me a new one.

I shook my head. "Don't want a new one. Even if I did, you couldn't get it—this came out a few years ago. You can't find it on a single anymore."

"I'll get you the album."

"She'd just break that, too."

He had no answer. I took the damaged record back to my own room, set the pieces together as carefully as a doctor sets a fractured bone, and fashioned a cast out of Scotch tape, though I knew this break would never heal.

That was the beginning. The next day I rooted around in the stack of Christmas wrapping supplies in the spare room closet, through bags of paper, ribbons and bows, a tower of used boxes, small ones nested inside larger ones, until I found a box that I considered big and sturdy enough: the white Marshall Field's box. My mother would never be able to part with my brother's possessions. They would sit there, objects to be occasionally dusted, taking up space in an empty room that would be part shrine, part storage locker. But she wouldn't love them as he did.

So I would take what I wanted. And the first thing I saved was *"Paint It Black."*

Now, years later, I pushed the broken 45 with its mummified adhesive tape down over the spindle onto the turntable and watched it spin. At forty-five revolutions per minute, the yellow edge of the tape blurred into the black of the disk, like caramel bleeding into licorice. This time, in the silence, I heard the sighs of the footsteps on the stairs, the snarl of the floorboard as feet reached the landing, the click and creak of the tiles as my father padded into the bedroom.

"Thought I heard music. Didn't think I was dreaming. Can't sleep?"

He came alongside me and peered into the record player. A ratty old bathrobe, blue plaid faded to muddy gray, hung loosely on his frame. His feet were bare, ugly, toes horny with calluses.

"What you got on there?" he asked, squinting.

I flicked the knob that turned the player off. The record slowly wound down to a full stop, the blurred edges of the tape and disk returning to crisp lines of demarcation. I lifted it gently off the spindle and held it before him, cupped in my hands like an offering. The way he blinked rapidly and thrust his hands in the pockets of his robe, automatically driven to root around for loose change, told me that he remembered.

"Did we ever think of her?"

His hands rose up out of his pockets and reached out, taking hold of the disk delicately between thumbs and forefingers. He stared at it briefly, flipped it over, glanced at the B-side, and then handed it back. The old mattress croaked a protest when he sat down. He cocked his head and appeared to look at me, but he was really looking through me, as if I was just a sheer curtain beyond which the real view lay, an open range of past, present and future, where truths and half-truths and outright lies grew side by side, bending to and fro in the prevailing winds like prairie grass. Which was he looking to harvest?

"Did she ever think of us?"

I stared at him, astonished. I had expected an excuse, a justification, a defense. But what gall to turn the magnifying lens back onto my mother!

"I can't believe you can sit there and ask that! After all she did every day. How typical! To devalue what a homemaker does— the cooking, the cleaning, the gardening, the shopping, managing the household, planning the budget, keeping the family business—because, make no mistake, that's what it is—keeping it running smoothly so—"

"That's not making a home."

His simple declaration was like a dam thrown up to block the torrent of my words.

"All that stuff, all that doing. It's just housekeeping. It doesn't make a home." He put his hands over the bony knees that jutted

112

out from his robe and pushed himself up, gasping and wincing a little from the effort. He slipped his hand under his robe, gingerly probing his left ribcage.

"For that matter, it takes more than one person to make a home," I retorted.

"Well, touché." His attempt at a grin looked more like a raw rift across his face. "And for that matter, housekeeping and nursemaiding—I guess I could use some of that right about now." His chuckle came out a dry rasp. "So who am I to pass judgment?"

His gait to the door was half-hobble, half- walk and his pace seemed to match the beat of Aaron's whispered refrain that was once again ambling through my head: *"be sweet, be sweet, be sweet."*

"A husband," I ventured quickly, if only to silence the voice and its command.

He paused at the door, looking through me again. "Some would say that was too generous a description." He pointed a finger at me. Was it my imagination or was it trembling? "Three sides to every story. But you, you're the daughter. So I guess your side is the truth."

Is that where I had learned it, the flippant exit that used to drive Aaron crazy until he reconciled himself to living with it, going so far as to say he enjoyed it now, since it allowed him to savor the view of my swaying posterior? Was it nature or nurture? Was it handed down in the genetic code that passed from father to daughter, this penchant for the quip and the pivot? Or was I merely mimicking behavior I had witnessed, like a little girl tottering around in her mother's high heels or running her father's razor over her hairless chin? There was, of course, nothing left to do but take the records off the turntable, close up the case, turn off the bedroom light and trudge back down the hall to my own room, where I lay sleepless in the yellow knife blade that the streetlight laid across the bed.

CHAPTER 8

The kitchen cupboards had little in the way of mood-lifting breakfast foods that could dispel the ill-humor left over from a sleepless night, foods that I would actually deign to consume. He had made a pot of beans and franks. The sweet smell of cooked onions enveloped me but I craved the carbs and sugar of cereal. He offered a cup of coffee. I scorned that as well.

"Never developed a taste for it."

His eyes flicked back and forth from the stove to the white cabinets sorely in need of a fresh coat of paint to the green Formica table with its chrome legs and the half-moon chip in its surface. It had mysteriously appeared one morning after a turbulent argument that had woke us kids at one in the morning with jagged voices and the shriek of a plate as it met a wall. I dug the end of my fingernail into the crescent gouge as my father wracked his brain, performing a mental inventory of his larder for something to offer that I wouldn't refuse.

"Toast?" He gestured to the loaf of white bread on the counter.

"Wheat?"

"Guess a trip to the grocery store is in order. Make a list." As he laughed, his right hand moved up from his hip to his ribcage.

"Still in pain?"

He flicked his hand and the question away. "Nah. Just a pinch or two. I'm not s'posed to wear my corset thing so much now."

"Taking your pain reliever?"

"Yeah, yeah, Nurse Claire. So, whaddaya gonna eat?"

The toasted white bread spread with strawberry jam melted on my tongue like cotton candy in an eight year old's mouth.

He wanted to shop for groceries first but I deep-sixed that idea. I was there to help him with Grandma Sophie's and the sooner we got to the job, the sooner we would finish, and the sooner I could get back on I-55 going in the opposite direction. From the resigned expression that deepened the wrinkles around his eyes, I could tell he knew what I was thinking.

Grandma's house was just three blocks away. Its location, a stone's throw from the EJ&E Railroad tracks where my grandpa had toiled as a switchman and a short drive from the steel mills to the east, played a large part in my parents' decision to buy one of the new brick homes that sprung up in the area after World War II. My father was the son who put down roots in the old neighborhood; his older brother, Pete, a bull-dog of man with a salt-and-pepper crew cut, his mother's broad face, and the striking brown, long-lashed eyes of his sire, Jakub, threw in his lot with competitor Inland Steel, married an East Chicago girl and settled his family over the border in Indiana. His younger brother Jimmie, the baby of the family, had, in his youth, often suffered the indignity of being called his older brother's name, so alike were they in their rangy stature and dark good looks, except that Jimmie had his mother's baby blue peepers. Jimmie enlisted in the Army just in time to be shipped off to Korea. He stayed in the service after his tours of duty were over, moving at the military's whim from posting to posting across the United States. Even after he left the Army and came back to Chicago with his wife and child, they didn't seem to stay in any one place very long, renting apartments and the top floors of two- and three-flats all across the Southeast Side. Of the two Sokol sisters who survived beyond infancy, dishwater blonde sparrows Dorothy and Frances, always referred to in the diminutive as Dodie and Frannie, both were younger than my dad. They married early and after the war their husbands carried them off further south, out beyond the city limits to new-made suburbs with old Chicago names like Burnham and Calumet City, where they lived in "ranches," churned out babies like good Catholics, and rode with pride in their husbands' new Buicks and Chevys. The distance and all those kids, as well as their mother's embarrassing Old World customs, made it inconvenient to visit the old house more than once a month.

The burden of looking after the aging widow defaulted to my mother, the daughter-in-law, who took it up with a genuine grace. She was a bit of an anomaly in those days, an only child of older parents who had, like Jakub, died before I was even born. Perhaps she embraced Sophie to fill that gap. She even allowed me to be her assistant. We brought groceries and performed seasonal yard work. In the spring and summer, my mother cut her grass with a push mower and washed her windows. In fall, we raked the brown and amber leaves that drifted down from the three massive oak trees that stood in her yard. In winter, we shoveled the snow from her sidewalk and scattered rock salt to melt the ice on her porch steps.

After the chores were done, my mother would wash her hands and comb her hair in the bathroom while I stepped into the living room to attempt a quick goodbye. It was always dusk in there, even at the height of a summer afternoon. The sun never penetrated the Venetian blinds and heavy brocade draperies that were pulled three quarters of the way across the picture window, leaving only a small opening in the middle. Grandma Sophie sat in a wing chair upholstered in an old-fashioned fabric with velvet floral flocking that had once been raised but was now irrevocably crushed, stained and faded. She sat for hours, watching her small world revolve and evolve. Her view had once extended for a mile or more across open land, over the cobblestone street to the railroad tracks and beyond to the marsh where cattails grew and spring peepers sang. Now she looked out on small brick bungalows and a street lined with cars parked in front and the people who moved in and out of the houses and the cars.

She never let me go with just a quick "bye bye" from the doorway. Always she beckoned me closer. Trudging across the dark gray carpet, my feet felt like they were encased in concrete. She waited, a patient semi-smile fixed on her wrinkled face, Mona Lisa as crone, her eyelids so hooded I could barely discern the fabled blue of her eyes. The fabric of her housedress, like that of the chair, was faded, the pattern of tiny purple and white flowers a ghost of its former exuberance. The flesh-colored stockings she wore sagged around her thick ankles like the skin of some matriarchal elephant. Up close, she smelled of must and crushed lilacs, like her house.

When I finally reached the chair, she would smile more broadly, making the creases in her face deepen. She inevitably started talking so rapidly in English so heavily accented it might as well have been a foreign language, so little could I grasp. She punctuated her sentences with numerous Polish phrases for good measure so that a conversation with Grandma Sophie was not a conversation at all but a trip to a foreign land where I could only nod dumbly and hope I using the appropriate facial expressions in response. At the end of her monologues, she would dig her fleshy, liver-spotted hand with its bulging blue-green veins into the pocket of her apron, pull out folded dollar bills and hold them out.

"No, Grandma, I don't need—"

"Take, take," she would urge, catching hold of my right hand and pressing the money into it. The skin of her palm always felt dry. I wondered that the touch of it didn't make a crackling sound, like parchment.

In the end, I always took it. She was too powerful to refuse, this crone of babble and babushkas, my strega babcia, grandmother witch.

The white frame house with its sharply gabled black roof resembled the house of my memory. The lilacs that fronted the broad porch were overgrown with dead wood and only one of the monster oaks that had loomed over the side yard, making it a shady, cool bower in the heat of a summer afternoon, remained. Inside, the house was still dark, darker than in my memory, and murky, moldy. A film of dust seemed to cover everything and motes of it hung in the air.

"If you see anything you want to save, just put it aside," my father said.

What could there possibly be in this house that I would want? I glanced to the corner where the grand piano had sat throughout my childhood. Never quite understood why it was there. Nobody played it except Uncle Jimmie, and he could only tap out a small repertoire of simplified classics and pop tunes. At family gatherings, he'd sit at the piano under his slick-backed hair and provide the background music, segueing from Broadway show tunes to a little light Mozart to Sinatra, eyeing his audience with the amused aloofness of a piano man in a hotel lounge. All he needed to complete the image was a shot glass for tips. Whenever I walked into the room he would launch into Debussy's *Claire De Lune* with a wink and a nod. He rarely mingled, even ate sitting at the piano, careful to close the case over the keys. His standard line when anyone complimented his playing, if they noticed at all above the drone of conversation and card-playing, was *"yeah, I coulda been a virtuoso,"* with a sneering whine that could have out-Brandoed Brando.

If my father was in hearing range, he would invariably launch into a spiel which amounted to a back-handed defense of his brother's talents—what I came to think of as the 'litany of couldn'ts.' *Couldn't tie his shoes 'til he was nine—had to do it for him. Couldn't pour a glass of milk without spilling half of it. Couldn't read 'til he was in the third grade. Couldn't run after the ice man or the coal cart without falling down and splitting open his lip. Couldn't stand up to the Ravitz brothers to save his life—had to fight his fights for him. Couldn't work up the nerve to ask Millie Daschle out. Even had to kiss her for him. Only thing he had going for him is that he looked just like me. But hell, first time he sat down at a piano, this boy could play.*

Jimmie would just grin and say, "Well, least I didn't need your help on my wedding night." Whatever woman was in the room would shush them at that point, nodding sharply with eyebrows raised in signifying arcs in the direction of whatever child was present. My father's lips would curl slightly in an arch smile, as if at first he didn't realize what his mouth was doing, and then suddenly he would lift his drink as if to hide it.

The piano was gone now, leaving a gap of blank wall and floor.

"I might have taken the piano just for the hell of it. Where'd it go?"

"Sold years ago. Jimmie sold it when they moved back down south."

We trod the long hallway that ran the length of the house. Rooms opened off each side. A shotgun house, I've heard it called, because you could stand in the doorway and shoot a bullet straight down the hall and out the window of the back porch. Grandma's bedroom was off the middle of the hall on the south side, right across from the bathroom. I peered around the door frame, expecting to see the bedclothes in disarray on the floor, pillows and blankets tossed this way and that. However, the bed was made, the linens neatly folded and tucked, the wine-colored coverlet drawn up to the massive, dark headboard. On the floor, Grandma's ratty terrycloth slippers peeked out from underneath the edge of the bedspread, as if awaiting the return of her feet.

She had died in that bed, surrounded by her things, in her familiar darkness, in her room with the moldering, brown-tinged wallpaper, under her ceiling with its star-shaped water stain. Images of the alternatives flashed: needles, feeding tubes and a respirator, rasping her inhalations and exhalations, forcing her chest to rise and fall in a monitored, even rhythm in the antiseptic glare of an ICU that turns even the healthiest skin a sickly shade of gray.

"Doesn't look like you've gotten very far."

"Tell you the truth, I ain't done shit. I just—I don't know where to begin."

We were poised at a moment: if I said the wrong thing, he would break down, I knew he would. I wasn't ready for that, re-fused to be ready for that. I hadn't come to be a shoulder for a maudlin old man, regretting his losses and choices, to cry on. I would never play that part for him. He'd lost the right to press that role on me years ago.

Snapping my fingers, I held them up in his face, counting off the steps we would take. "Pick a room, any room. Sort the stuff into three piles: scrap, salvage and possibly precious. Scrap goes in the big black garbage bags and we tote them to the alley. Salvage goes in the white garbage bags and we put those aside for Goodwill or the Salvation Army or whoever. Possibly precious goes in the boxes in case any of her heirs want to turn them into heirlooms. Same with the furniture, unless you were thinking of trying to sell it. Have you seen an attorney about getting named executor of the estate?"

He nodded. "Your cousin Linda, Dodie's daughter, is helping me with that. She's a lawyer, you know."

"I didn't. But I don't really keep in touch with anyone up here. I only spoke to her briefly at the … funeral. Well, good, at least you've got the legal side under control."

"Why is that?"

"Well, you can't do anything formal with her bank account or anything else until—"

"I meant about not keeping in touch."

I looked away, crossing to Sophie's dresser, running my fingers down the handle of her hand mirror. The mother-of-pearl inlay glowed with iridescent pinks, whites and baby blues. On the back, raised gilt flowers grew and twined around the mirror setting. The glass itself was cracked at the top. It reflected the crease running across my forehead.

"I'll start with this room. Pick one for yourself and we can get this show on the road."

Midway through the morning, after enduring obnoxious talk radio hosts, snippets of country pop songs and a repetitive cycle of "newsweathersportstraffic" from the static-cursed radio blaring in the kitchen, I made a mental note to bring Tally's Walkman with me the next day. I had emptied the tiny closet. Sophie's wardrobe was limited to cotton shifts and housecoats, appropriate only for the rag bin. One black garbage bag slumped in the hallway. I took a second one and set to work clearing the bureau. The drawers were recalcitrant, opening only after some hard tugs, as if they realized that alien fingers gripped their tarnished handles. The bottom drawer yielded a weak mothball odor and threadbare sweaters that had long since lost their ability to keep a body warm. In one corner sat a flimsy shirt box with a creased top and collapsed corners that overflowed with ancient greeting cards.

Artifacts. The good stuff, as Aaron would say.

Most of it was mundane. Sophie's children were not especially creative when it came to honoring their mother. Christmas and Easter cards, Mother's Day and birthday cards depended on Hallmark to craft their sentiments. They limited their contributions to "Love," and their varied signatures. And at some point, the sons' signatures transformed from tight, upright, masculine cursive into slanted, flowing feminine script when card duty was apparently handed over to their wives. When the grandchildren could grip a crayon or a pencil, they were given cards of their own to sign, once again full of flowery, pre-fabricated mush written by the creative arts department at American Greetings. Every now and then some lyrical little soul would add a phrase of his or her own making: *"I like the cookies that you keep in your cookie jar, Grandma." "I send you 1,000,000 kisses, Grandma." "I am sorry that Tecza died. He was such a beautiful bird."* The last was in my own immature scrawl, written upon the occasion of the death of her colorful parakeet, Tecza, which my father said meant rainbow in Polish.

Among the pile were two cards hand-made from construction paper and crayons. The edges were brittle and slightly curled, but the crayon markings were still vibrant. Haphazardly drawn Easter eggs—pastel striped, bright spotted, black and white zigzagged—decorated the pages. On the front of one card, a large, fat bunny stood upright juggling the eggs; on the other, they tumbled out of a squat yellow basket overflowing with bright green Easter grass.

We had made them on Easter Sunday, 1971; an April 11th according to the scribble on the inside corners. Jamie and I. Sitting out on the enclosed back porch at a rickety folding table. We'd been banished from the kitchen and dining room for being underfoot while the women bustled to and fro, mashing potatoes, slicing ham, whisking vinegar and sugar into sour cream to dress the cucumber salad, setting up the table for the buffet. Most of the other grandchildren were teenagers and they were playing hearts at the newer card table set up in the living room. Some, the married ones, like my sister Marjorie, weren't even there, having acquired new holiday obligations known as in-laws.

Aunt Dodie had produced a box of crayons and some construction paper and sat the four youngest down: me, Jamie, Dougie and Linda. It was chilly out there. The weak April sun, when it managed to burn through the overcast, had not yet been able to loosen winter's last, desperate grip on the air. Linda whined that her fingers were cold and wandered back through the open door into the stuffy, but good-smelling warmth of the main house. Dougie picked up crayons and tossed them back down without drawing so much as a scribble. He resented having been shooed out to the porch with us. He was eleven; he belonged at the other card table at the opposite end of the house. Where—precisely because he was eleven—he was definitely not wanted.

He twiddled a blue crayon between his fingers. "Come outside and throw the ball around with me," he said to Jamie. "I brought one—and my glove."

Jamie shrugged, head down, concentrating on his rabbit. "Maybe later. Don't have my glove with me."

"Big deal. I won't throw hard. Come on. This crap is boring. It's for girls."

Dougie was betting that those words would jolt any self-respecting nine-year-old boy to his senses. I thought so too, and anticipated the loss of Jamie's company, but hid my feelings by ducking my head down closer to my paper.

Jamie tapped his card with his finger. "I'm gonna finish this first."

Dougie snapped the crayon in two and flung it down. One piece landed on Jamie's card, leaving a blue dot in the middle of a pink-striped egg.

"Pussy," Dougie muttered as he stalked into the house.

"Talkin' to yourself again?" I mocked just loud enough to cause him to stop on the threshold and turn.

"What'd you say?" His face was blotched an angry red and a flustered white.

Jamie quickly shoved a crayon in my face in fake disgust. "Here, take the darn crayon. I don't need that color anyway."

Dougie's eyes narrowed and his nostrils flared, as if he could scope and sniff out the deceit. "Stupid babies." A feeble parting shot as he slammed the door behind him.

Jamie glanced up to gauge my reaction, his brown eyes wary. "Jeez, you're lucky I can think on my feet."

"Aaw, he wouldn't have done nothin'. He's all talk and diddly squat. Besides, it smells a lot better out here now."

"Yeah. Like my mama would say, that is one na-aa-aa-sty boy."

We had only seen each other two or three times since my brother's funeral the previous summer; once when Aunt Peach had called out of the blue in late August to say she was taking Jamie downtown to the Art Institute and would I like to join them. She invited my mother to come along as well but, as usual, she had some housewifely chore that just couldn't wait. She had thrown herself into her housework with a vengeance, doubling her previous efforts, always a blur with a mop or a dust rag in her grip, while my father, it seemed, wanted only to sleep. He had switched to afternoon shift—four to twelve they called it around the mill—and often slept until noon.

Aunt Peach looked as cool as a marble column in her whites that hot day: white capris, white sleeveless shirt, white espadrilles, white-tipped fingernails from her immaculate French manicure, white headband holding her blonde fall off her forehead. Even her lips were frosted a whitish pink. Next to Peach, my mother, in dowdy tan Bermuda shorts, her ashy brown hair shot through with gray, wiping her rough, red hands, looked grimy and bedraggled, though it was barely ten in the morning and she hadn't lifted anything much heavier than her coffee cup yet.

My feelings that morning were plain and raw: guilt for noticing the difference and relief at being ushered out of that house and into Aunt Peach's luscious red Impala convertible for the trip up Lake Shore Drive; flattered to hold her hand as we ascended the granite steps between the great bronze lions that stood sentinel on Michigan Boulevard; mesmerized as her voice flowed like honey as we strolled the galleries. We lingered in front of a large blue study of water lilies and she sighed.

"Oh, to be there, in Giverny, in Monet's garden, a lily on the pond, evoked by the hand of a master. Immortalized. Embraced."

No one I knew talked like that. So I closed my eyes and drifted in the blue-green pond, the water warm on my skin, the liquid thick with life: with algae soft as velvet; with undulating fish, fins fluttering in an unknown current; with the underwater forest of stems that held the lily pads in place. Above were trees that filtered the harsh summer sun into a liquid light, dripping down to mottle the surface of the water, splashing on a lily here and there, heightening the color of the petals. Oh, to float, languid, limp, lost. Then, without warning, my brother's face appeared above the water, breaking my reverie, his mouth a gasping O of horror, filling, filling with green: water, algae, leaves; his hands grasping my shoulders, my chest, pulling me under, weighing me down... As I ran headlong from the gallery, through the watery blur of my tears, bumping into other visitors who clucked and gasped their disapproval, I swear I felt his hands gripping my ankles and the slimy ooze of algae down my calves.

When she found me sitting on the soothingly cool marble stairs that led down to the main entrance, she said nothing. Just put her arm around my shoulder and squeezed. Gently. Once. She took my hand and led me out the great brass-encased doors. She posed Jamie and me before each lion in turn, snapping quick photographs, and then, laughing, instructed us to stand directly in between and pretend to browse our museum brochure.

"You are reading between the lions. Comprenez-vous?

We didn't—and she had to explain, and then we laughed, too, pretending to get the joke.

At lunch, as we rubbed elbows with the suits and skirts who worked in the Loop, she expounded on Georgia, where she'd been born and raised in a town just over the border from Tennessee. After spending several of her formative years living with her maternal aunt in downstate Columbus, she had attended the University there, but left before she earned her degree in art history to marry Sergeant James R. Sokol of the United States Army, who had been stationed at Fort Benning. She sketched out verbal images of heat and red dirt; of wild vines with funny names that crawled up telephone poles and across fences and could devour whole buildings while you weren't looking; of the smell of pines and mountain laurel that made the air itself succulent, edible.

"It sounds so pretty. Why would you ever want to leave?" I asked, breathless.

Jamie rolled his eyes. "It's so hot and humid in the summer you just want to lay down and pant like a dog."

Aunt Peach glanced at him out the corner of her eye. "No more so than Chicago. But to answer your question, Pie, a wife goes where her husband goes. I've had the opportunity to see many wonderful places."

Jamie snorted. "Army bases."

"That's enough sarcasm, sir." She fixed her blue eyes on me. "But you know, I do believe that, after Georgia, right here, Chicago, is my favorite place of all. Because the people I love are here."

She insisted that Jamie and I split a sundae to top off our cheeseburgers and watched with hungry glee as we lapped up the creamy vanilla ice cream and gooey fudge.

"Want some?" I held out a spoonful heaped with melting deliciousness.

She shook her head. "Thank you for offering, but a woman gets to be of a certain age and she just can't eat like she did in her youth. I have to watch my girlish figure. Besides, it's just as satisfying to watch you two enjoy it." And her eyes did seem to devour us, tenderly, lovingly, in a way that made me yearn to be consumed.

That evening, as I sat across from my mother at the kitchen table, I tried to tell her about the water lilies, but she just raked aimlessly through the tangle of spaghetti on her plate, her eyes wandering to empty chairs on the left and the right, to the stove, to the sink, to seemingly anywhere but my face. I willed myself to stay awake until my father came home in order to tell him about my revelations, but as the clock hands approached eleven, my eyelids sagged and my chin was drooped to my chest, and the tale of the water lilies would have to wait until the sun rose. In the end, it was a tale left untold. Whenever he finally rolled out of bed the next day, I was already gone, out into the light, jump-roping, hopscotching, Barbie-dolling, eating peanut butter and jelly sandwiches at a friend's house, wandering from alley to schoolyard to park on a child's summer odyssey to remain in the light, until it was finally time to amble home, coated with the grime of a day spent on the move. And by then he was gone again.

When I saw them again, on Christmas Day at Sophie's, Aunt Peach was in white silk and black velvet, her hair swept up and back in a French twist, her lips as red as the poinsettias she had brought to brighten the living room. That was the day I noticed that she didn't hang in the back of the house with the other women, scuttling back and forth between the kitchen and the dining room, dishing up the grub and gossip. She made the requisite trip to deposit her potluck offering, stayed just long enough to appear interested in the dishes, of both the edible and verbal variety, and then drifted back to the living room, where she would perch next to Uncle Jimmie at the piano or on the cane-backed chair next to Sophie's curio of china birds. That seemed her favorite place and the right place for her, for she was a rare bird herself, a peacock amidst a flock of house sparrows.

"You always look so beautiful," I blurted out that afternoon, not meaning to say it out loud, but unable to corral my thoughts when I passed by the bathroom and spied her applying a fresh coat of lipstick and tucking a stray strand of hair behind her ear.

126

She smiled. "You are just the sweetest thing. I could eat you up. But, at the risk of sounding arrogant, I will agree if there's one thing I know how to do, it's put a look together." Her eyes ran the length of my scrawny body, measuring me, taking in my red plaid jumper and white turtleneck, my red tights, my scuffed Mary Janes. "I think you have potential, too, Sugah Pie." She leaned in, her voice low and confidential, whispery as confectioner's sugar. "If you evah want any tips, any fashion advice, you come see me and we'll go to town."

On Easter, Aunt Peach wore ice blue, with her hair French-braided and her lips and cheeks just kissed with a delicate, petal-soft rose. Dougie had already greeted me with a blatant "Hey, Four-Eyes," a mocking reference to the recently acquired addition to my face. Peach cupped my chin in her hand and tilted my face up ever so slightly.

"They suit you, Pie. They add an air of mystery, n'est-ce pas? And those frames, very French. Do you know, I think Elizabeth Taylor herself has a pair of cats-eye glasses."

When I repeated this to my mother as she stood at Sophie's kitchen table, rolling up little triangles of dough into crescents, her thin lips paled under their coating of pink Maybelline lipstick as they spread into a scornful slash across her face.

"Meddle not with him that flattereth with his lips. Or her." It came out of her mouth like spit.

Edging away, I sought my father, who perched on the edge of the piano bench, coaching the card players who had switched from hearts to poker, critiquing his brother's piano playing, rolling his eyes, but sniggering all the same at the latest joke added to Uncle Bob's long-running comedy routine *("Yeah, after dinner, me and the boys are gonna go out and play kick the cans—Mexi-cans, Puerto Ri-cans, Afri-cans")*. He was showing Jamie, sitting at his feet, how to properly shuffle a deck of cards and do sleight of hand. He looked so vital, so awake in the midst of all that activity, as if he were the hot burning center of the solar system around which all else revolved, as if the quantity and mass of the satellites in the room had finally made the one that was missing less noticeable. When he saw me standing in the doorway, his hands dropped to his knees, like a juggler letting the balls fall, and he focused those burning eyes on me, beckoning me with one swift flip of his fingers. I told him what Aunt Peach had said, then I told him what my mother had said, then I waited for his take on the issue. He took a long swallow from his can of beer. His cheeks seemed flushed—from the human heat of the room, or the alcohol. His eyes strayed to Jamie, still sitting at his feet, his face raised expectantly for my father's reply, as if he were a fount for the wisdom-parched mind. He held out the empty can.

"James, my good man, would you fetch me another? Cuz when you're out of Schlitz—"

"You're out of beer!" Jamie shouted as he skittered off like a puppy playing a game of retrieve. My father leaned in close to me as Uncle Jimmie started in, as usual, on *Claire de Lune.*

"Well, you know you're beautiful to me, Miss Claire Josephine. And never let it be said that Joe Sokol didn't recognize a beautiful gal when he saw one."

I had expected no less, but I was not mollified. "But why did Mom say that? She's always so mean."

"Don't pay attention to her when she gets like that."

"And Aunt Peach is always so nice."

Something in the way his lips tightened and his eyes looked down and to the side told me that he had left me and turned his focus to someplace else. I tapped his shoulder to bring him back. When he finally spoke, his voice was a pianissimo rumble under the melody of the song.

"Claire, there are at least two kinds of women in the world. Your mother is one kind and Aunt Peach is another. And they're like oil and water—"

Jamie returned, holding out a fresh beer can.

My father's voice rose to forte again. "Why thank you, sir. Now why don't you take Miss Claire Josephine here and show her your neat card trick." With that, my father stood up and crossed the room to Sophie's armchair. He squatted down and took her hand in his, whispering something, his mouth close to her ear.

"Claire Josephine?" Jamie repeated incredulously. "Your middle name is Josephine?"

I scowled. "Yeah, what of it? It's from my dad."

"Claire Jo. Clairey Jo."

"That's my name. Don't wear it out."

Later, on the back porch, while we put the finishing touches on our Easter cards, Jamie leaned over so his mouth was not two inches from my ear and whispered, "My mama's right. You do look pretty in your glasses."

I couldn't be sure that it was just the damp chill in the air that made the goose bumps prickle up on my arms.

During the endless stretch of time between the serving of the dinner buffet, with its enormous ham centerpiece, and the arrangement of the dessert table, which boasted a huge lamb cake with black licorice eyes and shaved coconut fleece, we ricocheted from room to room, avoiding Dougie. He plunked himself on the sofa in the living room, pounding his fist into his mitt, glowering from under his thick uni-brow stretched like a millipede across his forehead, his lips, slimy with spittle, drooping under his nose like squashed red Play-doh. We cast furtive glances at him from our cave under the piano and then, shooting each other a wink, crawled out and scuttled down the hall. He either didn't get the hint that we were determined to leave him out or he was simply dead set on hounding our every move, his doughy face growing more mottled with frustration as the pursuit dragged on. At first it amusing, leading him on the hunt. We started calling him 'Elmer,' as in Fudd, the relentless but befuddled pursuer of a certain wascal wabbit.

We sang *sotto voce* as we trekked from bedroom to dining room to kitchen to porch and back again. *"Ooooooh, wait'll I get dat wabbit—what would you want wit a wabbit?"* But we grew bored with the game and decided to leave our nemesis behind once and for all. We formulated a diversionary plan: Jamie would head for the bathroom, then double-back to the living room. I'd grab our jackets and slip down the hall and out the back door. With Dougie torn between two quarries, Jamie would have a moment to sidle out the front door. We'd meet up in the back yard on the side of the garage where we'd be hidden from view. Our escape ran like clockwork, except we underestimated our opponent. He actually did have the intelligence to figure out that we'd given him the slip. Luckily, we spotted him trundling down the gangway before he saw us and we ducked into Sophie's old shack of a garage, praying that he would mistake the creak of the battered door for the complaints of the oak trees stretching their winter-stiff limbs against the fresh spring breeze.

The garage smelled of old metal and rust, of dirt and damp bricks. The dim, oblique light of the late afternoon barely diluted the darkness. Hulking outlines of strange forms loomed around us; the rafters arched above like the ribs and spine of some great gaunt beast into whose belly we had stumbled, little Jonahs swallowed by the whale. We crouched beside the door, hands clasped, fearful of what lurked within, unwilling to tread further into the gloom, but equally unwilling to face what lurked without.

Hold your breath, said the wet press of Jamie's hand on mine. *Don't make a sound or move a muscle, not even a gritty scrape of your patent leather shoe on the cobblestone floor. Here we are, just you and me, in the dark, and we'll be safe—if you only keep hold of my hand.*

My lungs were burning, my eyes tight to bursting in their sockets when we heard the muffled crunch of his shoes on the gravel just outside the door. I sensed, rather than heard, his sausage-like fingers pressing against the wood with its crust of paint, flaking and etched with lines like the skin of an alligator. The hinges creaked an eerie protest that sent a shivery finger flitting up my spine. I needed desperately to exhale, and to inhale again, as white sparks danced behind my closed eyelids, even as I realized how absurd I was acting, thinking, like a baby, that to not see is to not be seen.

Then we heard it—a little "heh" like phlegm caught in the back of the throat. Then the soft crunch again, an evaporating sound of retreating feet. We exhaled in a whoosh and inhaled in a great suck of relief, leaning into each other's giggle, heads butting, shoulders rubbing, smacking our fancy shoes together as we sat on the stones and reveled in the discomfort of being alive, as the cold and damp seeped up through our thin Easter finery. My dress was hiked up around my thighs and I could feel the grind of the cobblestone through my underwear and the grainy dirt against my legs. We gloated over our brilliance and Dougie's ultimate stupidity, and Jamie had his hand on my knee, waggling it back and forth in time to our singing: *"ooooohh, wait'll I get dat wabbit"* when the door swung open with one long, disapproving shriek.

"Come," was all my mother said, but that single word cracked like a slap across my face and the touch of her hand as she gripped mine and roughly jerked me to my feet was just as brutal.

"What? What did I do?" I asked just once as she hustled me down the gangway, the toes of my shoes scraping against the cement, marring their shiny new surface.

"You know," she replied as she shoved me into the back seat of our car and then took her place in front on the passenger side.

Perhaps she took my silence for admission of some guilt. But I knew better than to continue without a witness. When my father finally emerged from the house and got into the driver's side, he flashed me the briefest of smiles and arched his eyebrows. It wasn't until the car pulled away from the curb and passed the row of hedges three doors down that she let loose with a torrent of invective disguised in the form of questions. What was I thinking? How could I go into the garage with that boy? How could I do such a shameful thing? Didn't I know right from wrong? How could I have let Dougie—of all people—witness my wicked behavior, my disgrace? Didn't I care what other people thought about me, what they said about me?

When she paused to draw breath, I jumped in. "What did he say?

An erupting volcano would have looked less livid than my mother's face as she glared at me over her shoulder. "Oh, aren't you bold as brass?! He said you had your dress pulled up and your panties pulled down. And God knows, probably half the house heard him!"

My father quickly shook his head. "Nobody else heard him—you're—"

"What do you know about it? You were off in the front room with your beer!"

"He's a liar!" I shouted, the magma of my own volcanic core gushing out. It wasn't Dougie's treachery that incensed me; I was accustomed to it, expected it—though this false accusation sank to a new low even for him. No, what really drove the blistering hot anger up from inside me was my mother's automatic acceptance of his version of events as the truth. How could she? What was *she* thinking? How could she assume I was guilty without so much as an interrogation, her accusatory third-degree notwithstanding? Why was she always so ready to believe the worst of me?

I drew my legs up to my chest and was ready to kick out against the back of her seat with the full force of my fury when I caught sight of my father's eyes reflected in the rear-view mirror. The look they held and their quick shift from side to side arrested my feet in mid-launch. That look, even as it warned me to cease and desist, also said *I believe you.* Those smoldering eyes fumed and cursed in silence and let me know that I would just have to be content with that. It dawned on me, as I turned away to curl up to stare out the window for the short ride back to our house, that I perhaps could be.

I slipped the construction paper cards into my purse and set the store-bought ones into the "possibly precious" box. This was one time when I didn't want to weigh the value of someone else's artifacts.

Back at my father's house, after we called it quits for the day with the kitchen and bedroom empty of all but furniture and appliances, after a quick trip to the Jewel for fifteen minutes of power shopping, after turkey sandwiches on wheat bread and a hot shower to wash off the powdery film of disuse and decay that had settled over me like a shroud, I sat cross-legged on my bed and opened my box.

My intent was to add the home-made cards. However, as soon as my fingers brushed the other relics, they were compelled as if by reflex to examine and caress them. They lifted the red velvet jewelry box and pried open its clamshell lid. The ring inside gleamed like a new-made promise.

It fit perfectly now, as if it had been forged for my ring finger, as if the maker had known the exact measure of bone, tendon and skin that the gold band would encircle. Back when it had come into my possession, in the summer of '72, it had been too big, sliding dangerously back and forth over my knuckle. The fear of losing it drove me to secure it on a gold chain around my neck.

That was the summer of weddings ...

CHAPTER 9

"She's got her nerve wearing white."

"—off living in some commune out in Oregon. Coos Bay, I think—"

"I'm surprised she didn't stroll down that aisle barefoot."

"Well, didja notice how loose that dress is?"

"—peasant-looking—"

"Yes, well, I'm sure it's hiding a little pumpkin the peasant picked up in the patch."

Sidling along the back wall of the dimly lit banquet room, I couldn't see the faces of the hen party that roosted at the table near the door, the farthest from the head table, the outlier area where the least welcome guests were seated, but I could vividly imagine the raised eyebrows and pursed lips that punctuated the gossip they were pecking up like kernels of corn, blissfully unaware that a child was listening.

"—lived with some other guy out there—"

"I heard she went with a nigger for awhile."

Shocked into temporary silence, the cackle of women hoisted their coffee cups and highball glasses for a restorative sip. Across the dance floor, empty while the band took its ten minute break, I saw the bride, my cousin Diane, Aunt Frannie's oldest daughter, in animated conversation with Aunt Peach. Diane was a pretty hippie in her gauzy, high-waisted dress (Empire style, Peach later informed me), her long hair flowing, her circlet of flowers only slightly wilted after the long day. As usual, it was Peach who was truly stunning, her hot pink sheath and matching pumps a flamboyant accent to her tanned skin, her summer-bleached hair (or was it from a bottle?) piled high with loose ringlets that looked dangerously, temptingly close to coming un-done. She drew almost as many snide comments as the bride.

"Spends it as fast as he makes it."

"Who does she think she is—Jackie O?"

"Well, Jimmie is no Onassis."

"He *is* better looking than that old fart."

"Something's up in that bedroom—why only one child?"

"Maybe she doesn't want to spoil her figure."

"They're lucky to have *one*…"—a significant pause—"well, you know, he had the mumps when he was a teenager."

"So?"

"Well, sometimes that …" A hen in mint green leaned her beak closer to the other's ear.

"Really? I didn't know that."

A significant nod.

A sweaty hand grabbed hold of mine. "What are you doing back here? Let's go get us some screwdrivers." Linda's face was flushed, a thin film of perspiration grazing her full upper lip.

"Oh come on, the bartender's not going to give kids liquor."

Linda rolled her eyes. "You just have to say that it's for your Mom or Dad. He don't care." Linda tugged at the scooped neck-line of her dress, fanning the fabric back and forth. "It's hot in here. Come on," she whined.

If Jamie were here, he'd know how to get out of this. But Jamie was down in Georgia, visiting his maternal grandparents. Linda tugged my arm and I succumbed. The band, back from their break, launched into a chugging version of "Proud Mary" as we tottered over to the bar in our platform shoes and sizzle mini-skirt dresses with matching panties. We were poised in that mo-ment of pubescent youth where we escaped both condescension and condemnation; a little younger and the adults would have fawned and cooed *"how sweet;"* a little older and we would have been branded sluts for showing so much leg.

"Our moms sent us to get Screwdrivers," Linda said boldly, stepping onto the brass rail that ran along the bottom of the bar.

The bartender, young enough to be pimply, just grinned and nodded as he splashed shots of rum over ice and then filled the glasses with orange juice. He shoved them across the wet surface of the bar. As I reached for mine, he kept hold of the glass for a fraction of a second before letting go, running his middle finger over the back of my hand in a wet, electric arc that jolted me to my navel.

"Make sure you give that to mommy," he said with a wink.

"Okay, so he's an asshole, but I'm glad I don't look eleven," Linda snickered as we teetered away. We found refuge in the far corner of the room, hunched on metal folding chairs that felt deliciously cool on the backs of our thighs. Linda downed half of her drink in one long swallow, glancing around scornfully. "This place is such a dump."

The Jolly Club had seen better days, although it had never been within shouting distance of high-class. It was a neighborhood banquet hall, a stale-smelling box, dreary and smoky, with dark paneled walls relieved only by several opaque glass block windows. Its sticky floors hosted myriad rites of passage of the neighborhood: weddings, showers, christenings, retirements, and funeral luncheons.

"Diane seems like the type of person to have an outdoor wedding," I ventured after taking a tiny sip of my drink and tasting only the tartness of the orange juice on my tongue.

"My mom says this was thrown together at the last minute. She's knocked up, you know."

I took a sidelong glance at Linda, who was focused on the band's singer, as he warbled his way through Brandy, *you're a fine girl, what a good wife you would be.* Her vocabulary was not my vocabulary; her knowledge of the world exceeded mine. She had tapped into some pipeline of information that I, for all my bookish ways, had yet to access. She'd come a long way from that night—was it just two years ago?—when we lay in her bed and I fell asleep listening to her recite the rosary. I was eleven going on twelve. She was eleven going on thirty.

Noticing the puzzlement on my face, she rolled her eyes again, taking another slug of her drink. "Having a baby. Pregnaaaant." She drew out the syllables as if talking to the village idiot. "My sister's wedding is gonna be much fancier than this. She's having her reception at Marina City—downtown—with a four course dinner—and absolutely no Polish sausage! She didn't want to invite any kids, but my mom said she was getting too highfalutin. Plus, since I'm gonna be the junior bridesmaid, it was only fair to invite some other kids to keep me company. So you get to come."

Lucky me.

Cynthia's wedding, celebrated five weeks later in the blast furnace heat of late July, was indeed a far more upscale affair, but it had its own quirks. Breaking with tradition, the ceremony was held in the groom's air-conditioned church in one of the toney suburbs on the North Shore: one of the W's—Wilmette, Winnetka, *no, not Waukegan.* My father wanted to skip the church, but my mother insisted on going, sniping that she wanted to see just how the other half lived.

The endless car ride up from the South Side along the lake, through downtown, past North Side neighborhoods and finally up and down twisting, rolling ravines of money country, as my father called it, made my stomach curdle. Sweat beaded up on my face as unwelcome waves of heat, and then a sickly chill washed over me.

"Pull over! I'm gonna be sick," I blurted out and then I was, just barely managing to swing the door open in time to puke my guts out on some wealthy family's immaculately trimmed, emerald green lawn, where the animal sounds of my retching were happily drowned out by the hissing of automatic sprinklers and the buzz-sawing of cicadas in the mid-afternoon haze.

"Oh, Claire," my mother moaned in a moment of unexpected reserve.

My father handed me the handkerchief that had been peeking discreetly out of the breast pocket of his suit. "I won't be needing that back," he chuckled softly.

In the cool, modern, unadorned interior of the church—"so this is the Protestant idea of a church," my mother sniffed after an usher seated us in a pew on the bride's side of the aisle—I leaned against my father's shoulder, nursing my still mutinous stomach.

"We could go back outside," he whispered.

I shook my head. "It's cooler in here."

My eyes shifted to the groom's side. The pews were filled with men and women who obviously comprised the "other half." Every female over the age of eighteen had a strand of pearls around her neck and a glowing orb at each ear as well. Their hair was teased and lacquered to cotton-candy perfection. The scents of spice and flowers wafted with their every move. *That's the smell of money,* my dad whispered. And I knew, of all the women who had trekked up here from my half of the world to witness this sedate spectacle, only Aunt Peach might have the usher guessing on which side she belonged.

As it was, she didn't attend the ceremony. "Too far to go, and too snooty to boot," she purred later at the reception back in Chicago, in the elegant banquet room of the Marina Towers, overlooking the green-gray river. "They're like corn cobs," I had blurted, my nose pressed to the window as we circled into the parking lot. "Damn expensive corncobs," my father muttered, noticing the parking rate.

Peach grabbed hold of my hand and pulled me off to the side of the receiving line.

"She certainly is a bon-bon of a bride, isn't she, Sugah? I prefer a simpler, cleaner style myself." Her eyes devoured me in one long look. "You, on the other hand, are completely charming in your powder green, fresh and sweet, like an after-dinner mint."

Preserved by the freezer-like temperature of the restaurant, the bride did look like an edible marzipan doll in her spun-sugar confection of a dress, iced with lace and spritzed with pearls. Even her bouquet had the flawless perfection of candy roses, embedded in the stark white satin frosting of her skirt. But it was Aunt Peach who drew the longest stares of the evening, appraising looks of admiration from the men and barely suppressed flickers of consternation from the women. Peach wore black— and to make matters worse, black lace—over beige satin, which gave it the slight air of a peignoir, which brought to mind a boudoir, and all that other French stuff, excusez-moi!—well, it just wasn't anything an upstanding matron would wear to a wedding. Perhaps the most egregious faux pas that she so artfully committed was wearing it in the form of a strapless, gravity-defying dress and then, *quelle horreur!,* having the absolute brazen nerve to doff the little bolero jacket that hid her caramel-colored shoulders and cleavage.

"Sans gene, sans peur et sans reproche!" She laughed as her husband pulled her onto the parquet floor in front of the dais for a slow dance.

"What's that mean?" I asked Jamie, who was back, brown as a walnut, sporting a buzz cut on his head and a mush-mouth twang in his voice. We sat at an abandoned table in the far corner where we could observe the little dramas that inevitably played themselves out in a gathering of families, friends and newly-introduced strangers turned relatives.

"Without something or other," he shrugged, tugging on his shirt collar. "Man, I hate ties."

I gestured down to the white patent sandals that were squeezing my toes into an unnatural arc. "I hate shoes."

"You shoulda come down to Georgia with me. I was barefoot practically the whole time."

"Not if they give those kinds of haircuts down there." I ran my palm over his furry scalp. "You look like a Chia-Pet."

He glowered. "Aahm never lettin' my grandpa take me to the barbershop again. Christ."

"Well, I'm glad you're back, fuzzy head and all. Read any good books down there?"

"Besides the Bible?" We rolled our eyes simultaneously. "Just a whole bunch of Reader's Digests. Grandma had some Harlequin Romances but I'll be damned if I'm going to pick up one of those. 'Scuse my French. Besides I was mostly too busy helpin' my grandpa and my uncles out at the cemetery. They're the care-takers."

"He had you digging graves?"

"Naw, just cuttin' grass, prunin' trees. Stuff like that."

"Wow. Was it weird—being around the graves?"

"Naw, it was cool. After reading the headstones, I kinda liked thinking about all those old bones down under the ground. Some of the graves were really old, from the 1800's. I'd make up stories about the people to pass the time, imagining what they'd looked like, what they'd liked to eat, their favorite TV shows, whether they liked James Bond movies." He grinned. "Whether they liked their martinis shaken, not stirred. Whether they had ever even had a martini!"

We laughed. Our attention drifted to the bride and groom as they posed beside their towering cake, the groom's hand resting with a proprietary air over the bride's as they cut the first slice with a gleaming silver knife. They fed each other circumspectly, using forks, leaving nary a crumb nor smear of frosting on each other's lips.

"Man, it's better when they finger-feed and get all smushy with it. This is too hoity-toity for me," Jamie sneered. "If it was you and me up there, we'd show 'em how it's done."

"No, we wouldn't, because we'd be older and grown-up and probably hoity-toity, too."

"Never."

Our collective gaze wandered the room, from the matrons staunchly planted at their tables, sipping their after-dinner cof-fees, to the younger set on the dance floor twisting to a medley of Beatles tunes respectably covered by the four-piece band, to Peach and Jimmie, who stood on the fringes. His hands rested on her hips, which were swaying ever so slightly, like a boat gently rocking in calm water. His head was bent to her ear, then to her neck, as his lips swept down the curve of her to rest on her shoulder. Hoping Jamie didn't notice that I had spied their flagrant display, I quickly turned away to look for my own parents. My mother was sitting with Grandma Sophie and the aunts. She was following their conversation, but in a superficially solicitous manner. Her eyes were straying to that very display of heat from which mine had just fled. On the opposite end of the room, my father lounged back against the bar, nursing a highball. I expected to find his shifty gaze reconnoitering the lay of the land, but he too was staring fixedly. The shortest distance between two points was the imaginary line from my father's eyes to Peach's face. The curve of the glass at my father's lips might have hid his expression, but his eyes gave it away. I quickly, almost guiltily, glanced back at my mother. From the tightness in the stretch of her lips, I could tell she had seen what I had seen. She rose stiffly from the table and crossed the room, weaving in and out of the clusters of revelers. Her shoulders and back were straight and unyielding under the fabric of her steel-blue dress.

"Jeez, it's embarrassing," Jamie sighed. He grabbed my hand and pulled me down under the table, where our view below the tablecloth was restricted to knees, ankles, varicose veins, pumps, sandals and wingtips. Had he witnessed the little drama or was he merely commenting on his own parents' behavior?

"They love each other," I murmured, unsure of what to say.

"Yeah, maybe, but they fight a lot, too." He picked at the underside of the table with his thumbnail.

"My parents used to fight a lot. Now they barely even talk. I wouldn't complain if they acted like that sometimes." I gestured in the general direction of my aunt and uncle.

Jamie wrinkled his nose. "They're too old to be acting like that—in public, anyway. Christ, my dad's 43 and Mama's 37. How old is Uncle Joe?"

"My dad's 47."

"Almost 50!" Jamie's eyes widened.

"Dad told Marjorie not to make him a grandpa until he turns 50, but her baby's due in February, a couple of years early."

"You're going to be an auntie?"

"I told her I would baby-sit when she comes to visit, but I'm not changing any diapers."

Suddenly the lower half of a pink chiffon dress blocked our view. Two white patent shoes poked out from under the hem.

Then the apron of the tablecloth lifted and Linda's round face appeared. Her cheeks were almost as pink as her dress.

Her eyebrows arched. "What're you two doing under there? Playin' spin the bottle?"

"Hiding from your jerk brother," Jamie quipped.

Linda sighed. "Yeah, I know he's a jerk, but at least you don't have to live in the same house with him." She squatted down beside us. "Wanna get some screwdrivers?"

I shook my head.

"Oh, come on. I don't want to go up there by myself. You did it last time."

Jamie looked from my face to Linda's, trying to decipher the gist of the conversation and what important piece of information he was missing. He focused on me, my cheeks growing hotter every second his brown eyes lasered in on mine. *Why did I feel shame spreading over me like a layer of tar, hot, sticky, oozing, foul?*

"What's the deal?" Jamie asked.

"We scammed the bartender for drinks at Diane's wedding," Linda blurted proudly.

Jamie frowned. "You can't get away with that here. You'll get busted for sure."

"Oh, you're no fun. Come on, Claire." She pulled at my arm.

Jamie's eyes were as serious and sharp as reprimands. He moved his head quickly, furtively, from side to side.

"Chicken!" Linda spun on her chunky heel and flounced off, her skirt swishing like foamy pink waves in her wake.

"Horseshit. You're the bravest girl I know—but that's just stupid. I mean, ignorance runs in that family, but what's your excuse?" Jamie said as we watched Linda's feet cross the room until we lost her in a sea of skirts, legs and trousers.

"Good grief, I only did it once," I snapped, pretending to be affronted, rather than shamed by his disapproving tone. "Since when are you my keeper?"

That ought to put him in his place. I didn't expect him to answer, but he did, his voice barely more than a breath that hung in the still, small space between us.

"Since your brother died."

In that moment I wanted to be furious, to rage against his audacity, his presumption. *How dare he? How dare he?* And yet, when I pivoted to face him, my hands clenched in tight balls of wrath, bone and hot flesh, a stream of invective rising in my gorge, ready to inflict damage with fists and tongue, my brother was staring back at me, his eyes a sad shade of toffee, his skin a smooth caramel, his lips bubblegum pink, a luscious candy angel who lingered for a moment and then melted before my eyes, leaving Jamie in his place. He fumbled around in his pants pocket, then took one of my fists in his cool, dry hand, turned it over and opened each finger like petals unfurling. In the center of my palm he placed a gold ring, a curious trinket the likes of which I had never seen before. The ring was forged in the design of a heart encircled by a pair of delicate hands with a crown resting above.

Questions replaced the insults in my throat, questions that he heard without my speaking.

"It's called a claddagh. It's for you."

I ran a finger over it, examining the intricate embellishments on the crown. "Where'd you get it?"

"My grandma down in Georgia."

"This must be very precious. Why'd she give it to you?"

"I was keeping her company one evening, when everyone else had gone off to the tavern. She asked me about my friends up here and I told her about some of them..." He glanced shyly at me, then away, his cheeks ruddying a bit under his tan. "I told her about you. She told me about this beau she had when she was a girl—how they were friends, then—then it got a little more serious, and he gave her this ring. His family was from Ireland and it was kind of a ... a whatchamacallit, those things that get handed down?"

"Heirloom?"

"Yeah. He gave it to her before he joined up to go fight in France during the Great War. That's what my grandma calls World War I."

"It was her engagement ring?"

"No, he didn't ask her to marry him. She thinks he might have—if he'd ever come back."

"He didn't come back?"

"He was killed in a battle at some place called St. Mihiel, on September 13, 1918. I was amazed she could remember that. Sometimes she don't even remember where she left her glasses."

I ran my thumb over the plump, smooth golden heart, so strong, so impenetrable compared to the one of muscle and blood that beat in the human body and the one molded of hopes and dreams and wishes, fragile as glass, the one that would shatter from the blow of a knock on a door and a single telegram from a foreign land.

Jamie pointed out the different parts of the ring. "The heart means love, the hands mean friendship and the crown means loyalty. "

"You can't give this to me. I don't think your grandma would want you to give this away."

"Yes! Yes, she does. Well, she said I could do whatever I wanted with it. She never gave it to her own kids because she never told my grandpa about having it. It was her secret. He thinks he was her first beau. She said it was better that way."

"But now she's told you and that means you have to keep the secret, too."

"That's okay. I can keep a secret."

"But I don't know if I can. What if your mom sees it and asks me about it? I don't want to have to lie."

"Oh, my mama knows. She's known for years. She found it snooping around when she was a kid. Weaseled Grandma into telling her the story. Why do you think she took French in school? She said it was the most romantic thing she ever heard about her mother."

"Doesn't your mom want it for herself?"

"She said it's for a man to give to a woman, not for a woman to take on her own."

"Does she know you're giving it to me?"

"She first said I might want to wait til I'm older to give it to someone, but then she changed her mind and said giving it to you would be keeping it in the family. Seein' that her brothers seem determined to remain bachelors, it's mine. Try it on."

I slipped it onto the ring finger of my right hand but it was too large. I tried it on my middle finger as well as my thumb but the fit was still too loose.

"If I wear it, I'll lose it."

"I could get you a necklace and you could wear it like that."

Cradling the ring in my hand, it felt fragile and substantial at once, with both a delicacy and a heft to its gleaming circumference. "I have a chain I could use. But I don't know if—" I started to say that my mother would probably object, but the flicker of light that glanced off the heart at that instant—like a conspirator's wink—stopped my mouth. *He gave it to me; it's mine now; I will keep it.*

Grinning, he tapped a happy little beat on his knees. "This means we're going to be friends forever, you know, mon amie." He made his hand into a fist and rested it on my knee.

"Mi amigo." I balled up my own hand and placed it on top of his.

"La cousine, le cousin." He put his other fist on top of mine.

"Compadres." I stacked my other fist on top.

Something nudged my left hip and I turned my head to see a pair of scuffed black loafers. Our tower of fists tumbled as my gaze traveled up black trousers and an expanse of white shirt. Dougie, at his usual, red-faced, slovenly worst: jacket and tie long since abandoned, the tails of his shirt hanging dispiritedly out of the waistband of his pants, a grease stain blossoming like a miniature brown carnation in the middle of his chest.

"Wow, that tuxedo—it's definitely you." I bit the insides of my lips to keep from laughing. I was still pissed at him, seeking an opportunity for revenge.

"Shut up." He squatted, uninvited, on the floor beside us. "Let's play War, you and me." He pointedly looked at Jamie, while producing a deck of cards from his pants pocket.

"Only two can play," Jamie said.

"Yeah, so? That's the point. She—" he jerked a stubby thumb in my direction, "doesn't like cards."

"Yes I do, it just depends on the game and who's playing." I let a mischievous look fly like an arrow toward Jamie.

"What's that's? Old Maid with your girlfriends."

"There are just some rules I follow. Some my dad taught me and some I made up on my own."

Jamie slung a warning arrow back at me but I wrinkled my nose and blithely continued, enumerating on my fingers.

"Rule #1: don't play with belligerent drunks—you risk a fist fight when they lose money. Rule #2: don't play with happy drunks—they can't keep their minds on the game and will bore you with stories you've heard ten times before, which spoils your own concentration. Rule #3: don't play with maudlin drunks—they cry whether they win or lose. Rule #4: don't play with an old deck of cards when money is on the line—insist on a fresh pack. Rule #5: don't play at all unless you play to win. Rule #6: don't play at funerals—it's disrespectful. Rule #7: don't play at weddings—it's just plain tacky. And, ta-da, the most important rule of all! Rule #8: never, ever, under any circumstances, play with lying cretins who dribble gravy down the fronts of their shirts at fancy-schmancy restaurants." I stopped there with the middle finger of my right hand raised in salute directly in front of Dougie's pug nose.

While the wheels turned slowly in Dougie's head, I shoved Jamie in the ribs and we made our getaway, scrambling out from under the table.

"Try Solitaire, dick head," I quipped as we trotted toward the red exit sign that glowed at the far end of the room, bouncing off dancing couples and around trios and quartets of chatterers like pinballs in some mad flipper game. I looked back to see Dougie coming after us, the light having dawned.

Bad, ba-ad, ba-ad, my heart thumped out the warning against my chest.

"Jeez, jeez!" Jamie was shaking his head and laughing, trepidation and admiration mixed in his voice.

On the other side of the door, we paused to reconnoiter the nearest available hiding places. The hall was a barren waste of plush blue carpeting and flat walls covered in staid, pale blue wallpaper. I ran my fingers over its embossed floral pattern as my eyes scanned up and down. Not a nook or cranny in sight. Our only possible retreat was the ladies' room at the end of the hall. I grabbed Jamie's damp hand and dragged him after me. Halfway to sanctuary, I glanced over my shoulder and saw Dougie burst out of the banquet room.

When Jamie realized my intent, he squeaked, "I can't go in there."

"You have to—just let me check it out first."

The sitting area was vacant; no dowagers reposing on the blue velvet bench or the dainty floral-upholstered arm chair.

"The coast is clear," I hissed, hauling him in. I held a finger to my lips as we heard voices echoing from the interior of the toilet area. I slipped into the first stall and pulled Jamie in after, shutting the door and locking it. I gestured for Jamie to stand on the back of the toilet while I perched on the edge of the seat. He ducked down, his hands on my shoulders to help him balance.

We heard one toilet flush, then almost immediately a second one, then the squeak of stall doors opening, followed by the click of high heels on tile.

"She made her usual grand entrance tonight." The voice, vaguely familiar, trilled sharply over the spray of water from the faucets. "I think if she walked into a room and didn't turn every head in the place, she'd drop dead."

"She's an attractive woman."

My heart had been thrumming from the adventure but now it thudded even faster and I felt my stomach lurch as if a huge hand had just grabbed hold of it and squeezed. That second voice belonged to my mother and I could guess the focus of the conversation.

"Oh, it's such a put-on! I swear she's faking that accent. And dropping her little French words everywhere. Thinks she's Scarlett O'Hara."

"Well, she *is* from Georgia. You and I have never been there so how would we know?" My mother's voice, which in the two years since my brother's death had devolved into a weary monotone, had a curious edge to it, bland yet wary.

The grating whir and rasp of the hand driers rose above the voices for a moment.

"Moonlight and magnolias, my ass," the first voice scoffed over the roar. "You just know she's been the slut of the ball since she first sprouted tits."

I leaned back slightly and glanced directly up at Jamie, who had his eyes shut tight and his face squinched up like he was enduring extreme pain, his cheeks mottled red and white, his front teeth biting down hard on his lower lip, the ugliness of the conversation reflected in his countenance. I wanted to reach up and erase it from his face, take my hand and smooth his cheeks and forehead, draw his lips back into a smile with my finger.

As the driers died, I heard a familiar whine.

"I know they came in here."

"Douglas, Jamie would never go into the ladies' room. Maybe they went off to explore the lobby. Did you try there?" My mother's voice once again dropped into its tired cadence.

"They came in here. The both of them."

"Well, I did hear someone come in, but..." the other voice said.

I gestured to Jamie to stay put, flushed the toilet and opened the stall door, mindful to pull it back to a closed position.

My mother's face peered around the corner from the lounge area. She raised her eyebrows in surprise and her cheeks reddened as she stepped around to the sink area, her arms folded across her chest. In that instant I was struck by the *oldness* of her, the thinness of the skin beneath her eyes, its purplish tinge that made her look perpetually wan, the way her eyelids drooped a little at the corners, the way the flesh sagged just a bit at her jaw line, as if gravity weighed more heavily upon her than me, as if the earth was growing ever more eager to claim her.

I blinked away my thoughts and washed my hands, careful to keep the claddagh ring tight in my closed fist.

"When did you come in here?" The question was easy enough to answer truthfully.

"Just a minute ago." I lowered my voice and confessed. "I wanted to get away from Dougie."

"Was Jamie with you?"

That one was trickier. I pushed the button on the hand drier and it roared to life. "He wanted to get away from him, too." Whether it was the hot air on my hands or the anticipation of having to lie if asked a direct question about Jamie's whereabouts, I felt sweat tickling my skin on its way down my spine.

"Did he go to the lobby?"

I rubbed my fists together. "I don't know. I think he went to the bathroom."

"The men's room?"

I glanced over my shoulder and rolled my eyes. "Well, he *is* a boy."

"Don't get lippy. A simple 'yes' or 'no' would have served." She moved closer to me, leaning in to my ear so that proximity and the drier assured her words would be for my benefit alone. "You stay away from both those boys. They'll just get you into trouble. That's what boys do best." Then she turned on her heel and headed for the door. "We're leaving soon so come get your piece of cake."

A moment later the hand drier died. The room was as silent and cold as a morgue.

"All clear," I said quietly.

I heard Jamie hop down from his perch, his shoes tapping and scuffling on the tile. "Watch the door," he commanded, his gruff voice echoing off the porcelain.

I stood sentry as he made his getaway. Dougie was nowhere in sight, drawn by gluttony back to the banquet room and the promise of an overflowing table of cake and other sweet delectables. We should have been doubled over in laughter about our escapade, gasping for breath and clutching our stomachs, until we cried "uncle" with a wheeze: *"I can't laugh anymore—it hurts!"* But the pain in our guts came not from belly laughs but from a poisonous brew of confusion and shame, anger and embarrassment and something akin to that sick feeling you get when you see something dead on the side of the road and wished you'd have turned away, but, no, you just had to look and sure enough, there were the blood and the guts spilled out on the asphalt.

Instead of heading back to the banquet room, Jamie turned in the opposite direction and trudged toward the lobby, hands jammed into his pants pockets, shoulders slumped under the thin white cotton of his shirt.

"Don't you want any cake?" I ventured, regretting my idiocy the second the words left my mouth.

He shook his head and quickened his pace.

The lobby was not a quiet oasis in which to hide and lick one's wounds. A steady stream of people passed by the lounge chairs into which we sank, a mix of residents and revelers coming and going from street to elevator and elevator to street. Through the revolving doors we could see a kaleidoscope of city lights: the red and white flash of head and tail lights on passing cars, the stark glare of the streetlight as it caught the polished chrome of the door as it spun, the changing glow of stoplights reflected in the glass, red, green and, for mere instants at a time, a warm amber.

Presently Jamie shrugged and sighed, as if to signal he had reached a resolution in some internal conflict he'd been having as we had sat there, held in the velvety blue arms of the chairs.

"Why don't other women like my mother?"

It was half question, half frank assertion. Part of me wanted to let the lie slip out, a silly, soothing falsehood to contradict him: *They do too like her! Just because one old biddy ..."* and so on, slathering it on, layer upon layer, like a thick swath of frosting that hides a crack in the cake. But we were beyond that. Clenching my fist, I felt the hard circle of proof warm against my palm and its tiny crown press into my flesh.

"Jealous." I silently prayed that one word could put the matter to rest.

"Cuz she's pretty?" He sounded flabbergasted, as if the possibility that women might be so shallow had never occurred to him.

"She's not just pretty. She's—" I searched my mental thesaurus for the word to capture the essence of Peach in her fashionable clothes, her impeccable hairdo, her manicured fingers, toes and manners. *Beautiful, glamorous, gorgeous, radiant, ravishing...*

"Sublime."

He stared at me, his mouth hanging open a bit, lips pink and plump, brown eyes squinting through the black fringe of his lashes (*"to die for,"* Marjorie had once commented).

When do we begin to see our mothers as they really are? When do we stop painting the maternal canvas with a softly focused, blurry edged impressionism and use sharper brush-strokes to capture the acute lines, harsh colors and clarity of realism? Or do we ever? Is our perception forever distorted by our emotions, the feelings of love and hate, of aversion and desire that swell and ebb within, phases of human sensibility as cyclical as the moon or tide? Was I surprised that Jamie viewed his mother with such a calm, rational eye while the rest of our little universe seemed to ogle her through a feverish, hallucinatory fog of susceptibilities: infatuated, besotted, fixated, obsessed.

Only my father had seemed to share Jamie's nonchalance in the face of Peach's astral presence, neither drawn in by her hyper feminine gravitational pull nor repelled by it, as the women were, as the like poles of magnets push away from each other. And yet even his eyes had strayed into her orbit this evening.

Sitting there, staring at Jamie, my father's words echoing in my head (*"there are two kinds of women ... your mother is one kind and Aunt Peach is the other"*), I began to wonder what it would be like to travel in that orbit morning, noon and night, to bask in the warmth of that glowing sun, to be a satellite of that celestial face ... to be Peach's daughter.

At that moment of betrayal, I didn't picture her face, nor her slim form and chic apparel, the white capris that hugged her calves like lovers, the bolero jacket that caressed her shoulders and breasts. I didn't envision her freshly painted toe nails gleaming like tiny Chiclets through the straps of her sandals. I saw her hands; the way the long slender fingers tapered to nails filed the perfect length, neither too long, nor too short, extending just beyond the flesh of the surprisingly strong, square fingertips. No ragged hangnails or overgrown cuticles ever marred those fingers; no blue-green veins ever bulged from the back of those hands like subcutaneous snakes; no dry, weatherworn skin ever cracked over those knuckles; no calluses ever yellowed those palms. And yet I imagined those hands could do wondrous things, perform the hard miracles of a mother's work: the laying on of hands in illness, wringing out the cold washcloth before placing it tenderly across a fever-fired brow; the cleansing and dressing of wounds with the delicacy of a surgeon. Those hands could knead bread: fingers, knuckles and palms coaxing the dough out of its sticky intransigence into a state of smooth, pliable amiability, to be twisted into a fulsome braid, to be molded into a broad mound, and, later, to be sliced open by those same hands, gladly yielding up its tender, yeasty heart-flesh.

Those hands could transform human flesh as well, changing a frown to a smile with the merest brush of velvet fingertips across a cheek, drawing out sour humor like poison from a snake bite, spreading sweetness like a salve. Those hands would touch in only the gentlest of ways: never grabbing, never pulling, never pinching, never—not once—slapping. Hands like those would hold a hairbrush delicately and wield it like a caress from a hair's root to its end; would braid with ease, plaiting and weaving with nary a jerk, adjusting bands without a snag, and then softly tuck any loose strands behind the ears. Those hands would cup a chin while words oozed like mellow gold honey from sugar comb lips: *"Aren't you just the prettiest thing? Quelle belle jeune fille!"*

"Comment ça va?"

The immediacy of the nasal French filtered through a Southern lilt startled the imaginary voice into silence and froze those hands in mid-vision, leaving them poised like the gloved hands of a mime, paralyzed white against a black background in my reverie. Before me were the real hands and their very real owner.

"You missed the bouquet and garter toss."

Jamie's shoulders, first one and then the other, rose and fell in a stuttering shrug.

"I thought you were bound and determined to catch it."

This time just his left shoulder hitched while he stared fixedly at some point in the distance.

"It's time for us to go. Daddy's goin' to pull the car around." She stooped between the chairs, so her face was level with ours, her hands resting on the blue velvet arms. The objects of my fixation. I could have touched them.

"Did you two get into a fight with your cousins?" She glanced from Jamie to me, and back again.

That slight movement stirred the air and the scents that rose from her: the faded incense of her perfume, the dry bitterness of cigarette smoke, the sour ferment of alcohol, the savor of roasted meat, the milky vanilla freshness of just-sliced cake, the tang of human heat, and something else, a smell that I would come to recognize much later, the aroma of desire.

She was a banquet for eyes, ears and mouth.

"He's an oaf," Jamie spat.

Peach's head stuttered a little, as if she had started to nod and then caught herself, pursing her lips to rein in the smile that had tried to spread forth. She shook her head.

"I am not raisin' a man who blames his actions on other people." She took Jamie's chin in her hand. "I expect my son to be responsible and have some self-control."

She turned to me, her eyes stern, even as her lips twitched between reproach and revelry. "And you, Miss Claire. What sort of a refined young woman encourages a gentleman to join her in the ladies' room? Really!"

How did she know?

Her eyebrows rose and fell as she rolled her eyes, shook her head and heaved a sigh. She was serious; she was mocking; she was parental; she was conspiratorial. When she pulled us to our feet, I stole a glance at Jamie. He looked as shaky as I felt, like a tightrope walker in a cross-breeze, uncertain of which way the wind was blowing and which way to lean.

She strode to the revolving door, with just the slightest sway in her hips. Jamie tottered after her and I followed him, zombie-like, without a thought. The great chrome-and-glass door spun us onto the sidewalk where we skittered back and forth and whirled around like wooden tops freed from their strings, our arms outstretched, whipping up our own breeze. Jamie threw his head back and reached his hands to the sky, only to growl in scorn at the orange haze that lay over the night like a blanket.

"Damn, I forgot what it's like up here. Between the pollution and the buildings, you can't see nothin'. One good thing about Georgia. You can see a quadzillion stars."

Peach looked up, too, and stretched her hand skyward. "Oh, sugah, you're so right." Her voice had lost the mocking indecision of the lobby.

Then as Uncle Jimmie pulled up in the Impala, I heard my mother's voice behind me.

"Where do you think you're going? I've been looking all over for you. Your father's waiting in the parking garage. Let's go."

Peach pivoted on her heel and smiled faintly. "We were just trying to see the stars, Mary. But I'm afraid we're not havin' much luck."

"Sky's too orange. It's that haze, ruins everything," I whined.

My mother didn't bother to look up. "Maybe so, but that haze is part of what keeps you fed, clothed and housed. You're the poetic one in the family—maybe you'd feel better if you thought of it as the 'glow of industry'."

"It's not poetic at all, it's just dirty," I muttered.

"Take your pick, Princess, food or the stars," my mother snapped back.

Peach gazed at me. Did she wink or was that only the flash from a passing headlight? "What a choice to make, Pie. Food for the stomach or food for the soul?"

Uncle Jimmy honked his impatience and gestured up the street to where a traffic cop lurked, ticket book in hand.

"Bye, see ya soon," squawked Jamie as he clambered into the back seat. Then he leaned back out. "Hey!" he shouted and curled the fingers of his right hand so they formed a circle. I knew what he meant and thrust up my clenched fist with the Claddagh ring safely inside. *Power to the people, the poetic people!* Peach settled herself in the front seat, giving me a little backhand wave, and then they pulled away into the honking, heaving, stinking flow of metal and glass, rubber and chrome.

"Is that from a poem, or did she make it up herself?" I made the mistake of wondering out loud.

My mother jerked my fist down a little harder than necessary and propelled me toward the parking garage.

In the backseat of our car, as we sped back down Lake Shore Drive, with the warm breeze that came through the open windows clashing with the closed-mouth chill that rose from the frozen bodies up front, I cradled the ring in my palm as it winked fire under the highway lights and then pressed it hard against my cheek, where the thrill of it against my skin felt somewhere between a pinch and a kiss.

CHAPTER 10

Two weeks later, in mid-August, when the cicadas' frenzy had reached its height, and every human droned on, too, about dog days this and that, Jamie called. I was splayed out on my bed, held down by the humid morning air, wondering how I would possibly pass another day with my best friends out of town. It occurred to me that I wasn't likely to ever take another vacation again. *They won't make the effort just for me.* So in my dash downstairs to reach the phone first, all manner of possibilities raced through my mind: maybe someone came home early, or maybe it was one of the cadre of "lesser" friends whose company would do in a pinch. So to hear Jamie saying "howdy" on the other end of the line was truly joy in the morning.

However, at the word "beach," heat radiated off me like an aura, while something cold clenched at my stomach, that nasty, icy fist squeezing, releasing, and squeezing again. Oh, anywhere but there, I wanted to say—the zoo, the Field Museum, Kiddie Land, for God's sake.

When friends asked, I always found a ready excuse on my lips *… busy … going to my grandma's … my mom said no.* After awhile, they stopped asking.

I hadn't been to the beach since…

Yet the soles of my feet did yearn for the rough heat of sand. My arms yearned to lie down, spread wide and rise up again with tiny grains of it, mottled tan and white, clinging to the hairs, dusting the skin like cinnamon sugar. My fingers ached to sift, my toes to burrow... but my head and my heart beat a steady tattoo to drown out any other plea—*it's not safe, it's not right, it's not safe, it's not right.* Because there was no predicting what would happen if I ever set foot on a beach... much less in the water again. Would I curl up and blow away down the sand like an empty candy wrapper? Or start sobbing into a hole I'd dug, where my salt tears would commingle with the fresh water seeping in? Or get the dry heaves in the middle of a bite of ice cream bar? Or walk into the water and just keep walking?

It was like a wound that you think is pretty much healed, the scab plum-black, dry and itchy, like it's ready to fall off. But instead of waiting for it to fall off on its own, you get anxious and overconfident, or someone dares you, and you pick at it with a fingernail and off it comes. Then you discover that underneath, the skin is not healed at all and it starts to bleed anew, just as red and raw as the first time the flesh was pierced.

So when Jamie asked, I was about to say no, when I heard the word "okay" come out of my mouth.

Okay, it'll be okay with him.

"Cool! Put your mom on. Mama wants to talk to her."

"She's out grocery shopping."

"Uncle Joe home?"

I handed the phone over and headed upstairs to change, pausing to eavesdrop. The conversation was conventionally parental, with no hint of whatever feeling might have sparked his intense observation of Peach at the wedding.

He did utter a sharp "where?" followed by "you think that's a good idea?" and a few "uhm-hmms." I started up the stairs again, then jerked to a halt when I suddenly realized with another icy squeeze to the gut that I didn't have a swimsuit that fit. I tripped back down the stairs, waving my arms to stop my father from hanging up.

"Daddy, I can't go. I don't have a bathing suit." *Was that a cool hand of relief that brushed my forehead … or a clammy swipe of disappointment? As my stomach unclenched and my heart seemed to exhale, didn't my skin sag and my arms feel as useless as the dead trunks of trees?*

"Claire says she's doesn't have a thing to wear." He chuckled at something. "No, I really think she's outgrown it. Hey, I don't get involved in that fashion business… Okay, I'll tell her that. …When'll you be back?… No, I'm on afternoons… Okay. You enjoy yourselves."

He hung up and stood there in the tiny square entry space, staring out the screen door, rubbing his forehead with one hand, his other creeping into his pants pocket, his fingers seeking spare change to sift. "She'll stop someplace so you can get a suit. Something 'bout end-of-season sales. Half price." Pulling his wallet out of his back pocket, he handed me a twenty. "Keep the change. Buy yourself some ice cream at the beach."

The moment Peach pulled up, he shooed me out the door. "Don't keep 'em waiting." He waved her to stay in the car. "Have fun," he barked. Something kept his lips taut as he kissed me goodbye and his fingers cascaded his coins.

Peach tried mightily to convince me to go with a wild, neon print two-piece, as we trolled through the racks of leftover suits under the shiny sign that practically shouted, "75% OFF!" However, standing in the middle of a bustling Zayre, in all of its fluorescent harshness, with Jamie looking on and rolling his eyes, I grabbed the first tank in my size, a conservative, navy blue number with a little gold anchor embroidered on the bodice, something my mother would approve. Then we were back in the car. But instead of heading north up Ewing toward Cal Park, Peach steered onto the ramp leading up to the Skyway, heading east into Indiana.

I leaned forward, resting my chin on the front seat. "Where we going now?"

"Où est la plage?" Peach sang out.

Jamie translated. "That means 'where's the beach?'"

"What beach are we going to? Cal Park's the other way."

Her eyes in the rear view mirror were inscrutable. "Jamie, didn't you tell Claire we're going to the Dunes?"

This time the fist didn't just clench my stomach; it punched, hard. I turned to Jamie, my face itself tight as a fist. He was staring back at me, appraisingly, with eyes like open windows. *Yes, open for now... but when he sees me, really sees me, sees the fear, the weakness, they will fall shut in an instant.* Even with his ring hanging on a chain around my neck, I dared not believe that his friendship, his acceptance, was unconditional. *Only the dead are loved unconditionally... they can no longer disappoint.* It would gnaw— the pain, oh, how it would gnaw—if he saw the truth about me and turned away.

Well, then, he just wouldn't see it... because I wouldn't show it.

"I've never been," I said airily, looking back at him steadily, while the veins pulsed in my neck and temple. *He has to know, he has to, he was at the funeral, he knows how Joey died... and where... and even if they sugarcoated the truth to his face, adults always forget children are around, especially the good, quiet ones who play off in a corner, the ones who don't pester to join the adult conversation, but are content to merely listen... and absorb. It's a test—so I'll damn well pass it.*

"That makes three of us, Pie," trilled Peach. "We're heading off into the new frontier."

She twisted the volume dial on the radio as Aretha Franklin's voice cried out over the air waves, sounding exhausted and energized by turns, and the three of us joined her at the end and rode that bass line into glory: *"Rock steady!"*

The Skyway loomed high over the southeast side of Chicago. Not far past the Indiana border, it swooped back down to earth, where it threaded through the industrial landscape, skirting company-town neighborhoods in Hammond and East Chicago. Peach had a lead foot, so we zoomed past streets where two- and three-flats shabbily clad in ancient asphalt siding seemed to pitch forward or lean back five degrees past plumb, as if decade after decade of buffeting winds out of the northwest had taken their toll. We sped through Gary, pinching our noses against the rotten egg and burning metal stench of the mills, but it got up inside us anyway, leaving its nasty taint on our tongues, as if we'd been sucking on a mouthful of nails. When we finally exited onto a quiet two lane road, the air was suddenly fresh, even bracing, with a hint of pine from the groves that grew alongside the South Shore Line railroad tracks.

"Are we there yet?" Jamie asked the inevitable.

"Should be, almost. If your daddy's directions are accurate."

The sign for the turnoff loomed and the fist gripped my stomach again and sweat passed over my face like a clammy veil. I sat forward and turned my face and body to the window, to hide my rising anxiety from Jamie. It hit me suddenly, another blow to the solar plexus. I was seeing what my brother saw that day, the last things he saw, the stands of oak, hickory and ash that lined the entry road, the white pines and cottonwoods that replaced them as we neared the dunes, the camels' humps of sand that heaved up one hundred feet, two hundred feet above the parking lot.

A massive red brick pavilion hunkered down on the edge of the beach, looking almost too solid and set in its ways against the mercurial, ever-changing background of sand and waves. My brother would have set foot there as I did, if not to change into his suit, then to buy a hot dog and a cold, syrupy soft drink, or his favorite Nutty Buddy cone. Did the melting vanilla ice cream run out of the tip of the sugar cone in a sticky stream down his arm? Did his feet touch any of the grains of sand that mine now trod, or had those particles long since migrated on the near constant breeze, perhaps halfway up the bowl-shaped curve of Devil's Slide, or maybe to the very top of the biggest dune, Mt. Tom? Where had he and his buddies planted themselves? Far down the beach, away from the throngs of middle-aged mamas and their ankle-biters, or closer in, for quicker access to the concession stand and the cute girls who fawned around the lifeguard towers, tugging self-consciously at their bikini bottoms, wanting to reveal, but not too much? Did they lay out their towels carefully, as we did, Peach supervising the enterprise like she was planning a garden plot *("Sandals there, on all the corners, let's put the cooler over here"),* or did they just whip them from around their necks and toss them down any which way in a headlong charge for the water? Did he squint across the lake to try to view the Chicago skyline through the haze? Did he run to the foot of the nearest dune where the slope rose in a gentle curve and throw himself down, letting the gritty warmth cup his body like a giant, calloused, loving hand? Did he climb the dune and feel the burn in his thighs and calves, little tongues of fire licking at his muscles, as he fought for purchase in the inconstant surface and against the ever-present pull of gravity? Did he yelp as the sun-stoked furnace of sand scorched the bottoms of his feet? Did he stagger to the summit or bound up, as Jamie and I did, grim-jawed, determined to shed the shackles of the earth?

We waved to Peach, who reclined on her blanket far below, a tiny blue doll on a yellow postage stamp, in big, sweeping, double-armed, wind-milling waves, then fell back, laughing, into a patch of sand shaded by cottonwood and cedar. It felt wondrously cool and smooth against my skin, like a clean sheet on a freshly-made bed. We lay there a minute or two, our bellies ballooning and deflating, until we caught our breath and the flaming tongues of exertion ceased to singe our limbs.

"Now let's run back down straight into the water." Jamie sat up, his back encrusted, shedding sand like a dog sheds water.

Suddenly the shaded sand felt chilling, rather than refreshing. Here it was again, that challenge. *Do not ask that of me.* I could dig, I could sift, I could run, I could climb, I could endure the ever-present growl of the waves ravishing the shore and then retreating, ravishing and retreating. To be at this place now was to be there then, to see through my brother's eyes. And that brought answers to the questions that had been crawling around my head like centipedes—and perhaps even a kind of peace—but... *do not ask that of me.*

Out of the corner of my eye I spied the trail. Here at the top of the dune, the forest began to take hold: first, scrubby cottonwoods grew ensnarled with milkweed and willow shrub, then, where the sand and soil mingled, pines and junipers jutted out, and further back, where the earth was richer, oaks and maples rose in dense stands. And through it all wound a path.

"Come on." I hopped to my feet, grabbing Jamie's hand. "Let's explore."

We scurried across the super-heated sand along the ridge and followed the narrow strip of white sand into the copse. We left the heat behind as we entered a world of dappled light, green and ochre, which pooled here and there on the ground, liquid puddles of light that we sprang into and out of, like rainwater. Soon the sand path became a pepper and salt mix of sand and dirt, winding around the spindly trunks of stunted trees and under branches that twisted at bizarre angles, deformed and adaptive at once. Long, dried pine needles swathed the forest floor like brown velvet under our feet.

"How far do you think it goes?" Jamie asked, still clutching my hand.

"I dunno. Let's follow it."An idea struck me. "We're Hansel and Gretel and we've been left in the woods by our rotten parents."

Jamie squinted, thinking. "We don't have any crumbs or rocks to mark the trail—so skip ahead. We just escaped from the witch's house and we have to find our way back home."

"Okay. And it's getting dark and we have to gather pine cones for a fire," I added, stooping to pick up two ancient cones, their seeds long since dispersed to the winds.

"And sticks, too."

On we pressed, stumbling over exposed roots, stubbing our toes on hidden ones, until we came to a clearing where the path forked left and right. The path to the right wound deeper down into the forest, where the sand surrendered to the soil and the trees grew thicker, straighter, taller and the sunlight no longer poured liquid yellow through the leaves, but trickled down in tones of murky green and gray. A still path, close and slightly wicked. To the left, patches of blue and white stood out against the quilt of green leaves and the trail sloped gently upward.

"Which way?" I breathed, cradling the cones to my chest.

"Shhh!" Jamie was listening hard, his face scrunched in concentration as he cocked his head first to the right and then the left.

I held my breath and listened, too. From the right came nothing but the hiss of the breeze scraping through branches, scratching lazily against the trunks of trees, slipping between the pine needles. From the left came the unmistakable thrum and grind of wind, water, sand and rock—the lake!

"Mama might worry if we're gone too long."

We bore to the left. The path soon became steeper and sand began to overcome soil again. The sturdy trees gave way once more to thickets of scrub bush. Struggling up the slope with my arms full of pine cones and my head down, I bumped smack into Jamie, who had come to a stop just below the crest of the dune.

"Hey," I whined, grappling to hold onto both my treasure and my footing.

"Shhh! Get down!" He dropped to the sand, flat on his belly.

I squatted awkwardly as he wriggled to the top, a snake in blue swim trunks. I waddled after him.

"Why are we doing this?"

"Shhh—listen."

"I know, I know, the lake. I hear it."

"No. Liiiisssssten," he repeated, drawing out the word mysteriously.

Nothing. Just the aspiration and exhalation of the lake, *whoosh, haaaaa, whoosh, haaaaa.* I squinted and cocked my head. Still nothing but water. Wait... yes, there was another sound that rose up, just for a moment, a strange murmur, a pilgrim giggle, an arcing moan, a discordant mix of what sounded like longing and fulfillment, pain and pleasure.

Jamie squirmed to the summit and I scuttled behind, abandoning the pine cones so I could lie flat and peer over the ridge. We stared into a huge bowl of sand, bereft of vegetation, a Saharan gully transported to Northern Indiana. We gasped at our discovery.

"Jeeez!"

"Far out!"

But Jamie wasn't focused on the eerie beauty of the desolate landscape in front of us. I followed his gaze to a knot of wispy jack pines that overhung the ridge as it curved away on our right.

From under the tangle of thin branches and gray-green needles stretched a pair of bronze legs. No, three legs. No, four. Two a deep tan, the others paler underneath dark hair. They moved like snakes in a nest, twining, untwining, feet digging for purchase in the sand, undulating, straining, rising and falling in time with the weird harmonic moan, freezing with a sharp catch of breath and a rippling squeal, melting into rhythm again with a burbling grunt and the hushed coo of a mourning dove.

We lay there, our bodies pressed into the sand, motionless, soundless, two pieces of driftwood. Only our eyes were alive.

Eventually—was it seconds, minutes?—the legs ceased writhing and came to rest, straight and still on the sand under the branches. They became untangled and recognizable as two separate pairs, the tanned legs shorter and finer of bone than the pale ones, which had thick ankles and solid calves and that dark fur which oddly seemed to end at the ankles, leaving the feet the palest of all.

Jamie slowly eased himself back down below the crest of the dune, his chin leaving a narrow trail in the sand. But I couldn't move; my limbs felt numb, paralyzed by a strange brew of fascination and revulsion mingling in my blood.

"Whoa, Dougie told me, but I didn't really believe him. He's such a jive turkey—but, man, he was right."

I forced myself to look away from the legs, back down the slope. All I could see was the top of Jamie's head where the buzz stubble was growing out.

"What'd he tell you?" I whispered.

" 'Bout that. Makin' out."

What could he possibly know that I didn't? And yet, I was clueless, clueless, but for the whispery fragments that my friends and I pieced together in our bedrooms or up against the fence in the corner of the playground at recess. We laid those fragments down like stepping stones forming a path—to where? A look, a touch, the holding of hands, a kiss, an embrace. We presumed the destination was marriage… and babies inevitably followed, but there were gaps in our imagined path, stones missing. We had endured the squirm-inducing topics of anatomy and menstruation in Health with Mrs. Callaghan, while the boys went off with Mr. Reich, the gym teacher, for their own enlightenment in the mysteries of the human body. But the drone of the teacher's voice, the way she strung the words together in one, long, breathless slur, made it clear that she was anxious to cover only the required ground, quickly, efficiently, with no side trips along a scenic byway. Her territory was maintenance, not usage, and the no-nonsense biological aspect of procreation. But that only created more gaps. We instinctively sensed that our mothers could supply the missing pieces, but nothing could induce us ask them. Who wanted to suffer the indignities of a lecture—or the third degree? Or endure the aftermath of their growing realization that we, their baby girls, suddenly knew more than they ever wanted us to know?

But with Jamie, it would just be a conversation.

"So, what did he say?"

He tilted his head and arched his back to look at me upside down. His face was flushed, but whether it was from his awkward position or embarrassment, I couldn't tell. He flipped over onto his stomach and sifted some sand through his fingers.

"My grandpa says some things a gentleman doesn't talk about in mixed company."

"What!?" Jamie—holding out on me?

"Uh-oh, now you've done it. They probably heard that. Time to shag ass!"

He scrambled up, grabbing my hand along the way. "Follow me!" He let out a Tarzan yell to curdle the blood, took a flying leap up to the crest of the dune and lunged down the other side, arms pin wheeling, legs churning, spraying sand, singing the chorus of *"American Pie"* at the top of his lungs. I followed in full flight, but out of the corner of my eye, I just had time to see the tanned pair of legs scrabbling to withdraw into the safety of the thicket, like turtle legs retreating into their shell, and a shocked masculine face peering out from a tousle of shaggy black hair behind the snarl of pine branches, fleshy lips shouting *"fuckin' perverts!"* And then I was wind-milling, too, legs pistoning, out of control, headlong, gasping with that any-minute-now-I-am-gonna-tumble-head-over-heels-and-split-myself-open sensation, feeling gravity's pull consuming me, watching Jamie slowing ever so slightly as he reached the bottom of the dune, where his feet and ankles sank out of sight in the deep sand.

He was still whooping and singing as he tore off again. I straggled after him, struggling to keep the sand from swallowing my feet, my lungs and throat raw from the wailing and running and singing and laughing. This part of the beach was deserted but for an elderly couple taking a stroll. I thought they would scowl as we sped past them in our raucous glory, but when I glanced back I saw the old man smile and take the woman's hand.

We zigzagged from the pliant dry sand to the unyielding wet strip at the water's edge and back again, leaping bone-gray driftwood, skirting the occasional dead fish, scattering the herring gulls who scoured the shore for juicy tidbits thrown up by the lake or discarded by picnickers. When we finally fell onto our beach towels, panting and rolling like a couple of rambunctious puppies, a fire burned in my chest and mouth that seemed unquenchable, no matter how many gulps of cherry soda I downed or chunks of ice I sucked.

"All hail the returning adventurers," laughed Peach. "Where ever did you go and what did you see there?"

Jamie turned his head on the towel to shoot me a quick look. "Hiked on the trail up at the top of the dune. Wasn't much to see besides trees."

"We gathered some pine cones," I piped.

"And you didn't bring me any back?" Peach pouted, her eyes hidden behind her oversized Jackie O sunglasses.

"She dropped them all. What a klutz!"

"James!"

"He's right, I am. I lost them all when we took off down the hill."

"Man, we were haulin'!"

Jamie launched into a vivid description of the blowout that we had stumbled upon and our wild descent from the heights, leaving out certain details. I lay on my towel, eyes closed against the serrated glare of the sun, pondering the red glow that permeated my eyelids, waiting for the fire in my body to subside, drawing circles in the sand with my finger, half-listening to Jamie's travelogue. The image of the legs kept drifting in and out of focus: the way the tanned foot, elegantly arched, had run up the pale, furred calf, slowly, in a curious caress. Sitting up to take another sip of pop, I glanced over the rim of the can at Peach's delicate foot with its pink-lacquered toenails. Had it ever dragged its way gently along the back of a man's calf, Jimmie's perhaps? Watching as it played in the sand, moving idly back and forth, arching, toes burrowing tentatively, almost tenderly, I think I knew the answer.

My gaze shifted to Jamie's calf, straight and slim, tanned, practically hairless. What would it feel like to run a foot along that smooth surface? I watched in a blend of horror and fascination as my foot, with its stubby, unmanicured toes, nails embedded with sand, sidled over next to Jamie's skin, as if it were an entity separate from me, with a will of its own. I was not, could not be, causing my appendage to do this. No, it was doing it of its own volition, lifting itself, poised just bare inches over the swell of muscle that shifted rhythmically under the skin as Jamie flexed his feet in the sand. Unexpectedly, he raised his left leg to stretch and it grazed the bottom of my wandering foot, just the briefest moment of connection, a millisecond of foreign skin on foreign skin, not the familiar, everyday skin of his hand, but uncharted territory, a new frontier. It sent a ripple of thrill up the nerve of my leg to the base of my spine.

The wind had picked up and with it the waves, white foam fingers crawling up the sand. Over the loudspeaker, a male voice, distorted and nasal, droned.

"Repeat—swimming is only permitted in the area between the manned guard towers and the pavilion. If the waves continue to increase, swimming will be prohibited due to the possibility of rip currents." The speaker's breath rasped through the sound system. "Rip currents are impossible to predict. If you're caught in a rip current, do not panic. The rip current will not pull you under. Try to float on your back or swim parallel to the shore until you are out of the current. Then swim directly towards shore."

Jamie pushed himself up and sat back on his haunches. "I'm burning alive."

Peach pointed at the water. "I have been waitin' all mornin' to tell you all to go jump in the lake."

He jumped up and took four or five leaps before he realized I wasn't right behind him. Stopping just short of the water, he teetered on his toes as the waves rushed in to lick them. He looked over his shoulder. "Come on! Whatcha waitin' for?"

There I sat, hunched up, knees to chest, arms tight across my shins. *Revealed.*

Jamie trotted back and fell to his knees in front of me.

"Come on, we can swim. We're by the lifeguard tower."

Rifling through my mental file cabinet marked "EXCUSES" to find one that he might, just might, accept, I felt the Claddagh ring brush against my knee as it dangled on its chain around my neck. I clutched it like a life preserver.

"I don't want to lose the ring. It might slip off in the water."

"Silly Gretel. Take it off."

I hesitated, but the expectation in his eyes drove me to obedience. But my fingers seemed to have been transformed into awkward sausages, thick, rubbery, useless. I fumbled with the necklace's clasp until I felt a pair of hands close over mine.

"Let me help, Pie," said Peach. "I'll keep it safe. And your glasses, too." Her calm fingers eased the chain from around my neck and she cupped my chin in her hand. "You go on and have yourself a splash."

Still I sat, waiting, waiting for it to happen, for Jamie to give up, for the windows in his eyes to shut, for him to give up as the others had. Instead he reached out and took my hands, prying one, then the other, off my knees. Wordlessly, gently, he pulled me out of my tight little ball to my feet. He smiled and began to walk backwards towards the water, his eyes fixed on mine, that familiar skin of his hands warm and damp against my own.

"Close your eyes," he coaxed, with a wink.

I shook my head.

"Close your eyes," he repeated, this time a command.

I hesitantly obeyed, closing first one and then the other. The soles of my feet felt the fiery, dry grains of sand give way to a cool, moist, hard-packed surface. Then the firm footing began to feel water-logged, squelchy. My heels sank. I paused, sinking further, arms tensed.

"We have to go farther."

"I have to open my eyes."

"It is forbidden to look upon the sacred pool until one has been dunked in it."

"Jamie—"

"You have been invited to join the secret order of Poseidon. You cannot refuse without stirring up a great anger in the water. Come."

He was a lodestone, pulling me with a magnetic promise in the warmth of his hands. *Trust me. I've got you. I won't let you go.*

The first lick of the water's frigid tongue shot me up on my tiptoes, gasping. The second, around my ankles, made me squeal and tense my shoulders yet again.

"Come."

The water lapped at my calves as goose bumps rose on my arms. It swallowed my knees, mouthed my thighs, devoured me to the waist before Jamie would let me stop.

"Keep your eyes closed."

"Jamie—"

"Put your arms over your chest."

"No!"

"Like a mummy." He arranged my limbs for me, Egyptian style, folding my arms across my chest, pressing my hands flat to my sternum, where my fingers could feel the curved edge of bone below the skin.

"Now hold your breath and lean back."

"No!"

"Lean back."

"No!" Rising panic clenched my voice into a squeal.

"Lean back," he ordered in his commanding voice, and then "come on, it'll be okay," in a softer, coaxing tone.

"You're outta your gourd if you think—"

"Shhh, Poseidon and the sacred pool grow impatient."

I felt his hands on the small of my back and at my neck, still warm, still promising.

I won't let you go.

"It's okay," he whispered. "I know what to do. I watched Preacher Effingham baptize the entire Stokes family when I was staying at my grandma's." All the reassurance in his voice, in his hands, rock steady. "I know what to do. I promise."

I shivered, feeling the gooseflesh pebbling the skin up and down my arms.

"I can't."

"It'll be okay. I promise." *Rock steady.*

I leaned into that promise and the water consumed me.

Oh, the weight of it, the surprising liquid heft. Had my brother, too, been astonished by that when he was inside the lake's cold, fluid maw? The way it dragged a body down and buoyed it up at the same time. The way it swallowed up sound except for its own throaty gush and burbling hiss. Or had he been too frantic to notice, too locked in a struggle against its voracious appetite, alone, without solid, flesh-and-bone hands at his back and his neck to heave him back up out of the belly of the beast?

Gasping, dripping, dizzy from the sudden regurgitation back into an off-kilter, blurry world, I flinched at the box of stars that spilled, upended over my head.

"In the name of Poseidon, god of the sea, I name you Aphrodite, born of the water, goddess of beauty and love."

For a moment, the briefest moment, I raised my head and looked down my nose at him, the height of regal arrogance, my mouth set in dread scorn.

"James Joseph Sokol, you are so full of it." Then I pushed him hard, driving my hands into his chest with all my strength, yelling as he went tumbling backwards into the water.

"Mighty Aphrodite!"

And I leaped in after him.

At the end of the day, after the salami sandwiches and the ice cream bars were consumed, after the sand fort had risen and fallen into decay, after the skin on our backs started tingling, after the sand worked its way into every crevice of our bodies, we packed up and drove back to Chicago. Jamie and I sprawled in the backseat, achy, trying to find comfortable positions, shedding sand with every twist and turn. Aunt Peach switched to the classical music station for the ride home and turned down the volume so we were cradled by cello, lulled by harp. When the Impala glided to the curb in front of my house, the lawn was gray-green in the twilight and the lights were on.

"September's coming. We've already lost the best of the sunlight," she murmured, half to herself. She let the car idle for a moment, before reaching to turn the key.

"You don't have to come in." I quickly gathered up my towel.

She turned and regarded me. Her eyes were ringed with pale skin with the softest of wrinkles just beginning to creep out of the corners. "Are you sure, sugah?"

I nodded, glancing over at Jamie, asleep in the corner, his head resting on the door frame, his hands tucked between his thighs. "Thanks for taking me."

"Well, Pie, thank you for comin' with."

I was halfway up the front steps when I heard her calling softly and her sandals clip-clopping on the concrete. She held out something to me. It was the Claddagh ring on its chain.

"You forgot this." She spun me around and clasped it hastily back on my neck. Then she wrapped me in a lingering hug, enveloping, ravenous. "All right then," she whispered in my ear as she finally released me, "off you go." She clattered back to the car, but sat there, watching until my mother answered my knock on the locked screen door.

"It's about time. You should have been back hours ago."

"We were having so much fun Aunt Peach said she couldn't bear to tear us away."

"Go have your bath. You look like you brought most of the sand home with you."

That was it. She did not ask what we did, what we saw, did not request every last detail of our adventure, nor even a single one, just looked at me as if I was a cat that had dragged something unspeakable into the house, some vermin tidbit, a bloody mouse, a ragged bird.

I paused at the bottom of the stairs. "Are you mad that I went to the Dunes? It was okay, you know. I was okay. I am okay. I came back."

"Go have your bath," she croaked again, and turned away to shut the door.

Later, much later, somewhere in the very deep part of the night, they woke me with their fighting. It wasn't even that loud, just an unsettling vibration that rippled up through the floor-boards and the mattress, spreading discomfort.

My back felt tight and raw where the sun had scorched it. I swung my legs over the edge of the bed and eased my toes down, down, down until they touched the cool surface of the linoleum tiles. The door at the staircase was ajar so I squeezed through the narrow opening, groping my way down to my listening place, longing to press my flaming back against the cold, hard wood of the steps.

"No!" My mother's voice was shrill, dissonant as a warning siren.

There came no intelligible reply, just a heavy, grunting sigh and the whispery rustle of cloth sliding against cloth, the sound of insinuation.

"I said no. You're drunk!" A challenge in the tone. And disgust. And something else. "Stop!"

A long, jagged sound: the ripping of fabric, an intake of breath.

"Sonovabitch. Stop!"

I inched my head forward until I could see around the edge of the wall. It was hard to make out anything. Some light spilled in from the kitchen in a rectangular pool on the carpet and the glare from the streetlight sliced through the Venetian blinds, carving bands of light and dark on the wall, like the bars of a prison cell.

"Bastard!"

Movement, shuffling and then two figures appeared in those bars of darkness and light, figures grappling in what seemed at first to be a hug. But my mother was trying to push my father away, her hands shoving into his chest, only to slide futilely up past his shoulders, as he pressed her to the wall. Her face was cut in half by the shadow of the blinds, half black, half white, the glare catching her grimace.

"Let it go, Mary. Why can't you let it go?" My father's voice was soggy, saturated with liquor and entreaties.

"How dare you let her take her there? Without asking me!" Her fisted hands pulled his hair, first away from his scalp, away from her, but then—did they also press his head closer?

"You weren't around. God, just let it all go."

Then they were gone, out of the bands of light and dark. The sofa creaked.

"Bastard." Pain in the voice, and fury and, again, something else.

Pressing my damp palms to my ears, I crept back up the stairs to my room. Wrapped in a faded pink comforter, a relic from my infancy, chewing on its frayed eyelet edging, I rocked in the old rocking chair in the corner, clinging to the stuffed dog, Cuddley Dudley, another relic, whose matted fur, incongruously blue as a turquoise sea, had already absorbed an ocean of tears. Wide awake, my skin stinging as I leaned back into the posts, I waited for the storm to pass.

So press the skin against the chair, burn it again, break the blisters, bite the inside of the cheek raw, stab the jagged fingernails into the palms, you're so good at pain to drown out pain. Something's happening, it's happening, it's going on, like the legs at the beach, but there's no harmony here, only dissonance, no foot moving tenderly down the length of a calf, just the jarring clash of bone against bone ...

When the thunder had faded to a dull rumble, the sporadic snores of male sleep, I unfolded myself from the rocker, letting the comforter fall away. On practiced feet I made my way back to my post. From the darkness of my parents' bedroom, came sniffles and guttural murmurs, the hushed lament of a woman in

173

mourning. My father slouched in his easy chair, eyes closed, face heavy, flesh drooping, skin lit a ghastly blue by the glowing eye of the television set which reflected only white noise and black snow. The smoldering orange tip of a cigarette winked at me in the dark.

Inching down to the bottom of the stairs, I cursed the soles of my feet for sticking as I tried to lift and place them without a creak. The trek across the living rug—one foot forward, down, then wait, the other foot forward, down, then breathe—seemed endless. Standing at the side of his chair, my fingers tingled as I reached out and took the cigarette, with its lengthening ash, between my thumb and index finger and eased it from between his. I stubbed out the butt in the square glass ashtray balanced on the arm of the chair. As I turned to go, I felt his hand, hard, sandpaper rough, close over my wrist.

"Claire."

"You said you quit."

"Thought I did." He grabbed the pack of Camels off the end table and thrust it at me. "Go on, take 'em. Break 'em in two, throw 'em away. I want to be good. So help me."

As I leaned forward to take the pack, the Claddagh ring on its chain fell out from under my pajama top and swung back and forth in front of his face, glimmering in the TV glow. He reached up and caught it.

"What's this?" He rolled the ring between his thumb and forefinger.

"A ring."

"No shit. Where'd you get it?"

No use trying to lie; those eyes could always pierce a veil of deception. "Jamie."

"I'll be damned. Looks pretty darn expensive to have come out of a Cracker Jack box."

"It's not a…" I stopped short. *Spin on a dime, like he can.* "Candy-coated popcorn, peanuts and a prize, that's what you get in Cracker Jack."

"Didja have fun today?"

"Yeah, but my back's all burned. It hurts."

174

"Umm-hmm. Flyin' too close to the sun again. Well…" He leaned his head back and closed his eyes. "Time you got back to bed. Do me a favor and turn off the tube on your way."

"Aren't you going to bed, Daddy?"

"Think I'll sit here awhile."

I took a last look at his face. "Don't tell Mom."

" 'Bout?"

"Cracker Jack."

He moved his head from side to side, just once, as if the effort were exhausting. "Secret's safe with me."

I flipped the knob on the television and the picture-less picture with its eerie glow vanished.

" 'Night, Daddy." I padded back up the stairs, squeezing the pack of cigarettes in my fist.

"You should give it back," he whispered from the dark. "You should. He'll regret it. Someday he'll want to give it to his … true love."

I pretended not to hear. I dumped the crumpled cigarettes in the toilet and watched them swirl away into oblivion, picking brown flecks of tobacco off my hands and wondering why, of all the things I'd heard and saw and done that day, it was my father's voice, the jagged edges of those words that seemed to cut at his throat, that made me want to cry.

Now, years later, back in my father's house, when I moved to take the ring off and slip it back into its velvet crypt, it winked at me again so I left it on. I fell asleep with my face upon my hand and woke in the morning to find that the heart and crown had left a ruddy imprint on my cheek, like a brand.

CHAPTER 11

He'd never been one to talk much at the breakfast table, preferring to listen to morning radio while he sipped his black coffee and worked the crossword puzzles in the Tribune. When I was very young, I would climb on his knee and read the comics with him, sipping from my own cup of joe so diluted with milk and thickened with sugar that my father joked it was more lait au café than the other way around. Together, in silence, we read what he called the funnies: *Peanuts, Brenda Starr, Dick Tracy, Nancy, Lil Orphan Annie.* On those days when I just didn't get the joke, he would read a strip out loud, emphasizing the irony or sarcasm with his voice, or explaining a reference that only an adult would be clued in on. He'd let me help him unscramble the letters to the word jumbles, which he confidently wrote in pen, same as the crossword.

"Pencil is for sissies," he said.

But it didn't add up to a lot of verbalization, if you didn't count the news, weather and sports updates and Orien Samuelson's Farm Report, which for a city dweller like me prompted an instantaneous flight-of-fancy to the barnyard world of soil conditions, hog bellies, soy beans and corn futures.

"What's a hog belly?" I once asked.

"Just what it sounds like," he replied.

"An actual hog's belly?"

"The edible part."

I only had to ask him once why a city radio station would bother to broadcast farm news.

"This radio station broadcasts all over the Midwest. And what is most of the Midwest? Farm land. Maybe you better read some maps along with those story books."

So to find myself, thirty years later, sitting across the table from an effusive old man, jabbering on about the heat wave currently broiling the Plains states and exactly when the weatherman predicted it would hit the Chicago area, and how bad the one back in '95 was, but he survived it okay by laying up in a bathtub of cold water, but he'd be happy to run out and buy a room air conditioner if it would make me feel more comfortable during the coming onslaught, because, hell, he knew that once you were used to living in a freezer, it was hard to go back to more primitive conditions, but a major problem living in this neighborhood was there was no Home Depot close by, Christ, you had to drive all the way down to Cal City, and where was the justice in that, don't we all deserve a decent local shopping center, but, no, the corporate assholes won't invest in certain areas of the city, even though these people's money is as green as any, and damn, he wouldn't go to that hardware store over on 106th because it was a rip-off joint. He wanted to buy local, but damn, a man has a right not to get ripped off and overcharged in the process.

He must have noticed that I was staring at him, open-mouthed, because he stopped abruptly and drew breath.

"Somethin' on my face?" He wiped his mouth with his palm.

I shook my head.

"Well, you're looking at me like I sprung another eye or somethin'."

I blinked and looked down at my bowl of now-soggy wheat biscuits. "I just—when did you—I don't remember you ever being such a..." I trailed off, at a loss.

"A liberal? I been a liberal since way back. Voted for Truman, Stevenson. Hell, I voted for Kennedy. I did go through a conservative period when you were young. Vietnam, that whole business. Everyone does that. They say only the young and the old can afford to be liberal. When you're raising kids, paying bills, tryin' to be respectable, you buy some conservative clothes and act the part. I *do* regret voting for Nixon in '72."

I shook myself like a dog shaking off water after that particular deluge. "I was going to say that I don't recall you being such a conversationalist, particularly in the a.m."

He cocked his head and took a sip of coffee. "Yeah, I guess you're right. But I read somewhere that women like to talk. So I guess when I had the chance to talk before, I didn't take it. Now, my cup runneth over... makin' up for lost time."

I pushed away from the table and scraped the dregs of my cereal into the garbage. "It was okay by me back then—that you didn't talk a lot."

He squinted into his coffee cup. "I guess that's good to hear, cuz I know I missed a lot of chances—and it bothers me some-times... a lot of the time."

The clatter of my bowl against the sink sounded jarringly rude. I let the water run over it longer than necessary while I stood, a dithering female Hamlet: *to ask or not to ask... the question, whether to prolong the futile conversation which will lead to... nowhere... or to cut it short here and now... to tread the worn path... to blaze a new one ... to stand absolutely still and wait for time and the moment to pass without comment.*

Can I ever resist a comment?

"There are no second acts in American lives." The quote trailed behind me like a war banner as I headed through the doorway.

"Draw your chair up close to the edge of the precipice and I'll tell you a story." His reply, in a soft, low, almost tender murmur, tripped me like a snare wire. I paused in the hall on feet unable to move forward and unwilling to turn back.

"What was that?" As if I hadn't quite understood.

The table legs squealed against the vinyl as he rose, the soles of his feet whispered as he crossed the room, and the old wood of the door frame sighed as he leaned against it.

"If you're gonna quote Fitzgerald to me, then I'm gonna throw him right back at you."

What did he see in my face, my eyes, when I turned? What emotion played around my mouth? What expression was it forming? Surprise, scorn, a smile, a scowl? Whatever I presented, he parried with a shit-eating grin the width of the Mississippi River and a gotcha twinkle in his eye. He held up a finger and shook it gently under my nose as a chuckle burbled up his throat. He padded into his bedroom and was swallowed up by the dim interior. After a shuffling crackle of papers, he re-emerged with a tattered book in his hands.

"You left this here. I used to read it a lot—still do—at night, when I can't sleep, cuz *'in the real dark night of the soul it is always three o'clock in the morning.'*"

It was Bartlett's Familiar Quotations, my old copy from high school, second-hand and well-thumbed even then, the spine cracked, the gold leaf printing on the cover rubbed halfway to oblivion, the once-crisp texture of the binding now soft, loose and fragile as old skin.

"You dog-eared some pages. I started with those. I liked the quotes from Fitzgerald so much I wound up reading the books. Liked Gatsby so much I actually bought myself a copy. How does that grab ya?"

The heat of confusion spread across my cheeks and I hurriedly opened the book and brought it up to my face, breathing deeply. It still carried the smell of its original owner, her perfume layered with mine and my father's aroma, tinged with the salty, dry scent of old wood and the musk of decay.

"That's one of my favorite novels, maybe *the* favorite. *'So we beat on, boats against the current, borne back ceaselessly into the past,'*" I said, still inhaling.

"Yep, but I think I like the quote about Tom and Daisy even better."

I stared at him over the edge of the book. He gently pressed the book down from my face, wetting his index finger on his tongue to help him turn the pages. He found the entry and used his finger to guide his reading.

"*They were careless people, Tom and Daisy—they smashed up things and creatures and then retreated back into their money or their vast carelessness, or whatever it was that kept them together, and let other people clean up the mess they had made.*'" He tapped the page. "There's something to that..." He brought his hand up to cover his mouth and lapsed into silence. His eyes were no longer focused on the page but on something or somewhere off and out the back kitchen window.

I closed the book and handed it to him.

"You can take it home with you," he said, half with me, half somewhere else.

"I have two others. I bought one at college to replace this one. And I bought an updated edition a few years ago."

"I thought you might want it for your box." He turned his gaze from the window to me. The hanging skin around his eyes looked so delicate, as if it might tear under the weight of one clumsy finger if I should dare to touch it, like the sheerest tissue paper.

How has it come to this? This is not my father.

"I stopped collecting things for it a long time ago."

He nodded, a little dip of his chin, but kept his eyes on mine. My fingers twitched with the lie.

"Well, considering who gave it to you—"

"I never saved anything of hers." My fingers stopped twitching.

He was a fisherman playing his line: letting it out, reeling it in, softly, softly, then with a hard jerk. He must have felt himself losing me, like a long-awaited fish slipping off the hook. He'd had me, so close, he'd had me right there, with the unexpected bait. Fitzgerald of all people and Gatsby of all books. It wasn't a con. I sensed that it was, indeed, real, but it was bait nonetheless, as I struggled with the bitter, metallic taste in my mouth and the razor-bite of the imaginary claw-like hook in my cheek.

Suddenly, with a sag of his shoulders, he cut bait and let loose the line. "Wasn't much to save..."

He turned away and retreated back into the dark of the bedroom, where the sun, even in my childhood, at the height of a summer's day, never seemed to penetrate, closing the door behind him.

It took him awhile to come out, but when he finally did, it was all *hurry up, let's get cuttin'*, and so I forgot to bring the Walkman. At Sophie's, he chose to work in the living room and carried the radio in from the kitchen, so I took the dining room at the back of the house. He asked what I would like to listen to and I said it didn't matter. He surprised me by dialing to WFMT, the classical music station.

"You don't have to listen to that for my benefit," I called.

"I'm not," he called back.

I strode down the hall. "Oh, yes, you are. First, F. Scott Fitzgerald, now Mozart's Rondo Alla Turca. It's like you're trying to woo me. Stop. It should be enough that I am here, helping you."

He was crouched before the curio cabinet that held the china birds, so life-like in plumage and pose they seemed poised to fly out of their cramped glass aviary in a flurry of wings and twitters. He looked up, his face unreadable in the gloom. "I didn't miss this part of you."

"What?"

He didn't answer, but instead reached into the cabinet and pulled out a cardinal, its ceramic feathers bright as fresh blood, a fierce pride in the set of its sculpted head and the gleam of its black eyes.

"What?" I repeated, squinting in the murk. "Oh, for Christ's sake, we need to shed some light in here." I stomped to the picture window and pulled the drapes open, bringing a cascade of dust, but not much additional light. "What did you mean by that remark?"

"The cruel snob in you." He sighed. "I didn't miss that, but it's a part of you, so…" He shrugged and held out the cardinal. "You always admired these. Do you want these for yourself?"

"I didn't particularly like them. She did."

"Who?"

"Mom."

"Hell, I knew some woman did. Besides your grandma."

"And I'm not a snob. I just know a fake when I see one."

181

"Can you? Well, that's good, considering what you do for a living." He placed the bird in a cardboard box. "I myself can't always tell." He gathered two more birds in his hands, a brown-flecked sparrow and a gaudy bright bluebird. "Someone's got to want these."

"You're avoiding a conversation."

He examined the birds for flaws. "Living without a female of the species for so long made me forget how fickle you all can be. This morning you were insinuating that I was talking too much, now you're bitchin' that I'm talking too little. I'm just squattin' here doin' what we came here to do."

I took the bluebird from him, wiping a fuzzy layer of dust from its smooth head and back with my thumb, rubbing a finger over its claws frozen in a clench around a ceramic twig.

"Aunt Peach always liked these, too." I handed the bird back. My words suddenly struck me as absurd. "Strange that they should both like them. Must have been the only thing they had in common, aside from their gender. Maybe she'd like to have them. Why don't you ask her."

He set the birds carefully down in the box.

"Ever talk to her?"

He took more birds from the case and examined them. Then he shook his head. "No, not since your Uncle Jimmie died, almost—" he squinted at a chip in a Baltimore Oriole's tail, "damn, that's over fifteen years ago. After they moved, it was mainly just Christmas cards, then that kinda petered out." He took the last two birds out of their glass cage. "I guess I should wrap these in some newspaper." He dusted off his hands. "I shoulda brought some newspaper." He looked up at me, a bit of the old surliness at the corners of his eyes. "Ain't you supposed to be working the dining room?"

He stuck with the classical station until noon when he switched to newsweathersports. And there it was, floating back to me, that strong, solid baritone patiently explaining soil conditions across the Midwest and what they meant for farmers and consumers in the near future, Orion Samuelson's voice, still on the air in at the turn of the century.

CHAPTER 12

No one ever actually dined in my grandmother's dining room. It was too small to accommodate a banquet table large enough to seat all the members of her extended family: sons, daughters, their wives and husbands, grandchildren. At family gatherings, the walnut trestle table, which usually sat bare, was hidden beneath an ivory tablecloth that Sophie had embroidered with the names of her descendants, adding each new name as its owner came into the world. Each was scripted in a different color or shade of thick embroidery floss, a painter's palette of names stitched haphazardly over the fabric in no apparent pattern. We grandchildren would flock to the table at gatherings to run our fingers over our soft, raised names, tracing the shining cursive over and over, as if reading Braille. My name stood out in royal purple; Jamie's glistened in gold. Dougie's full Christian name was wrought in a shade that Jamie and I secretly labeled puke green. Served him right, we thought; it fit his personality. We never saw him fingering his mark once he passed the age of seven or eight. It was one of those "babyish" habits that he shed early, while we continued the ritual long into our teens.

The top of the table would be submerged under the tidal wave of gastronomic delights that swept in upon these occasions from all the Sokol, McConnell and Wojcik kitchens: the *golabki*, steamed cabbages leaves stuffed with meat and rice swimming in a sea of tomato sauce; the *kiszka* and the *kielbasa* sausages coiled atop platters of boiled potatoes and sauerkraut; the *pierogi* that melted in your mouth, oozing potato and cheese; the baskets of breads: rye, raisin and sweet-as-cake *chalka*; the roll of head cheese studded with bizarre, gelatinous cubes of—what? We never dared to ask. The table was, for its time, an equal opportunity buffet, integrated with foods that were not of Polish origin: crumbly cornbread and creamy-smooth sweet potato casserole from Aunt Peach's kitchen; a pan of some form of pasta, mostaccioli in a bland red sauce or a gluey macaroni and cheese casserole, and a jiggly Jell-O mold from Aunt Dodie who'd married Irish and whose half-breed children detested most ethnic foods, preferring hunks of Velveeta and bologna slapped between two pieces of Wonder bread. Of course, integration only went so far. The time Peach slipped a pot of collard greens onto the table, they sat there untouched except for the spoonful that she had taken for herself and the one Uncle Jimmie glopped onto an edge of his plate and ate out of uxorious loyalty.

We made a circuit around the table, gathering our favorite entrées and sides, and then scattered to every nook and cranny of the house to eat, the men carrying their heaping plates into the living room to their self-appointed places at the card tables, the children sitting cross-legged on an old blanket spread on the living room floor or, in decent weather, out on the front porch on metal lawn chairs or the steps, balancing full plates on our knees. The women took their skimpier helpings into the kitchen and perched around its little square table or leaned against the counter. They were always on diets, filling in the spaces that their meager meals left in their stomachs with periodic swigs of black coffee.

After allowing appropriate time for digestion and the resting of palates, a span which the women seemed to intuit by some internal clock, they swept the remains of dinner off the table and laid out the second wave: the sweets. This was what we children had been waiting for, even the older ones struggling to put childish things aside. This was a right they still clung to: that the

184

children had first dibs on desserts. And oh, the desserts: the *kolaczki*, edible diamonds of rich dough glowing with strawberry, apricot and blueberry preserves; the *royal mazurek*, a cobbler-like creation bursting with cherries; the *makowiec*, a poppy seed roll for sophisticated tastes; the honey spice cake studded with oily walnuts; the lemon bars from Peach, tart and sweet as they melted on your tongue; layer cakes from Dodie, her specialty, high and light as clouds; and always, a mystery dessert, a new recipe clipped from the food guide of the Tribune or the Sun-Times or the glossy pages of Ladies' Home Journal or McCall's.

"I've never made it before. I know you're not supposed to give guests something new before you've tested it—but you're family. Tell me what you think. The truth. Is it a keeper?"

The women promised to exchange recipes. The kids ate themselves to the brink of tummy trouble. The men, beer drinkers all, hung back, playing poker, preferring to sip their carbohydrates with an alcoholic edge, tipping back cans of Hamms or Pabst or Schlitz, whichever was on sale that week. Perhaps they might sidle back to the dining room at the far end of the evening to snatch a slice of poppy seed roll or to scarf a cookie from the plate just as the aluminum foil was descending, and pat their wives' bottoms for another repast well done. Then the horde would disperse, carrying off what was left of the flood of food, but always leaving the choicest tidbits in Sophie's refrigerator, which the women, dating themselves, all still called "the icebox."

By evening's end, the tablecloth would be stained, an abstract expressionist canvas of pale yellow grease spots and terra cotta tomato sauce streaks, with flecks of maroon, peach and brown that, if you stared long enough, might coalesce to convey the events and emotions of the day. One of the daughters would always volunteer to wash it, but Sophie just shook her head.

"Tomorrow—I wash." She would gather it up in a crumpled ball and carry it down to her cellar to soak it overnight in the laundry tub. Her steps on the wooden stairs were heavy, halting. Her breath rasped in her throat.

Then the table stood bare, all signs of the feast having vanished, except for the scents that lingered in the air of the closed rooms, the vaporous debris left after the flood. But they were only ghosts of their former selves: the licorice spirits of anise and fennel, the vinegar wraith of sauerkraut, a vanilla chocolate phantasm of marbled pound cake. At these times, when the others had departed and only the four of us remained, my mother sweeping the kitchen floor one last time, my father sitting on the toilet cover in the green-tiled bathroom chatting softly with his mother while she soaked her aching, swollen feet, and me standing in front of the sideboard, imagining myself living in the blue-and-white world pictured on the dinner plates, wearing wooden shoes, skipping along a canal, picnicking under the slowly turning arms of a windmill, then the table seemed like an empty altar in a deserted church, where silence hung like a shroud, disturbed only by the rustle of the custodian's broom and the discreetly unintelligible murmur from the confessional.

Now, as I eyed the table, it reminded me less of an altar than an autopsy table, or the yawning mouth of a grave. Shuddering that thought away, I started to open drawers and clear shelves. In the middle drawer, Sophie's embroidered tablecloth lay carefully folded. The fabric now was thin; the shadows of bygone stains had effloresced in brown and yellow blossoms across its length. The original brilliance of the embroidery floss had been dulled by too many washings and trips through the wringer. But the names were still there, whole, legible, not a single letter missing. Automatically my fingers moved to trace mine, Claire Josephine, and my brother's Joseph Matthew, Jr. and, last of all, Jamie's, James Joseph. I marveled at how similar the Josephs were, the stitches almost identical in the curve of the cursive J's, the length of the stems on the lowercase p's and h's, the nearly perfect circles of the o's. I'd never noticed that as a child. I folded the cloth and set it aside. That I would save for myself.

The other drawers contained the flotsam of a long life lived frugally throughout the pendulum swings of the Twentieth Century from profligacy to parsimony and back again. There was one set of silverware, badly tarnished, the "fancy" set used for special occasions until the family that gathered grew too numerous to serve with only 8 place settings. Sophie declined to waste money on a second fancy set and, instead, pressed the everyday kitchen stainless steel into service. As she aged and the daughters took over most of the party planning, they switched to plastic and paper, to her dismay. "You waste your money on this throw away—save the forks! I'll wash and use again," she scolded after every holiday meal.

One drawer held ivory napkins that matched the tablecloth, including the one with the brown scorch mark from Uncle Jimmie's carelessly placed cigarette one Christmas. Tucked in beside them were Waterford crystal salt and pepper shakers, a gift from her "Irish" son-in-law (never mind that he was a 3rd generation American born in Pullman). Next to these sat a cut glass candy dish full of buttons of all shapes, sizes and colors and a wooden box with an elaborate marquetry cover inlaid with mother-of-pearl that held a sewing kit. In the drawer below sat two pairs of tarnished candlesticks, one set low and squat, made of brass; the other, tall and slender, forged of silver, gifts from her children, flush with money to burn in the Eisenhower era. Beside them was a fan with an ebony handle which opened to reveal an intricately drawn scene: an exquisite Asian woman, a geisha unmasked perhaps, her face a pale petal with eyes and lips and the barest curve of a nose, her body swathed in a scarlet kimono streaked with gold, pausing to breathe in the delicate scent of pink cherry blossoms in a garden of oriental splendor, a souvenir from Jimmie's tour of duty in Korea.

In the bottom drawer were stuffed two brand-new, still in the original package, white lace tablecloths, in a modern blend of cotton and polyester. Gifts perhaps, but who would have been so thoughtless as to suggest she replace her old one which held all those memories? Did the purchaser intend to save Sophie from the bitterness that would rise in her mouth, and the ache that would weigh down her arms when she spread the old cloth over the table, when she ran her hands over the names and remembered there were some who would never walk the circuit around her banquet table again? Beneath the packages sat a large, white Marshall Field's box, startlingly similar to my own, but in pristine condition. Inside, cradled in a nest of still-crisp tissue paper, lay an oval silver serving tray, its finish dulled by years of neglect. But under the tarnish, the artisan's skill showed through.

A tree of life, thick of trunk, stretched its branches across the length and breadth of the platter. It was a mighty oak, its craggy bark etched deep into the metal, the veins of its lobed leaves traced more delicately, with tiny acorns scattered about its roots. Under those roots, the surname SOKOL was engraved in strong Roman letters and below that, in a romantic script, were etched the names *Zofia* and *Jakub*, matriarch and patriarch. All around the outer lip of the oval, more names were engraved, the same names that Sophie had embroidered on her tablecloth, preserved now in something impervious to the effects of time and use. The tree itself bore a remarkable resemblance to the huge oak that stood in the side yard, a venerable gray-beard even back then, and now, as I gazed out the filmy dining room window at its still-sturdy limbs and glossy fresh leaves, as yet untouched by the harsher side of summer, it seemed ancient and ageless at once, a Galadriel of oaks.

The occasion was her 70th birthday, early November, 1974. A mean, gray snarl of a day, when the sky intermittently spat down a biting, jagged edged rain that nipped our cheeks and the backs of our hands as we puddle-jumped from the car to the front porch. We hadn't been to a family gathering in almost two years, not since the summer of the weddings, when it seemed we saw everyone every other week, maybe far too much. Something had happened, was happening. In our small family, in the larger family. It was a mystery hidden in plain sight. But I felt it, under my feet, the earth trembling. The juxtaposed plates of all our lives had strained against each other, absorbing energy, building tension, building pressure, until it all became unbearable and the inevitable readjustment had to occur. The earth quaked and the edifice of our relations swayed to and fro in the magnitude of the temblor. Life according to the theory of plate tectonics. It's hard to take that into account when you build your house of family relations. You can make adjustments to the foundation and gird the walls to withstand the vibrations of the inescapable paroxysm, but you have to work with the basic materials with which you are surrounded, the bricks and mortar of blood relations. You can't choose to use granite if you are given sandstone. All the precautionary measures you take, all the safeguards you install, may succeed. The building may still stand after the ground has settled. But in the aftermath, when you inspect the exterior carefully, you may see the jagged rift, the fault line running down the façade, the displaced strata of the material, of the structure, of the earth of your life.

The fault line, the fault.

At thirteen, I did not fully comprehend what exactly had shaken the earth under my family, but I knew where the fault line lay: across my mother's shriveled, bitter walnut of a heart.

We were at war—yet again. It started with clothes. Shopping trips to Goldblatt's or the new mall in Calumet City deteriorated into skirmishes. She ambushed me as I came out of a dressing room in a halter top and the shortest of short shorts, all the rage among my peers, in an outrageous, eye-catching Day-Glo orange.

"You're showing more skin than you're covering."

"It's summer. It's hot. It's okay to show some skin."

"Not that much," she said, handing me a staid polo shirt and some twill shorts of a far more conservative length. Old lady gardener shorts.

"Bermudas," I scoffed, rejecting the ensemble, silently vowing to take a scissors to my old jeans when we got home.

In retaliation, I launched grenades at regular intervals, assaulting everything from her sense of style (or lack thereof) to her preferred shade of lipstick.

"Pin curls went out with the 50's," I sniped, passing the bedroom as she set her hair for the night, twisting it up to her scalp and securing it with a pair of crossed bobby pins.

"When was the last time you bought lipstick? When Jackie O lived in the White House?" I quipped, waving the tube of Maybelline with its squat nub of rosy pink wax that barely crested the edge of its metal cylinder. "Why should I listen to someone whose ideas of fashion come from the Sears catalog?"

Our mother-daughter angst was in no way original, for the battleground soon expanded to include my taste in friends. Of Lori, a gum-cracking blonde with the body of an 20-year-old and a mind not far behind, who'd recently moved with her mother (après-divorce), into her grandparents' house on the corner, who wore hot pants year round, braving Chicago winters by layering them over black knit tights and pulling on knee-high lace up boots, my mother remarked, *"If she doesn't slow down, she'll be pushing a baby carriage 'round the block before she gets her driver's license."* Of Yvette and Brenda, my oldest and dearest, and of whom I had thought she once approved, back when that mattered, she noted acidly, *"I don't know how their mothers let them out of the house. They look like a pair of streetwalkers from Uptown."*

This was hand-to-hand combat without subtlety or rules of engagement, no thoughtful parry and riposte. She bludgeoned; I punched back.

"What do you know about friends?! You don't have any!" A shriek, the thud of rubber soles on stairs, the reverberating slam of a door. The sounds of warfare.

The most dangerous combat zone, the one littered with hidden landmines, centered on the male of the species.

"Dogs. They're all dogs," she spat, when she spied me mooning over a photograph of Roger Daltrey in an issue of Rolling Stone that was making the rounds.

"You just don't like rock," I spat back.

"I don't care whether they sing or dig ditches—they're all after one thing and one thing only. Just remember that."

"Yeah? Would you be saying that about Joey, too—if he were still here?"

God, she wanted to slap me. How her hand trembled as she brought it up swiftly, but instead of swinging at my face, she laid it across her own mouth, staring daggers—*but a glare can never hurt me.*

I rolled my eyes, dismissing her, raising the magazine to my face, shutting her from view, leaving only the window of Roger's golden curls.

When she discovered the Claddagh ring while snooping in my dresser drawers under the pretense of putting away my laundry, which she hadn't done since I was eight and she decided that I should take responsibility for my possessions, she hauled me in for interrogation.

"Where'd you get this?" She held it away, with the barest tips of her fingers, as if it were a rotting alewife that had washed up onto her pristine beach. "And don't bother to lie. I can tell when you're lying."

"Jamie gave it to me."

"Why?"

"It's a friendship ring."

"When did he give it to you?" The ring swayed in the vehement breeze of her questioning.

"Last year."

"You've been hiding it that long?"

"I'm not hiding it. I wear it every day."

"Then you're hiding it under your clothes. And when you take it off, you hide it in your sock drawer."

I stood defiant, arms crossed, back pressed hard against the door jamb.

"You have to return it. This little crush you've got going has gone too far. He obviously stole it from his mother."

"No, he didn't. And I don't know what you mean by 'crush.' We're friends, cousins."

"A boy his age couldn't afford this. He stole it. What kind of present comes from a thief? And yes, you are cousins—" she seemed to spit again. "So if you think this is going to lead—"

I quickly cut her off. "Aunt Peach knows he gave it to me."

Her fists, already clenched, tightened so that the ridges of her knuckles strained white against the skin, ready to burst through. "I'm the mother in this house and I say it goes back."

"No."

Her lips flared to reveal her teeth, like an animal in full, triumphant menace. Possession is nine-tenths of the law, they say. She had the ring gripped in her fist as she marched around my bed and brushed by me out the door. All I had was a little missile to fire at her back.

"Daddy already knows about it."

It was enough of a blow. She stuttered in her step just a millisecond, then straightened her back and continued her righteous stomp down the stairs.

The fire fight began sometime past midnight when my father came home from work and lasted for nearly an hour, a fight unique in my memory in that the voices of the combatants rarely rose about whispers. Nevertheless, though the words were indecipherable, their fiery hiss sounded as if it could sear flesh. The only volley that rang clear came from my mother and even that was no full-bellied shriek, but a dull, flat shot from the gullet.

"She'll find out what you are someday. Sooner or later. She'll find out what you are."

The sounds of the battle trailed off into the opening and closing of bathroom, bedroom and cabinet doors, a groan of a couch spring under a body, the clink of glass upon glass, a rasp as the spring was once again released from its burden, and then the tap of hard-soled shoes on the stairs. I hurriedly turned my face from the door and, with a gulp of breath, froze into a semblance of sleep. The edge of the bed sank a little under his weight, and the air around him was heavy, too, with the smoke of the mill, the reek of the tavern.

"Hey there. I know you're awake. Here."

I felt a whispering itch on my left hand as it lay across my chest. Opening my eyes in just the narrowest slits, peering through a fuzzy fringe of lashes, I saw a glint in the shaft of light streaming in the window. A disembodied hand lifted mine and placed the ring in my palm, gently closing my fingers over it. The hand rested over mine for a moment.

"Promise me something."

I nodded, my hair rustling against my pillow.

"Always believe the best of me, never the worst—unless you see it with your own eyes. Can you promise me that?"

I nodded again.

He pressed my hand again as he rose from the bed and left the room, dragging the foul odors behind him, like Jacob Marley's chain.

After that, the open battles between my mother and I faded into a twilight war, more like armed neutrality. She took to watching the Watergate hearings. For hours. Every day. Dust bunnies appeared, tumbling along the floor in the breeze of our footsteps, curling up in the corners, tracking a gray film across tables and bookshelves. Dirty dishes piled up in the sink and dirty clothes in the hampers, until my father and I banded together to tackle the jobs of washing and laundering. I'd come home from school in the afternoon to find her as I'd left her in the morning, sitting in her nightgown and housecoat, staring at the television screen, or out the back window of the kitchen. Most often she was silent, but occasionally she'd murmur as I passed, *"Liars. You know, they're all liars. Born to it. Right down to the President of the United States."*

Then there was the scroll. That's what I came to call it. She'd sit for hours in my brother's bedroom, at his desk, her pencil poised over a piece of typing paper, staring out the window at the roof next door—or maybe the sky—and then quickly hunch over and jot down some thought in a hasty scribble. I'd peek in the doorway, sometimes in silence, sometimes with a purposeful noise—a bump of my shoe against the door, a tapping of my fingers against the jamb—but she never looked back to see who was there. When she had filled one sheet, she would start on another, first drawing a horizontal line with a ruler across the middle of the sheet, and then taking a long piece of adhesive tape and attaching the sheets along the short edges, as if she were creating a banner. Once I made so bold as to walk up to the desk to get a glimpse of her obsession. It appeared to be some kind of a timeline. I saw the numbers 1960 and 1961 written in large block letters near the top, and the names of months printed under the line, but before I could grasp the meaning in her flowing cursive notes at the vertical tick marks drawn with precision, she rolled the sheets up, secured the ends with paper clips, and kept it safe within her grasp as she resumed her vigil at the window.

Once I found her working her way through a stack of old photographs, bringing them close to her face to examine them carefully, then laying them down on the kitchen table, arranging them like cards in a game of Solitaire: several columns of pictures that somehow she felt were related, each photo laid carefully across the bottom of the one above: photos of my father and my mother, separate and together; photos of other family members: my sister and brother, Uncle Jimmie, Peach, Sophie surrounded by children, and there at the bottom of a column, a photo of an infant in my father's arms, the newborn me, and at the bottom of another column, a photo I'd never seen before, of another infant cradled in Peach's arms. When she realized I was standing behind her in the doorway, she picked up the photos as you would playing cards, column by column and laid them back in their shoe box.

"Ye shall know them by their fruits," she murmured as she brushed past me and into her bedroom, closing the door and remaining there into the evening, through dinner and beyond, my father tossing and turning on the couch when he finally stumbled in after his shift was over.

She stopped going to Sophie's to clean or grocery shop. She barely roused herself to do this for her own household. If Marjorie had been around, we might have called on her for help, but she was farther away than ever, on the opposite coast now, her husband having been transferred to San Diego the previous spring. With two little ones underfoot and a third on the way, it may as well have been a transfer to the moon. My father refused to even inform her about what he called "the situation," for fear of harming the unborn child with unnecessary worry.

"We can handle this," he insisted. So, faced with the yawning white mouth of a nearly empty refrigerator stocked with only the odd condiments: half a jar of mayonnaise, a crusted bottle of catsup, some mustard and pickle relish, a few sticks of margarine, a cloudy jar of brine in which a solitary olive floated, my father and I found ourselves behind the wheels of shopping cart, cruising the aisles of Jewel, salivating like a pair of yokels on their first trip to Vegas, struck dumb by the feathers and falsies on the Folies Bergere gals. We gaped like refugees from some Third World or Iron Curtain country, flabbergasted by the bounty, the choices, the products we supposedly couldn't live without. We loaded our cart with the national brands that leered seductively at us from the easy-to-reach, eye-level shelves; got lost in the snack aisle feeding our junk food jones. Into the cart went the Baken Snaps, the Pringles, all the artificially-flavored creations that ended in the wondrous, yearning, open-mouthed syllable—"O": Fritos, Munchos, Cheetohs. Bags of Baby Ruth and Snickers bars, sweet and salty at once—in they went, followed by a canister of mixed nuts.

In aisle four, past the bread and coffee and pancake mix, my father found a new fascination: Goober—peanut butter and jelly in a jar—together—side by side in vertical stripes, like an awning, purple and tan.

"Who thinks these things up?" he mused. "A more enterprising man than me, I guess," adding the jar to our load.

As novice shoppers we didn't realize we had completely missed the meat and dairy cases at the back of the store until we heaved the last bag in the trunk. Laughing, we drove to the Kroger a few blocks away and hastily scoured its refrigerator cases for steak and moo juice.

"Not bad, not bad at all," my father congratulated himself as we hauled our provisions home, his fingers tapping out the chorus of *Bad, Bad Leroy Brown* on the steering wheel. "I could dig that."

My stomach twisted and squirmed, like a worm on the end of a hook. It may have been fun, exotic even, this little daddy-daughter excursion, one of those events we would laugh about over the years, bonding over a bag of corn chips: *Ay, ay, ay, ay, I am the Frito bandito.* But it wasn't right. It felt *wrong.* "What about Mom?"

His fingers skipped a beat, and then resumed their tapping. "What about her?"

"What's her problem?"

He turned to look at me, his brow hanging heavy, his eyes suddenly marble hard. "I'm not sure I like the attitude I just heard."

"I just meant—what's wrong with her? Why's she acting... like she's acting, just sitting around all day? And that thing she's making, whatever it is... her scroll of paper. And just not doing... anything"

"I don't know. Maybe she's just tired."

"Dad, I don't think—"

He cut me off. "Claire, there's tired, and then there's *tired*. Bone-weary. Brain-weary. I think she's that kind of tired."

"What's that mean?" I persisted, for the first time in my life actually turning down the volume on the car radio so that I could focus, so that *he* could focus on this one thing that suddenly seemed to sit like an elephant between us.

"What's it mean? A bright gal like you, straight A's in school, all your highfalutin book learnin' and you can't figure it out?" His hands, clenched around the steering wheel, had that same white-knuckled look as my mother's had when she'd gripped the Claddagh ring. "It means maybe her life didn't turn out like she wanted it to. It means maybe the man she married ain't who she thought he was. It means maybe she never thought she'd be goin' at it tooth-and-nail with the only child she has left at home. It means maybe she never thought—no—I *know* she never thought," his voice, which had swelled into a bitter rant, now collapsed, "that she'd have to bury what she loved the most."

The blocks passed by. Men were out on this crisp Saturday raking leaves, balancing precariously on the top rungs of ladders to clean them out of the gutters, shoveling them into bushel baskets, dumping them into piles in the alleys, where, later, come the pale lavender of late afternoon or the bruised blue-black of evening, they'd set them afire. Then the children would gather round and watch the bright colors, the golds, the wild oranges, the scarlets, float up in the rising column of heat like swatches of rich fabric, only to shrivel and dissolve into shreds of black. They would warm their hands so near the flame they could feel their skin perched on the edge of singe, and laugh while the ashes danced to the fire's tune, breathing in the smoke that smelled of change, an incense of remembrance and loss, until, hypnotized by the spirit of incantation in the pyre, they would begin to sway and whirl and speak in tongues, calling on—what?—the goblin gods of Halloween? The trickster spirit of the dying season? The souls of the dead?

"Did she love him the most?" He didn't have to reply; even as the words left my mouth, I knew the answer—in every gaze she'd turned on Joey, even the heat of battle, it had been there in her eyes, at the corner of her lips, in the way that she rode him, hard, to be better, to be a better man... than the one she married.

We turned onto our block and drove down the hill in the silence that had settled between us, squeezed in there with the elephant.

"When will she be back?" I asked, unsure why I had framed the question in those particular words.

My father didn't seem to notice. Or maybe he, too, felt as if she was gone, leaving only an empty shell to hold her place in the corporeal world.

"Maybe when she's not so tired," he grunted as we pulled up in front of the house. The leaves from our elms were thick on the lawn, a yellow tide that covered the walk and lapped at the front steps. She was the one who took care of these things, but my mother wouldn't burn leaves that fall. My father and I raked them up in silence and dumped them in the compost heap at the back of the garden. There they sat, destined to decompose in the way of all things. No pagan, flaming pyre to honor these fallen. The spirits of the dead already hung too heavy on our house.

When my mother dropped the ball on caretaking duties at Sophie's, the other women had to pick it up. They divided the work between them on a rotating basis. When it was Peach's turn, Jamie would call and I'd meet them there. She would collect Sophie's grocery list, then head off to the store, leaving us to do any other chores that needed doing. We didn't mind. I couldn't really picture Peach cleaning windows and mopping floors in her peasant skirt and platform shoes, her hair falling in its wavy glory around her shoulders, her nails painted a dreamy mauve.

Jamie would cut the grass with the ancient push mower, the blades of which needed sharpening about every three rows. I would sit on the porch steps and talk. Of my friends, he was the only one in whom I confided about my mother's strange malady, and maybe he sensed that I wanted no advice, just an ear in which to vent. He would nod and push, nod and push, never attempting to explain or console something beyond explanation or consolation.

Sophie would croak at us through the screen door. "Lemonade—come." I'd take the tall, sweating glasses from her shaking hands and we'd carry them into the grape arbor at the back of her yard and sit under the vines which no longer bore edible fruit, only tiny purple nodes so sour they made your shoulders shudder. The vines' chief produce now were leaves; they grew so thick and lush that the light that managed to penetrate into the arbor was a jewel green and cast an alien tinge across our faces.

"I wish I'd known him, your brother," Jamie said, taking a sip, and then pressing the glass to his forehead, already wet with sweat from his labors.

"He was cool." I pulled a fringed, thick-stemmed leaf from an overhanging limb and sliced it with surgical precision, running my fingernail along its veins. "Sometimes I think I'm losing him though."

"What do you mean?"

"My memories of him. He's getting a little hazy. Like my life with him is a movie and I can't remember the entire story any more. Just some scenes, and some lines, and even those I don't remember from beginning to end. The rest is blurry, like the camera's out of focus."

"Maybe that's supposed to happen." He took a long swallow. "Maybe that's normal. Maybe the problem with your mom is that it's not happening."

We sat for a long while without speaking, with just the sounds of the ice hissing and clinking in our glasses and the far-off buzzing of gas-powered mowers and the occasional rumble and fart of a car engine.

"What's the best thing he ever did?" he finally asked. He was seriously into superlatives and extremes: best song/worst song, best book/worst book, best smell/worst smell—you name it, he'd demand the best and worst of it, from TV shows to toe jam.

I squinched up my eyes, thinking hard.

Waist deep in water. His face fills the frame as the scene runs, a grainy, herky-jerky moviola projected on the screen in my mind.

You know, it's not really blue.

Clinging, clinging, like a monkey, fingers clinging to smooth, wet limbs, legs wrapped around the slim but sturdy trunk of a walking tree.

It's not really blue.

Tiny droplets of water adorn the tips of his long lashes like seed pearls.

You can put your feet down. I've got you.

Freckles spice his nose and cheeks like a sprinkling of cinnamon.

That's it, let go. Now stretch out.

Water and hands cradle me. His face leaves the screen and only the blue background, violent with light, remains, so harsh I must close my eyes against its knife-edged glare. Its fierce memory glows orange against the backs of my eyelids.

Arch your back a little. Here.

A hand presses at the base of my spine.

I've got you. Now, be the water. Go on. I won't let go.

But he did. And then it was only the liquid hand that held me in a blue wish.

I am green velvet seaweed, a fish in the sea, a folded gull corking in the waves, a piece of driftwood rolling toward the shore. I am a nodding buoy, an oar set free from its galleass, a corsair with skull and crossbones flapping stark black and white against the blue. I am a royal barge carrying the Queen of Sheba, the Titanic remade, an island ...

...the water. I am the water.

I opened my eyes, slightly amazed to find myself dry instead of dripping, smiling at Jamie through the green murk. "He taught me to float."

Surprise wrinkled his forehead. "I thought I did—that day at the Dunes!"

I shook my head, sorry to disappoint him, eager to re-boost his male ego. "But you helped me remember how—and then I wasn't afraid."

He rubbed his chin and dug the rubber tip of his Converse into the dirt, only slightly mollified. "Okay, so what was the worst thing?"

The reflex action when asked to speak ill of the dead, at least with regards to most of the dead, the good dead, is to refuse. *De mortius nil nisi bonum.* Of the dead, nothing but good. Does this arise from some innate human decency which acknowledges that the dead can no longer defend themselves from slander? Or does it come from dread fear, a quaking before the unknown power of those gone to some other place? My tongue balked at forming an answer to Jamie's question. Not that I couldn't have run through a dozen fingers and toes counting off the outrageous acts and petty slights that one sibling commits against another: the beheading of Mr. Willoughby, the bloody nose or two or three that "just happened," the humiliation of being ordered to stay five paces behind on the walk to school, the casual disregard shown by finishing off the last scoop of ice cream in the carton without a thought of sharing or by stopping at Frank's corner grocery for a Milky Way and never thinking to buy even a penny piece of bubble gum for the little one who sat expectantly on the front steps, waiting, waiting, hands hugging knees, butt grinding sore on the pebbly concrete, just waiting for the hunter to come home from the hill, for the hero to take leave of his band of brothers and return to the faithful vassal, bearing some token from his travels.

But why speak of this? For wouldn't it be true that if I had to pick the worst day with him, the worst moment; if I had to relive over and over again the most brutal of our cat and dog quarrels, or endure the wintriest day of his teenaged indifference, a day when all I saw was his retreating back; if this was the price I would have to pay to have him back again, wouldn't I pay it in the blink of an eye?

He shouldn't have asked me such a question. I think he knew it the moment after the words escaped him, from the way his front teeth bit down on his lower lip and his gaze shifted from my face to the ground.

"He left me," I finally mumbled, grabbing hold of a thick branch and pulling myself to my feet. Was it then that I started to perfect the art of walking away? I strode out from under the cover of the arbor into the bare bulb brightness of mid-day, rubbing the wet glass across my cheeks so its sweat could camouflage the other, hotter liquid that had begun to ooze there.

"I won't leave."

I shrugged, as if it didn't matter. I could hear his steps on the gangway just behind me, feel the heat radiating from his body onto my skin. "Let's go see if Grandma has any of those vanilla fingers in her cookie jar. Half the time she forgets about 'em and they go stale. But I like 'em that way."

As we clambered up the porch, two steps at a time, he caught hold of my hand. A wet, hot current of electricity prickled up from my palm, shooting out to the far-flung points of my body: my stomach, my toes, the tips of my ears.

"I meant what I said." He planted himself in front of the screen door.

He'd grown. Somehow, somewhere along the timeline of days that had passed from one summer to another and yet another, without my noticing, he'd surpassed me in height, an easy feat to be sure, for I'd always been one of the runts of the amassed Sokol litters, but it was still unsettling to have to look up to meet his eyes, to know my forehead was level with his lips, to entertain the weird notion that my body could be enclosed entirely within his own.

"Okay, Horton," I smirked with a bravado I conjured out of that wet electricity.

He scowled, missing the allusion.

"Horton? The elephant? Dr. Seuss?" I heaved an exaggerated sigh, reveling in my momentary superiority. He may have gained the advantage in height, but I conceded nothing in wits. "*I meant what I said and I said what I meant … an elephant's faithful one hundred percent.'* Horton Hatches the Egg."

He rolled his eyes as recognition dawned. "Fuckin' A. That's me, elephant man."

"Shhh!" I hissed, gesturing toward the gloomy living room just beyond the screen, where I knew Sophie sat like a brooding hen.

"Aw, she swears—all the time—but in Polish so no one knows."

"How do you know? You don't speak Polish."

"The tone of her voice. What else would she be sayin' under her breath all day long?"

"Maybe her Rosary?"

"You ever say the word 'dupa' in one of your prayers?"

We stared at each other, struggling to keep a straight face, sucking in our quivering lips, holding our breath on the laughter that finally burst out in spraying, snorting giggles. We careened and caromed until we landed in the porch swing, the force of our bodies sending it lurching sideways. We slouched there until we'd heaved up all the laughter and our shoulders stopped shaking and our bellies ached a little and we were breathing again, rather than gasping. He flung his head back and breathed out sharply and those taffy-colored ringlets of his bounced gently with the motion. I wondered, maybe for the first time, what it would be like to run my fingers through that hair, to languidly stretch out one of those tendrils and let it go again, just to see it bounce back, to fathom its elasticity, or just to giggle and say "boing" and bring a smile to his face. His bony elbow and bonier knee rested against mine and the ratty fringes from our cut-offs twined. There we sat, the cookies forgotten, quiet but for the murmur inside where skin met skin, until Peach rolled up with two paper bags of groceries for us to unload.

President Nixon addressed the nation that very evening, August 8, 1974, to announce his resignation effective at noon the following day. I sighed, watching the sweat, which always be-trayed him in moments of stress, form a slick between his nose and his lips. It's over, I said to myself. There in Washington, and here. She'll snap out of it now. When our new President, Gerald Ford, declared, after taking the oath of office, that our long national nightmare was over, I assumed that our long familial nightmare was over as well.

Instead, its manifestations merely changed. As summer ended and our part of the world once again turned its face away from the light, so did my mother. She passed the ever shortening days in bed in the permanent gloom of her room, swathed in faded floral sheets and a nappy, blue blanket. She paced through the long nights, with the silent footsteps of one whose feet are intimately acquainted with the lay and feel of the floorboards. Only the creak of bedsprings gave her away. She left her marriage bed to walk the floors, downstairs and up. I'd awaken to the sharp click of her rosary beads against the laminated surface of my brother's dresser. She would hoist herself up from her knees before the relics she'd left there and the beads would sway and carom off the front of a drawer. In her white robe, she was, to my myopic eyes, as insubstantial and mysterious as the vapor that rose off the lake on the first frigid morning in January. Tangible, but not. The bedspring would creak. Then it would begin, the monotone whisper of a one-sided conversation in an empty room.

"Watch, O Lord, with those who wake, or watch, or weep tonight, and give your angels and saints charge over those who sleep.

Tend Your sick ones, O Lord Christ;
Rest Your weary ones;
Bless Your dying ones;
Soothe Your suffering ones;
Pity Your afflicted ones;
Shield Your joyous ones;
And all for Your love's sake. Amen."

Monologue turned into mantra: the Apostles' Creed, the Our Father, the Hail Mary, the Glory Be.

"O my Jesus, forgive us our sins, save us from the fires of hell, and lead all souls to heaven, especially those who have most need of Your mercy."

Lying there in the dark, listening, I wondered. Wondered if she meant my dad, if she meant my brother, if she meant herself. Wondered why she'd turned to this now. When was the last time we'd crossed the threshold of a church and dipped our fingers in the holy water? A lifetime ago.

The litany would repeat, on and on, around the chain of small black globes. I could picture the way she rolled them between her thumb and her fingers, and the way her lips barely moved as she uttered the prayers, the ends and beginnings of words bleeding into each other. Worry beads for the hands and the head, to ward off other actions best left undone and other thoughts best left unimagined.

Eventually, I would drift back to sleep. In the morning, she'd be gone, leaving no evidence she had ever really been there. The plaid coverlet on the bed would be smooth, wrinkle-free, the pillow, plump and rounded. I'd find her in the kitchen, sipping coffee, the violet-gray traces of a sleepless night smudged under her eyes. She would wait until my father hauled himself out of bed and then she'd crawl in, drawing the covers up and up until she became just a lump under the bedclothes and a hank of graying brown hair strewn across the pillow.

Finally he dragged her off, literally, to a doctor, a general practitioner who sent her to another doctor, a special doctor, as my father referred to him, a doctor who handled these kinds of things, who admitted her to the local hospital for "exhaustion" and "observation."

"A shrink. He's a shrink. Why can't you just say it?" I blurted out, fear masquerading as honesty.

He slapped my face, once, a swift, hard stroke of the hand. In the freeze-frame moment afterwards, he stared at that hand in shock as his other gripped the edge of the kitchen table, as if he was the one reeling from the blow.

She came home five days later with the basket of yellow chrysanthemums my dad had bought her and a little orange prescription bottle labeled "Tofranil." She didn't try to hide it, placing it right up on the kitchen counter next to the sink and a water glass.

Things didn't change overnight, as I expected. She seemed to sleep better and more in accord with a circadian rhythm: she went to bed at night and was awake during the day. She ceased her nocturnal visits to the shrine and her rosary mantra. One day she astonished us by walking into the kitchen and announcing that she would cook the meal. She ran the vacuum. She dusted. She asked me about school. She seemed to be with us. Almost. But not quite.

One morning I walked into the kitchen to find her standing over the garbage can, tearing paper into tiny shreds, methodically, with a careful precision, as if every rip was imbued with a significance beyond the simple elimination of clutter. It was garbage day and after she'd finished, she took the trash bag out to the can in the alley, just in time for the sanitation truck to trundle over and carry it off to the landfill. She spent a long time in the bathroom with the water running after she returned.

I would have welcomed an argument. But we weren't arguing. Everything was strangely civil. Every sound, every voice seemed muffled, every action kept under wraps. Maybe this was how normal people, those who hadn't suffered traumas like death, lived. Who were we to ask for more than that?

CHAPTER 13

Sophie's 70th birthday party loomed and a barrage of phone calls ensued. My mother answered some; others she let ring while she retreated behind her bedroom door. She promised to bring a pan of homemade potato salad, but when the morning of the party dawned, she had neither the potatoes nor the inclination, so my father ran out in the gray drizzle for a couple of cartons of store-bought. She wrote a note on the calendar to send a check to Aunt Dodie for our contribution toward the big gift, but at the party, my father had to slip the cash to his sister with an apology for the misunderstanding.

We had been the last to arrive on that ugly November afternoon and I knew, unlike in times past, we would be the first to leave. Jamie and I were squeezed into the corner in back of the piano, whispering, playing Rummy. From this spot we had a clear view of the proceedings, but were obscure enough to avoid our McConnell cousins, who, with each passing year, had become more foe than family. My mother didn't join the other women bustling in the back rooms. She sat on the cane-backed chair with its faded floral cushion and examined the birds in the curio cabinet. She'd take one out, hold it up to her face, inspect it front and back, then replace it in its exact spot, and close her hand over the next. She had neglected to put on makeup and her face was a colorless backdrop for their vivid plumage. Her lips, without the barest slick of her pink Maybelline, looked as pale as her cheeks. When Peach came down the hall from the kitchen, having completed the usual small tasks she took on, the kind of work that didn't involve grease or sauce, she looked amazing in black slacks and a turtleneck, like a muse for a Beat poet, and she headed directly for her usual perch near the curio. She stopped in mid-step when she noticed it was already occupied.

Pivoting gracefully in her black ballerina flats, she floated in the opposite direction, where she slipped onto the piano bench between Jimmie and my father. The three of them each faced a different direction: Jimmie toward the piano, his fingers launching into an exaggeratedly syncopated version of Heart and Soul; Peach, with her back to it, facing out into the room; and my father, sitting sideways on the edge, where he could keep an eye on Sophie or let his gaze drift just beyond her out the window into the gloom, with a set to his lips and jaw as if willing the clouds to part.

"Well, heah I am, between the man I love and his brother. This must be what Mr. Thurber meant by 'the catbird seat.'"

An odd smile played about her lips, feral and rapacious as it rose and fell and twisted, animating her face with the drama of a Greek mask, happy and sad at once.

Something passed between my father and mother when he turned his gaze from the picture window to her, still at curio. His jaw, in profile, was still jutting forward, and his eyes still seemed to will something in their dark intensity, but his hands reared up ever so slightly from where they rested on his knees, held for a moment, and then drifted back down. My mother's fist was pressed to her mouth, a skin-and-bone stopper for a hole through which it sometimes seemed nothing sweet ever flowed.

Peach leaned back and smiled up at her husband. "Hon, play somethin' good, play us a love song."

"I thought I was," Jimmie asserted, before he segued into the broken chords of an old Elvis crooner.

"You know the words to this, Claire? I used to sing it to Jamie as a lullaby."

Peach had a lilting voice, slightly, almost endearingly off-key. She swayed a little as she sang of wise men and fools and falling in love, her shoulders pressing against Jimmie's side, then rebounding softly into my father's back, a mesmerizing, tantalizing pinball bouncing between the bumpers.

"Come on, Claire, bet you any money your daddy sang this to you when you were a babe in arms. Sing it with me," she coaxed.

I glanced at my father, whose own gaze was still fixed on my mother, who was now standing in the doorway, looking at me, looking through me, her face, like Peach's just moments before, a mask. But unlike Peach's, hers was immobile, unchanging.

"Don't bet against her, she'd win," she murmured. Then she turned away and walked down the hall.

Uncle Jimmie shifted from one set of broken chords to another.

"Unchained Melody. Come on, Joe. We need a baritone in here. 'Oh, my love…'"

But my father stood abruptly and stalked across the room to Sophie. He stood behind her, his hands kneading the back of her easy chair, staring out the window again.

Peach soldiered on without him, through the verses and refrain.

She thinks he's in love with her. The thought exploded in my head like a flashbulb, illuminating everything in a stark, black-and-white split second, a frozen, light-and-shadow moment captured in a strobe, showing all and nothing.

My mother thinks my father's in love with Peach. She's jealous. Been jealous. Forever.

I had felt the chill, had sensed the undertones, and swayed in the tremors. I'd long been aware that women judged each other with tongues that dripped acid both subtle and harsh. I'd eavesdropped. I'd heard the snide comments, the petty snipes. But I'd thought it was just because she was younger and prettier and more "with it" and wore hipper clothes and dropped those French phrases here and there like rose petals. I'd thought it was about the surface; that the other women were foolish enough to let an image of Peach share their mirrors, even my own mother.

When she looked in the glass from herself to Peach and back again, she made the mistake of asking who was the fairest one of all, and let the gray-green filter of envy discolor her view.

But the truth was something darker.

Believe the best of me, never the worst—unless you see it with your own eyes.

Was there something to my mother's notion? Did he love Peach? No, if he loved her he would still be sitting there on that piano bench, reveling in the touch of her shoulder on his back. *But maybe he does, maybe he loves her so much it hurts to sit there and feel that touch, knowing that her husband is on the other side—his own damn brother. So to stop yourself from screaming, you'd have to get up and walk away.*

Peach had swung around so that she was now facing the piano too, her arm draped over Jimmie's shoulder, her fingers massaging the back of his neck. *No, no. It's insane. Peach and Jimmie love each other—they're always hanging on each other, for God's sake—and okay, maybe Dad thinks Peach is pretty, everybody does, and he likes to look at her, and why not? Men on the street probably look at her that way every day, and, yeah, he likes her, and why not? She's witty and enjoys a good joke, and she likes him because, hey, he's her brother-in-law and he's good-looking and he can tell a joke, and this is all just stupid jealousy from a sour, sour, SOUR mind—*

—and what wouldn't I give for Peach to be my mother.

There. I'd actually said it—if only to myself, for once, and that breathless thought, fey, reckless, was like a rough hand to my forehead that snapped my head back against the wall with an audible thump. Jamie stopped shuffling the cards and looked at me curiously.

"You okay?"

I shrugged his question off. My mother had walked back into the living room wearing her tan raincoat. She held out her hand to my father.

"I need the car keys. I have to run to Jewel."

He dug in his pocket. "Missing an ingredient back there?" He dropped his key ring in her palm. "Want me to go? It's pretty slick out there."

She shook her head, but stood there for a moment, as if weighing the keys in her hand. Her head turned toward me, and I thought for a second that she was going to ask me to go with her. Her eyes, dark holes in that pale face, locked on mine and she seemed to consider something. I quickly looked down at my playing cards and didn't glance back up until I heard the door close on my father's admonishment: "Be careful."

A bit later Aunt Dodie announced that dinner would be a little late so why didn't Grandma open her gifts now. She poked her head in the doorways up and down the hall, rounding up the poker players who'd been banished to the spare bedroom and the youngest cousins who'd been playing hide-and-seek in the basement. She herded everyone into the living room where she proceeded to arrange a tableau according to her grand vision. She shooed the children into a semi-circle around Sophie's feet, physically pushing them onto the floor with a forceful hand on the shoulder.

"Indian style," she barked, nudging knees with her foot.

The teens, and, for once, that included Jamie and me, hung back, slouching in the doorway and against the walls, determined to resist her directions. Where did she think we were, school? She eyed us warily, and then, deciding to avoid a potential clash with volatile adolescents, beckoned for the women to draw their folding chairs around in back of the kids. The men, like the teens, she let be and went bustling down the hall again. She returned with an armload of gifts wrapped in gold foil paper, big boingy spirals of white curling ribbon dripping over the sides. With a flourish, for this was her moment in the spotlight and she was milking it for all it was worth, Aunt Dodie set the presents down on the coffee table next to Sophie.

"I'll bet she practiced that at home," I sniggered into Jamie's ear.

"Happy birthday, Ma."

She gave a little flick of her fingers towards us, her chorus line, and we echoed the verse with subtle variations.

"Happy birthday, Ma."

"Happy 70th, Ma."

"Happy birthday, Grandma."

Sophie endured it with the infinite patience of an aging monarch receiving her due from the peasantry. She carefully removed the bows and set them aside with an admonishment to her daughter to "take these home—use over." She opened one end of the wrapping paper and slid out the box. "Paper, too." She got the recalcitrant lid off with a little eager help from Aunt Dodie, shifted the tissue paper aside and lifted out the engraved silver tray. She examined it, her expression neutral, yet another mask. Dodie yipped and yapped, explaining its significance, pointing out the tree and the branches and the acorns, as if she thought Sophie's eyes were too weak to read the fine script or her brain too slow to grasp whose names were inscribed there. Even after her daughter's elucidation, Sophie's response to the platter was decidedly lukewarm. Her lips cracked into a little smile, and then she set the tray back into the box and handed it to Aunt Dodie with a gesture that seemed to indicate she should put it somewhere.

"She means stick it up your dupa," Jamie hissed in my ear.

Sophie repeated the procedure with her next gift, which turned out to be a pair of lambs' wool slippers, over which she burbled with much enthusiasm, rubbing their ivory cushiness against her cheek.

Dodie's smile was tight and relentless across her face.

We didn't notice my mother's absence until after the call to dinner. Jamie and I squeezed back into our corner, sitting cross-legged, heaping plates on our laps, avoiding the card tables where the minors had been segregated. My father came and squatted in front of us, a plate of half-eaten food in his hand.

"Have you seen your ma?"

I shrugged and shook my head, chewing.

"Did she get back from the store?"

"Dunno. Maybe she's back in the kitchen."

He squinted a little, cutting a couple of vertical furrows into his forehead. "I didn't see her, but I guess I'll look again." His voice held just the beginnings of concern.

"She's better now?" Jamie asked after my father left.

I waggled my hand. "So-so. She doesn't sleep all the time like before. Actually gets up and does things. Talks to a shrink—oops, a therapist. But it seems kinda weird, like she's just going through the motions, you know? Sometimes I wish she'd start bitchin' at me again. Then I would know she's really back."

After we ate, Jamie brought out his recently acquired prized possession, a slightly battered, but still glossy Ovation acoustic guitar that he'd rescued from a pawn shop on Commercial Avenue. Peach suggested we retire to the spare room where we might find a more receptive audience than the men, who had now settled into their serious poker game, except for my dad who stood by the front window, hands in his pockets, fingers moving. He could only summon up an anemic jingle without that brass- and metal-loaded key ring. As we left I heard Peach remark, "Maybe she just got tired of us and drove herself home. We are a rather dull lot."

The small itch of foreboding that had been causing me to shift uneasily in the past half hour, like a scratchy label sewn in the collar of a shirt, evaporated in the wake of those sensible words. *Yeah, that's probably what she did—but not because we're dull. She can't stand to be in the same house as you—and she's forgotten the meaning of the word "fun," if she ever knew it in the first place. And now we'll have to walk home in this crap.*

As if reading my thoughts, Jamie tapped my shoulder. "We'll give you a ride home."

He sat on the old twin bed that had been pushed up against the back wall and turned into a makeshift sofa with a navy afghan and some throw pillows. I plopped down at his feet. Some of the cousins, playing Yahtzee at the card table, acknowledged our arrival with grunts. Linda, who seemed to be succumbing to Dougie's influence, rolled her eyes and hitched her chair around so her back was to us.

Jamie strummed aimless chords, then tried, with much starting and stopping, to pick out the opening melody of *"Stairway to Heaven."* Dougie muttered something to his tablemates and everyone tittered. Churlish and itching for a fight, any fight, I stood up.

"What did you say?" Jamie's foot nudged my calf and out the corner of my eye I saw the quick warning shake of his head. But I stepped over to the table and glared down at Dougie.

"I said, for a long-haired faggot he makes a piss-poor guitar player." Dougie tossed down his cards and folded his arms across his burgeoning, adolescent chest.

Fat ass tub-o-lard.

"I s'pose you think you could do better?"

"Well, I ain't no long-haired faggot so—"

"Bullshit. Go ahead," I gestured toward the guitar, which Jamie clutched protectively. "Show us your stuff."

Dougie sighed with a nervous exaggeration, regarding me warily. Then, falling back on the last resort, he flipped me the bird. "Sit and spin, baby, sit and spin."

"Chickenshit asshole." I slapped him hard, a good wallop across the cheek and jaw that slammed his face sideways and left a rosy brand on his skin.

"Bitch!" He thrust back from the card table, nearly upsetting it but for the quick hands of the others. Dice and scoresheets went flying and so did my heart, a prisoner thumping against its cage of ribs, and so did my hand again, but this time he intercepted it mid-swing with his own ham-hock.

"You're a goddamn looney tune, just like your mother!"

After that everything seemed tinged in shades of red: the tiny scarlet beads strung in an arc across Dougie's face where I scratched him with the fingernails of my left hand; the wet ruddy pink of his palm squashing my face; the crimson flash of the sleeve of Jamie's sweatshirt as his arm went around Dougie's neck; the coppery sparks that flashed before my eyes when my head cracked against the door jamb; the lobsterish faces of angry adults who loomed, scolded and man-handled; the henna-colored halo ringing the light in the bathroom where Peach sat me down on the edge of the tub and pressed my hand, into which she'd stuffed a cold, damp washcloth, threadbare and gray, to my forehead; my father's livid cheeks as he stood in the doorway, shaking his head, muttering "what the hell got into you…"; the rusty haze which seemed to hang in the air.

"We'll give you a lift," Peach murmured.

"We'll walk. She needs to let off some goddamn steam."

I flung the washcloth into the sink and jostled past him.

"Where the hell do you think you're going?"

"Getting' my coat. Goin' home."

"You wait for me outside."

The threat in his voice, obviously intended to make him appear parental and in control in the eyes of the other adults, didn't fool me. When had he ever punished me—really punished me? That slap? That was an aberration, a fluke, a cry of frustration that truly did hurt him more than it hurt me. He'd never raised his voice, much less his hand, to me. That was her job.

Refusing to run the gauntlet of scandalized hypocrites in the living room, into which Dodie, determined to rescue her precious event from catastrophe, had trundled Sophie's cake, I stomped out through the back porch and slammed the door. The sleety rain had ceased but the air was still raw, another slap in the face. The early dark of November pressed down on the houses and trees, making everything seem smaller, including me, as I shivered in the gangway, shoulders hunched, hood up, hands jammed in my pockets.

The door opened and closed behind me.

"Hey," came the soft voice. Jamie.

"Hey."

"You're missin' that yummy cake. Hoo boy, someone put it the refrigerator by mistake and the frosting's hard as a stick of butter. The Queen is fuming. Heads will roll."

I held up my hand, rubbing my thumb and index finger together. "This is the world's smallest violin playing just for me."

We huddled together, exhaling little clouds from our noses and mouths.

"You didn't need to do that. I can fight my own battles," Jamie mumbled.

"I know. I wasn't really fightin' your battle. Not sure what I was fighting. Maybe, just—everything."

I took his silence for understanding, but he had his head cocked to the side, as if listening to something else.

"What?"

It was the dinner hour; that and the crappy weather had left the neighborhood quiet. Quiet, except for a muffled purr that seemed to come from somewhere near, the faint huffing of a car engine in idle.

It was Jamie who pinpointed the sound's location, who headed for Sophie's tar paper shack of a garage; who leaned his shoulder into the warped, recalcitrant door, with its alligatored, peeling paint, forcing it open; who was hit with a nose and mouth and lung full of choke-inducing car exhaust. He knew—even in the pitch-black interior—and he pushed me back, a hard whack in the chest that took my own breath away.

"Go get your dad!" he screeched, "get your dad!" as he stumbled over the broken bricks that formed a makeshift path back to the alley.

But even as I turned, as my brain started to process the thing that Jamie already knew, as that old, cold fist started to clench around my stomach, my father was there, grabbing my shoulders, physically hoisting me aside like a department store mannequin, dashing in through the open side door as Jamie screamed for help in lifting the overhead door off the alley. Light from the hanging bare bulb illuminated the interior, threw a sheen on the roof of our Malibu, where beads of water left from the day's rain still shimmered.

We spoke no intelligent language now. The only sound was the panting of the beast, ranting, intoning, screaming incantation, in the hope that the clamor would rescue, would take the cup from our lips. We pled for mercy with one breath and cursed with the next. Did the words I had so rarely uttered since first I'd memorized them as a toddler scroll through Jamie's and my father's mind as well?

Oh my God—do not do this to me, I cannot bear it—*I am heartily sorry for having offended Thee*—she's not moving, she's not moving—*and I detest all my sins, because of Thy just punishments*—she's a ragdoll in his arms—*but most of all because they offend Thee, my*

God—my God, why? Why? Not now, not—*who are all good and deserving of all my love.* Breathe, breathe, breathe the cold, wet air, breathe—*I firmly resolve*—I'll do anything, anything, promise anything—*with the help of Thy Grace*—help!—*to confess my sins*—what have I done?—*to do penance*—I'm sorry, I'm sorry, what did I say? Do?—*and to amend my life.* Just let her live. *Amen.*

Take this cup from me …

A neighbor, glancing out a back window, might have thought they were slow dancing, two lovers closing a juke joint, sharing the last dance of the night, my father and my mother, hovering in the pool of light cast into alley. He had his arms around her, holding her close and tight to his body, swaying gently. Her arms were flung around his neck, her hands dangling. Her head rested on his shoulder, the blue-white pallor of her cheek stark against his black coat.

Her lips, relaxed, curved, parted to utter some lover's secret, were cherry red.

CHAPTER 14

Maybe it was the gong-like clang of Sophie's silver plated tray as it slipped from my fingers and crashed to the wood floor that brought my father to the dining room. What did he notice first? The open cabinet door? The platter? His daughter sliding down the wall, puddling on the floor, hands clutching stomach and mouth? What did he relive in that endless moment between action and reaction, in the seconds that he paused there in the doorway, as that first rush of adrenaline flooded hot and cold down through his body?

Whatever images raced through his mind in the time it took to get from the door to me, they had ravaged his face, left it drained of color, the flesh mottled, wet with fear-sweat. And his eyes, oh, his eyes—had they ever looked so panic-stricken, so pleading?

And then I knew. When he held my chin and spoke to me with those white-ringed eyes on the edge of flight-or-fight—no words, what use were words, just something more to come between us—I knew why he had called, why he needed me to help him do this thing, to be here with him.

He, too, knew what it meant to be haunted.

Whose face did he see on strangers passing by? His? Hers? Both? All three? Did he see my brother or Jamie in every hard-bodied young punk who slouched against the bricks at the 7-11 or boomed their bass-driven hip hop out the windows of their daddies' Cavaliers as they trolled the strip mall parking lot or lounged in boredom and anticipation in the outfield of a softball diamond, waiting, waiting, for the fly ball? Did he see her face on every woman of a certain age who pushed a grocery cart with weary grace down the aisle at the Jewel, pausing to check the saturated fat content on a box of Cheez-Its or the sell-by date on a gallon of skim milk, an air of purpose about her, secure in the import of her decisions, of her life? Did he see them all together, a ghostly trio walking down the street arm in arm, passing through the noisy rabble, pale, translucent faces and bodies performing a slow, regal pavane amid the gaudy, ragged parade of life?

We didn't speak of these things. We sat on the front porch in the old swing whose rotting boards creaked a warning under our weight and sipped from the cans of pop that we'd brought. We watched a litter of children tumble out of the brown-bricked Cape Cod across the street, a stair-step family, 2 boys and 3 girls, each with thick black hair and skin the color of dulce de leche and faces just as sweet.

"The Cantus. Good people," my father said, nodding in their direction. "Boys shoveled her sidewalk all last winter. Wouldn't take a penny. Glad they're neighbors."

"How times have changed."

"What's that supposed to mean?"

"Back in the day you were as quick as anyone else to laugh at Uncle Bigot's jokes about the spics, the wetbacks—"

"That's your special joy, ain't it? Reminding me of all the bad things I've done in my life?"

"It's my job."

He chuckled. "Well, that was more a sin of omission, laughing at that crap, going along to get along. I don't think I really felt that way—if I did, I wouldn't still be living around here. And if I did have some prejudices, well, that was back then. Maybe I have changed. A man can change, you know." He looked down at his can and shook it gently, releasing the carbonation. "Deathbed conversions. Happen all the time."

"I don't think you're quite on your deathbed yet."

He took a swallow of pop, his eyes fixed ahead.

"But if you live around people long enough you come to see them as human beings, not stereotypes."

"Something like that." He took another sip.

Laughter rippled out from the circle of Cantus as it exploded and they streaked in different directions, a Big Bang of children speeding away from the one in the middle of the front lawn, a little girl with her hands pressed over her eyes, counting in Spanish.

"I used to bring your ma over when we were courtin' and we'd sit out here and talk. I was a gandy dancer on the EJ&E, fixing track. Her father was a crew boss, and she was in some class with Jimmie over at Bowen. *She* actually went to high school. Me, eighth grade was the end of the line—I graduated and went to work. Putting food on the table seemed a helluva lot more important than reading Shakespeare. But she got her high school diploma. And she could draw. Jimmie showed me these little cartoons she'd pass around, making fun of the teacher and what not. They could've been in the funnies. I figured she was a step up—and I wasn't about to let Jimmie even think of making a play for her. Even without a high school education, I could talk a good game. So we'd talk. Talk, talk, talk, making our big plans. Or I guess it'd be more fair to say she'd listen while I talked about *my* big plans."

"Didn't she have plans, too?"

"If she did, she didn't share 'em with me. I told her she could be in the newspaper with those drawings of hers, but she just laughed it off, said she just did it for herself and her friends. I guess I figured my plans were her plans. And she was willing to listen—she had that way about her. She wasn't the most beautiful woman I'd ever seen, but she made me feel like she understood me, like she knew who I was. Even if I didn't always know myself. I told her I would take her places, if she wanted to go places, she should stick with me. Shit. Just holding her hand was something, sittin' here, listenin' to the trains, hearin' all the possibilities whistlin'." He balanced his can on his knee, staring off toward the little man-made ridge where the tracks lay. "We thought we had to get married. Thought she was pregnant. We rushed to get married before Lent—and then it turned out she wasn't pregnant after all. Or maybe she miscarried real early. I don't know. I had just let out a sigh of relief when all of a sudden she was pregnant for real—and damn, I admit it, I panicked."

"Wasn't part of your plan?"

"Long range, maybe... but all of sudden everything seemed to be happening so fast."

"So you looked for the honorable out?"

"Fighting Nazis seemed like a noble cause."

"See the world, slay some fascists, save democracy, miss out on all the 2 AM feedings and dirty diapers and colic. Sounds like a bargain to me."

"I needed to grow up."

"Or die trying."

He chuckled again, shaking his head. "She said the same thing. Told me I had an excuse not to go—my family obligations. Told me it was better to be a living coward than a dead hero. But she just didn't understand—"

"You just got through telling me she understood everything."

"I *thought* she did. That was a mistake. She thought it was about the war, but it was really about her, us."

"How many women did you sleep with in Italy?"

He glared at me. "Not one. Not a damn one." He uncrossed his legs and made a movement to stand, but I put my hand over his and pressed him to stay.

"I'm sorry. That was uncalled for."

All but one of the Cantu children had been found and now those three joined the little one in the hunt for number five, scouring the bushes on the fringe of the yard, trooping up and down the gangway, hands on hips, faces keen with envy and admiration at their sibling's cleverness.

"Did you grow up? Over there in Italy?"

"You had to, if you wanted to survive. And I did. Want to survive, I mean. You know that Army commercial, it's not just a job—"

"It's an adventure."

"It started out like one. I saw more of this country than I'd ever seen before, on the train to camp in Colorado, then to Florida, and then over to Italy."

"You got to go places and she didn't."

"We had a baby. You don't drag a baby all over the place."

"That's how Tally was raised."

"Well, it was different back then."

"Let me guess, your own little backyard just got too small to hold you—"

"No!" He flung himself up out of the swing. The wince that pinched his face betrayed the pain that his passion had cost him. "No," he wheezed, "that's just it. I was ready to come back." Pressing his palm to his side, he hitched himself over to the porch rail. His hand trembled before it found a firm grip around the post. "You see a boy younger than you, his guts hanging out, and he's gripping your hand, squeezing it purple, begging for some painkiller and asking 'bout some white lights he's seein' floating over your head and talkin' to his ma who's come to take him home…" His voice, a fraying thread, broke.

Cliché. Cliché. Your life's a cliché. You don't move me anymore. The automatic spite that filled my head appalled me. I bit down hard on my lip.

Be sweet …

It must have been Aaron's hands, strong-boned and sure, reaching out from 300 miles away, that prodded me up out of the swing and guided me forward to join my father at the railing. The breeze, warm and damp out of the south, might have been his breath against my cheek, in my ear.

Be sweet …

The last Cantu was found, somewhere off the back alley. We heard the squeals and giggles of discovery pealing like carillon bells.

"Did you bring your pain pills with you? You look like you need—"

"I'm trying to say something to you, Claire. But sometimes I think no matter what I say—it's just no good. You've just got this—you wear this—this suit of armor—and you never leave it off—and I can't find the chink... And I have been down this road before, with her."

I moved away, leaning back into the corner, noticing my arms automatically folding across my chest and willing them back open, gripping the rail, as he did, with slightly trembling hands.

"Why don't you just say what you have to say?"

"I came back because I wanted to come back. I was ready to be a man. I wanted to make something with her, to build something good and strong, the two of us together. I put my dog tags and my Bronze Star away and thought I was doing my best, but things were different. She was different."

"What? You couldn't stand a few stretch marks? The dark circles under her eyes? The medals of motherhood?"

His first reaction was to snarl back, but, very consciously, he folded his lips in for a moment, brought his hand up over his mouth, massaged the tension out of his jaw. "No," he finally said, shaking his head. "It wasn't anything to do with her appearance. She was just—different. And I was different, too."

"She was a married woman with a toddler who'd been without a husband for—what?—two years? What did you expect? Your teenage hottie?"

He resisted my bait. "No. I'm trying to tell you—it wasn't that sorta thing. I... I just got the feeling that she... she sorta looked at me like... like I was dirty, soiled. Like I was this mistake she'd made. I started to wonder if I was. She'd still sometimes do her little drawings, but she wouldn't show me. Sometimes I'd ask to see 'em, and she would just tear 'em up, say they weren't meant to be shared. Maybe I wasn't worth sharing them with. I started to wonder if maybe this was how I felt about myself, and that I was doing the chickenshit thing and blaming it on her. But no, I'd always come back to that look."

I knew that look. I'd seen it sweep through the house and linger on each of us, me, my father, my sister, even, upon the rarest of occasions for the briefest of moments, on my brother, like the megawatt beam of a searchlight scouring the perimeters of a prison yard. It was a look that pulled us in even as it froze us in our tracks; a look that thrust us away even as we scrambled to appease it. It was a look that occasionally spawned some of the rare comedy in our dour home, like the first time I heard Mick Jagger singing *"I Can't Get No Satisfaction"* and I asked Joey what that song was all about and he replied, with a perfectly straight face, "Mom's life," before cracking up with a big snorting guffaw. I didn't quite get it but I joined in the laugh at her expense. But the look provoked more tears than laughter, more dread than joy, discontent breeding discontent.

"What do you do when you realize that whatever you do or say, it's wrong? When just about nothin' seems to please? What do you do?"

A half dozen nasty quips jumped to the tip of my tongue: *"be like Avis and try harder," "trade up for a newer low-maintenance model"*, but I kept my lips pressed firmly together. In examining this tiny plot of barren ground, in which we both felt we had toiled but reaped very little, his view of the world was as valid as mine.

"I kept trying to fill her up, with whatever I thought would work—money, things, babies, but she wasn't a spender, didn't want the stuff other women seem to like, and she kept miscarrying. She lost four babies between your sister and Joe Jr. Those big gaps between you kids weren't planned, Claire, weren't part of some grand scheme. She just couldn't seem to carry a baby to term. She was pretty much ready to give up when Joey came along, safe and sound. After he was born, she didn't even want to tempt fate again, did everything she could to not get pregnant, but I guess I caught her with her guard down... and then there was you."

"The accident."

"The bonus," he asserted forcefully. "Cuz I knew that each of you was going to be better than me and her, that the whole was going to be greater than the sum of its parts. That's how I saw it, anyway. But she was protective of that pregnancy, too. Wouldn't let me come near her for nine months. At least, I thought that's why. But then I came to think that mostly she was just furious with me for putting her through it again, the waiting for the worst to happen. She would barely even look at me anymore, as if she couldn't stomach the sight of me. Yet, after all that, probably because of all that, when it was over at last, it was the sweetest thing and all worth it to hold you, cuz I knew you'd be the last little bit of me and her combined." He was looking at me, but for all I knew, he might have been seeing her, his emotions opaque, his face unreadable. "You know what I mean? Is it like that with Tally?"

With Tally? We were all accidental … baby, mother, father. Oh God, crazy, it was crazy, after Jamie… mindless, heedless, self-effacing, pretending how many boys were him? Saved from disaster only by that proverbial sheer luck and the occasional thin sheath of latex… and then by my own body, wasted, stripped down to jutting bones of hip and rib, shut down, turning the clock back to pre-pubescence. Fading away to nothing, a gray shadow in a corner of a room. But when you pass out in someone's class, or nearly so, struggling to keep hold of the edge of the black soapstone lab table, that brings on a certain level of obligation. And a closer examination. And a realization that the girl, underneath those shapeless sweatshirts, has no meat on her bones. In his own way, Aaron was reckless, too. Took me home. Gave me chai tea and bread he had made with his own hands. And at a time when I could eat nothing, would eat nothing… that—that simple loaf —that is what I could eat.

But I just nodded. "Of course, looking at her, you know who her daddy is. There's much more of him than me."

"Maybe it's just an old wives' tale, but that seems the case with most first borns. Come out looking like their daddies. But she's got your eyes. Every photo, there they are, staring out at me." He leaned a little more heavily on the rail. "Any particular reason you and Aaron haven't had any more children?"

The accidental family… gravitas, he had it, in a place that was already seriously serious—ho, ho, ho, the University of Chicago is NOT funnier than you think—despite the gargoyles. He talked ideas, but not in the pretentious, self-conscious way of my fellow students… nor in the "feed your head" way of my professors. Just in the same way as he cooked and ate spaghetti alla carbonara or drank a glass of beer or kneaded yeast dough. Yet he laughed, too, and as I got to know him, he seemed to laugh more. And he had that amazing ability to just be… still. To not shift from foot to foot, to not turn hot to cold with a passing cloud, to not spin on a dime, to not jangle. Do I dare disturb this universe? Friends two years and he never had a woman that I knew about… stopping in to visit him at all kinds of crazy hours: mid-afternoon, early morning, well past midnight after Regenstein Library closed… never a whiff of female around. His world needed to be rocked…

"Why try to improve on perfection? That would just be tempting fate. Plus, there is the little matter of us not being married. With one child, that can seem trendy, with-it—but with multiples, you know, it just starts to seem trashy, irresponsible."

"And why is that?"

"Oh come on, Dad, I would think a person of your generation would look down on—"

"No, I mean, why didn't you ever get married? I'm guessing he's asked more than once."

August is the wettest month in Chicago… big rains… biblical, 100-year flood rains… the kind of rains that just make a girl want to be a silly, puddle-jumping child again… and show up drenched on someone's porch, always the bedraggled waif… but now with some meat on her bones, enough to qualify her as a woman… enough to disturb this universe. He left me swaddled in his bed, under the sheet, the towel I'd used as a turban now unwrapped on the pillow. He padded into the living room and I heard the creak of the futon as he settled his body down, a deep shuddering intake and exhalation of breath, the dull thud of a glass set down on wood. I lay there, starkly awake, and breathed in the smells of his intimate life: the fresh detergent scent of the towel, the aroma of cedar that rose every time I shifted under the sheet, the vague odor of Dial soap that hovered like an aura around the pillow, the warmish smell of a body at day's end, a not unpleasant mingling of sweat and deodorant and the herbs and spices of an evening meal permeating the skin …

I scraped at a blistered chip of paint with my thumbnail. "Fidelity issues. Inability to commit."

My father's gaze lingered on my jabbing thumb. "Aaron doesn't seem like that kind of man ..."

No... he's the kind of man who says getting rid of it is out of the question ... 'maybe if we were just kids without resources, but I have been a grown man for some time now and I knew the possibilities and you are enough of a grown woman to understand them as well, and we need to accept the consequences of our actions and the responsibilities that come with the pleasure and besides, I love you'... uncharacteristically burying the lead. The kind of man to listen to my fears... telling me I'll be what you need me to be when you need me to be — because I need you...

"Not his. Mine."

All those ghostly boys... and he knew, he knew, but he was whipped, caught up in me like a fly in a spider's web, but this spider possessed the gift of changing what she had into the thing she needed, unlike some who scorn what they have and pursue what they think they need—the thing that's ever out of reach. The trick is to be more vampire than black widow, to take only what is needed at any given moment, instead of sucking the victim dry, leaving him an empty desiccated shell of a man forgotten in the corner of the web... he knew, he knew, and once, in the heat of it, threatened to leave, and the only reply to that? You won't leave me, because you know if you do, you'll be just like all the ones that did...

"For a long time, family was the one thing that I did not want."

The sudden squint that tightened the corner of his eye told me that he did not want to go there. Pressing his hand to his stomach, he rested his forehead against the post. "Shit, Claire, I'm hungry, I'm hurtin', and I just want to go home."

I didn't need Aaron's real or imaginary hand to propel me to him, to lay my hand on his back.

"You've been listening to that country station way too long. You're starting to sound like Waylon and Willie."

He wheezed out a tight chuckle. "Hey, ya'll, we play two kinds of music: country and western."

"Jokerman."

Across the street, the mother of all the little Cantus, a softly curved woman in jeans, her hair tucked up under a baseball cap, came out of the house with Freeze-Pops spread like a rainbow-colored fan in her hands. Her children clustered around her, clamoring for their favorite colors, each receiving a kiss along with their treat. After she had settled them on the stoop to eat, she noticed us and waved, a little tentatively.

We waved back and as my father's arm drifted down again, it settled around my shoulders. And damn, if my cheek didn't feel the pull of his chest like a lodestone. And damn, if I wasn't forced to admit to myself that it felt good.

CHAPTER 15

He was curled up on his bed like a fetus when I called him for dinner. When I ventured that I wouldn't have thought that would be a comfortable position for someone with a broken rib, he muttered that he ought to know what felt good to his own body, they were his ribs.

"You haven't eaten since breakfast. A piece of red meat will do you good, you old carnivore."

"Maybe later."

He was reliving it. The pain of the hours, days, weeks after her suicide. That's what had him coiled into himself, his face as gray as his worn-out sheets. Who knows how often he replayed those scenes in his head? Had he managed to keep them on pause for years, as I had? Or did he press play on a regular basis, hoping with each new viewing that somehow the script would change, the ending would be different, that he could make an alternative version, a director's cut of his own life?

What would he edit out? The nights he passed out on the sofa with a Jim Beam bottle that slipped from his hand and soaked the seat cushions and carpet? He switched to odorless vodka when walking into the house, its windows closed against the frigid Chicago winter, began to feel like the embrace of a sweaty, booze-drenched armpit. Or how about the day he spat on the floor of the church rectory, Our Lady of Guadalupe, the very church in which he'd been married, swaying in his alcohol-fueled fury, hocking up a juicy one and letting it fly at the feet of the elderly priest when informed that his wife should not have a full Christian burial because of the manner of her death? The old-school priest, with his Bassett hound face and drooping jowls, reluctant to discuss the matter in front of "the child," offered sympathy and the possibility of a prayer service at the funeral home, and, of course, spiritual counseling for the bereaved. That wasn't good enough for my father, heathen though he was, so he spat and grabbed my hand and we lurched past the little grotto of the Virgin, where the light from the candles in their little crimson cups glowed a lurid, unseemly red. The tiny flames flickered in the violent breeze of our parting.

Later that night I found him hunched in the bathroom. This time it was he who clutched the cold, unforgiving porcelain, pressing his forehead into it like a frantic ram sparring with a rival, snot bubbling out of his nose, his eyes wet red slits in an ashy face.

"Can't put another one in the ground," he kept saying, over and over, while I pried his arms from around the sink and wiped his face and sat on the edge of the tub with my arms around him and my head against his shoulder.

He had her body cremated and he secretly sprinkled some of the ashes over her son's grave and some of them in Sophie's side yard under the oaks where she had toiled without complaint and some in our own garden around the roots of the peonies that she would cut in the spring and bring into the house. The rest he kept in a tiny makeshift urn, an old perfume bottle that he washed and dried, replacing the atomizer with a corked stopper. It sat on his dresser until the day I stole it. Now its final resting place was my relic box, which, in turn, had made its way back here. Home.

After eating dinner alone, in silence but for the self-conscious scrape and ping of my fork and knife against the plate, I strapped on Tally's Walkman and popped in the ear buds before I started to clean up. Music can inspire the brain to recall a memory, but sometimes it's just as useful in warding one off. And nothing and no one compares to Frank Sinatra when it comes to lending a touch of glamour to any common drudgery. Having him inside my head made scouring the pans and washing the dishes seem a hep-cat, swinging thing to do. Almost.

Frank was purring, assuring me that the best was yet to come, and I was believing him with my hips, so I sensed my father's presence behind my shoulder before I actually heard him. I glanced around to see his lips moving.

I popped the right bud out. "Pardon me?"

"Whatcha listening' to?"

"My man Frank. Hungry now?"

He shrugged and raised his eyebrow in a question.

Frank was flying to the moon, playing among the stars, swinging at the top of his game. I reached out and fumbled to put the ear bud in my father's ear. It tipped back out but he caught it and fit it inside in one graceful motion.

"These itty bitty things have a good sound," he said, astonished, talking louder than necessary. "Didn't know you liked Frank."

"I didn't, until I got old enough—ahem—mature enough, to appreciate him."

"Like fine wine."

Frank segued into *"I've Got You Under My Skin,"* a live version captured onstage in—where else?—Las Vegas, with Count Basie and his orchestra loping along and Frank punctuating and syncopating the rhythm in the way that only he could. My father's hand slipped around my waist and he pulled the dish towel out of my other hand and locked his palm over mine. We were dancing, swing-time, clumsily at first, our limbs rusty, our rhythm out of sync with each other and the music, his from lack of use, mine from an over-reliance in my youth on the heavy, thudding beat of rock and disco and techno and house. This was different: the rhythm, the tempo of the heart. But even as we stumbled and stepped on each other's toes, it felt like we were slowly settling into a groove, and as the crescendo built irresistibly, the trombone starting seductively smooth and low and contained, then climbing and flaring out brass bold and cocky, and Frank letting out a joyous, spontaneous "hey!", we were there at the party, breaking away, falling apart, the cords of the ear buds stretched to the max, just our fingertips gripping, then swinging back together, palm to palm, face to face, and every word Frank sang was true.

He leaned against the stove, clutching his back, and the smile that split his lips was half a wince.

"Gotta get me something that plays those CD things. So we can both listen without these wires and plugs. Stereo's been broke for years. I kinda just let music go—don't even listen to it that much on the radio." He pulled the ear bud out and handed it back to me. "How much they cost?"

"You can get a decent player for under a hundred these days."

"Tomorrow. We'll go. You can advise me."

His face was a chiaroscuro of exhilaration and exhaustion, smile lines and furrows of worry, the pallor of his forehead contrasting with the ruddy glow of his cheeks, the bravado in his voice bumping up against the vulnerability in his eyes.

"Go to bed, old man. One dance and you're outta gas."

"But at least you can't call me a dead hoofer."

"That's true. You are coolsville, daddy-o."

He eased himself into a chair and threw me that grin of his.

"Hungry now?" I glanced around. "Shit, you don't even have a microwave to reheat a meal. How do you survive?"

"Lukewarm, cold, whatever it is will be fine."

He just picked at the beef and broccoli.

"Not into stir fry?"

"No, it's good, got a good flavor, I'm just not—how do you say it?—'into' food today."

My eyes followed a crack that ran along the vinyl from the foot of the table to the cabinet under the sink. The flooring there was heavily faded, the wear and tear of years upon years of feet shifting at the sink, rinsing fruit and vegetables, filling pots for coffee and pasta and soup, washing dishes, scrubbing pans, shifting and turning and grinding heel and toe, her feet, my feet, his feet.

"Why didn't you ever leave? You retired ten years ago. Hell, even the mill's been closed since, what, '92? Why didn't you sell this house, get away from all the… work? Takes so much work, so much upkeep. You need a new floor," I rambled on, hoping to soften that initial blow, presuming he'd take it the wrong way.

He blinked as he sat for a moment, the fork poised on the way to his lips. He set it back down on the plate. "You're mighty cavalier about it. But I can understand that, you left young and stayed away. It's my home. It's what I've known for fifty-some years. If I woke up anyplace else, I wouldn't know what to do with myself. How to be. And sometimes I wonder, you know… aw hell, sometimes something cold touches me on the back of my neck or my arm and the hairs just stand up on end." He pushed the plate away. "And then there was always you, back of my mind. I was afraid, if I left, moved away, how would you ever find your way home?"

The crack in the flooring drew my eyes again.

"Cuz times change, wounds heal up, things get mended. Hell, even the sky around here is black again. Some things are worth saving, worth sticking around for. Speaking of which, next time Aaron asks you to marry him, you should. Or you're so modern, maybe you should ask him."

There was that grin again, as he eased his way up from the chair and out of the kitchen, his hand still holding his back, but doing his damned best not to hobble. I sat in the front room, in the long June twilight that started out turquoise streaked with a pale parfait of yogurt colors, lemon yellow, strawberry pink, creamy orange, and then deepened to lapis and violet. Listening to the rustle of my father removing his clothes and brushing his teeth, the pad of his feet across the short hall, the creak of a floorboard as he paused to say goodnight, I realized that in the face of that proprietary smile, for the first time, in a long time, I didn't feel taken for granted.

He wound up buying a sleek silver-toned boom box and half a dozen compact discs to go with it, revealing his own eclectic taste in music. He chose Claudio Arrau playing Debussy to replace his old vinyl copy of *"Claire de Lune,"* which he claimed was scratched beyond aural recognition. In the same hand, he held a Johnny Cash greatest hits collection, a re-issue of Frank Sinatra's collaboration with Antonio Carlos Jobim, Kiri Te Kanawa singing *"Ave Maria,"* and James Galway with the Chieftains, while he contemplated a pop singer's pale, delicate face on the cover of a CD.

"I hear she's good."

"She's more than good. How'd you hear about her? Been scanning the radio stations behind my back?"

He shifted from one foot to the other, his cheeks reddening under their gray stubble. "Well, actually, it was your daughter."

"Tally? Tally told you? When?"

"Oh, she's mentioned her and some others in her letters. I always ask her what she's listenin' to, you know, tryin' to find some common ground." He added the CD to his stack.

His folksy nonchalance caught me off guard. As, I suppose, it was intended to do.

"Just how often do you communicate?"

He threw me a sidelong glance, as if slightly alarmed by the rising pitch of my voice, as if picturing me pitching a fit in the middle of the music aisle in Target.

"I don't know. We write. She writes. I write back. I knew you didn't know about it—at the beginning—but I kinda thought you'd know by now."

"By now? How long has this been going on?" I demanded, dropping my voice to a clenched whisper, propping a grimace of a smile on my face as chirpy little girl of five or six skipped past, beckoning to her laggard mother, who trailed four steps behind trying to soothe a whiny toddler who clutched her hand and a squawking infant riding in the baby seat of the shopping cart.

"Can we get another Raffi, mommy?"

My father took hold of my elbow, easing me out of the middle of the aisle, as the woman maneuvered clumsily around us.

233

"She first wrote after that time I came to visit. What's it been, nine, ten years?"

"You've been corresponding for a decade and I never—" Suspicion ignited and illuminated the circumstances of the situation, like a red signal flare on a dark road.

He grabbed my elbow again, pinching the bone hard between his thumb and fingers. "I have a right to communicate with my granddaughter—and Aaron understands that. I wasn't gonna let you shut me out of her life—the way you shut me out of yours."

"That's not what pisses me off. It's the sneaking around, doing it behind my back."

"Because you would have said no."

"You don't know that!"

"Oh, yes, I do. Admit it. And don't go blamin' Aaron. He's a good man, a good father. He didn't have nothing to do with it. And maybe if you were all under the same roof, you would have found out a lot sooner."

"Mr. Sokol? I thought it was you. Hi, there."

The gentle baritone voice arrested us in mid-argument. Behind us, with an armload of necessities, stood Strawboy, grinning shyly. He juggled his items, trying to free up his right hand to extend it to my father. His efforts sent a canister of shaving cream crashing to the tile floor.

"Klutz," he murmured as he bent to pick it up, but I was quicker and nestled it back into the crook of his arm.

"Claire," he nodded. "Back in town?" Then he shook his head, as if silently reproaching himself for stating the obvious.

"Helping my dad with Sophie's place. There's a lot to clear up—well, I'm sure you understand, you've been there."

And I sure am stupid for reminding him of his own loss.

He shifted his weight from left foot to right, glancing around as if looking for something, someone. "Well, hey, if you need any help with any heavy lifting, you know, grunt work—I'm good at that. I'd be happy to lend a hand, an arm, a strong back..."

My dad made a show of flipping through his CDs.

"Thanks, Kevin. Maybe we'll take you up on that. My dad here is nursing some broken ribs so—"

"Healing fast, healing fast," my father muttered. "But, yeah, thanks for your offer."

Before the inevitable awkward silence settled in, I smiled and patted Kevin's forearm. "Looks like we're both headed for the checkout lanes. Take care, and if we do need some heavy lifting, we know where to call."

"Well, yeah. Hey, do you—let me give you my card." He dumped his purchases on a checkout conveyor belt and dug into his back pocket, fishing out a battered wallet.

A lightning bolt surged across the little card, arcing over his union memberships and his home and work phone numbers. "An electrician? I never knew..."

"Signed on as an apprentice not long after ... well, I guess it was January 1980. Best decision I ever made." His grin was a little lopsided. "Knew the guitar thing wouldn't pan out."

My father wandered over to the next open lane, eyeing the selection of mints and gum.

"Take care, Kev."

"Hey, you too. And really, call me if you need some help— with anything."

I rejoined my father, but we suspended our active hostilities for the time being. Instead, a stone cold silence stood between us in the checkout lane and sat between us in the car on the ride home, a big old iceberg in the midst of the rising heat that had rolled in from the west. Funny how we'd get one melted and another one would rear up in its place. He set up his boom box and popped in his first CD, but I had already stomped up the stairs, slammed the door to my room, plugged in my ear buds and turned the volume up on the Walkman, forcing the galloping Emperor Concerto to fill my head before any selection of his could.

At the same time, the question nagged at me like the toddler in Target, persistent, inescapable: which one did he pick, which one did he pick?

Aaron felt the full force of my outrage over his betrayal that evening. Or rather, he would have if we'd had the opportunity for a private conversation. But considering the telephone's proximity to both the open front door and to my father, a truly frank discussion which would have included several expletives uttered at an obnoxious volume, was out of the question. I could close the front door to avoid putting my business in the street, so to speak, but my father was barely 30 feet away in the kitchen, working a crossword puzzle in the quiet that had resettled on the house after he'd listened to each of his purchases.

I was a teenager again, hunched up in the little alcove, knees to chest, trying to convey all the meaning and passion of my feelings in a convoluted, constricted code.

"You are in deep shit," I hissed immediately after his 'hello."

"And how are you, too, babe? I miss you."

"Mailman, when I get hold of you you're going to know the true meaning of 'going postal.'"

"Are you planning on telling me what you're talking about or do I have to get a translator?"

"You know what I'm talking about."

"Let's see if I can decode this: deep shit, mailman, going postal. The seething lilt to your voice."

"Yes."

"Are we talking about letters?"

"Yes."

"Certain, specific letters?"

"Yes."

"Letters exchanged between a particular old man and his granddaughter?"

"Yes."

His tone suggested that the world should still go on spinning on its axis the way it always had. "Okay. So?"

"So?" So much for code. "So I can't believe you would go behind my back like that. You—of all people—who once told me that you'd never lie to me."

"I didn't. I haven't."

The shrug in his voice made me want to scream. Instead, a tiny, clenched squawk escaped my tight throat.

"If you had ever asked, I would have told you the situation."

His logic infuriated me. "How was I supposed to ask, when I didn't know about the situation?"

"Definitely a catch-22."

"I'm not laughing."

"Well, babe, you should be. You should laugh a lot more. You're even more beautiful when you do."

"You should have told me, and you know it, so don't try to weasel—"

"Hey, you backed yourself into this situation because of your stubbornness."

"And stop calling it a situation."

"Joe has every right to be a grandparent and Tally has the right to have him. Whatever crimes you think he's committed, they are against you, not her."

Stretching out, pressing my back hard against the wall and the soles of my feet forward into the door molding, I felt the full force of being caught between two immoveable objects. The vertebrae along my spine, the ligaments in my knees, the muscles in my calves all protested.

"So, how's the house cleaning going? Getting much done?"

As if the subject was closed. Hanging up would have been the most satisfying thing to do. Instead I bent forward, giving in to my screaming bones, and answered his question.

"It's slow. We didn't go over there today, and tomorrow he has a doctor's appointment. Rib check, I guess. And she has— had—so much stuff."

"Imagine that. Any interesting artifacts?"

"A few," I replied, intentionally cryptic.

"How's Joe feeling?"

Glancing around the corner, I could just make out a sliver of my father's t-shirted back hunched over in his chair in the kitchen. "He's in some pain, more than he wants to let on, I think. Maybe he tried to do too much too soon. And yesterday…" I let the sentence wander off on its own, having no desire to accompany it to its conclusion.

"What?" Aaron forced me along.

237

I heaved an exaggerated sigh, wanting to make light of it. "Oh, we just got a little spooked, that's all."

"By?" Now he was the serious one.

"One of those artifacts."

His silence prodded me onward.

"This silly tray we all chipped in to buy for Sophie's 70th birthday. As if she needed anything like that. Seeing it made us think of—her—my mother. And what happened. I think he took it hard, like a punch in the gut. Literally. He just curled up in bed, didn't hardly eat."

"And now?"

"Better. Bought himself a CD player today. I think he's trying to woo me."

"That's a bit self-centered of you. Even though you are intrinsically woo-able. And how are you?"

"Okay."

"Okay?"

"Yes, I'm fine. I saw, I cried, and I got over it, and now— I'm fine."

"When you're flip like that, I know you're not fine."

To deny it would have been pointless. He would have just kept prodding and poking and digging and sweeping and peeling off layer after layer until he'd reached the bones of the issue.

"She was forty-nine. When I was little, she seemed old to me. I thought she was old, and then—after—I realized she wasn't, really. And now, from where I'm standing, with forty right there in front of me, I can see she was still young, but I don't think *she* knew that. I tick off the years and as I get closer to it... I don't know, it's like a milestone and I start to wonder what will happen when I reach it, if I will reach it. Will I get beyond it—or be stuck there, like her. It was the same with my brother. I dreaded sixteen and I longed for it. I wanted to stay there and I wanted to get past it. I went a little crazy."

"You'll get beyond it like you got beyond sixteen. And you'll breathe a sigh of relief and say why the hell did I ever let that bother me?" His voice in my ear was as sweet and soothing as a honey cordial.

"I went a little crazy when Tally turned thirteen, too. Times when she'd sleep over and I would get up in the middle of the night and tiptoe to her room and just stand there, over her bed, watching her sleep, listening to her breathe. Her eyes would flutter and I'd wonder what she was dreaming. I'd whisper all the things I wanted her to know, about boys and being true to yourself and living a decent life, because these were all the things my mother should have said to me when I was thirteen and didn't. And then she gave up the chance to do it altogether. And I thought to myself I'd better say these things now, even if I say them while she's sleeping, because, God knows, she won't give me the chance to say them when she's awake and will I even be around to say them when she's fourteen or whenever she is ready to listen. I wondered what the hell was I doing? Did I really think I was being a better mother, whispering in the dark, when I couldn't even face sharing a life, really sharing it, being there all the time, whether it suited my mood or not?"

He didn't reply immediately and I heard the meow of a cat and then the jagged thrum of a purr. "I never knew this," he finally said.

"Well, I guess I'm sane enough to keep my insanity under wraps."

"You're not crazy. You're human. Did you ever consider the possibility that your mother might have done the same thing, stood over your bed and whispered all the things she couldn't say in the waking hours?"

"No. Because I was awake those nights when she was wandering the house—and she wasn't talking to me."

"Have you at least forgiven her for what she did?"

I paused, listening to the cat's little motor gunning 300 miles away, picturing Aaron's strong, big-knuckled hands running over its sleek body, chucking it under the chin, scratching behind its ears. It was almost as soothing as doing it myself, stress relief by surrogate. "What I've realized is that there's nothing to forgive, because she really died the day my brother drowned. The next four years were just about finding a way to get her body into the grave."

I'd forgotten where I was and who was sitting just within earshot. "How's Tally?" I asked, quickly slamming the door shut on the other topic. "How's our camp counselor?"

"Don't think I'm going to let that other remark go."

"Let it go," I pleaded. "At least for now. I really can't elaborate. POS."

"POS?"

"Parent over shoulder—sort of," I whispered into the receiver.

"Ahh. Okay, we'll revisit it later."

"Much later. I'm going to sign off for now."

"Hey, before you go, remember, 'tis better to forgive than to seethe."

"Ha-ha. How about this one: honesty is still the best policy."

"To err is human."

"Yada yada."

"Whatever you do, don't blame him."

"Funny, he said the same thing about you. So where does the buck stop? Who am I supposed to blame?"

"How 'bout no one?"

"A blame-free, guilt-free situation? What a concept."

"Revolutionary. Think about it."

"I will."

"And while you're at it, you need to think about a wedding date."

"I do?"

"Yes, that's what you're going to say."

"I will?"

"That works, too."

"Aaron—"

"Night, babe."

CHAPTER 16

My father stubbornly insisted on going to his doctor's appointment alone.

"There's no sense in the both of us havin' to sit there coolin' our heels in some stinkin' waiting room. Damn places smell like sickness."

"I never really noticed. They smell more like antiseptic to me. I don't mind the smell. And I feel like as long as I'm here, I should keep you company, even if I am still angry with you."

"Shit, I'm not some doddering old fogie you have to help in and out of his chair."

I could have reminded him of his earlier pain and pallor, but he was like a fractious horse with the bit in his teeth and the whites of his eyes showing, so there was no finessing him. He hated going to doctors, always had, and so rarely did; hated the vulnerability and weakness that the need for them—in his mind—implied. So I let go of the bridle and off he went, snorting and stamping.

I read the two newspapers and puttered around the kitchen, putting away dishes, changing the garbage bag, marveling and cursing at how quickly I had fallen into domestic caretaker mode. Fighting a powerful urge to drag out the vacuum and attack the dust bunnies lurking in the corners, I went up to my room and flopped down on the bed.

Idleness. Wasteful idleness. Idleness that allows unwelcome thoughts to leap into an unoccupied mind, like children hopping on and off a slow-moving carousel. They wouldn't dare try it at the height of the merry-go-round's rotation, when the ponies and lights blur into a liquid, streaming ribbon of color. But when the carousel starts to wind down, when the ponies and poles again solidify into something tangible, something to grab hold of, then the children will jump.

So it is with thoughts. The whir of a busy, pre-occupied mind keeps the nagging, hungry, wolfish dreads at bay. My mother had thrown herself into housework in an effort to keep the merry-go-round spinning, keeping that despair from hopping aboard. Of course, it only worked for so long, until the carousel broke down and the unwelcome thoughts jumped on. Soon they were the only riders left.

I lifted the little, fan-shaped perfume bottle out of its nest in my box and let it rest in my palm. The ashes were obscured by its wondrous cobalt blue glass. The weight was all in the bottle, not in what was left of her, the merest ounces of a life lived. But once, it was a full-fleshed life, pendulous, with heft and substance. And before that even—before the disappointment, there was...something...some other life, light and airy, uplifted, springing like a deer. I'd seen it once, I thought. A photograph that captured that, the time before the road forked and my mother chose the path that she later decided was the wrong one.

My father's room was in gloom, as usual, but when I flicked on the light, it was surprisingly neat. The bed was made; no dirty socks littered the floor; his clothes, in the doorless closet, were hung primly, with shirts grouped on one side and pants on the other. On the nightstand sat two gold-framed photographs: a 5x7 of Tally's latest school portrait and a 3x5 of him and me at my high school graduation, my mortarboard and his grin set at rakish angles.

The top of his dresser was Spartan, with just an old West Bend alarm clock, his comb and a box of Kleenex resting there, so empty compared to the last time I'd walked into this room. I felt as much like an intruder now as I had then, my movements jagged with a shameful, sweaty furtiveness, the adrenaline of stealth playing up and down my spine like mallets on a marimba. Ping! My ears cocked to pick up the slightest grind of a key in a lock. Ping! My nose sensed the faintest hint of old soap and talc, of the bars my mother stashed in the drawers to freshen them and of the dusting powder she used that came in a round box with a fuzzy violet puff and filled the air with the ashes of roses. He may have finally put away her wooden tray of ancient, caked cosmetics and her hairbrush and hand mirror and the linen and lace table scarf upon which they rested, but her essence still lingered after all this time. And he had to have kept the photographs. It was just a question of where.

Top drawer? No, boxers, t-shirts, socks, and a stack of old handkerchiefs, the big square kind for nose-blowing in the days before disposable tissue and the small type just for show in the breast pocket of a suit jacket. The middle one, then. No, several bulky wool sweaters, pitted here and there with moth holes, a couple of pairs of worn winter gloves, black leather, brown suede, the material creased and thin between the fingers and across the palms, and a small block of cedar that had long since lost its scent. Had to be the bottom drawer, then. Nope, just thermal underwear that looked baggy and puckered from long, hard use. I plopped down hard on the floor in disappointment, only to regret the thud that I had made. I tilted my ear quickly in the direction of the front door. It was then, with my head at that oblique angle, that I saw it—a sliver of red piercing all those layers of faded white fabric.

It was an archaeologist's "aha" moment.

Here was his little cache of artifacts, the private ones hidden from public scrutiny. Anyone walking in off the street would have known that house was a museum of household relics from the 60's and 70's, from the hulking stereo cabinet in the living room to the Popiel's Vege-matic Slicer and Dicer in the kitchen cabinet under the sink. The rooms even had that impersonal, museum-like atmosphere, lacking a touch of the quirky individual who actually moved within them. Except here, in the inner sanctum. And even here the display looked suspiciously sparse, as if other important pieces of the collection had been hastily removed from view. It occurred to me that if I looked carefully I might see their empty places outlined in dust on the nightstand and the dresser, the ghostly evidence of their former presence, like the smell of my mother's soap and powder.

Perhaps there, in the red box—how apropos—I'd find them, his secret fetishes, the ones he would not risk even his own daughter seeing—or perhaps, *especially not* his daughter. This had to be the good stuff.

Tucked beside the shoebox was a small leather case which looked so beat up I was almost afraid to touch it for fear it might disintegrate. Indeed, when I lifted it out of the drawer, powdery brown flakes clung to my damp fingers. It smelled not unpleasantly of decay, a good decay, a natural decay, like it had seen the world, collected its dust and was now ready to return to dust itself. The rusted zipper clenched its teeth and refused to open without a struggle. After much tugging, it gave way with a low snarl.

It takes a fellow fetishist to truly appreciate another's collection. The case was an ancient toiletry kit, with little pockets and elastic to hold various objects: an old-fashioned safety razor and blades, nail clippers and a metal file, a comb, little bottles for cologne and shampoo, a brush to apply shaving cream, a shoe buffer. Other items were tucked inside as well. There was a stack of war ration books issued to Joseph Matthew Sokol, Mary Margaret Sokol and Marjorie Anne Sokol. The covers were dingy brown with age and spotted with stains, the edges of the paper soft as suede. The basic facts of their lives were written in blue ink that had faded to a watercolor purple: first, middle and last names, street number, city or post office, state, age, sex, weight, height, occupation, signature. My father, at age eighteen, stood five feet eleven inches tall and weighed 155 pounds. My mother, at age eighteen, stood five feet one inch tall and weighed 105. He listed his occupation as switchman, she as housewife. So quaint, these self-descriptions, these identifiers for a time before the mandatory photo ID. And the signatures, what did they tell? My father's was back-slanting but tidy, perfectly legible, while my mother's slanted forward, surprisingly elegant with a tiny curlicue flourish at the beginnings of her M and S. The books still held the miniscule rectangular coupons: some with a cornucopia of fruit printed in red, others labeled "coffee," still others graced by the torch of freedom held in liberty's hand.

Nestled in a corner of the case was a pair of dull metal disks on a bead chain. My father's dog tags. Another identifier—those numbers stamped in a row along the edge, readable to my fingers, like Braille. Under them, a small plastic case that held his Bronze Star. Peeping out of a pocket stitched into the lid of the case was a beige-tinged slice of card stock. Photographs.

A find, a treasure trove. My father in uniform, solemn and serious and surprisingly mature-looking, washed in shades of gray in an official studio portrait. My parents getting up close and personal in an instant photo booth. The strip of photos captured them in all manner of poses and personas: sexily snuggling cheek-to-cheek, my father, head tilted down, looking up suavely from beneath his sleek eyebrows, my mother, head thrown back just slightly, lips parted in a sultry come-on. In the next shot they had morphed into fresh-faced teens, smiling head-on at the camera, guileless, charming. In the third, they had switched positions and were serious, almost grim-faced, my father holding his hat to his chest, as if attempting their own version of American Gothic. In the last photo, they were goofs, plain and simple, adolescents mugging cross-eyed, tongues lolling. They were complete strangers to me, and yet, were there hints here, glimpses of people I had seen somewhere, sometime, if only momentarily?

There it was, the photograph for which I had gone snooping in the first place: my mother, *before*. One corner was sheared off and the edges of the print stock were tinged a burnt brown as if it had been rescued at some point from immolation. Who had taken a match to it? Him? Her? Impossible to know. But in the end it had been saved from the fire. That seemed the most important clue. And there she was.

Sweet-faced girl, baby fat cheeks under the glory waves of pin-curled hair. What to call this captured moment? Girl with Dog? Girl with Shoe Untied? For there they are, the laces of your white Oxford with its little curved heel, untied, splayed out, inviting. The hand ached to take them up and tie them, to brush the foot that rested there. Did you know they were loose as you sat there on the porch in your plaid tweed jacket and your wool skirt, one leg curled under you, the other stretched out for all the world to see: the passersby, the man who would develop the negative, the child to come who would gape at this photo and marvel at this person, who looked so like and unlike the mother she knew? Even the dog, a fluff of fur and pointed ears, a Samoyed, maybe, the one named Czygan, Gypsy, seemed to smile under your hand. The photographer captured himself, a head and shoulders shadow in the corner of the frame, an arty touch. Who was he? Your soon-to-be bridegroom? Yours is a broader smile than Mona Lisa's. White teeth gleam. There's no hiding what you feel. The autumn sun is warm on your face, but it's not so bright as to blind you. Are you looking at this man you think you love and presume you see the future?

A girl with possibilities.

Hers were mysteries I'd never solve. She'd left no note, no secret diary stashed away. In that strange year after her death, I had scoured the house for something, anything, set down in ink or graphite or blood, on any scrap of paper imaginable, loose-leaf, stationery, grocery receipts, secreted between hard covers or tucked into an envelope. I snooped in lingerie drawers and linen closets, felt with trembling fingers along the undersides of dressers, rooted through file boxes and hat boxes and shoe boxes, poked and prodded in the lining of old coats and the waistbands of old skirts, and under the quilted weight of mattresses. I hunted for the scroll she had hunched over, but it had vanished and all that remained was the image in my mind of my mother standing over the garbage can methodically ripping sheets of paper and carrying the bag out to the alley. I tore the house apart, room by room, while my father worked or slept or sat in a stupor in front of the television with a glass of vodka and 7-Up as his companion, but I never found the thing for which I was hunting.

I slipped the photographs back into the pocket and closed the case, struggling once again with the recalcitrant zipper. There was no need to sift further through the contents of the red shoebox; I'd seen what I needed to see. Still, the curator in me couldn't resist. The artifacts tucked inside might have been called the Tally Collection: school photographs dating all the way back to kindergarten when she was a gap-toothed munchkin peeking out from under a thick fringe of bangs; home-made greeting cards; a red construction paper heart glued to a tattered paper lace doily scrawled with a loopy, cursive sentiment: I ♥ U, Grampa; programs from her school theatre performances. There were letters, too, folded in their original envelopes, magnets to my hands and eyes. But I stopped my fingers from slipping the pink stationery out of its sheath and shut my eyes.

Some relics should remain undisturbed.

As I shifted the stack of letters, a strip of gold flashed and my nail struck something hard. A picture frame lay at the bottom of the box, under the letters. Peach and Jamie grinned at me from the small oval. Standing outdoors against some leafy backdrop, Jamie looked about thirteen or fourteen, his hair a wild tangle of corkscrew curls, tossed about by a breeze, frozen in mid-air by the camera's shutter. I'd seen the photo before—or at least that pose against that background. That hair of his caught blowing in the wind. I knew that hair, that grin… But something seemed to be missing. What I held in my hand was only a piece of a larger image. What else belonged there? What had I seen—and where did I see it?

Jamie in a white cotton shirt, the collar unbuttoned. Had he recently jettisoned a tie? Peach in a sleeveless white shell, sans sunglasses, squinting in the bright sun, little shadowed furrows branching out from the corners of her eyes, looking a little older, a little more matronly, a little less…

In my own box—that's where I'd seen this—but bigger, fuller, a more complete image, an image that put Jamie in the middle, not squeezed to the edge of the frame with half of his shoulder sliced away.

I tucked the shoebox and the leather case into the drawer, re-arranged the long johns over them, but I carried the oval frame upstairs. I didn't have to flip through too many photographs be-fore I found the original print. In it, Jamie stood between both of his parents, Peach on his left, Jimmie to his right. Jimmie's eyes were uncharacteristically hidden behind a pair of aviator-style sunglasses which made him look positively studly. The lush green backdrop was the arbor in Sophie's yard—and I remembered the occasion—eighth grade graduation. Three or four of us grand-children reached that milestone together. It wasn't the first time my father and I had been back to the house since my mother's death the previous November, but it was the first time we'd been there under the scrutiny of the extended family.

The air was thick with it. Cheated out of the cathartic scha-denfreude of a proper funeral, they—the aunts, uncles and cousins—seemed determined to release it somehow, even seven months later. Eyes and mouths—that's what filled the rooms. They spilled out onto the front porch and crowded under the small marquee that the men had erected in the yard to protect us from the elements. But nothing could protect me from the eyes. They oozed sympathy, but something else trickled out, too: curiosity, the kind that drags the gaze to a car wreck on the side of the road; and anticipation, the kind that keeps the stare fixed on an object of an unpredictable nature and asks the question, what will it do next? And the mouths, no escaping those. They were as irritating as faucets which gushed water that was never quite the right temperature and no amount of fiddling with the knobs seemed to help. They always ran either too hot or too cold: too flush with sentiment offered too late, as if this were the wake that never happened; or completely empty of it, as when Dougie joked loudly to his cabal that his dad had suggested confiscating all the car keys at the start of the party and only returning them to the owners who proved they were sober and sane enough to drive home.

Even Jamie seemed caught up in the teetering disequilibrium. He couldn't sit still. He'd plop down beside me on the porch swing where I'd taken up a permanent slouching residence and launch into a conversation, only to jump up two sentences later and stride away, sometimes only the length of the porch, sometimes halfway down the block.

We'd only spoken a couple of times since November and only once face-to-face, during an awkward, strained Christmas visit at which Peach was appalled to discover that we hadn't bothered to even hang a wreath. While my father alternately blustered a defense and stammered apologies for his shortcomings as a parent, Jimmie ran his fingers over the kitchen table like he was hankering for a keyboard behind which to disappear. Jamie and I wandered into the living room and sat on the floor half-heartedly playing with the gift he'd brought, a set of Weebles, little plastic egg-shaped people who wobbled, but never fell down. They were toys for little kids, the eight-and-under crowd, but we were getting into them nonetheless, flicking them with our fingers, smacking them with open hands. They'd tip and bobble, but no matter how hard we'd hit them they would always bounce right back up.

The adult voices occasionally drifted in.

"She's not going to be a child much longer. You're getting into the teen years. God knows it's a difficult stretch under the best of circumstances. You need to think about how you're going to deal with certain things."

Jamie set up a row of Weebles, poked the first with a finger, which sent it tumbling into its neighbor, which, in turn, felled the next in line and so on, like dominoes. But they all popped up, smiles fixed on their faces, ready for the next hit.

"You're father and mother now—to a female adolescent. Heaven help us all."

"Little kids today have the coolest toys. Too bad we're getting too old for this stuff," I said, the gravity of thirteen suddenly staying my hand from yet another swipe.

Jamie, too, drew back, folding his arms across his knees.

"I just bought 'em cuz they reminded me of you."

I picked up a dark-haired one with round glasses encircling its black dot eyes.

"I guess I should be insulted."

"Not the way they look, goof. I mean, this." He flicked one and it wobbled over, its little egghead brushing the carpet, then righted itself again. "They can take a punch. No matter what happens, they bounce back."

To reply would require me to either lie or admit the truth. I didn't want to lie and I couldn't risk the truth. Better to just sit quietly, nudging at the dauntless little Weebles with my toe, rather than admit that I had never felt more flat on my back. Better to avoid a conversation about problems at home, at school.

"What did you just say?"

Perhaps Mrs. Wainwright thought she had misheard my riposte to the obnoxious blonde bitch-in-training with her cheap pout who sat behind me in Social Studies, whining that her homework overload had cost her a trip to the mall and she just wanted to slit her wrists RIGHT NOW. Or perhaps my teacher assumed I would tell a convenient lie to make her think she had misheard me, thus saving both our faces.

But I wouldn't.

"I said that she's a silly bitch with shit for brains."

The way her cheeks flushed in two bright circles of red, like a doll's painted blush, and her eyebrows froze in astonished arcs made it impossible, simply impossible to contain the snicker that came bubbling up my throat and out my nose like a spray of carbonated soda. The way she asked me out in the hall if everything was all right at home made it impossible, simply impossible to swallow the bilious words that came raging up out of my stomach into my mouth—no, everything is not all right at home—my mother killed herself, you stupid ninny!

Even if Jamie found that funny, if he saw my acting out as a righteous response in the face of idiocy, what of the nights I spent huddled in my old rocking chair, clutching good old Cuddly Duddly yet again, unable to ward off the demon thoughts that surrounded me like ravening wolves, nipping at toes and fingers, waiting for the opportune time to move in for the kill? What would he think of my weakness, and those thoughts?

She saw it in your eyes, wicked child, saw who you preferred. She heard your thoughts as if you spoke them aloud—that one thought, that particular thought, on that particular day—"what I wouldn't give for Aunt Peach to be my mother"—*and all the times before when you had harbored that same notion*—*only not in so many words*—*but still the meaning, the desire, the wish, was there*—*in looks, in gestures, in the images that flashed through your mind. And that must have hurt the most*—*more painful than any wound that a husband could inflict, a cut to spill a mother's lifeblood, sharper than a serpent's tooth indeed.*

Wicked, wicked, thankless child... epithets hissed by a pair of cherry red lips.

Yet better to stay awake, berated by my mother's formless spirit, than to sleep and risk the dream. It always came with the smell of the earth. Heavy, musky, damp. A fertile smell. *I stand in a forest. Looking down, I see them, narrow and small. I follow the footprints pressed in the brown soil. Branches full of new leaves brush my face. Sometimes they cut my cheek or temple. But something about the smell drives me on. The footprints end at a place where the earth's been freshly turned, the soil disturbed. It's clotted. And then I realize what's happened. I fall to my knees and start to dig in the dirt with my bare hands, throwing the clods to the side and over my head. She's there, under the earth. She's been buried alive. The smell chokes me. The smell of her grave. The smell of guilt.*

I would wake to find my hands scrambling at my blankets, clutching and unclutching, jagged fingernails catching in the open weave of the fabric, huffing and puffing, trying to blow away the smell. And I would curse myself for being a fool; remind myself that she had never been buried at all, that part of her was downstairs on a dresser in a glass bottle. And begin to wonder if maybe that was part of the problem.

Jamie was wrong. I wasn't a Weeble at all. But it wouldn't do to tell him that. Let him go on thinking that I was strong. Living a lie was better than looking weak.

The façade cracked as they were getting on their coats. Peach, running her eyes down the length of me, consuming me as usual, clucked her tongue and shook her head, as if spitting me back out after discovering I was spoiled fruit.

"Sugah, you have definitely grown. Those pants are just waiting for a flood. Maybe I could take you shopping next week? We could have a girls' day out and get you some new clothes, some glad rags. What do you think?"

She was still in her "mod" phase, decked out in a pair of wine-colored gaucho pants, her legs laced up in black leather boots, her manicured fingers arranging the bell-shaped sleeves of her white cotton blouse. She smiled at me sympathetically, as if to say, *I heard your thoughts, too. And I completely understand where they came from. And it was okay to have them. Because, after all, you know what they say about great minds…*

It was one of those thoughts that wasn't supposed to actually come out of a mouth, my mouth, and create sound waves. It was supposed to just flicker inside my head, like a faulty neon sign, on and off, on and off, letting me know it was there, keeping me company in the dark. But out it came, with all the intensity and heat of an unfiltered, high-beam spotlight.

"You're just as guilty as I am. You and your clearance sale clothes, always a year behind the real fashion, but hell, next to her and all the other old cows in this family, you looked bitchin'. And I bought it- -ate it up! She knew. She knew. About me and about you. But you can never be my mother. So stop trying!"

A hand was on my shoulder, light at first, then heavy, restraining. I shrugged it off and turned on my heel. *Don't run. Don't you dare run.* At the bottom of the steps, I paused and faced them again: Jamie, forehead against the wall, his hand clutching his hair back from his face; Jimmie, head down, hands in his pockets; my father, his back to me, hands clasped together on the top of his head as if to ward off blows; and Peach, staring straight at me. I marveled at the contrasting colors of her face: stark white along the jaw line and forehead, still pink where she'd applied her blusher, grayish in the hollows of her eyes, where her mascara had started to flake and her eyeliner melted onto her skin. Then the colors began to run together and the contrast blurred into a mud-colored slurry, like sidewalk chalk in a rainstorm. There was nothing to do then, but to run and slam and fling and cry and to recall later that hers seemed to be the only dry eyes in the house.

Come spring, Jamie had called a time or two, his voice stiff and formal, inviting me along on bike rides and a trip to a museum, which I politely declined, pleading too much homework, too much housework. Algebra. Laundry.

We'd settled into a routine, my father and I, much like that last year my mother had spent in her twilight, undead, fugue state. We cooked, cleaned, went to work, went to school. He finally traded in the Malibu and went back to a Ford. He opted for day shift at the mill so he could be home in the evenings, although he spent more time interacting with the TV and his glass of Stoli and 7-Up than he did with me. Occasionally he rose to the challenge of fatherhood: grounding me for mouthing off at school, praising the A's and honors that I still managed to bring home, teaching me how to play Poker and Gin Rummy and Solitaire, especially Solitaire.

For me, schoolwork was my Stoli, my refuge, something in which to lose myself, something to keep other thoughts at bay. Mathematics makes sense; there is an order there, a logic which provides a focus, a discipline, for the brain. Elementary algebra is not random. Even with variables, the world is explicable, orderly. Numbers do not drown; polynomials do not kill themselves by breathing in carbon monoxide fumes. Everything makes sense and flows from and follows rules. The operation of addition has an inverse operation called subtraction, which is the same as adding a negative number. The operation of multiplication means repeated addition, and it has an inverse operation called division that follows a pattern for all numbers other than zero. Multiplication distributes over addition: $(a + b)c = ac + bc$; and can be abbreviated by juxtaposition: $a \times b \equiv ab$. This is all true. It simply *is*. The brain and hand work together to solve an equation, which is the claim that two expressions are equal. All one needs to do is prove it—by following the rules. Some equations are true for all values of the variables (such as $a + b = b + a$); such equations are called identities. They do not change on a whim, on a chemical imbalance, in the face of a trauma. This is again true. It simply *is*. All of this I could do—and do—and do—and not think about anything but the fact that I would be

Joanne Zienty

able to find the number, the solution, if I worked long and hard enough. Even the language of mathematics was calming: "rational expressions" and "functions" and "systems of equations." Rational. Systematic. Unlike life outside of mathematics.

Oh, English was easy, too. More subjective, perhaps, but still comprehensible, and conforming to a certain pattern. Exposition, rising action, climax, falling action, conclusion (or, if you're feeling pretentious, *denouement*). Every piece of writing we read followed the stages of plot development. Read a novel, a short story, a play. *The Diary of Anne Frank*? Listen to what the teacher is emphasizing by the tone of her voice and the lift of an eyebrow. *The Lottery*? Figure out what the teacher believes is the significance of the theme and the characterizations. Repeat this back using your own words. *The Tell-tale Heart*? Write three pages of what she wants to hear about method and madness. Read a poem. Look for imagery, simile, metaphor. Take in what she says and spit it back out again with a slightly different twist. And so on and so forth in the other disciplines; in science and social studies and art and music: nothing at all about you, everything about them.

Because then the world can still revolve and make a modicum of sense.

The graduation party was just another thing to get over with. It was hot, too hot for early June, and sticky humid; the air hung in your face like a damp, mildewed curtain. In my rattiest pair of cut-offs and a T-shirt that was just this side of the rag pile, I took the obligatory pass through Sophie's house from living room to kitchen and back out again, and then plunked myself down in the middle of the front porch swing and refused to budge. Aunt Dodie hovered behind the screen door and ventured that she could use some help in the kitchen. I kept my eyes fixed on a point in the opposite direction. Jamie was doing enough moving for the both of us. Something was crackling between us—the few words we spoke to each other snapped and stung like static shock. Maybe he felt the zap, too. Maybe that was why he couldn't sit still.

Finally he tried to pull out the burr that had been stuck in his ass and settle in.

"I forgive you for what you said to my mother."

My snort was deep and vulgar. "I didn't hear myself ask for your forgiveness. Or anybody else's, for that matter. And I'm not apologizing."

That sent him walking up and down the block. Every time he passed the house, he eyed me furtively from under his flowing hair and lowered brow. I fixed a stare on him and he'd turn his head, as if casually checking out the action on the other side of the street.

Guess who cracked open a beer the minute we set foot in Sophie's house and drank steadily all afternoon? By the time the meal was ready he was one churlish, exhausted sprinter lugging in toward the rail and looking too hard for the wire, baring his teeth at anyone who had the nerve to try to rein him in. Even the food was too heavy and boiled: hot lasagna in a tin foil pan where a cold pasta salad should have been, a bowl of mashed potatoes where chips would have sufficed.

Putting my plate aside on the wide porch rail after just a bite or two, I sat stone-faced, nursing a lemonade, watching as a wasp hovered over the chicken drumstick and biscuit, its wings vibrating so fast they seemed motionless, gossamer petals hanging in the air. Then it landed on a mound of melting green Jell-O mold and proceeded to feed.

The village drunkard stumbled out through the screen door, followed by Jimmie, who, for once, had climbed out from behind the piano. Sweat, probably 100 proof, trickled down my father's temples, pooling in his ears and at the corners of his eyes and nose and mouth.

"Who the hell are you to tell me enough's enough?"

"Your brother, man."

My father slammed his hands down on the porch rail, oblivious to me and his sisters, who had ensconced themselves, the better to keep an eye on me, in lawn chairs over on the opposite corner of the porch. He was oblivious to them all: the clusters of cousins who lounged under the canopy in the side yard; Sophie, who sat in her chair in front of the window, a fan at her feet; the husbands who bent over the cooler helping themselves to another cold one; Peach, a ghost image in white behind the gray mesh of the screendoor.

"Brother, little brother. You been chasing after me since before you could walk. You were crawling after me. You're still doing it." He may have been drunk, but he spat his words out with a laser-like accuracy, without a slur to soften their knife-sharp edges or their venom sting.

Jimmie's smile was tenuous, sad. "That's right. All those 'couldn'ts' you like to remind me about. Yeah, so I'm asking you to slow down again, so I can catch up." He put a hand on his brother's shoulder. My father jerked away as if scalded and lurched over to my side of the porch.

"Dad?" I offered, hesitantly.

He was unseeing, unsteady, and grabbed hold of the railing to keep his balance. It shuddered under the violence of his grip. So did my plate. The jarring movement startled the wasp. Its sleek body rose with a whispery buzz, levitated a moment, then settled back down on the Jell-O.

"Never will, that's the thing," he muttered. "Never will catch up. So stop trying. Stop following, period."

Jimmie's faced was still creased with that little smile. "You're my older brother, Joe. I've got no choice but to follow."

My father may have been heedless of his family, but they watched him with fascination; a nasty, heady concoction mixing consternation, anticipation and half-suppressed glee, spiked with just the barest pinch of sympathy. The women concentrated on balancing their plates on their knees and bringing their loaded forks to their mouths without losing a shred of cole slaw or a single green pea from their seven-layer salads, dabbing their lips with their paper napkins, keeping their heads down while their eyes ping-ponged, surreptitiously shifting their collective gaze from the food to my father and back again. The men didn't bother with discretion, but just stared as they chewed, smirks settling around their lips as they swallowed. Around their eyes there may have been just a touch of the *there-but-for-the-grace-of-God* squint. The younger kids tumbled about the yard, their half-eaten food long since abandoned, unaware of the drama playing itself out upon the front porch stage. The older ones, sensing the potential for some R-rated action in this hum-drum domestic event—*swears! insults! violence!* lit up on some imaginary marquee inside their heads—idled in the gangway or near the front stoop, leaning into each other, whispering and leering metallic grins.

"Brother. My brother. That is the problem. Houston, we have a problem. A big fucking problem."

"Language, Joe," chided Jimmie, warily crossing to stand just behind him. "Come on, let's go back in the house, get you some ice water, coffee."

"You're gonna get me somethin'?"

"Yeah, whatever you want, Joe, except booze."

"You're gonna get *me* something?" my father repeated, with a slightly different emphasis.

Jamie had made his way back down the block. This time, seeing his father, he stopped in front of the house where the sidewalk met the path to the porch steps. My father must have caught that motion and its cessation out the corner of his eye. He stared out at Jamie and his grip tightened on the porch rail, his knuckles raw white.

"How 'bout a son? You get me one of those?" he sneered, menace lurking behind the absurdity.

Jimmie's stomach contracted as if punched by an invisible hand. "Joe—"

"Naw, you're not the man to ask…" My father brought his hand up to his face and pressed it over his mouth, squeezing the bones of his jaw, as if to stop the words from spewing out.

Peach called out softly from behind the screen door. "Jimmie, Joe, come inside."

"Dad?" Jamie ventured from his spot on the sidewalk, his face taut with confusion.

Jimmie motioned for him to stay put.

"Get me something," my father whispered, as if to himself. "A wife? Nope, not the man to ask…"

He brought his hand down hard on the railing, just beyond the rim of my plate. The concussion sent it toppling over the side, startling the feeding wasp, which zigzagged for a split second before diving in for my father's flailing hand. It all seemed like some nasty, large-scale Rube Goldberg machine: the wasp stings the father who lets out a bray, which causes the brother to touch his arm, which causes the father to swing a fist, which connects with the brother's cheek with a sickening thwuck, which staggers the brother, which brings the son running and the wife slamming out of the screen door, which bashes into the two sisters on their way in, which causes them to drop their plates, while the brother lurches forward with his own closed fist, which lands squarely in the eye of his fraternal tormentor, whose head snaps back against the corner beam, and he struggles to keep his footing, but he must be seeing some spectacular fireworks shooting off behind his eyes…

As he slowly slides down and lands on his ass in the corner.

I should have been the first to get to him, crumpled there like something used up and thrown away. I should have been the first to touch his knee and shoulder; the one to lift his chin with a trembling hand and bring my face in close to examine the eye that was swelling up fast. It should have been my fingers that parted the black hair on the back of his head to check if the skin had split open. But in that instant when time seemed suspended, the restraining hands of Aunt Dodie, which perhaps meant to comfort but could only afflict, held me back and it was Peach who reached him first.

As she knelt before him, she glanced over her shoulder and a look passed between her and Jimmie. Reading that look was like trying to read a foreign language: most of what was there on the page was indecipherable. The most obvious meanings were recognizable: something akin to disappointment, something close to pity. Yet there were phrases and emotions there which required a translation that I lacked. Wrenching free of Dodie's grip, I slipped my arm around my father's shoulders.

"You okay, Dad?"

He grunted.

"Go get some ice," Peach commanded, her fingers tracing the line of his eyebrow. The left eye was puffing up so quickly only the barest slit separated the upper and lower lids.

"Jamie can get it." I shifted to my right, almost knocking her off balance.

She blinked and frowned at this unexpected retort, perhaps weighing if my jolt was intentional, and then turned to Jamie. "Ice in a washcloth, go on."

It was then I became aware of the silence, a previously unknown commodity at these gatherings. It wasn't a soothing silence, this absence of yammer and yakkety-yak. It was intrusive, prying. You can lose yourself in high-decibel chatter, can feel a certain, comfortable anonymity encompassed in the buzz. But kneeling in the midst of this hush was like kneeling in the glare of a white-hot spotlight with your acne and underwear showing, where anonymity turned to notoriety with one false step or look or word. Peach must have sensed it too, because she rolled her eyes and flicked a dismissive gesture to her husband.

"This town needs a sheriff," she muttered so that only the four of us could hear.

He nodded, and then circled the porch, making shooing, move-it-along gestures with his hands.

"Well, as they say, show's over, folks. Wasn't much to see in the first place. Just a brotherly misunderstanding." He opened the screen door and ushered his sisters inside. "Ain't it time to set out the desserts, gals?" He yelled over the porch rail to the canopy crowd. "I know for a fact that there's cheesecake, lemon meringue pie and a couple dozen chocolate chip cookies, as well as a tub of fudge ripple ice cream sitting in the kitchen just waiting for the locusts to descend."

The kids fell for his enticements and trooped off to the back door. The men didn't take the bait, but they eased back into their lawn chairs and the small talk hummed again, filling the void.

Jamie came out with the makeshift ice pack, the cubes wrapped in the same sad, gray washcloth Peach had applied to my own face back in November. She pressed it gently against my father's now gruesome eye.

"I'll do that." My hand tried to nudge her aside.

"Stop your nonsense. You're gonna hurt him more with your jostling. He could probably use some more ice for his hand."

A small pink welt was blossoming where the wasp had stung.

"I'll take care of him. He's my father."

She glanced at Jamie. "Hon, would you please get another cube for your poor uncle's hand?" She raked a look over me like I was a patch of the poorest, most unproductive soil she had ever seen, a look that asked how she could ever have thought I had possibilities, a look that said I was unworthy of her attention. In that small space between her eyes and mine, I suddenly became aware of the sharp odor of my unwashed hair, the tang of my sweat, the smell of my breath. I saw the frayed hem of my T-shirt, the grease stain on my cut-offs, the hairs growing on my knees where I had neglected to shave. I felt the tickle of the hole under my armpit, the burn of the hangnail gaping on my thumb, and the throb of a pimple growing on my chin.

In that moment, in that space, I truly was my mother's daughter.

How could I ever have been so mistaken? The revelation came and went in the snap of Peach's fingers in front of my nose.

"You'll take care of him? What a joke. Look at him. Look at yourself. You're doing a piss-poor job of it. I know you didn't ask to be put in this position. I know it's hard, probably the toughest thing anyone's asked to do. But you've got to rise to meet it, girl. That's what a real woman does. She doesn't just lie there and let herself get buried under all the crap she gets hit with—a real woman doesn't give up. She *gets* up and deals with it, with some spunk, some *savoir faire*. I thought you had it in you. I thought you knew better—than this." She ran her eyes over my barren ground once more, then turned back to my father.

"Joe, Joe, what are we gonna do with you?"

"Don't trouble yourself. You'll get that get-up all dirty," he mumbled, raising a shaky hand to try to fend her off.

"Well, now, if you were bleeding like a stuck pig, I might think twice, but there doesn't appear to be a major blood loss. Now, sanity—that's another thing altogether."

A grim smile struggled to stretch out across his face. He fought it, trying to keep his lips sullenly slack, but finally he gave in and let it light up his mulish face like a ray of stark, white sunlight piercing the gloom of shifting gray clouds.

Jamie returned with more ice wrapped in a napkin, which he held out to me. When I ignored it, stumbling back to my seat on the porch swing, he bent down and applied it to the wasp sting himself.

"Hon, help me get this man to his feet."

The two of them flung his arms over their shoulders and hoisted him up clumsily, with much huffing and heaveho-ing. Jimmie came out with a plastic tumbler full of ice water, which my father took with a curt nod of thanks, his eyes lowered.

"Let's you and me go for a walk," Peach murmured, after he'd drained the glass and started crunching on the cubes.

"I'll take him," Jimmie offered, but with a shake of her head, Peach slipped her arm around my father's.

"I think it'd be best if I went," she said with a calm, quiet insistence, throwing another one of those indecipherable looks at her husband.

I think she half expected me to try and tag along because she shot me an arrow of a glance as well, although this one's meaning was perfectly clear: you're not welcome. She needn't have made the effort. I was curled back into myself on the porch swing, knees to chest, arms tight around them, chin resting on knobby bone. I could have been difficult, could have argued, could have haunted their steps like a doppelganger. Minutes before, I would have.

When I was a child, I spoke as a child, I understood as a child, I thought as a child...

But now, in the split-second hereafter, I could wait.

When I became a woman, I put away childish things...

So I sat and watched them make their way up the block until they passed beyond my view, my father pressing the washcloth to his eye, wobbly as a toddler. And then I waited. Jamie perched on the edge of the swing, unsure of how close to me he wanted to get, unsure of how close I would let him come. Uncle Jimmie sat on the top stair, picking fitfully at his slice of cheesecake.

When they came back into view, just around the fringe of the boxwood hedge that grew three doors down, my father looked steadier on his feet. His head was bent and he was listening intently to whatever Peach was saying. Her lips moved slowly, deliberately. She seemed to be enunciating her words carefully, precisely, and ticking off some list on her fingers. They passed the house and continued on down to the other end of the block. By the time they returned again, they were practically sauntering, just a couple out for a stroll on a summer Sunday afternoon.

What lay beneath the calm surface of their faces, the masks they wore? The sheepishness clouding my dad's eyes when he passed Jimmie on the steps and tousled his hair like you would a child—what was that hiding? Was that supposed to pass for a proper apology? The dismissive roll of the eyes that Peach flashed for Jimmie when she saw that gesture and the soft, leisurely kiss that she planted on her husband's cheek when she sidled down next to him on the step—what did that conceal?

She ate a bite of cheesecake from his fork, her lips lingering along the tines.

Jesus. I'd been at war with the wrong woman. I'd been an ally on the wrong side. Frolicking with the enemy. The realization, and the shame that came with it, burned hot on my face, like the wind out of the southwest in mid-July. But I noted with a peculiar pride that this same heat kept my eyes dry, like the sockets of a skull in the desert.

My mother had lost the battle. I vowed to win the war.

CHAPTER 17

The vodka bottle was the first casualty. I poured its clear, bracing contents down our kitchen sink drain as my father sat at the table, cradling his pounding head in his hands.

"You should watch this." He just moved his head a fraction of an inch from side to side. His shoulders shuddered at the finality of the thud as it hit the bottom of the garbage can.

"If you bring more home, I'll do the same with them," I threatened, hands on my hips, chin thrust forward, an apprentice Amazon, ready for action.

He started to mumble something—an apology, an explanation, a pledge to reform—but I cut him off in one clean stroke.

"Don't tell me—you can say anything! Show me!" I stalked out of the kitchen and, though it was late in the afternoon, too late in one sense and too early in another, I showered.

Afterwards I lay on my bed in the steam sauna that was my room, watching the thunderheads roil and build in the west, plotting strategy.

She was a formidable foe, this I knew. What I couldn't be sure of was the extent of her encroachment on my territory. Had my mother been correct? Had this interloper seized a portion of my dad's heart? If so, to what extent and how strong was her hold? Was it a flirtatious, temporary incursion or a full-fledged occupation? And what was her intent? Was she merely collecting hearts for snicks and grins, to dangle for her amusement and vanity like charms on a bracelet? Or did she envision an eventual total conquest?

My plan of attack would vary, depending upon reconnaissance, but I prepared for the worst-case scenario, adopting a scorched-earth, take-no-prisoners, war policy. I would launch an assault on two fronts: in my home and in hers. I considered the moves I might make and her possible parries, as we glided like two queens over a life-sized chess board.

Even then I realized that Jamie would be the pawn.

To defeat an opponent, you have to put yourself in her shoes, both figuratively and literally. Peach outwardly had always professed a longing to give me a makeover, to buy me some 'glad rags,' as she put it. *What was she tripping on? Old Rod Stewart songs?* While my mother lived, she could never do it without implying a certain lack of taste on her sister-in-law's part and committing an outright usurpation of motherly duties. Now that my mother was out the way, she could step in and appear magnanimous with her guiding hand. But perhaps she secretly preferred me in the guise of an ugly duckling. That left her the only swan in town, with the most photogenic offspring to boot. *So confound her then, defy both her faces.*

It started with contact lenses, continued with a new wardrobe of tight, flared Dittos jeans, clingier tops and Candies platforms, and included a painful period of recovery after an ear piercing session involving an ice cube, a match, a sharp needle and a length of black thread, which resulted in infected lobes. *("You musta let 'em get dirty," Lori accused, refusing to accept any responsibility. "Didn't happen to me.")* When my wounds finally healed, the small gold hoops that my father bought me looked fabulous dangling from my ears, shooting sparks when hit by light. They felt exotic against my skin, like cool, hard feathers, stiffly sensual.

Then there was my face. Like Cleopatra and Elizabeth the First, Mata Hari and Elizabeth Taylor, Julie Christie and Farrah Fawcett-Majors and millions of females in between, famous and anonymous, I chose to paint it. With the experienced hand of

Lori guiding me, like an Avon lady in training, up and down the aisles of Walgreens, I waded into the vast and wondrous ocean of femininity: a throbbing sea of sights and scents, delicately floral and invigoratingly spicy; glamour, glitz and promises poured and pressed into tiny bottles and tubes and tins, lined neatly on bracketed shelves and hung from hooks for our purchasing convenience. My journey through the waters of womanly transformation ended with a drawer full of drugstore cosmetics: Maybelline blackest black mascara, thick and waxy on the bristles of its wand; Cover Girl blush, silk in powder form, in pinks and peaches; fruit-flavored lipsticks and glosses by Bonne Bell, a slick, sugary goo. I could have painted a rainbow between my lashes and brows with all the little compacts of eye shadow I bought. Spring greens and baby blues turned out to be highly unflattering, pushing me over the sweetly sexy borderline into skanky rock groupie territory ala Lady Marmalade. (*"Voulez-vous coucher avec moi?"*) Violets opened up my brown eyes and made me looker slightly older, in wholesome, Karen Carpenter sort of way. (*"Mysterious," Lori opined. "Long ago, and oh so far away..."*) Taupes and browns, on the other hand, were boringly mature. (*"Like yer going to the office, eeew," was Lori's judgment as she shook her head.*) Glittery pinks and bronzes made me feel like a back-up singer left over from David Bowie's Ziggy Stardust tour. (*"Awww, wham-bam, thank you ma'am!"*)

Being glamorous wasn't easy. But the ceremonial aspects of the process gave me the feeling that I was practicing some form of hyper-feminine witchcraft handed down from generation to generation, from one true woman to another. It was a sorcery to luxuriate in, a voluptuous voodoo ritual in the silken charm of drawing the kitten soft brush of shadow or blusher across my eyelids or over the apples of my cheeks. Application was the act of casting a spell. Too little—and the desired effect was too weak to take hold. Too much—and instead of turning into the enchantress Circe, you wound up the Gorgon Medusa, turning your own body to stone as you stared at your hideous reflection in the vanity mirror.

I wanted a natural-looking beauty, a look that Mademoiselle and Glamour magazines promised I could achieve in just five minutes if I followed their quick and easy grooming regimen. However, natural beauty, which encompassed attire, make-up, scent and hair, was impossible to produce in anything less than half an hour, particularly if the mascara clumped, as it often did, coagulating my lashes into three or four thick, goopy, ridiculous uni-lashes, which no amount of coaxing with a brow brush could separate. The only option was eradicate the mess with a fistful of cotton balls soaked in make-up remover and start over. But no matter how time-consuming, it was a magic worth perfecting because it gave me power. The power that Peach had been wielding all those years. The power of thrall.

I noticed it in the boys when school started in September. The queasiness and doubt that I felt as a freshman, the lowest peg on the high school totem pole, wading through streams of unfamiliar faces down unfamiliar halls, were hidden behind my enchanted façade, beneath the charms and potions on my skin. Freshman boys, scrawny and cowed by the abrupt deterioration in their status, having gone from being the kings of elementary school to the abused serfs of secondary education, looked longingly as I and my coterie of friends passed, swathed in a perfumed haze of Jovan Musk. Sophomores were bolder, venturing low whistles, chatting us up between classes, leaning casually against the lockers next to ours, their eyes traveling surreptitiously over our bodies, while ours flitted back and forth from the textbooks hugged tightly against our burgeoning chests to their angular faces, counting the zits erupting in glorious pink and yellow there. We didn't rate more than a glance or two from the juniors and seniors—yet. But we smiled behind our folders, knowing our time would come.

We were young lionesses, pretending to be at ease in our skin, even as our bodies surprised us, confused us: hardening and softening; stretching and tightening; shrinking and expanding all at once. Our lifeline in that vortex of confounding, frightening change was our belief in the power of thrall.

I noticed it in my father, in the way he looked at me as if catching sight of me for the first time. He'd come upon me studying and I'd glance up from my book with a smile, to find him standing there, looking a little shaky on his feet, with a wide-eyed look of astonishment on his face, his forehead creased with befuddlement, as if he'd come looking for one thing and found something quite different from what he'd expected.

He promised to stay on the wagon and I held him to his word. If he came home late from work, even by the narrowest of margins, I'd give him the smell test disguised as a hug. An embrace and a quick, unobtrusive sniff reassured me he was toeing the line. Part of me longed to trust him completely, the part that was still a little girl. The wiser part of me, the woman part, knew better and understood that eternal vigilance was the price of many things, not just liberty. I still wanted to believe the best of him, particularly now that I thought I had seen the worst. Because now that I had, we could move on, together.

He asked me one day, awkwardly shuffling his feet, if we needed to have a talk about boys. I glanced up from my polynomials and grinned quizzically.

"Right now, I'd rather talk about quadratic equations."

He rolled his eyes and held up his hands. "I can't help you there. But boys, that's a subject I know so—"

"Look, I know all about the behavior of the male of the species—just from watching you all these years."

His face reddened as he shoved his hands in his pockets and commenced to jingling. His grimace spoke the unspoken words of doubt and remorse. "That's what worries me."

"I still believe the best of you."

Emotions scudded over his face like fast moving clouds: confusion, recollection, shame, determination. He nodded more to himself than to me. Turning back to my equations, I pondered the one I was currently working on: beauty to the second power, plus three times the intelligence, plus two times the wit, plus acceptance equals the perfect daughter, the shining star that would blind him to all others.

Jamie was another story, a tough customer who didn't easily fall under the spell of thrall. Perhaps he'd lived with it in his own house for so long that he had developed an immunity. Jefferson High was a big school, both in number of students and physical size. It was a sprawling, tan brick building built in the early 60's to accommodate the baby boom and neighborhood growth. All those steel mill families, eastern European stock, breeding like rats. And then the Mexican immigrants followed. The neighborhoods were lousy with kids. So English, second period, was the sole class that we shared. I wasn't sure he even recognized me that first day. He sat in the far corner in the back row; I sat on the opposite side of the room near the front. The bracing, industrial smells of glass cleaner and floor wax kept us alert, even through Mrs. Leary's droning of the standard first day spiel about rules and procedures, textbooks and required reading, goals and expectations and the far-too-detailed overview of her syllabus for the semester. When the bell rang, we bolted to the accompaniment of scrapes and squeaks of chair legs over the freshly polished tile floor.

I was halfway down the hall to my next class when I heard my name called from somewhere close. He was right there, a half step behind me.

"Wasn't sure it was really you," he puffed, falling into stride beside me. "What's with the war paint? I didn't think you were into that crap."

I kept my eyes on the hordes through which we were dodging. "Whatever happened to 'hey, what's happening?'" I turned into my classroom with just the barest hint of a glance over my shoulder.

At lunch, I plopped down amongst the clique, whose members were all swathed in the intense scent of freshly applied musk. Scanning the cafeteria, I located him off in a corner, in animated conversation with a wiry boy with droopy eyelids and hair the indistinct color of straw after a long winter lying afield. I stared at him, silently willing him to glance my way, the old Vulcan mind meld technique, but when he finally did, giving me a little grin and nod, I coolly shifted my gaze back to my tablemates, joining my laughter with theirs, though I hadn't the slightest idea what they were laughing about. The goal was to maintain a façade of nonchalance, despite the voice inside that insinuated I'd be having more fun sitting with him.

"Isn't that your cousin over there—in the corner, with Kevin Straszewski?" Lori bleated, licking jelly from her fingers.

I dipped my chin, the most perfunctory of nods.

"He's kinda cute. Is he going with anyone?"

"No clue."

"Too bad he's a freshman. And Kevin—I'm not sure he even knows how to talk yet. To girls, anyway." She and the others tittered and turned away to scope out more promising boyfriend material. My eyes strayed back to the corner.

Tomboy girl, all dressed up with your scabby knees hidden under a skin of blue denim, but your scabby nature still shows through. Wrong, wrong, everything's wrong, but you pretend it feels all right. You'd prefer the wind in your hair to these ribbons taming you, containing you, bending you into a different shape, a smaller space, hobbling you…

…til you are less than half of what you started out as—like the foot of an ancient Chinese concubine—beautiful and perfect on the surface of its tiny silken shoe, deformed and useless underneath.

A bite of apple, a flick of hair over my shoulder, a spritz of eau de cologne back at my locker scattered those thoughts and held them at bay until the next time I passed him in the halls or sat in front of him in English class or sensed him watching me from across the cafeteria. When the push and pull became intolerable, I knew that it was time to cut the invisible cord that held us together, sever the ties of childhood, come what may.

I gave back the Claddagh ring.

He glanced from me to the ring in his palm and back to me, in the slightly slack-jawed way of adolescent boys.

"You'll be wanting to give that to someone else soon—and I wouldn't want you to be embarrassed about having to ask me for it. So I'm returning it now. Ahead of time."

He squinted in confusion, as if my words were a murky pool through which he just couldn't see.

"Your mom'll feel better about it, too."

269

I turned to walk away, but he caught hold of my arm.

"This was a gift. I'm not asking for it back."

"I know you're not. Right now," I said slowly, enunciating carefully, as if talking to a small child or a foreigner with little grasp of the English language. "But some day you'll want it back. You'll be kicking yourself, saying 'why did I give that ring to my silly old cousin, when I could be giving it to'—oh, I don't know, let's call her 'Cathy.' This saves us both a lot of hassle. Now you'll be able to give it to Cathy."

He swallowed hard. "There is no Cathy." He didn't seem to catch my drift.

"But there will be. Or maybe her name will be Laura or Susan or Jennifer. I don't know—I'm not a psychic. I'm just thinking ahead."

"There is no Cathy," he repeated dumbly.

Your lips are the color of Bazooka bubblegum and just as thick and sweet and juicy—if I could only taste them now, candy boy, and only inches away, if I could only just take my tongue and—

"Jesus, just stick the damn ring in your pocket and take it home." I jerked my arm out of his grasp, turned on my heel and stalked off, biting down ferociously on my lips, tasting the warm, salty blood, hearing him call after my retreating back.

"There is no Cathy."

But you are Heathcliff—and so I am.

Okay, so it was a calculated risk on my part. I handed it to him on the Friday before Christmas break, fully aware that I would encounter him at Sophie's for the holiday get-together. We circled around like wary cats that day. If he came into the front room, I moved to the kitchen. When he sat down with the poker players to eat, I perched on a footstool next to Sophie, merely picking at my own plate.

"Where is your tail?" she croaked, blue eyes glinting between their heavy folds of skin, like the flash of embers buried in ash.

"My tail?"

As she nodded, her jowls shuddered. "You the cat, Jamie the tail. Always like this." She held up two wrinkled fingers together. "Today, the cat is here," she moved one finger to the right arm

270

of her chair, "and the tail is here," she moved the second finger to the left. "Why is that?"

"We grew out of that kind of thing."

Her eyes sparked again and a smile puckered her sagging cheeks. "A cat grow out of its tail? A tail grow out of its cat?" She shook her head, sending her jowls wriggling again. "No, no. One needs the other." She brought her fingers back together.

I rolled my eyes. "I'm sure a cat can live without its tail. Manx cats are born without them."

"A cat without a tail," she shrugged. "Yes, but only half the cat it should be. And a tail without a cat?" She raised her wizened gray eyebrows and slowly drew a finger across the wattle of her neck.

Jamie didn't look anything like a lifeless length of fur and bone. He'd brought his guitar along and, now that he was done eating, was strumming chord progressions off in the corner, looking totally absorbed and happy in his skin.

"The cat-less tail looks fine, Grandma." I kissed her papery cheek and moved off in search of bigger game.

I had thought that Peach would be the wariest, the most elusive of my quarry, that her feminine intuition and intimate understanding of female wiles would have inoculated her against their use by others, but apparently subtle flattery and imitation can conquer all because she took one look at me in my black Bobbie Brooks slacks and my white velveteen sweater, at my carefully painted face and nails, at the gold hoops dangling from my ears, and heaved a sigh of conspicuous surrender and approval.

"Well, just look at you, sugah." She took my hand and drew me into the dining room where the feast was slowly being disassembled. She didn't seem to hold a grudge, commenting that I obviously didn't need anyone's help choosing a wardrobe, that I had my own certain something—*je ne sais quoi*. She asked about school, about boys, about how we were doing at home. Through it all, I smiled and nodded, smiled and nodded, uttering minimalist replies which she could interpret as the natural reticence of a fourteen-year-old girl, a contrite girl who has seen the error of her ways and who wears her apology unspoken, on her body.

As the other aunts began to hustle back and forth between the kitchen and the dining room at an accelerated pace, bearing platters and tins of desserts, eyeing our idle hands resentfully, she slipped her arm around mine and gave me a conspiratorial wink, as if to say, *'you and I were meant for better places and far better occupations.'* She guided me down the hall and into one of the spare rooms where coats lay slumped across the twin bed and a few wrapped presents were stacked behind the door.

Taking both of my hot, damp hands in her cool, dry ones, she looked earnestly into my eyes. "I know you gave back the Claddagh ring. Jamie told me. He tells me everything, the dear boy. I just want you to know that you absolutely did the right thing. I'm not sure he quite understands. You know, us girls mature much earlier and we are so much more in tune to these matters." She punctuated her remarks with an arch of her brows and a flutter of eyelashes. "Men, even grown men, can be so obtuse about these things. I confess, I probably am at fault for letting him give it to you in the first place—but it was such a cute, sweet thing to do. It's always been more than just a crush with him. However, now that you're older and being what you are to each other, well…" she blushed a most feminine petal pink that contrasted beautifully with her swimming pool blue eyes. "You both need to channel that affection elsewhere."

The further down the path of explanation she trod, the less sure-footed she seemed, as if she had only marked the trail so far, expecting to stop at some pre-determined point. I just stood, mouth closed, gazing attentively, focused on her as if she was the fount of all womanly wisdom and I was the parched traveler aching to quench my ignorant thirst. So she floundered onward, attempting to live up to my expectations.

"Of course, you can still be affectionate—as cousins—but that—special kind—of affection…" Her eyes veered away from mine, to the door, to the stack of presents, to the bed. "Well, you know what I mean." The pitch of her voice rose with tinge of exasperation, as if she was waiting for me to cut her off, hoping I would cut her off, with adolescent squeamishness.

"Sex." My utterance snapped her eyes back to mine like metal to a magnet.

"Not in so many words," she stuttered. "I mean, romance, flirting, dating—all the wonderful things that come before."

"Before sex?"

She cupped my chin in her hand, her eyes now the wintry blue of a January sky. "Way before."

She peered into my blank slate of a face and I saw for the first time an off-kilter Peach, a Peach unsteady on her feet, teetering like a woman unsure of her stiletto heels. Was that a chink in her invisible armor?

Now to exploit it, to break it open, lay bare her vulnerable underbelly—and then go in for the kill.

She turned from me, fumbled with her coat and purse on the bed, and then faced me again, holding out a thick, rectangular package wrapped in red and green plaid Christmas foil and graced with a hand-tied gold fabric bow. I took it, marveling in spite of myself at its weight.

"I wasn't sure whether to wrap a hand-me-down or not," she said cryptically.

Curiosity overcame resistance. I eased the bow off and ripped the paper open. The hand-me-down was a copy of Bartlett's Familiar Quotations.

"The wisdom of the ages pressed between two covers. Along with some of my own annotations." She patted the book and then pressed her palm to my cheek, leveling those eyes at mine. "I know I can't be your mother, but I wish you'd let me be your friend."

I flipped through the pages of the reference. A number of them had notes written in the margins in a neat, fluid cursive. Next to a quote from Mary Wollstonecraft: "It would be an endless task to trace the variety of meanesses, cares and sorrows into which women are plunged by the prevailing opinion that they were created rather to feel than reason, and that all the power they obtain must be obtained by their charms and weakness..." was the comment "*What's important is the power—not how it is obtained!*" Scribbled under the Kipling quip: "The female of the species is more deadly than the male" were three words in red: "*She'd better be!!!*"

I snapped the book shut, grinning. "I love quotes! You know, I was at my friend Lori's house one time, and we pulled this same book down from the shelf to look something up—and you'll never guess what was hidden behind it." I paused dramatically, as if waiting for her to take a guess.

She just stared, looking flummoxed.

I leaned in and lowered my voice to a whisper. "The Sensuous Woman by J. Talk about the wisdom of the world between two covers." I tucked the book under my arm. "But thanks. I'm sure I'll get a kick out reading this, too."

I don't believe I ever saw her that pale, like a magnolia in the moonlight, indeed.

CHAPTER 18

1976—the 200th anniversary of the birth of our country. *Hoo ha.* But before the party, we had to get through another winter. January, February, and March slogged along under layers of dirty snow pitted and pockmarked by rock salt sprayed up from the wheels of passing cars. The salt dulled the black asphalt in parking lots, leaving zigs and zags of crusty white etchings. It ate away at the street pavement, gnawing cracks here and gaping holes there, which lay in wait to swallow the wheels of cars and the feet of unobservant pedestrians. For days upon weeks, the sky was a low gray ceiling breeding claustrophobia and drooping shoulders, bleeding color from the bricks of buildings. Even my skin looked gray.

Jamie and I had not yet reached a rapprochement. Our only conversation occurred in the context of our English class, and even that was under duress, when we were thrown together for some group activity. We pointedly kept our eyes focused elsewhere if we had to share a literature circle: on the clock, out the windows, on the words which swam on the page—anywhere but each other. Once, when the sides of our fingers accidentally brushed as we reached simultaneously for the dictionary in the middle of our table, we both jerked away as if zapped by a thousand volts of current. He pushed the book toward me; I nudged it back to the middle and we both struggled to decipher the meanings of words from the context of the sentences we were reading.

He watched me in the cafeteria, leaning back, one heel resting on the edge of his chair, hands clasped behind his head, in that studied, practiced pose of self-conscious cool. He'd scan and pan like a movie camera, jutting his chin out to direct his straw-haired buddy's attention to the daily pratfall that some unfortunate nerd would take when the soles of his shoes met spilled milk or a dropped pat of margarine or the infamous cubes of strategically planted Jell-O. His eyes might stray to the squad of freshman cheerleaders who giggled just a little louder than everyone else— in unison—and who would invariably pop up out of their seats as if about to commence a pep routine—*we are the Trojans, the mighty, mighty Trojans*—before heading for the bathroom together. But I know his eyes found their way back to me. I know because I watched him, too.

Surreptitiously. Under lowered eyelashes. With corner-of-the-eye stares that gave me headaches.

Sometimes our stares met and glanced off each other to opposite ends of the black and white tile floor, like billiard balls smacking head on and ricocheting to the far corners of a pool table. Either one of us could have broken the impasse, could have stood and walked across the fifty or so feet that divided us, but it felt as if that fifty feet consisted not of tile, but molten lava, impossible to ford.

The spring thaw finally revealed the grass, in all its sickly yellow dismay. Easter in Chicago is often cold and damp, leaving women and children shivering in their light-weight, short-sleeved finery on the way in and out of church. It had been a long time since I had strapped on a pair of Mary Janes and I was ready to break from the tradition of going to Sophie's as well, sick to death of the whole phony routine and the phonies who planned and perpetuated it. That was my new catchphrase after having discovered *The Catcher in the Rye*. Holden Caulfield might have been my brother. But my father insisted, turning it into an issue of respect for one's elders.

"Can we just make an appearance then?" I pleaded. "Eat and run, fast?"

A glaze of civility had hardened over these gatherings, clear, cold and brittle, like the first layer of ice to set over a pond in winter. The rowdy joy of letting it all hang out with people who knew you and didn't seem to care how far it hung, people who loved you in spite of how far it hung, was gone. Had it ever been there in the first place? Maybe it had all been smoke and mirrors, or smoked kielbasa and Schlitz beer.

Recalcitrant contact lens, an eyelash that refused to be fished out of an eye, and a favorite blouse that mysteriously popped two buttons all helped to delay our arrival in purgatory until the approximate moment the ham made its way onto the table. No time wasted in forced chitchat, no awkward wandering through the smog of pity and barely concealed hostility that precipitated out of this mix of strangers bound by blood.

Eat and run, yes, that was the plan.

Leave it to Dougie to spoil it. He was one variable that I failed to factor into the equation. By now we were implacable enemies, a pair of Siamese fighting fish flaring in iridescent anger at the mere sight of each other. Without Jamie to surround me, to contain me like a fishbowl, I was prone to foolishly attack—and vulnerable to a counterattack as well.

He was in the midst of the only group that still seemed boisterous and carefree: the poker players. They were switching back and forth from Draw Poker to Five Card Stud, letting the dealer call the game. Uncle Bob had some rolls of gleaming Bicentennial quarters with the marching drummer on the tails. He was handing them out to all the kids and using them for his antes. He flipped one to me as I passed the card table, as the lord of the manor might toss tuppence to a beggar, but I flipped it right back, saying I already had some.

I paced the long dark hall that afternoon like the big cats at Lincoln Park Zoo paced in their iron-barred cages: from corner to corner, with a rippling tension born of ferocity submerged in boredom. Jamie was holed up on the back porch with his guitar and his cafeteria kimosabe, Kevin. Given his chaff-like head of hair, pale skin and general wasted appearance, I had started referring to him—in my head—as 'Strawboy.' Strawboy had brought his guitar along, too. They were warding off the chill wearing their jean jackets and gloves from which they'd cut the fingers, playing Neil Young songs, mumbling the lyrics, their voices just audible through the closed door.

A look from him, a gesture, the slightest tilt of his head in invitation, and I might have joined him, but he never glanced up through the window, at least not while I paused there on the other side of the door.

What a poser! Just who the hell did he think he was—the next Sweet Baby James? He'd even brought the damn thing to school a couple of times and used it for his demonstration speech in English class: "How to Play a Guitar." What a harem of little groupies he'd had at lunch that day, each with a special request. *Can you play an Eagles song, like 'Best of My Love?' How about Fleetwood Mac? Maybe 'Landslide?''' Do you have an electric guitar, too? Can you play Aerosmith? Dream On?* And he'd pluck out a few bars, just enough to leave them sighing for more and me wanting to alternately vomit and rake my fingernails across their fleshy pink cheeks.

The memory of it made me turn on my heel and walk back up the hall to the living room, where the chink and tinkle of quarters being tossed into the pot punctuated the rhythmical murmur of conversation.

"Whaddya think? Sox going all the way with Veeck this year?"

"All the way to the circus. Man's a clown."

"Nope, he's a showman—a ringmaster."

"Hey, at least they're still in Chicago."

"See ya and raise ya two bits." Metallic tang.

"Shee-it. Too rich for me."

"Here ya go—I call."

"Sumbitch."

My father had been sitting with Sophie since we arrived. He glanced up and gave me a slice of smile. I tapped my wristwatch and raised my eyebrows. He swallowed the smile and his eyes slid away as he turned his attention back to his mother.

Shit.

The configuration of the poker table had changed. Uncle Bob's place was now filled by one of the sons-in-law, whose names always escaped me: Kenny? Keith? Karl? Dougie still hunkered there but then abruptly shoved his chair back from the table.

"Hey, no pay, no play," drawled the K-man, tipping back his Pabst Blue Ribbon. "This kitty don't take IOUs."

Given the look on his red face and the way he clenched his ham-hock fists, I half-expected Dougie to upturn the table in retort, but he just mumbled something about the "goddamn Cosa Nostra," then stalked off down the hall and into the bathroom, slamming the door behind him.

I felt a hand on my elbow.

"Why don't you help us clear and set out dessert?" Aunt Dodie's voice scraped like sandpaper against my ear.

I let her guide me to the dining room where the ritual was underway. I grabbed a bowl of graying mashed potatoes and a platter of grease and made the short walk across the hall to the kitchen, glancing out the back door as I passed. Jamie happened to be looking up and our glances met, blinked and caromed away. On my next pass, I looked in the opposite direction. The hall floor was checkered with rectangles of light cast from the doorways of the room that lined it. As a little girl I used to jump from one patch of light to the next, imagining they were stepping stones across a rushing stream, back in the day when a passage of the hall was an adventure—for who knew what delights were waiting on the dining room table? Now it was all tedium and awkwardness and the knowledge that there was no new dessert under the sun.

On my third trip, I peeked back toward Jamie. He was still looking up, his chin resting on the curve of his guitar, a thoughtful expression on his face. With my fourth pass-through, I turned my head back to the hall. A rectangle of light was missing, the one that would have been made by light cast from the spare bedroom down the hall on the right. Odd. The only door that ever closed in that hall was the bathroom door. Even the door to

Sophie's bedroom always stood wide open, as if the open doors stated we are all family here, what's to hide?

An open door invites the passer-by to walk in, and a closed door invites speculation, but a door that's somewhere in between, a door that's not quite closed, ajar with just a sliver of empty space between its edge and the jamb—that's a door that begs for attention; that entreats the curious to creep up and bring her face as close as possible and peer through that slit of possibilities.

The heavy, four panel door was just barely open and the gap was dark, but as I focused on the sliver and my eye adjusted to the dimness of the interior beyond, I made out a bulky form bent over the bed where everyone threw their coats and the women often deposited their purses. The back of the figure bent and straightened, then bent again, a motion accompanied by rasps and metallic clicks and a papery rustle. A hand of the figure stuffed something into a pants pocket.

I knew it was Dougie.

And I knew what he was doing.

Strange how watching *his* crime made *me* break out in a sweat, cold beads of it strung like pearls along my hairline. Why should that familiar fist be clenching *my* insides when he was the guilty one? He tossed the purse he'd been rifling back on the bed. From its narrow rectangular shape, I recognized it as Peach's robin's egg blue clutch.

It was one thing for Dougie to pilfer money out of his own mother's purse—despicable, rotten, lowdown were adjectives that jumped to mind—but to steal from someone else's mother, from your aunt—that was just plain thuggery.

Before he turned around, I hustled the three or four steps to the bathroom and slipped inside, shutting the door quietly. My smile in the mirror could not have been wider—or more cruel. *Oh, sweet payback.* Big time payback. Payback for all the petty crap over the years and payback for that damn lie about me and Jamie playing doctor and payback even for Uncle Bob's racist jokes and for Aunt Dodie's holier-than-thou-arranged-to-a-T-to-suit-me-and-my-shit-doesn't-stink attitude.

When I sidled into the front room, Dougie, flush with his infusion of cash, was back at the poker table. Perhaps the other players assumed he begged it off his mother, because no hue and cry arose when he exchanged a few dollars for quarters. They were all cutthroats, eager to part him, sucker that he was, from his wad.

In wielding my weapon, I chose sheer, blunt force over subtlety. My father was still sitting on the arm of Sophie's chair, nursing a tonic water. I leaned into his shoulder, my lips barely an inch from his ear.

"Gee, I thought Dougie was broke. Now he's back at the poker table."

He shrugged. "Guess he visited the National Bank of Mom."

"Oh, he made a withdrawal, but it wasn't from his mother."

A muscle in his jaw twitched. "What's that s'posed to mean?" His voice was like the blade of a knife veiled in gauze.

"He stole it," I hissed, struggling to keep the triumphant malice out of my voice, worrying that my accusation had vibrated across the entire room, like ripples from a stone dropped in a pool of stagnant water. I half-expected heads to turn our way, faces contorted in shock, eyebrows raised, jaws dropped.

"Think about what you're sayin' before you say it, Claire Josephine." An intensity lit my father's eyes; a sudden tightness pulled the skin across his cheeks and forehead.

I refused to wither under that high-beam glare. "I saw him."

In one fluid motion, he craned around to pat Sophie's hand and excuse himself, then pivoted up off the chair arm to guide me over to the door, a firm hand on my elbow.

"You wanted to leave early, so let's go." He fished for his keys in his pants pocket.

"What? I just told you—"

"I heard what you told me."

"Aren't you gonna do something about it? Or don't you believe me?" It was my turn to glare, hands planted on my hips.

The muscles in his jaw shuddered again, almost in rhythm to the faint jingle that rose from his pocket. But he didn't look away.

281

"I believe there's been bad blood between the two of you for a long time. And it's only gotten worse the older you get. And I'm sayin' that sometimes you have to be the one to let things go. What did he do to you this time?"

"This isn't about him and me. He stole money out of someone's purse. I saw him. And I'm pretty sure the purse belonged to Aunt Peach."

His gaze slid past me. There she was, down at the end of the hall, leaning on the now-open back door, gesturing to Jamie, maybe telling him to get his dessert while the getting was good.

"I'll see you another two bits," Dougie called as he flung more of the filched money into the silver puddle in the middle of the card table.

Jaw set and eyes flashing fire, my father set off. I started to follow, but his right hand snapped a stop sign and I froze, adrift in the middle of the room, a lone swimmer treading water in a sea of sharks. Down the hall, his head inclined to Peach's, his hand gestured, the merest flick of his fingers toward the front of the house. Then he straightened and appeared to shrug. Peach looked up at him without replying, then pivoted on her heel and strode to the bedroom. She ducked inside for a minute or two, and then reappeared, purse in hand, a tight frown squeezing her face. She leaned against the casing, perhaps deliberating on a course of action.

What would a "proper Southern lady" do? Accuse or not? Approach the mother or the culprit? And how to make a strong case, given the fact that the lone witness was known to be biased against the suspect? She was a diver poised at the end of the board, toes curled over the edge, pondering the distance to the water, and the depth of the pool, and whether her entrance would be smooth and efficient, with nary a trace of whitewater left in her wake, or would create the kind of riotous splash that only a novice or a fool would desire. She was hesitating too long on that diving board. It could only mean that she was leaning away from making the plunge, with resignation hanging in the corner of her eyes and mouth. So I moved to head off her retreat back to the ladder and the safe way down.

Even with my father shaking his head at me, I walked straight up to her. "I saw him. He took your money. And you know that if the shoe was on the other foot, if it was Dougie accusing Jamie of stealing from Aunt Dodie, she'd be raising holy hell."

Actually, I didn't believe that for a minute. Dodie, in reality, would probably not have even considered climbing up to that diving board. She would have soldiered through, and hushed Dougie up by shoving a slice of chocolate cake in his mouth, maintaining the appearance of a warm, wonderful family gathering—because that's what mattered to her—that smooth, calm surface of the pool. Deep down, Peach probably realized this too, but, as I calculated, tossing Jamie's name into the mix was enough to make her take the plunge.

The resulting splash proved spectacular. Peach tried for a clean, clear, knife-edge entry. She left me standing at one end of the hall and my father at the other, while she ducked into the kitchen. She came out with Dodie and they both stepped into Sophie's bedroom. When they emerged barely a minute later, Dodie was in the lead, her face the mottled pink gray color of ground pork. She marched down the hall to the front room, brushing past me without so much as a look, tapped first her husband and then her son on the arms, and gestured with a quick nod of her head.

Uncle Bob might have followed her out of bored curiosity, but Dougie was engrossed in the poker game, bent on recouping his losses, and paid her no mind. So really, in the end, as in the beginning, it was his fault for all the white water spray.

Or the shit that hit the fan.

Later, on the short ride home, I saw the comic potential in the incident, in the whole running string of incidents. It was made for TV: an updated sit-com version of the Hatfield-McCoy feud or an All in the Family rip-off set on the South Side of Chicago. But in the hot, roiling middle of it, all I could see was ugly: harshly gaping mouths, bared yellowish teeth, the jut of jaws and the furrowing of brows until the faces surrounding me seemed to belong to some sub-human species. The sounds were ugly, too: guttural oinks, high-pitched squawks, braying neighs.

The pool into which we'd plunged was full of some primordial hideousness—and we were covered in that slime. Drenched in it, drowning in it—and though I could feel that smooth, flat surface of the wall up against the bones of my back and the palms of my hands, I felt that I would slip away into the depths of the muck at any second. I was gasping for breath, grasping for something to hold onto, an obscure memory flooding into my brain, of my father and me in the closet in the storm and afterwards watching the lightening. *Never be afraid of truth and beauty, there's too little of them in this world...* So where was he now? Why was he just standing there, leaning against the wall, shaking his head? And then, in the midst of all that ugliness, I found something beautiful and true to cling to.

"I saw him too."

Jamie.

It was enough to keep my head above the muddy roiling swamp.

"He's lying," Dougie mooed.

Was it a lie? Maybe. Maybe not. He never said he saw Dougie take the money from the purse. And, glancing through the window of the back door, he may have seen Dougie step into the bedroom. Likely? No. Possible? Yes. He could have noticed me hovering at the door, peering in. He might have watched Dougie come out and head straight for the poker table. It was all within that tenuous, expansive, undefined realm of possibility. Just not in the neighboring, fenced-in realm of likelihood. Whether it was a lie on his part or not, he stuck to the script that I'd written: Dougie entered the bedroom. Dougie rifled Peach's purse. Dougie rejoined the poker game flush with new cash.

When Dodie snarled, "Well, of course, he would stick up for her—they've been a pair of troublemakers for years now," a curious thing happened: Uncle Jimmie, who'd been hanging back outside the mudhole, wearing an expression that could only be read as "here we go again," suddenly plunged in and put his hand on Jamie's shoulder.

"No son of mine would lie about this sort of thing. If Jamie said he saw something, he saw it. So the only thing left to say is this: Douglas, be a man, admit what you did and give your aunt her money."

The simple, quiet power in his voice. Amazing. Stunning. The words. Beautiful. True. Moses parting the waters. The sort of thing I wanted my father to say, had expected him to say, and would later ask myself why he didn't say it. But he had been mute except for the disgust on his face.

Dougie wasn't anywhere near being a man. He maintained his innocence with a Nixonian flair: deny, deny, deny. When Uncle Bob fished two rolls of his Bicentennial quarters out of his pockets and attempted to shove them into Peach's hands, she stepped back as if he was trying to hand her fistfuls of dog crap.

"It's high time we said our goodbyes to Sophie," she murmured, sidestepping her in-laws like they, too, were piles of waste.

My father and I followed, but not before I let fly a triumphant arrow of a smirk at Dougie, whose glowering return shot promised murder and mayhem when and if we should meet again. I heard my father whisper "sorry about that, Ma" as he bent to kiss Sophie's cheek.

"Under my own roof," she muttered. "Under my own roof."

I'd expected our parents to engage in a post-mortem outside, but Peach and Jimmie headed straight to their car. Jamie hesitated, looked back, opened the door to the back seat and stashed his guitar case, then came bounding over the grass to the sidewalk, where I knelt, pretending to tie the laces of my shoe.

"Call me," he said.

"No, you call me."

"Fine, I will—so make sure you're waiting by the damn phone."

"I may not feel like talking."

"Be there."

It was a command. And only a fool would not want to comply.

When he finally did call, it was nearly ten o'clock, way past the time my father considered acceptable for such congress. And with him slumped in front of the TV watching the tail end of Columbo, with the rumpled detective shuffling around, fishing for clues in his wrinkled trench coat and too-long pants, it was impossible to have any kind of a true conversation. We skirted around topics, speaking in fits and starts, trying to say much in as few words as possible.

"You've been avoiding me."

"I haven't."

A scoffing sound on his end. "Yeah. Why?"

"Why what?"

"Jeez—you never used to be like this." His voice was very low, as if there were parents in his vicinity as well.

"Like what?"

He was silent for such a long time that I thought he might have abandoned the phone. "Hey? Are you still there?"

"Unfortunately… Look, is it gonna be the same or different?"

Now it was my turn to pause.

"Hello?"

"From when," I finally replied.

"What?"

"Same or different from when?"

"Huh?"

"Same or different from when," I repeated, trying to enunciate for emphasis, yet at the same time, struggling to sound cool and casual to my father's ears. "You know, how it's been or how it was."

"Jesus, you're—I don't even know what to call it—Byzantine?"

"Thanks."

"So?"

"What?"

"You never answered the question," he sighed.

"Different. From both."

"Both?"

"From how it's been and how it was."

That cracked him up, although he sounded exasperated as well, trying to muffle his laughter.

"Hey, I've got to go cuz it's late. But ..." I dropped my voice another decibel. "Thanks."

"For?"

"Today."

"You mean at Grandma's?"

"Yeah."

"Il n'y a pas de quoi."

Now it was my turn. "What?"

He sniggered. "You should take French instead of Spanish."

"Buenos noches."

"Bonne nuit."

Still we both hung on the line. "Okay, well, I'm going."

"Okay."

"Okay, so 'bye."

"Bye."

"Hang up the damn phone," my father muttered from across the room.

Things were different after that. Both from the way they had been recently and the way they were before. It was in the way he loomed over my locker in the morning, his arm slung over the top of the door in a proprietary fashion, his hip casually jutting out, his foot blocking my path, the way he took up my space so that some form of contact was inevitable: an arm brushing an arm, a knee bumping a thigh, an elbow grazing ribs. At lunch, he'd pass behind me on his way to his usual table and slip cryptic notes onto my tray, little folded squares of loose-leaf paper that I'd hastily tuck into the pocket of my jeans to decipher later in Spanish class. While everyone else was conjugating verbs, I was solving rebus riddles sketched in blue ink:

                                                     U

He introduced me to his buddy. I inadvertently slipped and called him 'Strawboy' to his face. They laughed and the nickname stuck: from then on he was, indeed, Strawboy of the wiry build, droopy eyelids and wheat-colored hair. When not at school, we arranged to meet on neutral ground: on the swings at Cal Park, in front of the Walgreen's on 106th Street, on the steps of St. Francis de Sales church, and in Straw's garage, where they'd sit in old metal lawn chairs and pick riffs of songs out of thin air.

He'd ride his bike past my house, stopping only if he saw my father's car was gone. We'd sit on the stoop and talk fitfully about the most inconsequential of things: what we ate for breakfast and how we nearly wet our pants laughing at the latest Killer Bees skit on *NBC's Saturday Night* and wasn't *"Shake Your Booty"* just about the stupidest song ever recorded? But as we talked, our shoulders would gravitate together and when he reached down to re-tie his Adidas, his knuckles would graze my calf.

We were in a strange purgatory: not in one place or the other, but somewhere in between, a place where we were old friends and strangers at the same time, comfortable and discomfited, a burning, yearning place without signposts to guide us, only our own hyperactive senses of sight and smell, hearing and taste and, above all, touch.

By the time the last week of school rolled around, my body was in a permanent state of something that I didn't quite have a name for: a feeling of constant flow like warm running water and a coiled, tense giddiness that bubbled up from deep within and washed over the surface of my skin in waves, waiting, waiting, for—what? I ate little, slept less, with my throat tight, my teeth grinding, my heart pounding, a fist on a closed door. Whether my eyes were open or closed, I saw him.

When we all exploded out of the school doors on that last day, and the clique squealed its joy at our liberation, my gaze naturally sought him as he bent over his bike lock. What would summer mean for us?

He pedaled past my house after dinner. My father had answered an urgent call from Sophie to come and do some emergency plumbing. Something was leaking somewhere, he mumbled, so he might be awhile.

"If I'm not back before you leave—when are you leaving anyway?"

"Lori wants us there by eight."

"Well, have fun at Lori's. Not too much, though. And be home by eleven," he cautioned as he went out the door.

"Dad, that's only three hours—"

"That's enough time for a get-together. Eleven—not a second later."

When his reconnaissance showed him the coast was clear, Jamie wheeled his bike around and walked it up to the stoop, where I was already waiting at the screen door.

"Whatcha doin'?" he asked, peering in through the louvered glass and mesh.

"Getting ready for Lori's party."

"Oh," he replied in the clipped manner of someone lacking an invitation.

"But you can come in for awhile."

He looked around uneasily, as if scoping for Joe's car again.

"He's gone to Grandma's to fix a faucet or something. He'll be gone for awhile. And even if he comes back, what's the big deal? You're allowed to be here."

As he followed me up the stairs, I felt a prickly tingle, like the teeth of a comb running along the skin of my back, as I wondered what part of my body his eyes were watching. When I stepped into the bathroom, he hesitated a moment in the doorway, then, seeing me pick up a tube of mascara from the counter, he joined me, flipping the lid down on the toilet and having a seat.

"So, who's gonna be at this party?"

"Oh, the usual suspects. My silly girlfriends, as you call them, some jocks from deSales." I stared into the mirror as I carefully applied the wand to my lashes. "You could come with," I ventured airily.

"Not really my crowd."

"Maybe you should expand your little circle of friends. You could bring your armor with you." From his squint, I could tell he didn't understand. "Your guitar."

"Oh, so that's what you think—that I hide behind it. The truth comes out."

"Come on, admit it, you do hide behind it sometimes."

He raised his eyebrows and cocked his chin. "Just like you hide behind that crap."

"This," I gestured to my cornucopia of cosmetics, "is a woman's prerogative. If I really wanted to hide, I *wouldn't* wear it and I would just fade into the walls."

Most guys on the make would have hastened to say something flattering, something about my natural beauty, but he just stared at me thoughtfully as I wielded the wand, elongating each lash to its full glory. We were silent for a time, the length of which grew until I started to feel uncomfortable. I dusted my cheeks with blush, and in my nervousness, applied too much, so that I had to grab a tissue and wipe the excess pink away.

"What's it like?" he finally asked.

"What's what like?"

"Being you. Being a girl."

The question arrested my hand as it held the tube of lip gloss just inches from my lips.

"What a weird thing to ask!" I glanced over at him to see if he was truly serious or just cracking a joke. His face was solemn.

"I don't know," he mumbled. "It's just—I used to think we were so alike. I never thought it mattered—boy or girl—we were just—us. Just the two of us, together. And then… something—happened." His face collapsed and he pressed his hands to the top of his head. "Shit, I don't even know what I'm saying any more. I can't explain what I mean." He looked like he was in real physical pain, doubled over, head to his knees, hands clenched behind his neck, rocking slightly, as if nursing some internal wound.

"You're just noticing the difference now?" I quipped, hiding my own breathless confusion. "Didn't you watch the movies in health?"

"Go ahead, laugh at me, torture me. That's what seems to get you off lately. Maybe that's what it means to be the female of the species."

The Kipling quote popped into my head. *Thank you, Bartlett.* "More deadly than the male."

"I *am* dying," he croaked.

Turning away from the reality of him, still hunched over on the toilet, to stare at my image in the mirror, I pondered how to answer his question.

Silk and sandpaper... honey and lemon... July and January... feather and elephant... to seem one and to feel the other... hiding in plain sight... fitting in, standing out... being less, being more... walking around with a mouthful of words and lips stitched together like a corpse... a butterfly pinned to a display board... a queen bee trapped in amber... a mouse in a maze...a hamster on a wheel... going round and round and nowhere... and always under someone else's eyes.

Was that really me looking back from the glass or just someone that I thought everyone else wanted to see?

I stepped in front of Jamie and waited until he straightened and raised his face to look at me. "I can't explain either."

Then I reached out and touched the gloss to his lips. I expected him to flinch, to pull away with a 'what the hell,' but he sat there, unmoving, while I smoothed it along the curves of his mouth, until it was slick and shiny, promising as an oasis, and there was nothing left to do but press my dry lips against his wet ones and drink.

Is this what a baby feels nursing at her mother's breast? This strange, tense yet fluid connection that starts in the lips, and then spreads throughout the body, blurring the boundaries of self and other? Who is who? What skin is yours and what is mine? Where do you end and I begin? When I had imagined this, you tasted of bubblegum, a sugar plum boy, but no, you're really a green apple, sweet and tart at once, and all the flavors in between ...

That magnetic force that held our lips together traveled along the rest of our bodies so that the weight of his hands on my hips, pulling me down onto his lap seemed inevitable. The heat, the pressure, the movement—it was all as natural as the laws of the universe—biology and physics and chemistry come alive. And yet it was awkward, too: prickly and strange to find the hands which had pressed sand into castles at the beach alongside my own now pressing at my waist, weird and unnerving to open my eyes to the delicate, blue-white skin of his eyelids, the fine brown hairs of his eyebrows, the single tiny pimple on his forehead. It

was the uncomfortable sensation of thinking you know something so well, inside and out, and then being shocked by the
revelation that comes from seeing that thing from a new per-
spective, like looking down at the city from the dizzying heights
of the Sears Tower and finally seeing the patterns of that urban
grid that you've been scurrying around all your life.

It felt incredibly right and incredibly wrong. So I found myself leaning forward and arching back, giving in to the magnetic
force and resisting it, all the while under the spell of that
sensation that flowed from Jamie's lips through mine.

But in that moment when we had to break apart, to catch our
breath, to give ourselves a visual pinch to see whether we were
still separate beings; that we hadn't morphed into Siamese twins;
to reassure ourselves that this wasn't all some wet dream, something else grabbed hold of me. How to explain the force that
prompted me to pick up the tube of mascara, whip out its wand
and draw it gently over his eyelashes? He laughed and blinked at
the unfamiliar sensation, leaving black dots in an arc on the skin
under his left eye.

"Hold still!"

He let me wipe the smudges away with a damp tissue, but
when I whisked the brush over the lashes of his right eye, he
flinched away.

"What the—you're crazy!"

"You said you wanted to know what it's like to be a girl."

"Yeah, but not—"

"Shhh, just hold still."

"You are out of your squash!"

"Shut up and be still."

Amazingly, he did, submitting to my perverse will, allowing
me to manipulate and decorate his face as if he was a mere lump
of clay and I was the sculptress. He had never been a rugged,
boy-faced boy, had always been a little soft around the edges.
With every stroke of my brushes and wands and fingers, he
became softer still until I had molded his angular face into its
feminine form. I finger-combed his hair and pulled it up into a
high ponytail, leaving a few tendrils to spiral delicately down to

frame his face. *If he'd been born a girl, this is what she would look like.* I took his hand and pulled him to his feet, turning him to face the cabinet mirror, to meet his twin sister in the flesh.

He was speechless for a moment, and then a soft "shit" escaped his glistening pink lips, like air escaping from the pinhole prick in a balloon.

"We could go down to River Oaks Mall, walk into the Limited, try on some clothes and nobody would suspect a thing," I crowed, awed at my artistry.

"Shit," he hissed again, then laughed and mumbled a few lines of Lou Reed's *"Walk on the Wild Side"* about hitchhiking Holly who went from he to she with a little help from a razor and tweezers.

I grabbed my Polaroid SX-70 off the bookshelf in my bedroom and started snapping shots. The camera motor whirred and purred as it spat out the photographs one after another. I laid them carefully across the top of the toilet tank to develop.

Pink-cheeked girl-boy, angel-haired, chocolate kiss eyes, dream baby with seashell ears, only that down on your upper lips and cheeks might give you away, up close and personal, and yes, those eyebrows need plucking—and maybe your arms, long and tight-sinewed would betray your secret… or your shoulders, a little too square and broad, or the shape of your body, slowly molding into a masculine V-shape.

I could have been lost in that androgynous reverie for hours, peering through the camera lens as Jamie posed with an élan that would have given supermodels Christie and Lauren a run for their money, admiring my handiwork like Cinderfella's fairy godmother, but the bleating of the telephone downstairs jolted me forward.

"Shit—what time is it?" I ducked out of the bathroom and checked the clock on my nightstand. Half past eight—I was late to the party. I dashed down the stairs with Jamie at my heels.

"What's your story? Get your ass over here!" Lori squawked through the receiver.

She berated me for minute, then launched into what I was missing, which didn't really sound like much, finishing with another exhortation to get my buns moving.

"Hey, can I bring someone with?" I asked with a glance at Jamie, who was lounging against the front door. He snapped to attention and shook his head.

"Who?"

"Oh, a cousin of mine."

Jamie's head was swinging from side to side like a dog shaking off the excess drool after a long slog of water.

"Is she some uptight priss or what?"

I barely held back a snort. "Uh, no."

Lori heaved a sigh, weighing the merits of allowing another female to compete for the attentions of the limited number of males in the room. "Oh, fine, bring her."

"See you in a few."

"All right, get this crap off me," Jamie said the second the receiver hit its cradle.

"Oh come on, go with me. It'll be bitchin'."

"Wait—you mean, like this? With this crap on my face? Now I am positive that you are out of your gourd." He blinked under the unfamiliar weight of his Maybelline-caked eyelashes.

"Hey, you said you wanted to know what it's like to be a girl. So be one for awhile. Go all the way."

"Look—I—"

"Don't you want to see if you could pass?"

"Pass? For a girl?"

"In mixed company."

"Shit no!"

"Come on, it'll be worth it to scam all those idiots."

"Yeah, the whole de Sales goon squad—uh, I mean baseball team. Just my luck they'll have their bats along with them and start bashing me for being some kind of faggot. That's a lotta risk for a few shits and grins."

"Then do it to make me happy."

"Yeah, so what do I get out of it besides total humiliation?"

I reached up and pulled one of his tendrils back into place. "Whatcha want?" I asked breezily, mentally rifling through my closet, searching for a blouse or scarf that might camouflage his Adam's apple and lack of tits.

294

He fumbled in his front pocket and then held out his hand. From the tip of his index finger hung a gold chain. Swinging gently at the end of the loop was a gold ring. The Claddagh.

"I want you to take this back."

I flicked a finger at his curls. "Still no Cathy? Poor Heathcliff. But then, the way you look tonight, I could be Heathcliff and you could be—"

"You talk too damn much," he sighed in sweet exasperation. "Just shut up." In one graceful, gentle movement, he drew me up against him, slipped the chain over my head and down around my neck and then riveted his mouth to mine.

It is a daring thing, a kiss. Daring and full of consequence to open your body that way to another. Curious, too, how the touch of a tongue, just a small, supple muscle, can cause the rest of the body to quake, and lava to flow, and strange, shuddering sounds to erupt without warning. A soft, falling note in a minor key from Jamie when my hand came to rest against his hip was answered by a moan that slipped from me when his fingers brushed up my side and lingered near my breasts. And while our bodies were rocked by this volcano of sensation, the rest of the world—its sights and sounds—was obscured by smoke and ash.

So how could we have possibly heard the faint click of a key turning in a lock?

When the force of the door opening threw us, entwined, into the opposite wall, we upset the little table, sending the telephone crashing to the floor with a harsh jangle followed by the grating flat-line buzz of a dial tone. Jamie caught me by the elbows as I teetered back and steadied me against the wall before he turned to face the intruders.

In the end the memory was all about mouths: Jamie's mouth consuming mine; my own mouth, ready and willing and open, bathed in liquid velvet; my father's mouth shocked into a near-perfect O, and the fourth mouth—Peach's—contorted into a snarling grimace, like something cruel was pulling at the corners of her lips, stretching them into a harsh, red gash.

I'd seen that mouth before: on cornered cats, hissing with their ears folded flat against their heads; on defensive dogs, growling behind fences at an approaching stranger, the clear, elastic strands of saliva suspended from their yellow canine teeth; on my own mother the day she'd confronted me with the Claddagh ring clenched in her tight, white fist.

In the dim light of the early evening, in that little eternity that it took my father to cross the room to switch on the lamp, Peach had merely murmured, in a vaporous voice, "Jamie? Is that you? What—what are you doing here?" Something was off-kilter in the way she emphasized the word *"here;"* something almost self-ish, almost proprietary in her tone of dismay. And in the bright white incandescence that followed the clicking turn of a knob, there was more to read in those wide blue yonder eyes and slack jaw than just disbelief and disapproval.

I expected a shriek, but when she finally spoke, it came out a whisper, as if perhaps she never intended to let it out at all. "What the hell have you done?"

Denial was automatic. *They couldn't have seen us, couldn't have heard us. We were just standing by the door; we had just got off the phone with Lori; we were just about to head over to the party...* It was only when I noticed that her eyes were fixed on Jamie's face and I saw Jamie's hand reach up and tentatively press the tips of his fingers against his cheek that I remembered some things couldn't be denied.

"What have you done?" she repeated, louder this time, with deliberate precision.

"It's just—a joke. We were just goofing around," Jamie mumbled, wiping his hand across his mouth, desperate to remove the remnants of his already smeared lipstick and gloss.

"Were you headed out the door—that way?" Peach gestured, her hand slashing the air as sharply as her voice, all traces of Southern honey washed away. "Going out on the street—looking like that?"

"No, it wasn't—"

"You go wash your face! And scrub it good, boy!"

Shoulders sagging, Jamie headed dutifully for the stairs. I started to follow him, but my father grabbed my elbow.

"He can wash his own face." His voice had a clenched calmness to it.

"You were going out, weren't you?" Peach practically spat the words once she heard the water running upstairs. "You were s'posed to be at some party. You put him up to this—tartin' him up and then—"

"You heard him! It was a joke!" I shot back, trying to wrench my elbow out of my father's vise grip.

"But it was your idea, wasn't it? Your joke?" Peach stepped closer, stabbing the air in front of my face with her index finger, that polished pink talon just inches from my nose.

"My idea?" *Why was it so important to her that it was my idea?* Realization dawned an ugly, angry red on the horizon of my mind. "What? Worried your precious little boy is turning into some kind of queer? That's it, isn't it? No fags allowed. Well, you don't have to worry about that. If you hadn't walked in, we'd probably be doing it on the floor right this minute."

It all happened in a microsecond: Peach's hand swinging to slap my face; my dad's hand arcing to intercept her wrist; my hand clawing to free my elbow. We were caught in this strange, seething trinity in which Peach's electric anger seemed to surge through the conduit of my father's body, from the hand that held her wrist to the hand that gripped my elbow, to scald my skin and shock me into submission.

Instead it jolted me to a stark awareness. I stopped struggling to free myself and stood, accepting my place in that charged triangle, feeling that furious energy vibrating through the three of us, staring at the woman across from me.

"Why are you here?"

At once the electric geometric current was broken. My father released his hold on both of us, dropping Peach's wrist like a lit match he'd held for too long. He let loose of me more gradually, transferring the grip from his fingers to his eyes, where a brown gold fire flickered. Something I hadn't quite seen before. Centuries ago, when men drew maps of the seven seas, wherever the ocean extended beyond the grasp of their knowledge they would draw a monster and write *"here there be dragons"* and all ships would beware. Something in that flash of fire told me I was poised on the edge of the known world.

To her credit, she didn't ask me to repeat the question to buy some time in which to formulate an answer. Her eyes didn't skitter around in their sockets, veering left or right or up or down, reflecting the brain's search for the appropriate words. Her gaze was steady, imperious even, as if to say her right to plant her feet in this living room was equal to mine. My god, she was truly accomplished at this art.

"To pick up my son."

You lie! You lie! You can keep your eyes from giving you away by riveting them on mine. You can clench your fists and suck in your breath and hold your body ramrod straight in the pose of the righteous—but you lie all the same. How do I know? I can smell it. Your body betrays you even now, as the sweat beads up between your breasts and mingles with the perfume you sprayed there. It wafts out around you like swamp gas with every thumping beat of your heart...

Cuz you gave it away when you first walked in ...

"Wow—that's amazing. Cuz when you walked in the door and saw us here I swear you almost peed your pants."

That'll crack that veil of ice you're wearing across your face...

But instead of watching her façade shatter into a million lying shards, I saw my father's fury-colored face looming before me— the dragon rampant.

"Just what the hell are you up to?" His breath singed my skin.

Is this the face my mother saw when they squared off to do battle? The eyes that scorched everything in the path of that merciless gaze; the lips that spewed verbal napalm; the lowered, scowling brow that asked no quarter; the jutting chin that thrust and parried and promised no quarter in return? What had she thought the first time she saw it, what had she done? Did she stand mute, transfixed at the horrifying transformation? Did she turn and run from the hideous beast? Did she say to herself—here is where the myth of werewolves was born? Or did she do as I did, look the dragon in the eye and merely tell him the beautiful truth?

"You are ugly—the ugliest man I have ever seen. Go look at yourself in the mirror."

It pulled him up short like he was a dog rather than a dragon, like someone had yanked back on his leash. But the eyes still smoldered with red flame above flaring nostrils. Even the smell of sulfur and charred carbon seemed to hang between us.

I needed no knight charging in on his noble steed to rescue me, but I was still glad to hear the muffled thuds of Jamie's gym shoes on the stairs. He crossed to stand next to me, wet and bedraggled, Cinderella after midnight, his face scrubbed a raw pink, his damp tendrils plastered against his cheeks. Peach headed him off, closing her talons around his upper arm and squawking a clipped, "let's go." I grabbed his other arm and stretched up to kiss him, but my mouth just barely brushed his, a glancing, tenuous connection that felt sloppy, and emptier than if I had not even tried to kiss him at all.

The glass panes in the jalousie door shrieked as Peach slammed it behind her, the couch groaned as my father sat down heavily, the bottom stair squealed under the weight of my foot — the sounds of people wading through wreckage.

"What are you up to?" my father said again, but quietly this time, as if half talking to himself.

The answer bubbled up involuntarily, like a burp or a sneeze. "My mother's business."

And I could have sworn I felt a cold kiss on my cheek as if she was there to say "well done."

Of course they sent him away. They packed him up and shipped his ass down to Georgia, where I guess they presumed the only chance of makeup coming in contact with a man's face was by a kiss from his female sweetheart's lips. He thought it would just be for the summer: one of those temporary exiles with time off for good behavior and a sworn promise to live a reformed life. But in August he wrote to say that his grandmother had enrolled him at the local high school so he'd be spending at least part of our sophomore year down there in purgatory. I tacked the Polaroids of Miss Jamie on my bulletin board, silently daring my father to remove them. He didn't. Instead, it was me that he tried to remove.

The family drama followed its own stages of the narrative, with all the required elements. First, The Talk, full of self-recrimination. *("I've been a lousy father, I know that. I just can't seem to get it together—to be both a father and a mother, I can't do it. I just can't seem to cut it.")* Then the Abdication. *("You need a mother at this point in your life. I can see that — everyone can see that. But I can't be that for you. I'm helpless in the face of it. Marjorie is willing to take that on. You could stay with her out in San Diego for awhile. It'd be good for you. You'd get to know your little cousins…")* Oh, how he blamed himself. How he accepted the fault. How weak and ineffectual he'd been. How this would be so much better for me—although it would tear him up to let me go. God, it was cheap melodrama and all I heard was Peach's voice coming out of my father's mouth. I'd sworn to myself to be rational, but I let that cheap crap suck me in and that, in turn, allowed the fury to overcome me. So the Expressions of Angry Intent followed. *("You send me out there and I swear I'll run away—or fucking slit my wrists!" "Don't try to threaten me with that, goddamn it! After what we've been through and what we've lost, don't you even dare threaten me with that!")* After the heat and clamor of raised voices and slammed doors, the Chilled Silence settled, with a cessation of dialogue and minimal interaction. However, this being a melodrama, after the sensational incidents and violent appeals to the emotions, a happy, though tearful, ending must ensue—and so it concluded with the Apologetic Finale: the knock on the bedroom door, the peace offering in the form of a silver-wrapped chocolate kiss, the embrace, the shaky promises sobbed *("Don't send me away. I can be good. I will be good. I need to be here with you." "And I need you here, I do. I'll do a better job of it. Stupid, I can be so stupid…").*

Fingers crossed behind our backs…

The Polaroids hung in a neat, yet flamboyant row, like butterflies pinned in a specimen case, until the day before I left for college, when I took them down and tucked them away in my box and laughingly warned Jamie that if he ever tried to run for public office I had the goods to blackmail him.

The years had not been kind to those photos. The flesh tones degraded from a juicy peach to a jaundiced yellow. Everything in the pictures—the pink tiled walls, the chrome towel bar, Jamie's brown eyes—seemed muted, filmy, lacking the original gleam that radiated from the feeling of being slightly out-of-control and on the brink of something MAJOR. Yet sorting through them, fanning them out across my old bedspread like a deck of playing cards, brought back a glimmer of that heady light, a shiver of that blood rush, and the weird sensation of a pair of phantom lips pressing up against mine.

"Once he drew, with one long kiss, my whole soul through his lips…"

CHAPTER 19

When Joe finally returned from his doctor's appointment, hours later than expected, his face was washed out and weathered, like something left too long in the sun.

"Long wait?" I ventured.

He brushed past and trudged into the bathroom. The water gushed for a long time. When he eventually emerged, his eyes were red-rimmed. He dismissed the glass of iced tea I offered, and poured a tumbler of water from the faucet instead, drinking it in one long, trembling swallow.

"Problems? Rib not mending right?"

He sank down on a kitchen chair. "Fine. Everything's fine."

"Don't try to bullshit me, old man."

"I'll tell you what's bullshit." He shot back with a burst of energy, stabbing his finger in the air. "Getting prodded and poked by a coupla ninnies who don't look old enough to know their ass from a hole in the ground."

"Believe it or not, those ninnies have medical degrees and actually do possess skills and knowledge that you don't have."

He just glared.

"You need a laugh, daddy-o. And I've got just the thing." I laid a quartet of Polaroids down on the table in front of him with a flourish, like I was revealing a winning poker hand—four of a kind—all queens.

His lips, instead of softening into a smile, drew into a tighter, pale grimace, like a faded scar running from cheek to cheek. He exhaled, long and slow, grappling with something. "You just can't let it go, can you? You keep dredging this crap up. The other night it was that damn record—now this—garbage." He brought his hands up as if to shove the pictures away, but stopped just short, as if he couldn't bear to touch them. "Why can't you just let these old ghosts go?"

Let it go. Why can't you let it go? He'd spoke those same words years ago, to the other troublesome woman in his life.

"Because that's the thing—they're not old ghosts. They're everyday ghosts. And I'm not holding onto them. They're holding onto me. And I'm guessing they're holding onto you, too."

Another sigh escaped him like air from a punctured balloon, leaving him even more deflated, as his eyelids drooped, then his chin and shoulders, until he was just a colorless damp rag of a man hanging limply across a chair.

"And I think they're holding on because of things we've never talked about—things we should've talked about... a long time ago. But we didn't. We haven't. So we need to... talk about them. Now."

No response. Not even the flutter of an eyelash or the twitch of a cheek muscle to indicate that he'd heard me.

"I don't know how to start this—conversation—so I'm just going to... start."

You're nine years old again—wanting something—another cookie—some silly little toy hanging at eye level in the grocery store—a puppy—any goddamn thing that you are preparing to ask permission for—and you're already anticipating the "no," with sweat beading up on the back of your neck. Stop it! Suck it up! You're not nine anymore.

"At Sophie's funeral, Dougie O'Connell said something really weird—unbelievable. I was... I couldn't... He said Jamie Sokol drowned—in the lake. That he didn't die in a car crash."

He brought his hand up to cover his eyes, slowly massaging his temples, his fingers digging into his skin in tight circles.

"I figured he was lying, just like always. But I asked myself why? Why would he lie? I can't come up with a reasonable explanation. It doesn't make sense. So I'm asking you—what really happened? Was it a car crash—or did he drown?"

Where was the boom of thunder, the ear-shattering blast of a dam bursting, the sibilant roar of a tidal wave as it overwhelms the shore? It felt like a busting out, an explosion—there should have been a bang. Where was the bang? *I'm waiting for the bang.*

But there was only the raspy whisper of his hand sliding down his unshaven cheek. He kept his eyes closed.

"Car crash? What in the hell are you—" His hand slid back up and kneaded his forehead. "Where'd you ever get the idea it was a car crash in the first place?"

There it was. The brute force of it pushed me back against the counter. Its steel edge dug into the small of my back.

"Did Jimmie tell you it—"

"Peach," I croaked.

His hands slid away from his face. "Peach."

"I called there looking for him and she told me he'd crashed the car—and that he—that they'd already taken his body down to Georgia."

He was staring at me, but it seemed he wasn't finding what he was looking for. Something was moving around in the back of his eyes, hunting. "You believed her."

"Of course I believed her. She's his goddamn mother!"

"Why didn't you call me?"

Now it was my turn to stare at him and search. "I did," I finally replied.

"Bullshit."

"I did call you. Right after I got off the phone with her."

He shook his head. "You never called. I would—"

"You were drunk off your ass. In-co-fucking-herent."

He winced. *You damn well better not try to deny that.*

"Yeah, that was some lost weekend, wasn't it? Or was it a whole week? Maybe a fortnight? Hell, I'm betting a month!"

"Enough," he mumbled under his hands, which had found their way back to his face.

In some other place and time, I would have pursued him in retreat, under the cry of "take-no-prisoners!" But now it was enough to see him give way, to see the sag of his jowls, the gray stubble against his paler skin, the hanging head of a Mustang broken. And the taste of this victory was bitter in my mouth.

"Why would she say that?" he muttered, more to himself than to me.

"I've been wondering about that, doesn't really make sense on the surface. But I keep going back to it—and I think I've finally figured it out. Guilt."

He squinted as if trying to bring the idea into focus.

"She wanted to put a hurt on me that would make me eat my heart out for the rest of my life."

He gazed at me dumbly, like a lost tourist in a foreign country confronted and confounded by a language not his own.

"Jamie was supposed to come see me at college that Thanksgiving weekend. I called and asked him—begged him—to come. He said he would leave right after dinner on Thursday. He never showed up. So I figured—okay, something came up, he'll be around tomorrow. But Friday, Saturday, no Jamie. Then I thought maybe he was paying me back for not calling him for a couple of months. I finally called on Sunday. No answer. Monday, Tuesday, Wednesday, nothing. I kept calling. On Sunday, I guess it was, Peach finally answered."

"And told you Jamie died in a car crash." Disbelief coated and hardened his words like a thin layer of ice.

"You don't see it, do you? Jamie was coming to see me, got in that car because of me. I asked him to get in that car. I bore that burden. Can't you feel the weight of it? How it dragged me down?"

The tears were there, waiting behind my eyes, blurring the edges of my vision. One gesture from him, a hand extended, and they would have fallen. But he just sat there, rubbing his chin.

"You're telling me all these years you've felt responsible for his death—and you think Peach meant for you to feel that way?"

"Yes." Saying it felt like setting a copestone in place. *On a mausoleum.* "So this has been all about you, then? All these years?

And you could never see fit to forgive me for my own grief, for being drunk?" Something was stirring in his eyes. "So now that you've heard the truth—there was no car crash—what? You feel some relief? Some of that weight sliding off your shoulders?"

What was rearing up in those eyes? *What rough beast?*

"In a way, yes, but not—"

"Relieved that this boy—this boy you loved—like a... Ha!" He spat a croaking laugh. "I was gonna say 'like a brother'—but it wasn't like that, was it? Relieved—you're relieved that this boy you loved maybe committed suicide—cuz that gets you off the hook?"

"No—I didn't say—wait, suicide? What are *you* saying?"

"Good! Good!" He stood abruptly, grabbing the edge of the table with a shaking hand to steady himself. "No, it's good you know the truth. Now you can spend the next twenty, thirty years wondering what made him say to hell with this shit and walk out into that water. Yeah, think about that. Ache over that. I guarantee it'll eat away at you like a—yes, like a cancer."

He scanned the room wildly for a moment, a penned stallion searching for a gap in the fence, gauging the height of the rails. "Everyday ghosts," he brayed, as he staggered past me. "I'll show you everyday ghosts!"

"Don't walk away! Don't you dare walk away!" I shouted after his shirt, a gray ghost trailing behind him through the front room.

The only reply was the screech of the glass in the jalousie door as it slammed behind him and the grunt of exhaust from his car as it lurched away from the curb.

CHAPTER 20

On college-ruled notebook filler paper, in a tight, left-leaning cursive, with angry visages of hand-drawn monsters and demons, fangs bared and dripping in red ink, glaring from the margins:

June 1976

Don't know whose idea this was—so I don't know whose murder to plan. Maybe it was them both together. I don't know which way to play it, either. Be a model prisoner and get out of jail early for good behavior – or be so damn bad that folks down here just give up and send me back cuz they won't know what else to do with me. It's a game and we've got to play it— play it right. In the meantime, they're trying to break me with hard labor— got me out in the cemetery, mowing grass and cutting shrubs and cleaning up around the graves. No wonder my uncle's so creepy, hanging out with the dead people all day. And Gramma's just trying to find out the whole story, asking snoopy questions. But I am just keeping my mouth shut. Got slapped for being "sullen" the other day. They ain't seen nothin' yet. Play it like you said, with fingers crossed behind our backs.

Prisoner X

On the flip side of a postcard showing a spectacular view of the Tennessee River valley over the barrel of a cannon:

September 1976
Greetings from Chickamauga and Chattanooga National Military Park!

Dante missed one very special circle of hell—summer in Georgia. Help! I'm drowning in sweat, nuts and crackers. Oh yeah. This is the place where Sherman and Grant opened up a can of Whup-Ass and killed some of my ancestors. Bloodiest two day battle of the Civil War. 35,000 dead, missing or wounded. I think they're the lucky ones. At least they're not living in Georgia anymore.

Jamie

On fringed, blue-lined paper torn from a spiral notebook:

November 1976
Hey! I can't believe the rest of the country would actually vote for a peanut farmer from Georgia for President. Uncle Lem says he shook Jimmy Carter's hand when he was the governor—Carter, that is. Ha, Ha! Says he's a good and decent man. Might as well believe him. Nothing else to do down here in purgatory.

Thanks for the pix of you in your Anne Frank costume. I wish I could have been there to see your shows. Hey, did you really have to kiss that guy—what's his name—on stage? In front of everyone? Was it a real kiss or just a peck? Just asking…

Jamie

Inside a homemade Christmas card decorated with a fir tree cut from a scrap of green velvet and strung with tiny, hand-drawn music notes:

December 1976
Merry merry and happy happy and all that jazz. The old fogies are coming down here for Xmas so I guess I won't get to see you like we hoped. Not looking forward to this family reunion at all. Guess I'll have to hide the Cover Girl. Ha Ha! Seriously, I'm not sure how I'm gonna get through the whole charade. One of my buds from shop class offered to split a bag of grass to help me out. He guaranteed it would keep a smile on my face throughout the farce. Might take him up on that… J

Inside a construction paper heart glued onto a paper lace doily:

February 1977

Roses are black
And I'm pretty blue
Since I'm down here
Not up there with you.

...Okay, it's lame, I know. But it's the thought that counts. Right? Don't worry—a few tokes on a few joints is not going to turn me into a junkie. You laid it on pretty thick in your last letter. Hey, Miss "I scam for screwdrivers," you never used to be such a goody-two-shoes. I thought that was my job! HA HA! It's just that some things in this life are a whole helluva lot more tolerable when I'm high...

Besides, you were always the straight-A student, not me. I just want to pick out some chords on my guitar, maybe write some words to go with them. You're probably not ever going to catch me reading War and Peace. Though Strawboy just turned me on to some books. They're called The Lord of the Rings by some Brit named Tolkien. Strawboy's really into this Dungeons and Dragons game scene so he digs the whole wizard/hobbit/orc crap. Anyway, this hobbit—Frodo—and his buddies go on this quest to destroy this magic ring—whoever has the ring has the power to rule all of Middle Earth.
Speaking of the one ring – are you still wearing it? ...J

On a strip of cash register paper that came wrapped around a Maxell UDXL cassette tape:

June 1977

Thought about getting you a Hallmark card but couldn't see how that would show that I care enough to send the very best. So I took this paper from the Sinclair station where I've been pumping gas. Fringe benefit— along with dirty fingernails and the scent of eau de petroleum. Hey, it's money, honey. Strawboy showed up on my Gramma's doorstep the other

309

day. Well, not exactly. I had to drive in to Chattanooga to pick him up at the Greyhound station. Brought his guitar with him so we laid down a few tracks just for you. Happy Birthday, Sweet Lil' Sixteen!

Scrawled across the label on the cassette was the title: *"The Birthday Tapes by The Tuneless Wonders."* Captured on the tape were two tenor voices wailing *"Today, It's Your Birthday"* like Lennon and McCartney over a pair of twanging acoustic guitars. On the next track, the singers warbled that I was sixteen, beautiful and theirs. They crooned through Sam Cooke's *"Only Sixteen,"* lamenting that I was too young to fall in love and they were too young to know. But it was on the last song, a parody of another Beatles' tune, that the voices really broke through to the truth of harmony, one high, sweet and slightly nasal, the other low, smooth and rich, blending like a warm creamy mouthful of syrup and butter.

"Two of us getting carsick
Wearing lipstick,
From May-bel-line!
You and me wearing dresses,
Making messes,
On our way back home.
We're on our way home,
We're on our way home,
We're going home…

At the end, laughter cascaded and a voice spread thick with an Elvis Presley growl mumbled *"Happy Birthday, Baby."* Then came a click as if someone had turned off the recorder. Several seconds of the faint hiss of blank tape elapsed before a voice abruptly cut back in: *"Hey, it's just me and my guitar now. And something I wrote for you…"* And then just a simple, three chord melody, soft, slow under the voice:

"In the sky blue and bright,
In the darkest part of the night;
In the wind that brushes my cheek,

In the water that sings in the creek;
In the heart of every flower,
In the clock that chimes the hour;
In the sun, in the moon,
In January, in June;
In weather foul or fair,
In every word of every prayer;
Claire,
It's you. It's you. It's you."

On an index card:

October 1977

Supposed to be doing research for a paper on Robert E. Lee. Wanted to do William Tecumseh Sherman just to spite my history teacher—I'm thinking he's got a hood and a cape stashed in his bedroom closet. Just kidding—he's harmless—just a bit moldy around the edges. I found some people who don't hold my growing up in the North against me. We're getting a band together. Thinking of calling ourselves The Dead Elvises — or would that be Elvi? Or maybe The King is Dead, Long live the Kings. Too long? Ha-ha! We've got a drummer, a bass player and me on lead guitar so far. We're hoping for a rhythm guitar and a keyboard player, too—and some gigs, although I think a couple of the guys might just be in it for the chicks. Not me, of course. Though I was pissed to hear from Strawboy that you went to Homecoming with some jock. Strawboy said he was a <u>minor</u> jock—a pole vaulter?!?!? – but still. So did you want to go to the dance with him—or did you just want to go to the dance? Maybe you shouldn't answer that—I'm not sure I want to know... Jamie

On a sheet of Howard Johnson's Motor Lodge stationery:

January 1978

It's 4 am and I'm hunched up in the bathtub here, trying to get some sleep but I can't because Magilla Gorilla the bass player is screwing his girlfriend in the bed just on the other side of this cheap door. And the springs are creaking and the headboard is thumping against the wall and

311

she's moaning and he's grunting and shit. Christ, I wish they'd just get it over with.

Came down here to Atlanta to see some band Rolly was all hyped up about. He's the drummer in our band—I told you about him—thinks he's the second coming of Keith Moon. So he drags us down here to see this band from England—the Sex Pistols. Yeah, I know—how lame is that name? These jerks got all this publicity for being complete punk—green hair, safety pins stuck through their cheeks—the local rags even wrote they vomit onstage and commit other acts too perverse to spell out in a family newspaper. Shit like that. The place was packed—with TV crews, reporters and cops. I'm shitting bricks, worried we'd get the boot because we didn't have tickets. Rolly knows someone who knows someone who let us in.

So the band finally comes on after 10. Four skinny, sickly-looking, pasty-faced punks with bad haircuts. Faces like they are permanently constipated. B.F.D. They couldn't play for shit either. People started throwing popcorn and crap at them. I was trying to get into it, just for the hell of it. Rolly was hopping up and down, called it 'pogoing.' Just made me want to vomit. Then some bruiser musta got wind that we didn't belong there cuz he asked to see our tickets and then threw us out into the rain. Man, it was pouring! Rolly was so pissed he started kicking car doors along the street. He was wearing these big shit-kickin' romper stomper boots. Left a few dents.

We tried to get in some other clubs but we looked like half-drowned rats and our IDs didn't pass the bouncer test. But Magilla managed to fool a liquor store clerk with his and then he got us the room here at the HoJo. Hey, with his facial hair he could probably pass for 25. Rolly drank half the Jack Daniels himself without bothering to put much Coke in his glass. So he's passed out on one bed, Magilla's humping his skank in the other, and I'm stuck here in the tub, thinking about that day we went to the Dunes. Remember we went for a hike and snuck up on that couple making love? Don't be mad when I say that when I picture them now they look like us—they are us. Don't be mad, Claire—cuz what I remember most is holding you in the water, baptizing you—and the way you trusted me. I know you were scared. I know you were afraid of the water because of your brother—but you trusted me. You put yourself in my hands.

Would you still trust me now? Would you put yourself in my hands?

On a postcard from Ft. Lauderdale, Florida:

April 1978
Spring break = sand + sun + surf + foam (not necessarily from the ocean waves) nudge, nudge, wink, wink. Rolly got us a gig down here at some private frat party—some people he knows from Athens. We all piled into his dad's big ole Chrysler and trucked down. It was a 2-kegger at somebody's daddy's beachhouse. Shit, the place looked like a mansion to me. Musta been a real open invitation cuz the place was packed. God, we were wasted—but so was everyone else, so I don't think they noticed how bad we played. They were joking that we take our pay in beer, but Rolly got them to cough up the cash in the end. I think some threats might have been involved—but I stay out of the business end of things. Hey, congrats on making the National Honor Society in your junior year. Little Miss Smarty-Pants. Next stop, Harvard? Maybe you can hire me as your valet—or your fool/minstrel... In the mean time, you can find me on the beach, watching the bikinis stroll by. Don't worry—I'm only looking. The ones I've met seem pretty—vacant—if you know what I mean...J

On the back of a paper placemat from a Waffle House restaurant:

June 1978
I drove almost 700 miles in an old Chevy beater—10 straight hours of praying the transmission wouldn't drop out from under me and the radio would give me more than just static—stopping only to pee and grab a greasy burger and a peanut log roll at a Stuckey's and fill up the tank—and what do I get at the end of my odyssey? A fucking can of Pepsi from your dad, who tells me with a cackle that you're spending the next six weeks out in San Diego with your sister and her passel of ankle biters. Then he points out a photograph on the end table of you and some dork posing like a pair of mannequins under some fake-ass Roman arch at the junior prom. Is that the pole vaulter? Have you been climbing his pole?
It's a fucking conspiracy... though it may be my own fault cuz I told my gramma when I bought the hunk o'junk that I'd be taking a road trip in June. You know, I love that old lady but she can't keep a secret to save her life. She probably spilled it to my mother who probably told your father who

must have decided he needed to get your sweet ass out of town because GAWDDAMN—they don't make chastity belts anymore.

Please don't spoil my illusion by telling me it was your idea to vacate the premises. If it was, I don't want to know …

What I really wanted to tell you was… Happy Birthday. —Jamie

P.S. You should have told me about the dork and the prom. That's called a sin of omission.

P.P.S. If you tell me it didn't mean a thing, I'll be fool enough to believe you.

P.P.P.S. You looked beautiful.

On a sheet of loose-leaf notebook paper folded in the shape of a star:

October 1978

Can't believe I let you talk me out of quitting school. Musta been hypnotized by the sound of your voice on the phone. After we hung up, I hopped in my car and drove around. Wound up at the cemetery. One of the benefits of working there is you get to know all the ways to sneak in after hours. Not that many people want to. But I like it there. To me, the graveyard is a place of peace—and permanence, too.

The dead don't change.

My great-grandpa's buried there and his father, too, and my grandpa will be laid to rest there when he passes. We've got a family plot marked by a slab of marble with the Emory name carved into it. All our dead are planted there, in the ground, in even rows, like seeds that never sprout. We own the land—but the land owns us, too. Has a stronger grip on us than we have on it. We pick up some soil and it slips through our fingers—but once the clods of dirt have covered our coffins, that's it, we're caught and it'll never let us go again.

Unless you believe in the Second Coming and Judgment Day and all that holy roller shit. Which I don't. After I got busted, Grandma took me to Preacher Effingham and they tried to convince me to accept Jesus Christ as my personal savior and be born again in his name, but I just told them that Jesus died for somebody's sins, but not mine—okay, so I stole that line from Patti Smith. That preacherman looked like he wanted to beat the crap out of me so I knew all that Jesus love stuff is just bogus. But walking in the graveyard tonight it hit me that if it's true that all we've got is the here and now, then we can't waste a minute of it. And it feels like that's what I've been doing for the longest time—just wasting it.

All the Emory graves rest under a live oak. When I worked here in the summer, I used to bring my lunch pail and my guitar and sit up under that tree and eat and make some music. Dead folks make a great audience. They can't boo or make requests for songs that you don't know. Tonight I wished I'd brought my guitar along, but I hadn't so I just sat down under the oak for awhile. Then, I don't know what happened—it was almost like someone took my hand or grabbed my elbow and pulled me onto my hands and knees—cuz I found myself crawling. Something was pulling me over to the graves. It was too dark to see the names so I read them with my fingers, running them over the headstones like a blind man reading Braille. The newer ones, carved in granite, felt warm and smooth, like they were still holding on to the heat of the afternoon sum, but as I kept crawling and the stones got older, they got colder and rougher. They felt fragile under my fingers, like they'd crumble into a thousand pieces if I pressed too hard. The older graves have ledger stones—these huge slabs of limestone—laid over them, like legless tables or doors to an underground fortress. But do they keep the living out or hold the dead in? When I came to one at the far end of the graveyard, where the ridge drops away to the valley and you can see the ages of the land in the layers of sandstone, my fingers read this epitaph on the slab:

> *Behold and see as you pass by*
> *As you are now so once was I*
> *As I am now you soon must be*
> *Prepare to die and follow me.*

I stretched out on the stone and closed my eyes and felt the slab press up against my back like a hand holding me, but it was cold and clammy, uncaring, almost evil. It was an altar and I was the sacrifice. It was an autopsy table and I was the cadaver. It was a butcher's block and I was the side of beef. And then I began to feel like I was closed up inside of something—a casket, a burial vault. I could feel the cold sides up against my shoulders and the bottoms of my feet and the top of my head and I was gasping for breath—because it was all closing in on me, pressing in. There

315

wasn't enough space to just BE anymore—something needed to happen. I had this flash that this must be what it feels like to be born—to have the only walls you've ever known start collapsing in on you, caving in, bearing down, until you have no choice—it's either leave or die—choose death or choose birth.

So I opened my eyes and looked up at the night and stared and breathed and breathed and stared—gulping it down like it was the first air I'd ever breathed and blowing it all out again 'til there wasn't a molecule left in my lungs. The sky looked deep and dim and almost starless, like some dark celestial ocean. Finally I saw one star, one solitary star, silvery white in that vast empty space. At first I thought it was the Pole Star, but it couldn't be because I couldn't find the Dippers and then I realized I was lost—no idea where I was or what to head towards or how to figure that out. I panicked and started scrambling around, half on my knees, crashing into headstones, stumbling. I knocked over something that sounded like it shattered to bits—a flower planter, maybe. Christ, I was like an ant that's lost its leader line, scurrying helter-skelter, first in one direction, then in the opposite, desperate to pick up the trail again. Until I ran headlong into something. I hit it mid-thigh and went sprawling, scraping my chin good, getting the wind knocked out of me. It was a box tomb—they're like big stone tables sitting above the graves. Part of me wanted to just push off and keep running, but another part, the smarter part, said no, you need to stop and rest and wait. Get your bearings. So I boosted myself up on top of the tomb and lay down and just closed my eyes for the count of 10, breathing in and blowing out, feeling my heart slow from a boil to a simmer in my chest—and when I opened my eyes, there they were. Cassiopeia, a big W in the sky, like some eternal question "why?" And Andromeda, her daughter, the chained lady. And there were the Dippers, the drinking gourds, the stars for travelers looking to find their way. The big one was just above the horizon, the little one was higher up, with the two stars at the tip of the big bowl pointing the way to the last star in the little one's handle—Polaris, the Pole Star, the North Star.

I remember being at Grandma Sophie's one night, and we were sitting on the porch burning punks. Do you remember that? Your dad was out there with us and it was time to go home, but we were just sitting, burning the punks to ward off the mosquitoes, and looking at the stars—the few we could see in the haze. And we found the Big Dipper and the Little Dipper and your dad pointed out Polaris at the tip of the handle. He started talking and it sounded like poetry. He said it's the fixed and true beacon for the adventurer, the guide for lost souls, nature's compass that soothes the sailor when his magnetic compass washes overboard in the storm. It tells you everything will be okay if you just keep going. Polaris gives hope when all hope is lost. It blew me away—cuz he wasn't a man to talk like that—at least not around me. Then he laughed and said he stole that from a better writer. But I never got it out of my head.

Don't you see? It's you. It's always been you—since the day I saw you crouching under the table at your brother's funeral. I only know where I am when I know where you are—my body, my mind, the way I'm feeling. Does this sound corny? Are you snickering? Well, fuck it, I guess I don't care. You know, that day Dougie stole the money, before the shit came down your dad pulled me aside and said that all of life is navigation—finding yourself physically, orienting yourself mentally and emotionally, finding some kind of compass. Well, if that's so, then you are the star I steer by. My Polaris, Stella Claire, my bright, clear star.

I love you.

Jamie

CHAPTER 21

Footprints. In the sand, the eternally damp sand where the tongue of the lake laps at the shoulder of the beach. Prints of bare feet that fade as fast as I follow, the water spilling into the shallow cups molded by heels and toes and balls of the feet, dissolving the impressions in its liquid embrace. The waves sing as I trip alongside them, sometimes a lullaby, sometimes a siren's song... until the crashes break in, a sharp alien intrusion into a sibilant world. The crack of something hard against something even harder, a sound that sand and water could never make.

The light is harsh and growing harsher...

My eyelids were crusted over, stuck together with goo, but the glare from my desk lamp managed to slice through.

"Damn." The slurred curse came from a distance and a mouth other than my own.

The crud came away on my fingers as I rubbed my eyes open.

A thud. A groan. A slip-sliding hiss. A moan.

Gripping the arms of the rocker, I pushed myself up, sending a lapful of letters cascading to the floor in a paper waterfall.

Jamie's letters.

But I didn't stop to gather them because the groans and dull thuds coming from below called to me.

He sat propped against the wall in the front room like a scarecrow that had slipped off its post, a sagging man losing his stuffing, suddenly too small to fill his denim shirt, pounding the back of his head against the plaster. I could smell the tavern on him from the stairs.

"Oh, jeez…"

"Stay away!" He swatted the air in front of his face like he was trying to part a swarm of gnats, still banging his head back on the wall, with a dull thump, thump, thump. "G'way."

"Come on, let's get you to bed." I took hold of his upper arm, but he wrenched it out of my grasp, muttering curses, struggling to marshal his straw legs to support him. They kept sliding out from under him, his jeans whispering in protest.

"Stop banging your head and shut up, old man, before you say something you'll regret," I said, without rancor, putting my hand behind his head, wincing as the impact of his skull ground my knuckles into the wall.

When he stopped wrestling and let me pull him up, his lack of weight astonished me. I could have believed he was indeed made of straw, half-expecting to hear a dry rustle and crackle as I slipped my arm around his waist. He allowed me to guide him to his bedroom but batted my hands away as I tried to unbutton his shirt.

"You reek—you don't want to sleep in that."

"Still undress myself," he slurred, even as his fingers kept missing the buttons and sliding away across the front of his shirt. Finally he gave up and staggered over to his bed, half climbing, half crumpling onto the mattress. I leaned against the door, watching his sad efforts.

In another time, in another place, what things I would have said to you. Ha! What epithets I would have spat! What curses and insults I would have flung at you—about your weakness, your inconstancy, your betrayal— but here and now, the words just careen around in my head, glancing off each other like billiards, changing directions, missing connections …

I flipped the light switch and turned to go.

"You're wrong, Claire."

I hesitated in the doorway. "About what?"

"It's the things you don't say that you regret."

My fingers groped the wall to find the switch again. But when they did, they merely hovered over it, without flicking it up.

"So say them," I finally whispered.

But the only reply was the creak of the mattress as he turned over and a shuddering sigh that might have been his head shifting on the pillow.

Or another little piece of a heart being torn away.

I picked up the scattered letters, folded them neatly and pressed them back into their resting place in the white box. Where were their companion pieces, my replies? Had Jamie kept them, as I had kept his, secreted away from prying eyes in a manila envelope duct-taped to the back of my tallest bookcase? Or did he destroy them immediately after reading them, obeying the command I'd written in block letters on each last page just below my signature, using a permanent marker that dried brown-red, an almost perfect imitation of blood: BURN THIS!!

I gave this instruction even though I rarely committed incriminating evidence to paper; wrote no impassioned declarations of love or hate, just sketched out the barest bones of a life, the skeleton stripped of muscle and nerves and blood. And soul.

He told me everything.

I told him nothing.

In some ways, there was nothing to tell. When he was sent away, the real me went with him and what was left was just the shell, a simulacrum to fool a father, a teacher, a girlfriend, a boy. A ghost-image that reflected whatever it was they wanted to see: a dutiful daughter, a perfect student, a caring friend, a fun date. It was easier to be who they wanted me to be than to be myself.

Only Strawboy may have recognized the charade; may have suspected that a pod person had taken possession of my body or that a zombie could walk the earth in the guise of an attractive female or that androids and fembots exist outside of the realm of science fiction. He hovered: sentinel, watchman, guard.

In the morning rush, when my locker jammed, he was there to pry it open, nod and be on his way, like the quiet good

Samaritan or the silent gunslinger who rides in to clean up the town and departs with just the barest tip of his stetson. At lunch, on those days when I craved a Hostess Fruit pie or any of those highly caloric treats that, upon consumption, make a beeline for female thighs and buttocks—when the clique scorned these delights with looks ranging from disgust to wistful, unrequited desire, he was there to split one with me—sometimes cherry (my favorite), sometimes apple (his). How did he know? How did he recognize the need in me? Did he study me as I meandered along in the line of hungry teens flowing around the serving station in the cafeteria? Did he notice my gaze linger on the display rack where the succulent, fat-laden things rested in their Christmas-colored packages? How did he know? Even then, at the breaking of bread, we didn't really talk beyond a few mumbled phrases on the most mundane of adolescent topics: homework, the game, the latest Samurai skit on Saturday Night Live.

So how did he know about those days when the desperation was on the rise inside me, like mercury in a thermometer on a scorching summer afternoon? How did he know to show up at my front door, sometimes with his guitar in its battered case, sometimes without? If he brought it, we'd sit in the front room and he'd strum out chord progressions or challenge me to "Name That Tune." *I can name that tune in five notes... name that tune and if you do, hoo-ha, you're going for the Golden Medley.* If he came without, we'd wind up at Buzzie's pinball arcade down on Commercial Avenue. He's the one who taught me how to release that pent up aggression on the machine, hauling back the plunger, wailing on the buttons to send the flippers flying back and forth, bruising my hipbones with body slams on the edges and corners, but never so hard as to tilt, racking up points on Fireball and Joker Poker and Captain Fantastic. Afterwards, no matter what the weather, we'd hit the Tastee Freeze on Ewing for chocolate dipped cones, vanilla for me, chocolate vanilla twist for him.

"Some people just can't make up their minds."

"Guess I'm bi," he mumble-laughed.

He's the one who sat next to me in the movie theatre as the words crawled up the screen. *"A long time ago, in a galaxy far, far away…"* Was it a date or not? Yes—he asked. No—I paid my way and he didn't try to hold my hand or kiss me. Maybe…

He was the one who made me laugh hysterically at Turnabout when he parodied John Travolta disco-dancing in his white polyester suit. Who would have thunk it—him being capable of such a display, having the willingness to expose himself to public humiliation? Some in the crowd on the dance floor laughed derisively, of course, but others joined in the joke, dozens of fingers swooping low and shooting high as we all burned with our own Saturday night fever. Even the conversation leading up to our going was a hoot, possibly the first time we exchanged more than 10 sentences at a time:

"Did anyone ask you to Turnabout?" Folds cherry pie to split, hands me a half.

"Straw, the girls do the asking—unless you're a couple, and then it's assumed." Bite into mine.

"Oh, well, yeah. But did anyone ask you anyway?" Bites into his.

"No." Chew and swallow.

"So did you ask anyone?"

"No." Another bite. *"So did anyone ask you?"*

Rolls his eyes. *"What do you think?"*

"Maybe that's cuz you hang with me too much. Girls think you're already taken." Dip finger into oozy filling, lick. No visible reaction.

"Oh, you think so? Well if you believe that one, I have some prime real estate to sell you on the east side of Chicago."

"Oh come on. I've seen you with several likely candidates. What happened with you and that girl you took to Homecoming? What's-her-name? Laura?"

"Talked too much." Avoids spilling additional information by taking a large bite of pie.

"That's what kissing's for. Stops 'em from rambling on and on."

Chews on but his cheeks grow a little pink.

"So, you wanna go? Just for shits and grins?" Fish a sad, squishy, deflated pink cherry out of the crust with my tongue. Flush on his cheeks doesn't appear to deepen.

"Yer askin' me?"

Nod. Chew and swallow last bite of pie.

He verifies. "Just for shits and grins?"
Nod again.
"Well, alright, now yer talkin'."
Well alright then. "Okay, it's a… shits and grins night."

Then he showed up in that cream-colored leisure suit and shiny black polyester shirt, sporting Cuban heels and a shit-eating grin that spread his lips wide. The wonder of it was that he could actually dance. *A woman's man? Who knew?*

Passing time in high school purgatory, hanging with a friend, someone who didn't need to try to crack me open, someone who was happy to skim along the surface, someone who was just in it for shits and grins. Because, hey, if he wished for something more than that, he kept it well hidden, another boy with guitar armor. *Well alright so I'm being foolish, well alright let people know, about the dreams and wishes you wish in the night when lights are low…* And if he was just doing his duty to an absent friend, keeping an eye on the precious thing left behind, well, alright, he seemed to be having fun doing it.

As little as we talked about anything, we never talked about Jamie.

And as for his last letter, there had been no reply to burn.

The force of his words, the raw strength of his convictions had knocked me over like a rip current, dragging my feet out from under me, leaving me thrilled and terrified, thrashing in my bed at night, crying into my pillow. It pulled me under, pulled my hand to pen and the pen to paper and I struggled against it, wanting to respond, unwilling to respond, feeling victory, fearing victory. If I called out to him, we would both drown. *You're not the one I want to hurt.* And as I floundered, the words of the lifeguard from that day at the Dunes played over and over in my head:

"If you're caught in a rip current, do not panic. The rip current will not pull you under. Try to float on your back or swim parallel to the shore until you are out of the rip current. Then swim directly towards shore."
You're not the one I want to hurt.

So I left his letter unanswered and swam.

CHAPTER 22

The morning was too bright and hot, the hangover glare of the sun punishing my eyes as I stood squinting in front of Sophie's house. I'd left my father flat on his back, snoring fitfully in his rank-smelling bed. *Useless*, I'd muttered as I watched him from the doorway, a part of me raring to walk in and douse him with a pitcher of ice water to haul his sorry ass out of bed. Yet his chest, as it rose and fell, looked astonishingly fragile, the fingers of his left hand hanging off the edge of the mattress looked so delicate, that it seemed to disturb him would be to risk breaking him. So I left him be and walked the few short blocks to Sophie's alone, thinking the exercise would do me good, but finding instead that it only left me sweaty, recalcitrant and scowling at the foot of her front porch.

Yet there was nothing to do but climb those steps, even if my feet dragged; unlock the door, even if I struggled to fit the key in the lock; and begin the work of the day, even if I longed to be home—truly home—sitting in the shade of my maple tree, my back resting against its solid trunk, a book in my hand, an iced tea to my right, and Aaron's head resting in my lap. Like it used to be… once upon a dream.

Yeah, right…

There was a household to dispose of and a Salvation Army pick-up to supervise. Responsibilities. Yet as much as I struggled to get caught up in the flow of purposeful activity, I kept tripping over odd thoughts that lay like loose pebbles in a streambed.

This is the first time I have ever been alone in this house...

How long will it take for these rooms to lose her scent? Will it dissipate when the house is completely empty of her possessions or will the smell still linger? Will it be overcome by the odors of fresh paint and varnish? Be chased out by the fresh air that's coming in through the open windows? Or will some small bit of it survive, hidden in the back of a closet, clinging to some tight tiny corner of wall near the ceiling, where the painter forgets to run a brush. And when the next family who buys the house moves in, when the mother or father or child opens the door, just the merest whiff of crushed lilacs and talcum powder and Lydia Pinkham's tonic will escape, like tiny Hope taking flight from Pandora's box...

The salvagers arrived at the appointed time, two tall, lean black men in clothes that looked two sizes too big, one middle-aged with a graying beard, the other barely out of his teens. They swooped in and out like graceful birds of prey, quietly and efficiently carrying off the beds, the night stands, the end tables, the lamps. They gestured to the little empty curio in the living room and I was about to nod when something stopped me. My father had left the box of china birds on the floor beside it.

"No, not that. Leave that. But you could take the sofa."

They took one look at its worn fabric and strange bulges where the springs had popped and shook their heads.

"That's felt the weight of one too many asses. No offense, ma'am," said the older man.

The unexpected truth and poetry in the man's turn of phrase jolted a snorting laugh out of my mouth that surprised both them and me. "None taken," I quickly mumbled, struggling to stifle a fit of giggles.

They grabbed the last end table and took flight, the tails of their gray work shirts flapping in the breeze of their haste.

I stood on the porch and watched their truck rumble down the street. It was noon and I'd done nothing. I walked to the porch rail that overlooked the side yard. The enchantment of its tangle of lilacs and climbing roses, of the narrow dirt paths that wound around peonies and behind hydrangeas back to the grape arbor was gone. All that remained was overgrown shrubs.

Out of the corner of my eye in the midst of all the green and brown and black, I caught a flutter of white—the sleeve of a T-shirt, perhaps a scarf. I squinted, but in that same instant, a car engine backfired down the street and its shot-gun report startled me. I shuddered and blinked. In that split-second, the glimpse of white disappeared—but the sense of motion hung in the air, like an after-image of something or someone who had flitted past the arbor.

One of those everyday ghosts…

It occurred to me as I walked down the gangway that I was behaving like a character in a horror flick—the kind of person who does exactly the thing that she shouldn't, the kind of person that makes you want to shout at the screen, *"No, stupid, don't walk down that alley!"* or *"Hey, moron, don't open that door!"*

But if they don't, there's no story, is there?

I'm following you, wherever you lead, from now on.

The arbor was no longer the cool shade-drenched bower I remembered. The wood of the grapevines was too old to succor a healthy growth of leaves. It was a gnarled gray skeleton to which shreds of green flesh still clung. Sunlight flooded through the bare bones of the branches, bringing heat and glare.

Ah, but in the summer of 1979, it had been at the height of its emerald green glory and the only things that haunted it were the living.

It was the perfect place to brood. *My* place to brood. When I acquired my driver's license, I had taken over the grocery shopping for Sophie. The aunts were thrilled to relinquish this chore. For me, it was another dutiful brick to shove into the façade that I was building. In winter, I'd perch on the stool at Sophie's elbow and sip a cup of her strong black tea. We'd stare out the window in cozy silence that she'd occasionally punctuate with a question: how was I doing in school? Was there a boy to talk about? Did my father seem content? I kept my answers minimal: fine, no, seems so.

In summer she'd croak: "Go out, go out, too nice to sit here in the dark with an old baba."

I'd take my lemonade to the grape arbor. I'd drag an old metal lawn chair in under the vines and there I would sit and meditate. Even the sounds of summer: the giggles, shouts and splashes of the neighbor children in their kiddie pool, the far-off roar of lawn mowers, the raw hum of window air conditioners, could not spoil the mood.

But Dougie could.

After the purse pilfering fiasco, he had been sentenced to the family equivalent of community service: doing chores for Sophie. Aunt Dodie obviously figured it would prove to the world—that is, the relatives—that her son was really a fine, upstanding young man and the event had simply been a figment of my misguided, overactive imagination. Since then he'd been doing time mowing, trimming, painting and window washing. During our senior year, I chanced to walk into the kitchen with a bag of groceries and saw him tucking a twenty dollar bill into his wallet. Sophie shrugged guiltily when our eyes met.

Later, when we were alone, she made a brusque attempt at explanation. "For college," she rasped. "I pay you, too, take."

"I don't want your money, Grandma." I said, refusing the bill in her shaking hand.

Hard as I tried to make sure our paths never crossed, it was impossible and that spring, just before graduation, it seemed that every time I was there, Dougie was, too.

His presence began to ruin the arbor as my refuge. He never actually entered it while I was there, but he would hover around, taking forever to mow the grass, dawdling with the hedge trimmers around the boxwood that walled off the yard from the alley, sweeping and re-sweeping the gangway until every single blade of clipped grass was banished from the cement. Once, when he did darken the arched trellis entrance, I threatened that, if he dared to set foot inside, I would tell Sophie that he'd stolen money from the purse that always hung over her chair in the kitchen.

"And you know she'll believe me."

After that, our paths crossed less frequently. To my profound relief, for graduation, there was no joint family celebration. My father took me to dinner at Phil Smidt's in Hammond where we talked, laughed and sampled frog legs (yes, tastes like chicken—with the consistency of white fish) and gooseberry pie and probably looked, to the casual observer, like a model father and daughter. Summer arrived early and with a vengeance. On mid-afternoons in early June, after putting in six hours on my feet cashiering at Jewel, bombarded by fluorescent lights and crying babies and clanging shopping carts and the constant thrum of the check-out line conveyor belt, the arbor was the sanctum to which I fled.

So, on a particularly tiring day, when I'd driven there without even stopping at home to change out of my uniform, when I hadn't even peeked in the house to say hello to Sophie, but just parked the car at the curb and hurried down the gangway to sit in my cool, green place with my eyes closed and simply *breathe*, it was maddening to hear the snap of a branch and open my eyes to a tall dark form looming in the arch. Backlit by the stark white light of the afternoon sun, the edges of the figure glowed with a red-orange aura that made it impossible for me to distinguish the features of the face. But I knew who was.

"Just get the fuck out of here. I told you what I'd do if you ever came in here."

The figure paused in the opening for a long moment, and then stepped inside the arbor.

"You talkin' ta me?" The voice was Robert DeNiro as Travis Bickle filtered through a Southern drawl that ended in a snorting laugh. "You talkin' ta me? Sheee-et. I do believe that's the first time I've ever heard you say the word 'fuck.' Guess I'm just gonna have to haul your sweet ass down to Georgia for one of Grammie's 'come to Jesus' meetin's."

I blinked once, twice, three times before my eyes readjusted to the green gloom—although I knew the face that would loom toward me even before he squatted down and took hold of the arms of my lawn chair.

"What are you doing here?" I half-laughed, half-gasped. "When'd you get into town? Christ, I thought you were Dougie! Why didn't you tell me you were coming up? God, I haven't heard from you in—ages!"

He cocked his head and regarded me with a look that bordered on reproach. "Seems to me you're the one who went all incommunicado."

The foot of space between us was suddenly filled with an awkward silence that crowded out the moment's initial glee. It was one of those uncomfortable interludes when your gaze just automatically longs to travel down to your fingernails or sideways to examine a splotch on the wall or upwards to study a crack on the ceiling. But I forced my eyes to stay focused straight ahead— on Jamie's face.

It had lost some of its girlish softness; the jaw had tightened, the cheeks had hardened; the flesh seemingly transformed from warm, pliable clay into cool, immutable marble. But when I reached out to stroke the smooth surface of his cheek, the yielding velvet heat of him throbbed through my fingers. His hair still cascaded in ringlets to his shoulders. And his chocolate kiss eyes still beamed sweetly, though a new wariness seemed to tug the corners down and add weight to his brow.

When I leaned in to kiss him, he drew back, leaving my lips hanging inches from his.

"That would be the easy thing to do, wouldn't it? Just take up where we left off?"

His words, and the bitterness that flavored them, jolted me back in my chair.

"That's not what you want?"

His hands squeezed the metal arms of the chair. "It's not a matter of wanting. Wanting's what I've been doing for a long time. It's—it's about what's right. Getting things straight between us." He stopped, looked away with a pained wince, then stood up, shaking his leg as if chasing out a cramp. "You never answered my last letter. It's been—what? Seven, eight months? You never wrote back. I'd call, you were never at home. Your dad always said he'd give you the message. I don't know, maybe he didn't. All I know is you never called back. Never wrote, never called. What the hell was that all about?"

I dodged the question by throwing out one of my own. "Are you here to stay? Or just for the summer? The week? The day?"

"You didn't answer my question. And my answer depends on yours."

His voice had changed, like his face; the timbre had darkened, deepened. The boy with whom I'd spent hours chatting about everything under the sun was gone. I was now talking to a man. *Succumb to the terror in that realization, let it pull you under, or use it to fight back.* "You scared the crap out of me! That's why I didn't answer!" He looked astonished at my sudden vehemence. "You did! I was terrified. How can I be someone's North Star? Help someone else find his way—when I don't even know the way myself?! When I'm just as lost! You asked too much!"

His eyes shifted from left to right, weighing his response, just as clearly as if the scales were tangible and right there in front of us. *He wouldn't have done that before. He would have just spoke out, right off the top of his head.*

"Oh man," he finally groaned. "Claire, shit. I was so high that night I don't even remember what I wrote. Man, I'm so sorry. You should've just told me to fuck off and get my shit together. I'm surprised you didn't. Christ, what an idiot, I'm sorry." He was shrugging and shuffling, another bojangles man, his eyes looking everywhere but at me.

He wouldn't have done that before.

"You sounded pretty lucid earlier that night on the phone—and even in the letter you—"

He dug in the dirt with the toe of his Adidas. "Well, a good girl like you wouldn't understand this, but there's high—and then there's wasted. And it's like the difference between swimming through crystal clear water and wading through mud."

"So, are you high right now?"

He squatted down in front of me again. "I've been straight ever since." He stared at me, like he was memorizing the contours of my face. "I didn't mean to frighten you. I was just—just looking for something. Everybody's looking for something." He paused, appeared to consult the invisible scales again, then shrugged. "Whatever it was that I wrote."

Something was off, out-of-kilter, the scales unbalanced, but it was easier to not try to figure it out, easier to push those thoughts aside and let things be.

"So how long are you staying?"

"Til Grandma Sophie kicks me out."

"You're here—you mean you're staying *here?*"

"Been on my dad's shit list for years now, even before I got busted, and mama—she's turned into a freakin' harpy. They don't even want me up here. I crashed at Strawboy's for a couple days, but his parents were startin' to hint I needed to move on. Grandma said I could stay as long as I needed to. I told her I'd pay rent as soon as I found a job. In the meantime, I'd do her handyman work."

I grimaced. "She's been paying Dougie to do that."

"Yeah, she told me. She also told me she didn't want any problems between him and me under her roof. I promised to stay on my best behavior." He leaned in closed and whispered in my ear. "But I kept my fingers crossed behind my back." He brandished his hand before my eyes, like a magician introducing an elaborate illusion, fingers firmly crossed.

The nearness of his lips, the heat radiating from his body onto my skin, the seductive movement of his hand, made me sway a little, like a reed in a sudden wind.

Nothing... there is nothing like this... not the anticipation of a roller coaster climb when your skin goes taut against the bones of your face and your eyes feel gravity pulling them back in your skull... not the freefall down the other side of the arc, that stretched-to-the-limit, leaving-your-heart-behind-you, dry-mouthed surge... not the gasping effervescence of that first plunge into a white water wave when even your blood tingles... not the breath-taking sting of winter wind on your cheeks... not any drug rush like a liquid flame in the veins... nothing... there is nothing like this...

And like a junkie hurting for a fix, I took up the needle with trembling fingers.

My fingers did quiver as I unfastened the top two buttons of my uniform shirt and reached down inside. But when I had fished up my hidden treasure and held it out to him, the palm of my hand was as steady and solid as a marble altar bearing an offering to a god.

"I've had my fingers crossed for three years," I said.

He stared at the Claddagh ring.

"What a pair of actors—you playing the oh-so-good girl so they couldn't find an excuse to send you away, me playing the bad boy doing my worst so that they'd have to bring me back. Prevaricatin' swine, as Grammie would say. And all for what? I ask myself that every day. Why? They made us what we are. What're they afraid of? The truth? Truth is first cousins can marry in over twenty states. I looked it up. So what's the big fucking deal? It's not like it's illegal or immoral or—"

"Shhhh." I pressed the ring against his lips to silence him. "Shhh. It doesn't matter now."

Nothing mattered that summer in the gingerbread house of delights that we built together in the clearing we had suddenly found in the dark, brutal, confusing woods through which we'd been stumbling, lost, alone. It was a house built of chocolate and peppermint kisses, painted with honey smooth caresses, perfumed with the bittersweet, burnt sugar scent of cotton candy. It was a magical house where the more we nibbled at its sweet temptations, the faster they were replenished. It was a house of cravings, where the more we consumed, the more our hunger grew, a house without satisfaction where the need for, the addiction to, that candy overwhelmed every other need: for food, for sleep, for reason itself.

Once a week became twice, then three times, then four, until by mid-July, it was a daily need that drove us, shaking with withdrawal and desire, into the arbor. For the two hours we had between the end of my work day and the start of his, hauling carts and re-stocking shelves at the K-Mart, we were strung out in its emerald shadow, high on human candy.

Drugged we were, yes. Hyper aware of the passage of time, understanding with a piercing clarity Einstein's theory of relativity: how the hours we spent apart dragged by as if the hands of all clocks had been dipped in molasses; how the minutes we had together raced past as if time itself had been injected with amphetamines. Hyper aware, too, of every assault on our physical sensations: the two-ton heat of the midsummer sun after a morning spent in the featherweight chill of air conditioning; the gunshot snap and crackle of paper bags as the baggers shook them open; the pendulous, succulent nectar scent of the over-ripe cantaloupes and honeydews that I hefted onto the cash register scale. Every light was the brightest I'd ever squinted at; every color the most vivid shade possible. The nose- and lip-tingling fizz in my ginger ale might well have been the bubbles effervescing in the finest champagne. It was an altered state of consciousness, living life in perpetual arousal.

But into every junkie's life reality must eventually fall, piercing the haze like a knife cuts through gauze. It came with a restlessness, a vague bud of dissatisfaction that grew and blossomed into full-blown peevishness. More, he wanted more, *they always wanted more.*

Don't pretend you don't want it yourself. I do and I don't. I can't and I won't. There is no place. Not here. Not in a car. Not in Sophie's house. Not in my house. Definitely not in your house. All the nots running in my head and out of my mouth until I feel like I am being hounded by Seuss's Sam-I-Am. I will try it, you will see, but for now, just let me be. Why not? I don't know why not. And yet I do. A million reasons. Why did it have to become an issue? When did the arbor and its delights become less than enough? What is it about human beings? Especially the male of the species! They just have to go and spoil everything … never content with anything, always wanting more, looking for something else, asking, pressing, needing…

The last week of July it rained every afternoon. The sun rose on hot, sticky air that stank of wet dog, rotting fish and sulfur. By noon the thunderheads would rear up in the west. They rolled over the city in waves of violent white flashes of light and soul-shaking crackles and the booming footfalls of the gods. Torrential downpours overflowed the old gutters on Sophie's house and pelted a steady tattoo on window panes and roofs.

It kept us from the arbor, providing relief and aggravation in equal doses. Kept us penned up in the gloom of Sophie's house, moving restlessly from kitchen to front room to back porch.

Kept our hands busy with inconsequentials: the haphazard strumming of random guitar chords, the arranging and rearranging of wayward strands of hair, the scratching of mosquito bites. Kept our mouths pre-occupied with the perfunctory nibbling of almond windmill cookies and ginger snaps, gone softly stale in the humidity, and with the sipping of tart lemonade whose edge quickly dulled as the ice melted in our glasses. We attempted a game of Scrabble but abandoned it when the letters on our trays repeatedly defied arrangement into comprehensible words. Or maybe it was our minds that were defiant… empty of sense.

"I can't think with you sitting there jiggling your sandal like that, with that stupid slap-slap. It's like the Chinese water torture."

"I'm just trying to drown out the sound of your fingers drumming. Do you know how annoying that is when you're trying to think?"

"Yeah, well, I can think of something else I'd rather be doing with my fingers." That last under his breath, as if Sophie were in the kitchen with us, rather than in her chair far down the hall.

"Will you just use your tiles and play a word?"

"If I had an O, I could make 'tongue.'"

"Stop."

In the end we childishly pushed the board back and forth between us and then away, scattering our hard-won words back into a jumble of meaningless letters.

Neither of us would accept a suggestion by the other. A jaunt to a museum? *Not enough time.* The library? *Card expired.* So renew it. *Some other day.* Space Invaders at the arcade? *Too noisy—can't deal with that today.* Wanting only what we couldn't have left us sullen, shutting cabinet doors with a force just this side of a slam, rolling pencils to and fro over the kitchen table, chewing ice.

He wouldn't even touch me under her roof. Said he'd made her a promise of good behavior and he meant to keep it. Refused to listen, sticking his fingers in his ears like a petulant schoolboy when the temptress in me reminded him that the promise applied to his dealings with Dougie, not me. Then when he did abandon his chaste ideals in a fit of physical exasperation, and grabbed my wrist, recklessly pulling me into the dining room and pressing me up against the wall, I slipped under his arm and away, with a mocking smirk. *"Where's your good behavior now?"* *"Come back here and kiss me."* *"In your dreams."* To retaliate, from then on, he always kept something between us: a table, a chair, several feet of unoccupied, uneasy space. Wouldn't even entertain the notion of sitting together in the spare bedroom like we used to until Friday, when Strawboy showed up for some attempted comic relief with his guitar, his goofy grin and a basket of fried shrimp from Calumet Fisheries over at the 95th Street Bridge.

"Damn, some Catholic traditions are still worth honoring," Jamie chuckled, hoisting a golden-battered, thumb-sized shrimp to his lips.

"S'long as it's not god-awful fish sticks, I can deal with the whole meatless Friday scene," Strawboy agreed.

"Don't wipe your greasy fingers on Grandma's afghan," I sniped, disgruntled by the fact that they had consumed way more than their fair shares of the bounty.

They ran through their repertoire, Strawboy reclining into the worn pillows on the converted twin bed next to me, Jamie sitting cross-legged on the floor against the opposite wall. Beatles' covers segued into acoustic Led Zeppelin. *Baby, baby, baby, I'm gonna leave you…* Page and Plant morphed into Townsend and Daltrey, who bled into Elvis Costello and The Clash. They stumbled through the ska rhythms of *"White Man in Hammersmith Palais,"* cursing as their fingers fretted the wrong notes. The angry music of angry young Brits fed off the heat and the charged ions already in the atmosphere. Some sort of pissing contest was taking place, the two of them trading leads back and forth, not trading so much as seizing hold and then surrendering, a tug of war of chords and notes and hammer-ons and pull-offs and double-stops, and the thrashing of strings. Maybe Jamie was letting all that frustration seethe through his fingers onto those strings. Maybe Straw was just rising to the challenge. The battle hopped across the Atlantic and mellowed slightly for a leering *"Louie Louie,"* and then an epic struggle through *"Darkness on the Edge of Town."*

"Ain't the same without the E Street Band."

"Where's Clarence when we need him?"

"What you two need is some talent."

"She's still miffed about the shrimp."

The duo headed west, bringing Neil Young into the fray, and then taking on Fleetwood Mac with savage renditions of *"Go Your Own Way"* and *"The Chain."*

"That's how it should sound, in Chicago, surrounded by the mills, not some pansy California beach. Not that I'd mind laying up on some California beach."

"Lying."

"What?"

"Lying on some California beach."

"That's what I said."

"No, you said 'laying.'"

"What's the difference? Laying, lying?"

"To lay is to set something down, to lie is to be at rest in a horizontal position."

"So then it should be *Lie, Lady, Lie*? You're saying Dylan has poor grammar?"

"And should it be get lied instead of get laid? I think Mr. Webster would take exception to that. He's laying—er—lying over on that shelf next to you. Drag him out here."

"Vulgar cretins."

"Nope, nope, lookie here, missy. The word 'cretin' already implies vulgarity, so you are being—what's that word I'm looking for, Straw?"

"Redundant?"

"Right on, man."

They rifled through the yellowed pages of Sophie's ancient dictionary for a few minutes, hunting for dirty words. Finding little in the way of titillation, they tossed it aside and let their guitars rumble down South to channel Johnny Cash. We were all sweating by then in that close, seething, electric-hot little room, trickles running down the sides of Strawboy's nose and along his sharp jaw, the sheen of it glistening on Jamie's forehead and slicking back his hair at the temples, the spidery feeling of it crawling down my back and we all sang to the blood-throb rhythm. Oh, it did burn, burn, burn, that ring of fire.

"Damn, we need a bass," Strawboy moaned as we finished, wiping his seeping face on his already damp T-shirt. *A flash of skin so pale, but taut, stretched over contoured muscle.* "Shit, we were at my house, I'd grab my Fender. And the basement would be a helluva lot cooler."

"Who'd play rhythm?"

Strawboy gave me a sideways glance. Jamie gazed at me, cool speculation under the beads of sweat that clung precariously to his curls. Then they looked at each other and burst out laughing.

"I shoulda taught her years ago."

"Shit yeah, you shoulda."

"But she's always going on about it being 'my armor.' Never seemed interested in learning."

"I said that once, just once! You're the one who—"

"Shit, what time is it?" Jamie growled, never one to wear a watch.

I glanced at mine. "Twenty minutes til your shift starts, you jerk."

"Shit." Jamie sprang up. "Okay, man, you'll have to teach her the first lesson. Go with chords A, E and D. If she's as smarty-pants about it as she is about everything else, throw in G, E-minor and C and she can at least play some oldies." He thrust his guitar into my lap. "Go ahead. Take it." He nodded at Strawboy. "Don't let her drop it."

I kicked at his shin, but he pivoted out of the way and squinted at my left hand. "She needs to trim her nails. There's some clippers in the medicine chest."

"Asshole!"

Alone with me and the two guitars, Strawboy wiped the sweat away again, this time with quicker, more furtive, almost apologetic movements, bending his head so he didn't have to lift his shirt up quite so far and again expose that white, hard-packed belly.

"It's just joking, you know. We were just being stupid."

"So what else is new?"

"Aw, don't be mad, Claire. You don't have to learn—"

I cut him off. "But I want to."

"Really." It was more a statement of disbelief than a question.

"Yeah, I really do. So shut up and show me."

He regarded me warily, still unsure. After a moment, he shrugged, leaned his own guitar up against the wall and eased his way around back of me. Feeling the awkward press of his thighs surrounding mine, my own body contracted, giving up my right to the space. He took hold of the neck with his left hand. "The A chord's like this." He positioned his fingers along the strings in the second fret, reaching his right arm around me to strum, straining a little, or so it seemed, to keep his flesh from touching mine. "Don't play the top string on an A chord. Start with the one below that." Under his fingers, the chord rang out, gorgeous and full. "Okay, your turn."

Taking the shallowest of breaths, I sat, still sucked up into myself. He took my left wrist—cautiously, as if taking hold of a stem studded with thorns—and arranged my hand around the neck of the guitar, tentatively pressing my fingers to the correct strings, easing my thumb along to a comfortable position.

Well alright. Friends. Just friends. That's how it is that you sit here, up against me, just the barest sheaths of fabric between my skin and yours, and you cover my hand with yours and press my fingers and lean your head up close to mine, so that I can smell the citrus of your aftershave—Brut? But how is it that I am not sure whether the taste of salt on my tongue is from my sweat or the nearness of yours?

"Okay, strum. You can use the backs of your fingernails, or your thumb. It's up to you. Or I can get you a pick outta my case."

I ran my thumb down the strings, producing a grating buzz.

"Really press on the strings up here. Keep 'em down. It'll start to hurt—and it'll hurt for awhile, until you build up some calluses." He pressed his fingers down over mine.

I strummed again. Better.

"Okay, try it yourself." He lifted his fingers from mine quickly then, as if releasing some hot thing that he'd held for too long. I kept mine pressed down firmly and strummed away.

"Good, that was good. So that's A."

He plucked each string from top to bottom. "E, A, D, G, B, E. Einstein Ate Drano, Good Bye Einstein. Okay, so lemme show you D chord."

We weren't meant to know about this—the fit of one body to the other, the way a hand rests just so at the place where waist flares into hip. Not together, not me-and-you. This wasn't meant for us… that's why we flinch at every accidental touch, like it's the sting of a whip… isn't that it? Yet, we keep coming back for more…

By the time we got to the G chord, he had a hard-on. I could feel it between us, and the feathery touch of his breath on my neck, and his fingers following the path of the seam up my shirt.

This wasn't meant for us…

A quick shrug of the shoulder, a nimble flick of hand to the neck, an agile lie on the lips to save both our faces: "Must be a mosquito in here—and god, it's hot. My fingers are killing me already." I eased myself up out of the curve of his body and put the guitar on his lap. "Think I need a recess, teacher. And I'm thirsty—how 'bout you? Let's have some lemonade."

We slumped at the kitchen table, making a great show of sipping, of swirling the ice in our glasses, of pressing their cold curves to our cheeks and foreheads, avoiding each other's eyes.

CHAPTER 23

Mid-August found us saying goodbye to friends, as one by one they packed up and headed off to the next big adventure: dorm life at the U of I or NIU or Southern. The University of Chicago ran on a quarter system, so it started much later than most colleges—my freshman orientation didn't begin until mid-September. Some acquaintances were still around, taking classes at Moraine Valley or Prairie State community colleges. Even Jamie succumbed, moving back into his parents' house, letting Peach talk him into signing up for a few courses, but he chose the grittier scene at Loop College downtown. Labor Day came and went and then it was my turn. I gave my notice at Jewel, hung up my uniform shirt, packed suitcases and a trunk with clothes and memorabilia to carry me through—and headed for the beach for one last time.

"It's not like you're going across country. In fact, this is the perfect set-up. You're gonna be in a dorm room maybe twenty-five minutes away—a dorm room…" He turned his head to look at me as he lay on his towel idly scooping sand with one hand. "With a bed."

"And a roommate," I added, heading off what I knew was coming.

"Hey, roommates have to leave the room sometime… to go to the cafeteria, take a shower, maybe even a night at the library."

"How would you know? When do you ever hit the library for a night of studying?"

"Hey, between seeing you and stocking shelves, I've got no time to study."

"U of C's different. I'll have to study—a lot—if I want to compete."

He shrugged, physically, maybe mentally as well, and let that sleeping dog lie.

Here we go again. How can you know you don't like green eggs and ham? Have you tried them? Why won't you try them? What if we all refused to do things simply because we haven't done them before? Sam, Sam. Jamie, Jamie, let me be.

Spoiler.

After that, I couldn't find a comfortable place to stretch out on my towel. The sand felt unyielding as granite, irritating as steel wool; the sound of the ceaseless waves as harsh as a chainsaw to my ears.

"Wanna swim?" he asked when I had flip-flopped from stomach to back for the hundredth time.

"No." I jerked myself up into a sitting position.

"Hungry? We could go downtown for some pizza."

I shrugged. "Well, this is boring."

"Okay, then let's blow this popsicle stand."

As we shook the sand out of our towels, he couldn't help but nudge that old dog again.

"So, are you saying we won't be seeing each other as much?"

"Well, that's kinda obvious."

He shoved his towel under his arm. "Not sure it was, to me."

It was my turn to let the beast alone.

Would you, could you in a boat? On a train? In the rain? Sam, Jamie, I am weary, weary, weary…

He wanted to shower, so we were silent all the way to his house, where I opted to wait outside in his Malibu, scratching mosquito bites, trying to read *Sophie's Choice*, my eyes straying from the page to the front windows, wondering if *she* was looking out them at me. When he came busting out the front door and bounding down the steps two at a time, I couldn't help but smile at his exuberance, but as he neared the car, I noticed a streak of red at the corner of his mouth.

Blood seeped from his split lip.

"What happened?" I fumbled in my purse for a tissue.

He flinched away from my hand as I reached over to daub the wound.

"Jamie?"

No reply.

Not a sound.

Nothing.

Just the click of the key in the ignition, the growl and shudder of the engine roused from slumber, the squealing protest of tires pressed too hard and fast against asphalt.

And my own weak, jittery chirps. "Was it your dad? Your mom? What? Why did he—was it me? In the car? Aren't you going to tell me?"

He drove angrily, braking hard at stops, and then jack-rabbitting away, tailgating, swerving around cars as they paused to parallel park. But he said nothing, not even a muttered curse under his breath, until he pulled to the curb two doors down from my house.

"Hair. It's always the fucking hair. It's an excuse to start in on everything all over again since…" He shook his head quickly. "No, not even since that—it's everything that's ever been wrong with me since the day I was born. So just fuck it. Fuck it. Cut it off. Get a pair of scissors and cut it off, Claire."

Confusion and frustration splotched his cheeks like a sunburn and the dried black blood cracked and seeped an angry red again.

"Come in and we'll—"

"No, just get the damn scissors. Bring 'em out here. If I go in there, I'll just do something stupid—start heavin' tables around."

He closed his eyes, slumped into the seat and the sigh he let out seemed a dismissal of life itself.

"I'll be right back."

Get in and out as quickly as possible. No muss, no fuss, no questions asked. If I was lucky, my father would be ensconced in his recliner in front of the TV, pondering the hell-in-a-hand basket state of the world presented to him in living color on the evening news. *Slip in the back and grab the scissors from the junk drawer in the kitchen.* They weren't nearly as sharp as a barber's shears would be—but they'd have to do.

I shook off my sandals, edged in through the outer door and, hunkering low, crept up the back porch steps and over to the kitchen window.

Deserted.

The kitchen door was blessedly unlocked. He wouldn't be able to see me from the angle of his chair. Now to avoid being ratted out by any loud squeaks from the old floor or the junk drawer that never opened without a tug. Heaven forbid dropping the scissors. But as I inched across the kitchen, with each careful placement of my foot, it struck me that something was… odd… wrong.

Something was… missing.

No measured baritone intoned the latest developments from New York or London or the Mideast; no flippant jingle underscored a burning consumer need for some new and improved product. The TV wasn't on.

He was home. Had to be. His car was parked out there under the elm.

So get the scissors and go.

I eased the drawer open and clasped the cool blades in my sticky hot fingers, lifting them slowly out of their bed of loose string, rusted nails and eraserless pencils.

And froze.

That sound. Those sounds.

Something missing… and something present… something that didn't belong.

That didn't belong *here*—in this house.

I've heard this before. Those sounds have even escaped my own lips…

But not here.

And the second voice—if one could call it that?

I'd shed my sandals at the back door, so why did my feet feel so anchored in place, like they were encased in a pair of steel-toed boots? Yet move they did, and soundlessly—or maybe I just didn't hear them, so full were my ears already.

The door to my father's bedroom was ajar, a good eight inches of open space between it and the jamb.

It should be open—or it should be closed—not in this halfway, netherworld state.

You have been here before.

Don't. You know what happens when you peek through these types of doors. You know what goes on behind these kinds of doors.

Don't put your face up into the gap. Don't will your eyes to focus in the gloom.

On the bed, bodies heaved. Flesh hard and soft in the glimmer of sweat. *See how the skin of the elbow bunches and sags? Older flesh of a body slowly giving itself over to gravity. Milk white spreading over honey gold. She always did tan—but not too much, never mocha, just caramel. And see the chiaroscuro on the pillow of the dark hair and the light.*

You knew. You knew before you ever peered in. You knew what you would see.

You knew.

Yes.

And did she know? Is that why she shifted her head over his shoulder and opened her eyes? Or did she hear the foolish, useless gasp, and feel the cool exhalation rush past her cheek and fear it was a ghostly presence of… that other woman.

No. Only me. Only her daughter.

If it had truly been a revelation, a bombshell, an earthshaker, something would have happened. Some thunderclap moment. I'd have dropped the scissors or thrust open the door with such swift violence that its glass knob would have shattered against the wall. I'd have screamed or shouted or laughed hysterically; grabbed my mother's gilt hand mirror from the place on the dresser where it still lay, five years after her death, and flung it at their heads. I'd have thrown alarm clocks, toppled the bedside table lamp, yanked curtains down from the windows. I'd have pummeled their bare backs with closed fists, scratched and clawed the thinning, fine-lined skin around their eyes. All the violent acts that passed through my mind, I could have committed… if it had truly been a shock.

What was the term we learned in English? Anagnorisis – the point in the plot of a tragedy at which the protagonist recognizes her or some other character's true identity or discovers the true nature of her situation. Electra, Antigone, I could play… but this was no Greek tragedy.

This was just... a confirmation. The firming up of a viscous feeling that had oozed and curdled inside for so long. The what-took-you-so-long recognition of a notion that had clung like snot for years… the vaguest of suppositions, suspicions... but there it was… the clearest of evidence. Even a virgin can understand that bodies that move like that, in perfect intimate unison, have been molded to fit together with such delicate precision, such honed familiarity, only by time and practice.

How long? How long would it take to achieve that level of union, communion, complicity? Months? Years? Decades?

How many times?

It was a familiar voice that whispered the words in my ear, so close, so cold she might have been inside it.

Many. Many. For a very long time. Going back to even before you were born.

And in reply, bitter words to pound in my head and heart with every silent footfall back the way I had come.

Tell me something that I don't already know.

"Alright," Jamie hissed when he saw the scissors in my hand. "Do it. Right here. Right now."

"No. Drive. Now."

Something in my face perhaps.

"What? What happened? You and Joe get into it, too?"

"No. Just let's go. Come on, you were pedal to the metal a few minutes ago."

"Fine."

But as he turned to head north, I jerked my thumb in the opposite direction. "No."

"No? What?"

"I don't want to go to Uno's."

"Okay, so what you got a taste for?"

"Not hungry."

"By the time we get there, get a table, order and finally get the pizza, you will be."

"No. Take me..." *Where?* "Take me... to the Dunes. Let's go to the Dunes."

His sidelong looked asked if I was crazy. "The Dunes? We just left the beach."

"I don't care. I changed my mind. A different beach."

"It'll be after six by the time we get there. We'll only have another hour or so of daylight."

"I don't care."

He gave a defeated shrug as he put the car in gear. "Okay, we'll go. Then maybe you'll tell me what just happened back there."

"Nothing."

Sand at dusk is comforting to the feet, like a massage by a pair of cool, strong hands. It revitalizes, tantalizes, inspires a longer stroll than one originally intended. We'd climbed one of the smaller dunes and sat on top, watching the few other beach idlers below as they paused to admire the growing tangerine glow of the sunset.

"Think this is still part of the park? Or one of them private beaches?"

"Dunno. It's a beach. And there's hardly anyone else on it."

"No shit Sherlock." When he kissed me I could taste the onions from the Big Mac he'd wolfed down as we drove along Route 12.

"I'm just wonderin'—if this is still the park—how often the rangers patrol this stretch at night. After it closes."

"Who cares?"

"Well, hey, Miss Goody-Two-Shoes—"

"Who's that? Can't imagine who you are talkin' about."

"Hey, if it's danger you're looking for—it's my middle name. Danger. James Danger. At your service." He jumped up and bowed with a windmilling flourish.

"Yeah, we all know about your illegal tendencies."

He clutched his chest as if struck by a bullet and crumpled to his knees again in the sand, then extended a hand. "Don't underestimate the power of the dark side of the Force."

"Still want me to cut your hair?"

He nodded vigorously. "Yeah, do it now."

"Remember what happened to Samson."

"Losing my hair won't take away my power. It'll take away theirs—to get on my fuckin' case."

"They'll just find something else to ride you on."

"Cut it."

His hair had a mind of its own, as always, renegade strands escaping my fingers as I struggled to braid it into one neat, easily-snipped plait. The purple twilight, suited only for romance, not barbering, aided and abetted the resistance.

"Why dontcha just cut it?"

"Shhh. We do it my way or not at all."

After that he sat patiently under my hands, accepting the tugs and jerks that a good, tight braid requires, enduring without a flinch the pinch of rubber band on the skin at the back of his skull. In the end, it was a beautiful braid, not really long or thick, just even and neat, perhaps my best ever, but with the last sunlight slipping away, there was no time to admire it. Both ends secure, I took the scissors from my purse and severed it from his head.

It lay like a little snake across my thighs as I sheared the rest of the waves from his scalp, the loose strands tickling my skin as they fell to the sand.

"You're going to look like a shorn sheep."

"Don't care. Keep going."

Down on the beach, the strollers had departed with the sun.

With the last snip of the scissors, Jamie leaped up, rubbed his fingers back and forth through the couple of inches of hair left on his head and went barreling down the dune.

347

"Come on," he shouted over his shoulder.

I stuffed the sacrificial braid and scissors into my hobo bag and bounced down after him, my weight shifting back and forth from one foot to the other in the yielding sand.

"Look at that!" Jamie shouted, pointing.

The moon was rising up in the east like a second dawn, a less flamboyant dawn—the sun's subdued, subtle sister with a pock-marked face that glowed with its own quiet grace. It was a peach, golden amber with the hint of a blush, ripe and juicy, just hanging there, its succulent inner fleshy secrets barely contained by its velvet skin. I almost blurted the metaphor aloud, but the sudden remembrance of the other Peach filled my mouth like the sharp bitter pit of the fruit and stopped the sweet words from flowing out.

"Let's go for a swim." He shed his button-down shirt like he was shedding a too tight skin and peeled his white t-shirt over his head.

"You're crazy."

"Yes, I am." He grinned a bedlam leer. "Come on. You've still got your swimsuit on."

"Yeah. But what are you going to wear?"

"My birthday suit, babe, and that means nothing at all."

"You're nuts."

"What about 'em? Yeah, I know the water's cold, but—hoo hah—I am goin' in!" He unbuckled, unzipped and let his jean puddle around his ankles. "Are you comin'?"

"No. You're certifiable." I sank to the sand like an anchor.

"Chicken." He shoved down his briefs, starkly white in the now gray world, hopped out and kicked them into the pile with the rest of his clothes.

"Maybe so—but at least I'm not a lunatic." I glanced to the horizon, to that low-hanging moon. It was not quite full, missing a sliver at the side to mar its perfect circle. "You can't even blame it on a full moon."

When I looked back down he was in the water, walking backwards away from me, slowly, carefully, like he was dragging his feet to test the pebble-strewn sand bed. He beckoned with his hands.

"Come in," he crooned. "Come in, Claire de Lune."

I didn't. I sat on the sand and watched him move between the moon and me. He dove under the water and shot back up again, his newly-shorn hair slick against his head, gleaming and dripping like a seal's skin.

Beautiful. A thing of beauty. An object of desire. A body perfect. A body electric. A long thin line of fluid grace. The slender pale column of a Greek temple made from flesh and bone and heart. A male Aphrodite rising out of the black water. A working class David. A Saint Sebastian before the arrows pierced and desecrated his perfect form. Perfect.

So take it. Make it yours and yours alone. Do with it what you will, that perfection. Subdue it. Master it. Bend it to suit you, hold it next to you, love it if you must. Or mar it, sully it, break it if you want. Your will be done.

Thy will be done.

"Come in," he implored again, in a shuddery voice that sounded like it came from behind chattering teeth.

"No."

I resisted the recklessness of the moon and the water and his body.

When he finally came out of the lake, the moon was on its way up the sky, no longer a wondrous peach, just a bright not-quite-full satellite reflecting the hidden glory of something bigger and more fabulous than itself. He used his t-shirt as a towel and then stretched out on the sand beside me. The skin of his thigh was clammy on my own and pebbly rough with gooseflesh. But I didn't flinch away.

"I'm cold," he mumbled, slowly turning toward me and easing a leg over mine. "And don't say 'I told you so,'" he growled, flinging his arm across my chest and pressing himself against me.

"Told you so." Even as the words left my mouth, I was up and running, struggling against gravity and shifting sand to reach the top of the dune.

And then he was after me, and when we reached the summit, he fell upon me, as I anticipated he would, as I wanted him to, and we were wrestling and rolling, laughing and squealing, gasping and panting, his lips seeking to pin mine, but my mouth always managing to twist away, so he kissed everything else instead, my cheeks, nose, eyelids, chin, until gradually our frenetic action eased into a gentler motion, a melting together, where everything was touch because even with the moon it was too dark to see.

"I want you—and I know you want me—I can feel it," he breathed shakily into my ear. "You're so ready. So don't say no tonight."

Take him. Take him inside. Make him truly yours. Feel the way the bodies rise and fall... the motion of it... that motion... and the heat... feel the heat of him even now... the heat and the motion...

It will hurt.

Only for a moment. Nothing is to be gotten without pain.

I'm afraid.

We fear what we do not know. You want to know ... how the bodies join and fall apart, the angle of union, the melding... the motion and the heat, the hardness and the softness, inside... and this is the victory... the sweetest victory ...this is how you win.

But even as he knelt there and felt his way in the dark to enter me, pausing, breathless, as if not believing the moment, the image rose in my mind of my father kneeling between Peach's spread legs, pausing himself, maybe breathless, as if not believing the moment, and I thrust myself away, scrambling over the sand on my back, scuttling like a crab until he grabbed my ankles.

"Claire, stop!"

Even then I struggled on, twisting and contorting, spitting sand, flinching as grains ground in the corners of my eyes.

"Claire!"

"Let me go!"

"Not until you stop."

"I won't stop until you let me go!"

Children even then.

He let go.

I stopped.

And at that singular moment in time, the laws of gravity seemed undeniable, a force to bind all things permanently to the earth, even birds, planes, rockets.

And, most permanently, me.

"I can't do this."

No reply from the black form hunched in front of me.

"Not now. It's all so confusing…"

Silence, and then a whine-tinged mumble. "What's so confusing? I love you. You say you love me. People who love each other make love."

"But what are we to each other, really? What are you? What am I? Cousin, friend… girlfriend, the fucking North Star! I've been what everyone wants me to be for so long, pretending, acting. Jesus, I don't even know what I am anymore or what I want, really want. And now going off to school—that's scary. Who am I going to be there? Myself at last or just another someone that they want me to be? I mean, is this really what life is— just playacting through it all? I don't want the world to be just another stage, damn it. I want it to be real. And all I keep thinking—and I know it's selfish, but when is somebody going to be something for me?"

Quiet. A long quiet, underscored by the hiss of the waves stirring down at the shoreline.

"I thought I was," he murmured, just a breathing in and out, then the whisper of sand shifting. "What do you want me to be? I'll be anything for you, you should know that by now." His voice was dull, flat, as if he knew the answer would be something he didn't want to hear.

"I don't know, Jamie. I just… I don't know… a brother, a friend, for now."

It was only half a lie… the first I'd ever told him… I think.

"Like before," he said, his back still hunched.

"I don't know."

"Can't force the genie back into the lamp. I can't stop myself from wanting to touch you."

"I know."

"But you're telling me I have to."

"No—God, I don't know what I am saying."

"I can do that... be a friend, a brother when you need it... if that's what you need... sometimes, for now."

"Yes."

"Just don't ask me to stop touching you. Because that would kill me."

"I won't."

He sighed and stood, a dark figure moving in the dark. I heard the slap of his hand against his skin. "Shit, this sex on the beach crap is highly over-rated. Sand is not a good thing to have stuck in your privates."

Safe. Cozy. Riding in the night along the back roads of the northern Indiana dune country, secure and warm in the green and amber glow from the radio and instrument panels, hands intertwined over the gear shift, lit intermittently by white flashes of streetlamps, hearts thumping in time to the thrumming beat of guitar, drums and harmonica from the all-night blues station. A harbor, a haven, a nest in which to shelter, and although most of the stars were obscured, in leaning my head back against the headrest, gazing up out the open car window, I knew they were up there somewhere, just like they were a long time ago, in another car, in another state, with another brother by my side.

"On a cloud of sound I drift in the night, any place it goes is right. Goes far, flies near, to the stars, away from here..."

When he turned onto my street, I told him I didn't want to spend the night there. Without asking why, he drove me to Sophie's. Using the key he'd kept just in case, we let ourselves in and crept across the darkened front room floor, silently cursing the creaks in the old wood, slipping into the room where he still kept some clothes. He fumbled in the bureau drawer, and tossed me one of his T-shirts for pajamas, flicking on the desk lamp and watching sleepily as I popped my contacts out. We curled up together under the thin coverlet on the twin bed.

And slept.

There was nothing left to do but pick up the luggage and leave. He didn't say a thing, my father, that morning when we showed up. No reprimand, no question, no comment on the fact that I was still wearing a man's white T-shirt. Just offered us a breakfast that we'd already had at McDonald's and insisted on going along to the university.

After a brief tussle over which car to drive and a pissing match over who would carry the suitcases and a rapprochement over the steamer trunk, they managed to get everything loaded into Jamie's car. My father looked affronted when I slipped into the front seat next to Jamie and they both sat befuddled when I undid my seatbelt and hopped out again.

"Potty," I shrugged helplessly and took the front steps two at a time. But the bathroom was not my destination.

The bedroom was dim, blinds closed against the sun as always, the bed made, blue coverlet drawn up over the pillows.

Did you change the sheets, you sonovabitch? Or do you like to wallow in it, night after night?

There it was, on the dresser, its blue glass dull, almost black in the gloom. The perfume bottle full of my mother was cool in my hand as I cradled it and it lent a not-unpleasant weight to my purse, where it nestled between my wallet and a pack of Juicy Fruit. The freshening breeze that greeted me at the front door could have been her congratulatory embrace.

You are what you have always been... my daughter.

"Drive on, James," I ordered as I eased myself regally back into the car. "Drive on."

Sitting through the rambling, boring welcoming remarks offered by several grand poobahs of the university, my father kept a grim smile on his face. He gawked at the gray Gothic spires and arches of the central quadrangle, willing to play the working class lout from the sout' side of Chicago. He inspected my cinderblock dorm room with a critical eye and wiped a cobweb from the corner of my tiny closet. He hugged me tight to his chest in the parking lot, whispered "be good," and turned away quickly, climbing into the car without a backward glance.

The better to miss the sight of Jamie's lingering, decidedly unbrotherly, kiss.

"Sorry… I forgot who I was supposed to be today."

"It happens. It's okay."

"So when can I come see you?"

"You're seeing me now."

"After I leave now… again."

"I'll call you, silly boy."

But I didn't.

I wrote. Long letters filled with tedium about the social structure and living habits of the Trobriand Islanders as described by Bronislaw Malinowski *("a Polack, who woulda thunk it!")*, and the misery of rooming with someone whose facial expressions and vocalizations were distinctly toad-like, and the revolting qualities of the mystery meat served in the cafeteria under the name of 'ranch steak' *("we call it raunch steak")*. Letters that expounded on the hideousness of the cockroaches that inebriated boys torched with aerosol cans of hair spray and cigarette lighters in the bowels of the dormitory, that lamented the mind-bending impossibility of calculus, and that pondered the significance of gargoyles… letters filled with every mundane thing… but purposefully empty of longing, need, desire.

When he called, I made the toad lie and say I was at the library or in the shower or playing intramural Frisbee. When he showed up, unannounced, I met him in the commons with an excuse of tests and papers due. I let him buy me a coffee at Ida Noyes Hall and allowed him to walk me to Regenstein Library and gallantly carry my books, but blew him off at the entryway with kiss on the cheek. In his infrequent letters, he always asked when we could get together. I somehow forgot to give him a definitive answer in mine. But each night I slept in the soft, safe embrace of a white cotton t-shirt which I had conveniently forgotten to give back… and for the return of which he'd never asked.

In November, when my father called to ask what time he should pick me up on Thanksgiving, I said he shouldn't.

"The cafeteria is open for lunch for those who can't go home. There's money to be made serving."

"Well, I'll come get you after. I bought a little turkey, ten pounder. Figured you'd be ready to spend a couple nights home by now. Haven't had much of a chance to talk with you. Every time I call, you tell me you've got to go do your homework. I guess that's a good thing."

Dead, awkward air.

I sighed and caved. "I'll come for dinner but I'm not staying over. I have a paper to write."

"You could bring—"

"No, I need to get to the library for some research."

"Well, okay then, just dinner. I guess I have to admire your dedication. So when—"

"Two o'clock."

He was early, waiting in the dorm parking lot until I dragged my unwilling ass out at 2:05. By 2:30, I was home, bouncing off the kitchen walls, literally. By 2:45, I had exhausted all topics of civil conversation: schoolwork, the cafeteria food, my job, the weather, the hostage situation in Iran.

"If Carter has any guts, he'll send in the Special Ops to kick some ass."

"I don't think you can just drop Army Rangers into a country that's situated inland between—"

"That's the problem, exactly. What do my daughter the college student and the idiots in Washington have in common? Too much intellectualizing, not enough action."

"That's right. We're all dithering, navel-gazing pansies."

By three o'clock, I had my jacket on and was out the door on my way to check on Sophie.

"Better to go later. Bring her some leftovers. Turkey'll be ready at four."

"Grandma's not really fond of turkey anyway."

"And you can't seem to sit still in your own goddamn house."

A thousand replies rose in my throat… *must be genetic… learned it from the best… it stopped being my house when you let her into it…* but I let the door do the talking for me.

By 3:15, after walking at a brisk pace, I was bounding up Sophie's front steps, waving to her through the picture window, shuffling my feet against the chill as I waited for her to hobble over to let me in.

But when the door opened, it was Dougie who received my dazzling, only semi-fake smile. Expressions don't really freeze on a face—they congeal, lose their glistening transparency, grow opaque, meaningless. As he gave me the once-over, I felt self-consciously shabby in the maroon sweatpants and drab gray sweatshirt I'd grabbed that morning thinking comfort, not style. He, on the other hand, was dressed for an occasion in pressed jeans and sweater over a—Jesus, was it actually a button-down shirt? Was he turning into some fucking preppie?

"Claire, come sit. So long, so long. Much to tell, yes?" Sophie patted the arm of her chair. "Dougie, bring her a cup of tea, please. Yes?"

I agreed just to be rid of his smirking face. "What's he doing here?" I muttered, once he was safely down the hall.

"Came to visit. Like you. Off at college, too." She patted the chair arm again. "Now, you tell me about you."

I perched there and gave her cheek a quick peck and chattered inanely for a quarter of an hour on the nature of college life, skittering from topic to topic, a verbal manifestation of a physical desire, so did I long to flee, but doomed to stay, a bird grounded by clipped wings and the cage of Sophie's silent smile and Dougie's sullen stare.

By 3:45, my tea had gone cold and my tongue numb, and I had bored myself, while my limbs felt like strings stretched taut to the snapping point.

"Got to go, Grandma. Just wanted to stop in, see how you were. I wish I'd brought the car. You could've come back to the house and had dinner with me and Dad…"

Sophie brushed the idea aside. "Everyone asks and everyone gets 'no.' I don't want to go. A quiet day with a little chicken soup, that's good."

I kissed her cheek again. "Aren't all your days quiet?"

"Jamie and his friend always over playing their guitars. Not so quiet. But I like." She grinned and leaned closer. "Some. Not all."

"I'm gonna head out, too, Grandma," Dougie said, bending to her.

"Dzięki, dzięki, for coming to see babcia." She beamed. "And you can be friends now, yes? No more jealous children, all grown up, go to college. Yes?"

Best to leave that one unanswered except for tight smiles, which lingered only until the door was shut behind us.

To attempt to be civil or not… that is the question.

"What? Needed some cash, so you stopped by the First National Bank of Grandma? Maybe she'll install a drive-through for your convenience." *Oops, that one just slipped out. Too late for civil.*

"Well, bitch, unlike you, I can't make a quick twenty with a blow job in the alley."

My grin was wicked, glaring up at him from the bottom of the porch stairs. "Oh you could, you could, in that candy ass jacket you're wearing. That's not real leather, is it? Get yourself on up to Boys Town."

Mistake… even as my lips curled around the words and spewed them out… *how many times do we do this to ourselves… knowing the error of our ways, our words, and still following them down that stupid, dark, crooked, echoing path?*

Even as he trod slowly, deliberately down the steps, I was checking my escape routes. *Down the sidewalk… down the gangway. Sidewalk…*

But with him looming over me, blocking that path, the other way seemed the only way.

"Where you going, bitch? Need to go potty? Guess you're going to have to pee yourself again, cuz I don't see your fucking Siamese twin on your hip to save your sorry ass."

The air suddenly smelled funny… metallic… acidic. Fear. Rank fear. And now the cold fist clenches the guts while a strange heat flushes sweat in the armpits and across the forehead. *This is absurd... I am walking away and he is following... and for once, we are alone in our anger and hate... where did this all come from, really... where? What was the root? It had to have a root... didn't it? This kind of hate doesn't just happen... does it? And how did it come down to this ... no one to intervene... all the windows in the neighborhood closed to the late November chill... almost to the back gate... would he follow into the alley?*

Then I felt it...the searing grip of his fingers around my wrist, singeing my skin, jerking me back...the clammy rough wood of the garage door scraping my cheek...the scalding nip of a jagged fingernail across my flank... the icy bite of rusted iron against my belly...the scorching sting of his boot rammed against my ankle...the cold press of ancient dust pursing my lips...the white hot explosion as my skull connected with a blunt edge of the old oak tool chest...the frigid slap of his belt buckle on the bare skin of my hip...the battering heat and the savage cold meeting as he pushed himself up against me, icy hard knuckles gripping something warm and sticky and soft... and soft...

And soft.

Even as he shoved up against me, the brute force of his frustration grinding my pelvic bones into the edge of the iron worktable, I felt the laugh bubbling up from my belly and all the insults gleaned in moments of boredom from Roget's Thesaurus ping-ponging around my brain... *limp dick moron can't even do a rape right... impotent weakling... eunuch... castrato... gelding...* I tried to swallow it back down with the dust but it had a life and will of its own, bursting out of my pursed lips with force enough to ram my head against the tool chest again. Stars floated amid the dust motes. Uncontrollable, the laugh was uncontrollable, one of those laughs that just keep on going, shaking a body to its core, shaking a body until its insides feel ripped and raw, tendons stretched to the cramping point. It was a laugh that leaves a mouth gasping...*can't breathe, can't breathe...* that breeds hyperventilation. And total release. It was a laugh that only paused for a brief gasp, a mere hiccup, when the pain knifed up from my groin, and then it resumed at the realization that it was only a finger that he had savagely thrust up inside me.

One more vicious shove and he reeled away, spewing more filth from his mouth that my laughter still drowned out. . .

There is some grime that even the longest, hottest shower will not wash away. It clings to the skin like a film of grease. Its odor lingers in the nose and no perfume can displace it. Afterwards, the thing my body wanted to do was hop aboard a CTA bus and make its way north. But that would have necessitated a phone call and some convoluted explanation for my behavior—or run the risk of being the subject of a missing person's report. So although my body cried out for the expediency of flight, my mind clamped down like a hand over an open mouth, stifling the screams, willing my legs to walk, forcing me to pick up my purse from where it had fallen in the gangway and dig out the little compact mirror so I could examine my face and rub away the black smudges on my cheek and forehead with spit-covered fingers, steeling my spine to sit erect at my father's table and eat a portion of his turkey.

It came back up later in the empty bathroom of my dormitory, and it was a relief to be rid of it. But no matter how hard I scrubbed, under the scalding sting of an institutional strength shower, the grime would not go away.

She answered the phone, the sweet syrup of her "hello?" thinning and sharpening to a vinegary "hold on" when she found out who was on the other end of the line. Silence, then a vituperative hissing in the background. A blunt "shut up." Then a low "hey" in my ear.

"Hey."

"I'm sure you heard that. Just another happy Thanksgiving at the Sokol manse."

"Sorry to cause a hassle."

"It's okay. In fact, it's great to finally hear your voice after almost two freakin' months."

"I'm sorry. I should have called before but—"

"Don't even say it."

"You're angry."

"Damn straight."

"I'm sorry."

The promise I'd made as my fingers dialed the number had echoes of a deodorant ad: remain calm, cool and collected. *Wasn't so hard.* I'd made it through a fucking turkey dinner with my father. And blessedly, the toad had gone home for the holiday weekend. I'd vomited, showered, thrown my soiled clothes into the trash bin in the common room, knowing that no amount of Tide would ever get them truly clean or induce me to wear them again. *Wasn't so hard. Stiff upper lip, mind over matter, just suck it up, hold it in…*

It wasn't his anger that cracked that façade. Anger is easy to resist. It was a random thought that floated over the transom, an image that slipped in of those large yet fine-boned hands, fingers long and tapering, tipped with thick calluses from his years at the guitar, nails trimmed neatly, and clean, so clean.

"I need to see you. Can you drive up?"

Did he hear the tremor under the words?

"Tonight?"

"Yes. Can you? Please."

"You're crying. What's wrong?"

"Can you please come?"

"Yeah… I was gonna head over to Strawboy's, but he'll be cool with it. Claire, why are you crying?"

"At my dorm, in the common, there'll be that lady at the reception counter. Give her my name and she'll buzz me and I'll come down to let you in, like that other time."

"Okay, look, I'll be there in—oh—maybe forty, forty-five minutes tops."

"Okay."

"Okay, bye."

I waited to hear the click and hum on the other end before I hung up. I waited, wrapped in my blanket, propped up against my pillow in the corner where my bed met the wall. I waited in the semi-dark, the only light coming from the bulb hanging in my closet. I waited, rubbing the tip of my index finger over and around the cuticle of my thumb, digging in where it was dry and cracked, worrying it raw, reveling in the heat of it all: the throbbing of the flesh, the ooze of blood, the taste of metal on my tongue when I sucked at it. I waited through the bob-and-jerk boxing match with sleep. I waited even as I lost that fight. I waited, knowing the phone call from the desk would come any minute to yank me out of the semi-conscious pool in which I floated. I waited as blacks faded to grays, until the streetlights winked off.

I waited… but he never came.

Friday and Saturday, it was about me. *He's angry at me for two months of nothing. He's decided to make me wait instead of rushing over. It's payback—and I deserve it. He'll be here in a little while—this afternoon—he'll call and say he was mad, but now he's over it and he's hopping in the car and it will be fine, and we'll be even.* But one day dragged into the other and my eyes kept straying to the phone on the wall. *I should leave, go to the library, that would serve him right, showing up and I'm not here.* But in the end, I couldn't risk it. I sat at my desk and tried to work on my essay but the paper remained a bare plane of straight blue lines.

Sunday and Monday, it was about her. *The bitch.* She forbade him to come, told him some outrageous lie, threw a screaming fit, pulled the phones from the walls, took his car keys, feigned illness. Irrationality reigned. But how convincing could it be, with payphones at every gas station and convenience store and bus stops on every major street corner? Could I possibly convince myself that she had him locked in his room, shackled to his bed? He could get in touch with me, if he wanted to. I kept my eyes off the phone and on my notebook paper which I slowly, excruciatingly filled with poorly written sentences in support of a poorly constructed thesis, a house of straw that my professor would blow down in one huff.

Tuesday and Wednesday, it was about him. In a car crash, his face bloody and raw, hunched over the steering wheel, thrown forward by the force of impact from behind. Some idiot didn't brake in time, slammed into his Chevy. He was probably bounced around pretty bad, broken limbs maybe, on lots of painkillers, lying in a hospital bed too doped up to call. And then the creeping horror of the other possibility set in, a head-on collision, perhaps a drunk driver returning from a Thanksgiving celebration, southbound, reflexes addled by one too many cans of beer or shots of peppermint schnapps, blissfully unaware as his car drifted over the dividing line into the northbound lane. It could happen anywhere, on any street, with Jamie swerving, but swerving too late and then there is nothing but blood and broken glass and mangled metal and his hands, strong but still, so still and white under the ceaseless red-and-blue rotation of squad car lights, fire engine lights, ambulance lights.

Stomach roiling, fingers trembling, I finally dialed his number at noon on Thursday. Five rings, seven, ten, thirteen. Then Sophie's. I'd have to let her phone ring awhile just to give her time to make it down the hall in the event she wasn't sitting in her chair by the window. Eight, ten, fourteen, twenty. *Jesus, she never leaves the house.* As much as my fingers tried to resist, I dialed the number to my father's house. Five, seven, nine, eleven...

He was dead. Jamie was dead. They were out burying him and no one had called. *No, he's just hurt. He's in a hospital, and they are at his side, even Sophie, who barely leaves the front room, much less her house—but for him, he was a great favorite, she would venture out. For him, she would put on her thirty-year-old coat and one of those knit hats that the grandkids gave her every Christmas, and brave the raw November wind. For Jamie, she would do this. It must be so.*

I prayed in a way that I had done before—for another lost soul—with the act of contrition, with the grim delusion that admitting and begging forgiveness for my sins could somehow change the course of history for another... because this time it *was* my sin.

Take the bus. Swallow your pride and take the bus to your father's house. 'Home is the place, when you have to go there, they have to take you in.' Then you will know for sure. And that is exactly why I won't take the bus—because then I will know for sure.

When Sunday dawned again, my fingers were ugly and raw as they dialed Jamie's phone number for the twentieth or thirtieth time, the cuticles shredded by teeth and nails. The sting of each wound had kept me alert in my classes, had kept me living in the pain of the moment.

When she finally answered, Peach's voice sounded squeezed, her "hello" a constricted question, like a hand was gripping her throat.

"It's Claire."

Dead space, iced over.

"Is Jamie—" *How to say it? What to ask?* "Is Jamie there?"

A hissing, the quick intake of air through nose and mouth, then the abyss of silence again.

"May I speak with him, please?"

Another hiss. Then finally "Jamie's in Georgia."

A leap of the heart, so strong it felt like it would burst through my chest. "At his grandmother's?"

Yet another hiss, like ice shifting underfoot.

"Okay, well, I will try calling him down there."

"Can you talk to the dead? Is that one of your many talents?"

"He's dead." It was almost a relief to finally say it aloud. As a statement, not a question. Almost a relief. Almost.

"You stupid little bitch. What were you thinking, calling him up like that?" Her voice, still tight, switched from cold to hot in an instant, building that heat on the friction of the words seething from her mouth. "Asking him, crying for him to come see you? And he wouldn't listen to me, "no" doesn't work on an 18-year-old boy. And then he told me about the two of you, what had been going on all summer—and I couldn't believe it. The two of you... after I'd made him swear. So I told him. I told him!" That voice was fever-hot now, but her words seemed more a soliloquy, not a rant aimed at me. "I told him, but of course, he didn't believe me, didn't believe me, but what did I expect? Stupid! To slam out of here like that, to go off and then get in that car... Stupid, stupid!" Who was she berating in her sibilant mutterings? Me? Him? Herself?

"He crashed? It was a crash?" The well-rehearsed words came easily. They seemed to catch her by surprise, though, as if she'd forgotten someone was on the other end of the line.

"Well, you are your mother's child, aren't you?" It was a raw murmur. "You and your dry-eyed cruelty. Why did you call?"

My tongue was thick, foreign in my mouth. "I just want to— I need to know…"

"Crash?"A pause, another hissing, snake-like intake of breath. "Yes, a crash. On his way to see you. How does that make you feel? Live with that, you little bitch."

The wall against my back was the only solid thing in the room. *Melting. It's all melting. Nothing to hold onto. I need something to hold onto. Something to hold onto. The ring tones. Grab onto them. Two, three, four—pick up, dammit—the world is melting, the colors all running together, bleeding—five, six seven—bleeding into a brown mess of nothing— eight…*

He picked up on the ninth ring. "Yuh?"

"Dad?"

Long pause punctuated by a jangling crash.

"Whoops."

"Dad?"

"Drop the phone."

Drunk, he's drunk, the world is melting away, and he's drunk.

"Dad, it's Claire. I know about Jamie. I need—" What did I need?

"Claire. Claire Josephine." A sputter snort. "You—you were s'posed to be Claire Marie—for your mother." Another snort. "Christ, if you didn't come out lookin' like me—so Josephine. Sorry, lil girl."

"Dad." *But I can't get the sharpness in my voice, the needed edge to cut through his liquid haze. Cuz everything is melting, me along with it.* "Dad, I know Jamie's dead." *But my voice is melting too and I don't think it can even make it through the phone.*

"Been readin'—tryin' to, but eyes ain't workin' too good. But I'ma tell you a story. That I read. Never told you 'nough stories. So here's one. Man whispers, God, speak to me and a meadow-lark sang. Man din't hear. So man yells, God, speak to me! Thunder an' lightning roll. But man din't listen. Man looks around an' says, God, lemme see you. Star shines. Man don't see. So man shouts, God, show me a miracle! And a baby is born.

But man don't notice. In despair, cries out, touch me, God, lemme know you're here. God reach down and touch the man. But the man just brushes the butterfly away and walks on."

I wondered vaguely as I gently placed the receiver back into its cradle how long he would talk into the buzz of the dial tone.

At the moments of my greatest need, when did you stop being there for me?

CHAPTER 24

He found me on the cobblestone floor of the garage, hunched and rocking, my arms clasping my knees tight to my chest, no sound, no tears, just rocking.

"Should've torn this thing down years ago," he mumbled, wrapping me in his frail embrace.

Your mind is on something else, focusing on a scene I've already played ... you don't even know the other one, and I will never tell you... and yet you smell good today, a warm, clean laundry scent rises from the soft worn cotton of your T-shirt, but soap-and-water sympathy won't wash this away ... and you will never know, never know... unless I tell you... and yet, under the soft film of fabric and skin, beneath the supple muscle, lies the hard bone, solid, fitting so well into the hollow of my cheek.

"Just another one of those everyday ghosts," I murmured.

Finger bones pressed nail-sharp against my back, a prod to get me up and moving.

"Let's go, let's get you outta here."

"It's no good walking away. Can't do that anymore. They're everywhere. Every day, everywhere."

"I can't sit here."

"If I can, you can."

He shook his head. "No, I mean, it hurts—physically, Claire. I'm in a lot of pain."

Even in the dim light, it was visible there in the deep lines that creased his forehead, at the tight, turned-up corners of his lips, in the way his hand clenched his bent knee.

"I don't give a shit."

So he hunkered there with me, so full of pain that it started leaking out the corners of his eyes. "I can't tell the story you want to hear. I don't know the story."

"How can that be?"

"Didn't want to know. By the time I did, the one who could tell me didn't want to talk about it anymore."

"Peach?"

He shook his head as the pain inched down his cheeks. "That friend of his. Like his shadow," he croaked.

"Strawboy? He was there?"

His lips twitched an affirmative as more of his anguish leaked out his eyes.

"He cared enough to come to Sophie's funeral. He'll tell me the story."

"You tell me one first."

"About?"

"Why She Left and Never Came Back."

"That's a very short story. And I think you already know it."

"Tell me, damn it."

It took awhile of sitting there, watching him drink his tears, but the words found me at last.

"Once, there was a little girl who had a father who was a good man—not perfect —she knew he made mistakes—but he was an honest man who talked about truth and beauty and the North Star. And he loved the little girl and showed her that he did and kept her safe. When others, out of jealousy, cast aspersions on him, he told the little girl *'always think the best of me, never the worst—unless you see it with your own eyes'* and he asked for her promise and she gave it willingly. And she did think the best of him through the dark times that followed, even as he made bad choices, and led her into a dark forest. She thought the best of him because he was a man who would never bend to the will of others to forsake her and he would never leave her there alone, to fend for herself. So she believed the best, not the worst. Until one day, one late afternoon, when she saw it with her own eyes."

And there it is, laid out like all those corpses that we have viewed together and apart. Another dead body—and even in the gloom of this forsaken place, I can see the muscles of your face move as your jaw flexes and tightens. Oh, to peel back the ruddy skin and see the red flesh and the pale sinew, and to flay that open to the purple veins and arteries pulsing, and to pull those aside and dig deeper down to the white bone—to truly be under your skin—like a burrowing tick or a bacteria or a mutating virus that becomes one with its host—like a cancer… Will you ask? Will you be so obtuse as to ask for a time and a place? Or will you spare us both that final humiliation? Because you know, you know, you already know…

He leaned back against the upright, his eyes closed.

"How many sins do you get? Two? Three? Venial, mortal? How many? How many before you stop being the good, decent man that you're trying so hard to be and turn into—something else?"

"I don't know."

"You have an opinion."

I shrugged and my t-shirt snagged on the rough wood of the upright. "I don't know. By whose standards?"

He cocked his head, opened his eyes and stared at me. "The only ones that count. Yours."

I shifted and the cobblestones ground through the denim of my shorts down to my bones, as they had so many years before when I'd crouched there with Jamie.

This had to be over. For him, for the memory of him, this had to be over. No more using physical pain to block out the thought of something worse. And so I grabbed hold of the edge of the work table and hauled myself up, then extended my hand to my father. "Let's get outta here."

Again how insubstantial he felt as I helped him to his feet, and it struck me as I followed this shrunken man out the door that I had known at least one truth about him since the first night I'd come home. *How strange that I would think of it that way— coming home.*

Whatever was physically wrong with him was more than just a cracked rib.

After the dust-laden veil-like gloom of the garage, the sunlight was a nail in the eye and the heat a hammer on the head. We took refuge from the blows on the front porch, easing into the old swing, exchanging looks tinged with fear and amusement as it creaked and sighed under our combined weight.

"One day—it's just gonna let go—and we'll be down for the count," my father muttered.

"So when are you going to tell me what's really wrong with you, Dad?"

Jesus, when had I last called him that?

"Don't even bother to hem and haw. And forget about lying. Just can't do that anymore," I babbled on, buying him time. "You didn't just call me to come up here to help you sort out Sophie's mess and as far as your body goes—it's not just a cracked rib. I know that."

Were we both staring at the corner post where my dad had fallen years before, stupid belligerent drunk, after taking his brother's fist in his eye?

"Truth and beauty, Dad. Don't be afraid of it. Too little of it in the world."

There he was in the corner again, knocked flat on his ass. But this time I could be the one to get there first, to be there with those gentle, soothing hands.

"I can say it for you."

He bit down on his lip and his right hand worked on the arm of the swing, clutch and release, clutch and release.

"Cancer? And it's either too late in the game or you're just too—" The word 'frightened' almost escaped from my lips but I sucked it back. "Too stubborn to think about letting them do anything about it. You can just nod your head."

He wanted to glare at me, to rage, to rear up, the stallion, but he was broken and his eyes were wet and the liquid pain again seeped out at the corners and gathered in the grooves of his face and trickled down the rough edges making them soft, as water always will.

"Where? Or where was it before it spread?"

His hand worked the swing arm.

"You have to talk to me on this one. Don't make me run through a list or call your doctor."

"Pancreas." He spat the word out, the taste of it gall and wormwood on his tongue.

"And it's late in the game."

His chin barely rose and fell.

"They offered some form of treatment but you refused."

Under the squeaking disapproval of the swing as he pushed himself up and out, I heard a muttered curse and then mumblings. "Man" and "dignity" were the words I could distinguish.

All the years, the months, the weeks, the days, hours, minutes that I have wished for this moment, to see you beaten and humbled, to see you broken, tamed, blanched the color of fear, a gaunt man, a hollow man, head bowed, shoulders arcing toward defeat, even your pelvis sagging and bent, like a chastened dog with its tail tucked between its legs. This longed for, heart's desire moment is here—and there is no joy, no triumph, only a small hole along the seam of your t-shirt where the sleeve meets the shoulder, an insignificant tear in the fabric that needs a quick stitch before it grows into something larger and threatens the integrity of the garment. It is this rip which holds my gaze until my eyes water, this rip which draws me up out of the swing and over to you, this rip which draws my cheek to your shoulder and my arms around your chest… something that needed mending.

We stood there as time passed. The light changed as the sun rounded the house and its heat reached us. "Come with me," I whispered into his sleeve.

"Where?" His voice seemed to come from somewhere a long way off.

"To see Strawboy. Kevin Straszewski. Come with me."

His right hand released its white-knuckled clench on the railing and eased its calloused rough way along my arm that still hugged his chest, until it reached my hand, and covered it, his fingers willing their way between mine, until our hands were clasped comfortably, soothingly tight.

"Is that a yes?"

His hand squeezed mine.

The Straszewski bungalow on Avenue L looked the same as it had years before, except the evergreens that shrouded the foundation bore blade markings as if they'd recently been hacked into submission. The white paint on the trim looked fresh.

When I called the number on his business card and identified myself, the long pause on the other end of the phone made me reconsider the wisdom of my request, but the real warmth in his voice eased my doubts.

"Yeah, sure, I'd love to meet. Uhm, why don't you come over here? I can grill us some dinner—"

"Kevin, I'll be bringing my dad along. We need—we need to talk to you. It's about Jamie. I know it's been…"

A pause on both our parts. I could hear him suck in a deep breath.

"Yeah, well, I guess—I guess that's a conversation that's long overdue."

His living room was clean in an obvious sort of way, as if he'd dashed around, grabbing old magazines that he'd left lying haphazardly and arranging them in a neat stack on the end table with one hand, while wielding a dust cloth with the other. The tangy bouquet of Lemon Pledge hung in the air. Even his blue Oxford cloth shirt and khakis looked freshly ironed. Strawboy in business casual—that sight alone made the corners of my mouth twitch.

The mummified corpse of youth encased in its Dockers sarcophagus, while the ghosts of the people you have been hang in your closet and rest uneasily in your dresser drawers: the shrink-to-fit Levis, faded naturally by time and Tide, the t-shirts from every concert you ever attended. Or do you wear them still—like a lost boy—suspended in time, trying to get back to some moment—and this, this middle-of-the-road skin is just a camouflage to—fool? To please? Who? Me?

My father and I sat on opposite ends of a lumpy sofa whose bright blue floral upholstery had faded in all the obvious areas where human weight had pressed. His leg jostled up and down. Kevin perched in the blue-striped arm chair across from us, and then quickly bounded up again, remembering his duties as host, offering us beer, wine coolers, soda.

371

"I should have made some iced tea. Don't drink it myself."

We shook our heads, and then finally accepted glasses of water, to give our hands something to do. He had just settled back into the chair, when up he leapt yet again.

"Want to show you something," he said, ducking down the hall.

My father's fingers flicked something only he could see off his knee, then commenced a muffled drumbeat. "Maybe this wasn't—"

"Yes, it is."

He stopped drumming and rubbed his chin, then the back of his neck. But his leg still jiggled and his fingers soon found their way back to tapping on his knee. Then Kevin was standing before us, cradling an acoustic guitar with a glossy amber soundboard and a sound hole ringed with a translucent inlay rosette. He held it out to me, and when I opened my arms, placed it gently into them, like a nurse placing a newborn into his mother's first embrace.

"He brought it over with him that night. And they never asked for it back. At the time, I guess it was just another thing for me to be angry about, like, man, they are so oblivious to who he was, they ain't even looking for his guitar, they don't even give a shit about something he cared so much about."

If my dad winced at that, I didn't notice, so engrossed was I in the familiar yet unfamiliar body in my arms, in its weightless bulk, the way its curves rested easily, naturally, over my thigh, like a lover. My fingers circled the neck and fretted the strings, producing the faintest of tones.

"I know it was wrong—or I guess I finally figured out it was wrong, but by then, it just seemed too late to give it back. Then when I finally decided to just go do it, they were gone. Someone told me they moved to Georgia—and I was like, shit, I ain't going down there. I visited him down there a couple times—hated it."

It was possibly the largest number of words I'd ever heard him string together: sentences, a full paragraph, even.

"It's beautiful."

His eager face was pink-tinged and glowing, lit from within. "I went back and forth on it. You know, leave it the way he left it, or take care of it, restore it. And you can't just, well—guitar-players, you know—we can't just leave a guitar to sit. It would ruin it. So I took it in to this shop where I hang out and they did a little work on it. Still plays like a champ. I just put some new strings on a coupla weeks ago."

"Too bad I never learned how to play."

"Shoulda given you more lessons." The words sounded rough-edged, as if they caught in his throat on the way out. Those long, big-boned fingers, callused and moist, closed over mine and guided them up the neck. He arranged them over the middle strings and pressed the tips of them down. "Press and play."

I ran my thumb over the strings. The sound was slightly discordant.

"Not the top string."

I strummed again. The chord was sweet, rich and full.

"The A chord. Remember it this time."

We stared at each other, and I knew he was remembering a rainy afternoon spent on a twin bed pressed up again a wall and laid with pillows to form a makeshift couch.

It was Joe who pulled us back by rattling the ice cubes in his tumbler. "Whatever you thought about Jamie's parents, I think they would have appreciated having that guitar," he said. Ignoring the look I shot at him, he went on. "But I'm guessing Claire here would have appreciated it even more."

The glow lighting Kevin's face faded, like the embers of a fire, leaving only grey ash. He nodded and drifted down into the easy chair, settling lightly, soundlessly, like dust.

All the hollow, weightless men... enough of it... enough!

"It's beautiful, Kev. You took the time to take care of it. He would have wanted you to do that. He would have wanted you to keep it."

He shrugged, like he was trying to dislodge something unwanted that had settled on him. "Who knows what he was thinking? Or not." Another rise and fall of his shoulders. "That was the problem, maybe he wasn't thinking." His eyes were downcast, focused on something, the lace of his shoe that was slowly coming loose, the dark spot on the carpet midway between his feet and mine, Joe's still jiggling leg? The wheels were turning somewhere behind those eyes.

Always the moon to his sun, reflecting his light, the shadow behind his substance, the grey to his bright hot white, the pastels to the jewel brilliance of his rainbow palette, the pallid chaff left behind when the golden wheat is threshed... straw.

"Just what do you want to know?" he finally asked, lifting his gaze to meet mine.

There it was at last, no more bullshit, no more beating around that proverbial bush.

"What happened."

He massaged his temples, digging deep, as if dredging up the memory like something long buried in the muck. He jerked his head in my father's direction. "What? He never told you?"

"My father was—incapacitated for—"

"She means drunk," Joe cut in. "Drunk off my ass—for awhile. All I know is what..." he hesitated on the name. "What his mother told me after—and that wasn't much."

"And she lied to me." I took a sip of my water and stared at Kevin over the rim of the glass.

He swallowed and nodded. "He was angry at her that night. More than angry—I mean, he got angry at her a lot that summer. Over stupid shit. But that night—Thanksgiving—he was just crazy furious, just spewing shit—I'd never heard him talk about her like that. She'd taken his car keys and grounded him." He chuckled bitterly. "Grounded! At eighteen?! What was she think-ing? So he just slams out the house and walks over here with his guitar case and a duffel bag. At first, he's like, just pacing back and forth in my basement, going on about his ma being a liar—this and that—but he's not really saying much about whatever it was they got into. I got him to sit and have a beer and we smoked some weed and he calmed down a bit. Then he started talkin' 'bout going to see you and he wanted to borrow my wheels. And I'm shakin' my head, no—cuz I had to be at work in the morning and I didn't really trust him to have it back in time. I told him, I'll drive you there, man, but shit, it's already near midnight. Is she gonna be up to let you in? And he said you'd be waiting for him. So we loaded his shit in the Mustang, grabbed a coupla six-packs and left. We get all the way up to Jackson Park, we're just heading around that freaky statue of that woman standin' in the middle of the road, you know that one with her arms raised up, holding some kind of—I don't know—battle lance?" He paused, waiting for my nod of recognition.

"Yeah, I know who you mean. The lady green giant." The bronze woman with her heavy green patina, a Hyde Park landmark, a replica of the original Republic from the 1893 World's Fair.

"Yeah, that's the one. They fixed her up a few years ago. Scraped all the green crap off. She's the golden girl now. Still scary as all hell, though, like the attack of the 50-foot woman or something." He paused again, searching for words to bridge the gap in his stream of consciousness.

"Shit, yeah, so we just round the bend past her and all of a sudden he goes, stop, I can't do this—and I'm like, what the hell? He's just shaking his head—can't go there, can't go there—starting to freak again. By then, I'm starting to freak a little myself. So I drive down 59th past those open fields there—the Midway something?"

"Plaisance."

"Yeah, and so I'm thinkin' I'll park; we'll get out, go sit and have another beer, smoke another joint, and he'll be fine. Maybe I can get him to tell me what this is all about. So I get him out of the car, but he don't want to sit. So we walk. We passed this huge church set back from the street and then we were into this block with these old-looking buildings—I mean, old style, like Old England—and I'd never been to Hyde Park before and I'm thinkin', what the hell is this? Did we stumble into some flippin' time warp? These buildings had these heads hanging off the corners. These heads grinning and gaping down at us—frozen in stone. And I said, shit, Jamie, this is like Sam and Frodo in frickin' Mordor—and he laughed and asked what was I high on and they were just gargoyles."

"I asked him where your dorm was and he pointed in one direction, but then started walkin' in the opposite direction and we went back down to 59ᵗʰ and walked along those fields for awhile until we came to where the grass ended in a plaza and there was this concrete pool, I guess it was a fountain, but it wasn't on and the water'd been drained away for the season. There was some kind of massive, hulking shape, like the Grim Reaper, but without the scythe—and in the back there were these creepy figures, more statues—people, babies and kids and men and women, like some kind of parade caught in concrete—like they'd just been walking along and someone drenched them in Quikcrete and caught them there forever. And the streetlights just made it look creepier, with the shadows and all. I was like—freak time again—but Jamie just sat down against the side of the pool with his back to it—didn't even faze him. I lit up and passed the joint to him and he took a big hit and passed it back. Then he said, just outta nowhere—'she's my sister.' And I'm like—excuse me? And he took another hit and nodded. 'That's what my bitch of a mother told me tonight. She's my sister, no, wait, that would be my half-sister.' I guess I was well on my way to wasted, cuz I said 'your ma is really your sister?' He giggled and I knew it was the weed. 'No, asshole, Claire, she said Claire is my sister.' My jaw must been just hanging there cuz I had trouble closing my lips around the joint. 'Man, don't shit me like that,' I said. 'It's no bullshit.' 'She said that? Your ma actually said that?' He just nodded. 'You believe her?' He shrugged and said 'not when she first said it. But now, thinkin' 'bout things—things I saw and heard over the years—since I can remember, putting it all together—yeah, she's probably tellin' the truth. For once in her miserable life.'"

The torrent of words stopped gushing, like the flow of water cut short by the twist of a spigot. Kevin sat there, eyes wide open, lips clamped shut, cheeks puffed out, like he couldn't believe the ugliness of the toad that had just leaped out of his mouth, like he was waging a valiant effort to keep anymore from escaping. My father sat perfectly still, his eyes closed, his hands resting easily on his thighs, not a taut muscle on his face, at ease as I'd never seen him before, all that jangly, nervous energy becalmed, dissipated like steam into the summer air. Kevin, his eyes brimming and on the verge, propelled himself out of the armchair and down the short hall to the kitchen. I followed more slowly, cursing the happy-sounding slap of my sandals against the soles of my feet.

The thuds of Kevin's forehead against the dark cabinet added a sad contrapuntal beat. I slipped my hand in between his head and the door to soften the next blow, letting my fingers take the punishment. He let his head rest there against my palm momentarily.

"Kev, you didn't tell me something that I didn't already know." And in saying it out loud, I realized it was true. What had been intended as a kind lie to salve his self-inflicted wound became a statement of fact, an acknowledgement of the truth, at long last.

Yes, you've known it for a long time now. You knew it years ago. You knew it that night at the beach. You knew it and that knowledge is what sent you crab-scuttling out from under him and up the sand dune. You knew it from the moment you saw them together, Peach and Joe in your mother's bed, the way they moved together, the smug look that narrowed her eyes when she'd opened them and stared at the door, as if she knew you were just behind it, as if she could see you there in the gap of the open door. And maybe you'd known it before then—going back, way back, all the way back to that moment under the table at the funeral parlor when you'd opened your eyes and saw your brother's face staring in at you—those eyes, those brown eyes, those intense brown eyes that could only have come from one man.

"I'm sorry—for the burden of it all—that you must have felt you were forced to carry." I put my hand over his tightly balled fist and worked away with my fingers, plying and kneading until his softened and yielded like warm dough and he let me lead him back to the front room.

Joe had moved to the bank of windows, staring out, his back to us, his hands clenched behind his back. Hearing us, he turned, presenting an incongruous visage of equine pride, head erect, shoulders thrown back, teeth gripping the bit of the situation. When his lips parted to speak, I shook my head quickly, like a pitcher shaking off a catcher's sign. It wasn't his turn. Yet.

I guided Kevin to the sofa and tugged him down beside me. "How'd you wind up at the beach? You're in Hyde Park, sitting by the fountain of Time and then?" I asked, coaxing him back into the memory, squeezing his hand to start the flow again.

He kept his eyes fixed downward on his shoes or that spot on the carpet. "Yeah, the fountain of Time. I found out that was the name later—I looked it up. Weird, huh." He either shuddered at the eerie memory or shrugged to shake it off. "We sat there for awhile, smoking. I was sorry I'd left the beer in the car. Didn't say much for a long time. I remember thinking how life was just one fuck-up after another and how did that happen? Was that just the way it was? Just one long string of mistakes that you make or someone else makes and either way you get screwed. And in between all those mistakes you maybe get a little breather to suck it up and get ready for the next punch or do a quick fix— but you never seem to get enough time to truly make things right before the next one hits." Kevin glanced over at me, seemed about to say something, then apparently thought the better of it and looked back down. Finally he continued.

"We were pretty mellow after that joint—at least I was, cuz when he said, hey man, let's drive to the Dunes and watch the sun rise, I was like, you're cracked in the head, man, but what-the-hey, I've never done that before, so let's go. I guess I was thinking this was the breather—and not the next fuck-up. Roads were empty. We hopped onto the Skyway and then we were flying up over the East Side and gliding over Wolf Lake, radio blaring. We're singing *Should I Stay or Should I Go* along with Joe Strummer—like it was flippin' summer, like everything was okay, like it was no big deal—what his ma had said. Like he had made up his mind to not believe it—or he accepted it as the truth and was cool with that. I mean, afterwards, that's how I was thinkin' about it all. At the time, while it was happening, I was just flying along, high, enjoying the breather, stupid shithead that I was."

He craned his head toward me, lips curved into something that ached to stretch into a full-fledged smile. "You were never like that. You always had a—whaddaya call it—a seriousness of purpose. Eyes on the prize."

Fragile—under the skin and muscle, like bone china, brittle as glass, oh you tough men, as easily torn as paper…

"Didn't take us long to get there—of course, when we did, we kinda realized we wouldn't be able to just drive in, lot's closed, no shit, Sherlock. So we parked the car on a side street in some town, maybe Beverly Shores, grabbed the beer and started walking. It was flippin' dark and I'm askin', how do we know we're headin' in the right direction? Two things, he said, I can smell the lake and there's a sign. Seemed to me we were walkin' for a long time past these squat frame houses and it was pitch dark and you knew nobody was home. They were all summer cottages and it's the end of November. But I remember thinkin' someone must live here year round cuz there's a school bus stop sign and why the hell would a town of just summer homes have one of those? Some part of me remembers climbing a fence, then I felt the sand under my shoes, soft and gritty and I could hear the push and pull of the lake and we were there on the beach. I just wanted to sit down and drink a beer, but Jamie kept walking so I followed. Finally I said screw it—I'm not going any farther and he stopped. That sand was cold and damp and I was back to thinkin' 'what the hell are we doing here?' so I hunted around until I found a piece of driftwood to lean back against. The beer was lukewarm, but that wasn't a bad thing considering how raw it was out there. I think I asked out loud exactly why are we here again—and he said to see the sunrise and I'm like, man, it's too damn cloudy and the sun's not going to be rising over the water anyway, cuz, the lake's mainly north here, right? And he just laughed and grabbed a can of beer and sat at the other end of the log.

"I'm guessing you're gonna ask me did he want to talk about what he'd said before? About you and him being…" Kevin shrugged. "He said something about your brother—at first he said 'my cousin' then he's like—no, wait, my brother. He talked about how he drowned in the lake—and that's how he met you. At his funeral. He said that's when his family moved to Chicago. He said if he, your brother, hadn't died—but he didn't finish the thought—he just stopped talkin'." Kevin paused, his mouth slightly open, in the midst of forming words. He shrugged again. "There was a voice inside me that wanted to ask him more about it—but we just don't do that. Men, I mean. We don't ask." He glanced over at Joe, as if seeking confirmation.

My father's face was wet and he brought his hand up slowly and wiped it openly without a shred of furtive shame. "You're right about that," he muttered, clearing his throat. "We don't ask and we don't like to tell either and we are damned afraid to hear. Kinda like those three monkeys: seeno, hearno, speakno. That's us, apes hanging from a tree."

Kevin ran his hands through his hair. "Look, I wish I could tell you something—I don't know—something profound. Something he said, something he did that might help you understand or find some—comfort. I don't know." His voice took on a serrated quality, the jagged edge of a knife. "There just—he didn't really say anything. I can't remember him sayin' anything. He just kept drinkin' and maybe I shoulda told him to slow down, but I was pretty wasted by then. Claire, I'm wracking my brain, but I fell asleep—the weed and the beer, you know. I just fell asleep." He savagely swept his fingers up through his hair again, digging into his skull and yanking handfuls. "I just fell asleep. I just... fell asleep."

At the touch of my hand on his back, his hands ceased their frantic clawing. He simply sat, hunched over, elbows on his knees, hands hanging limp, a spent man.

Oh you weak men, you truly hollow men, not stuffed with straw, but with regrets and things left unsaid and undone... you men made of soft wood, pine, easily scratched and gouged, covered in soft skin, not a hard shell like you may think... easily bruised fruit...

"And when you woke up?"

Those large hands, those strong hands, hanging limp and still, those hands fluttered momentarily, flexing out and in, a gesture of something being gently cast away, the whimper at the end of the world. I could have finished the thought for him, but how would that have helped him, so I took his jaw firmly in my hand and pulled him to face me, my face up in his, nose to nose, our lips so close I could feel the electric thrum of blood and nerve.

"Say it."

Three seconds—maybe less—into our eye-to-eye and his eyelids shut tight, like shades yanked down by a frightened hand.

"Say it, Straw."

"Gone. He was just… gone."

It was out in a whisper, as his jaw strained to move under my grip.

"Dead." I replaced his euphemism with the stark truth.

"I didn't—" His jaw strained again under my hand.

"Know it at the time? I know, Straw, I know. Hold it together. You only have to say a little more." I relaxed my grip and let my fingers slip over his cheek, surprisingly still smooth from his morning shave. "Or I can say it for you."

"You found that house—the one that had some people who lived there at the beach town year round. And you pounded on the door and the man answered because everyone else was still asleep on the morning after Thanksgiving, but he was getting ready to go to work, maybe at the steel mill over in Gary—or maybe he'd just come home from his midnight shift—and he stared at you, the feral thing just beyond his storm door, sand matting your wild hair and dusting your cheek and crusted on your disheveled, slept-in clothes. And he probably would have slammed the door in your face but he's a man, he's a steel man, a man made of steel, so how can he be afraid, and he listens to your incoherent, rambling speech and manages to pull out the important words: *missing—friend—drunk—beach*. So he agrees to call the police, but he makes you stand outside. And when the cops arrive, you lead them back to the beach—and it's easy to find the way now, because the sun is up and it hurts your hungover eyes—and then it hits you. You never even saw it rise."

They cried for a long time, Kevin convulsively, with the violence of one who had been still too long, with heaves and snot and half-choked moans; my father with the absolute stillness of one who had finally found rest, the soundless trickle of tears in classic ebb and flow, as his thoughts and memories came and went. They cried in the living room. They cried in the car as I drove to the only place we could go, Kevin in the backseat, my father riding shotgun. In the rearview mirror, I watched Kevin's red-rimmed eyes fill and empty and fill again, as he bit down on the knuckle of his thumb to thwart a sob, as he stared hard out the window at the barn red shed the length of a football field that housed Krazy Kaplan's Fireworks emporium. "World's Largest!" its sign bragged in black and white letters over three feet tall.

"Seemed even bigger when we were kids," I smiled, trying to catch his eyes in the mirror. But he kept them fixed on the scenery flashing by.

My father stared straight ahead, occasionally drawing the back of his hand across his eyes, ignoring the pocket pack of tissue that I tucked into the cup holder between our seats.

Steel men, iron men, men of the forge and of the anvil; like the ore and coke you feed into the ovens and the blast furnace, your liquid core is revealed by fire—oh you weak men...

It hadn't changed much in twenty years. Route 49 up from Chesterton wound through growths of oak, hickory and ash trees, which cast cooling shadows against the harsh sun, still high at seven o'clock as the summer days stretched out to their fullest length. At the gate house to the park, the dense forest thinned out to jack pine, cedar and cottonwood. Then suddenly the sand reared up before us and the dunes seemed as mountainous as when I was a child and first felt the burn in my calves and thighs as I climbed their steep slopes.

The parking lot was full of families packing up to go home: children made petulant by exhaustion leaning up against open car doors, beach towels hanging limply around their necks as they waited for the oven-like interiors to cool down; cranky mothers shaking sand from paint-flecked blankets and worn comforters; a few tired dads dumping water and ice remnants from coolers and hoisting them into trunks. The beach was still a crazy quilt of blankets and sun umbrellas near the pavilion where the lifeguards sat on their white wooden perches, but the crowds thinned out further down past the Devil's Slide.

Kevin took off his shoes and socks, tied them together by their laces, slung them over his shoulder and walked in the heat of the dry sand, his feet sinking up to the ankles. I slipped off my sandals and walked close to the water's edge, listening to the sand sing in a high, clear ringing tone, the sweet result of friction and moisture playing on quartz crystals. My father kept his shoes on and stayed between us on the fringe where the moist packed sand just gave way to the dry.

Wind and water, things with soft edges have shaped the land for eons before man came along with his sharp-edged creations, the knife, the axe, the plow, the bulldozer. Their work is never done, always evolving over time that can't be measured by the hands on a watch; the water eroding the rock, the waves carrying the sand up to the shores, where the wind blows it away and piles it up into sinuous mounds, like the shoulders of a drowsing woman, shifting under even the lightest touch.

When we'd walked far enough down to claim the beach as our own and came upon a bleached log, Joe eased himself down onto it and sat hunched forward, hands hanging over his knees, his blood-shot eyes glaring out at the lake. Kevin made a movement to sit, but I grabbed his elbow and propelled him forward, guiding him inland, up a little dune, where we could rest in the modest shade of a scrub pine. We sifted sand through our fingers for a time.

"Sometimes it feels like you're all that's left of those who knew me back then—you and my dad. Truth be told, I couldn't run from it fast enough—and I thought I left it behind, but it caught up."

He was silent, still sifting sand through his big fingers. He grabbed a big handful and flung it to the side. "All I know is that you were supposed to fall for me. Not him." He pushed himself to his feet. "Damn, I'm sorry that came out. I wasn't going to let that out."

I reached up to clutch his hand, tugging him back down to the sand. "But you're right. That's what should have been."

"Yeah, shouldawouldacoulda—that really gets you far in life."

It was veering off into the bitter territory, the barren land where only regret and recrimination and doubt can grow. We needed to right the path, to skirt the wasteland and come out into the blue-sky land... so where was the blue-sky land? There had to be a blue-sky land.

"You've got to lay it all down, Kev. Now that you've told it, really let it go."

"Claire, it's not as easy as that. Christ, you know, they call it baggage—but that doesn't begin to describe it—cuz it's not like a piece of luggage that you can just drop along the way when it gets too heavy. It's up inside you, part of you—so it's like cutting out a piece of you—and how do you do that without bleeding all over the place? And how do you know you can really live without that piece?"

I squeezed his hand. "But you've got to do it all the same."

He stared at me, hard, as hard as tear-soaked eyes can stare. "Have you let it go?"

"No, and I never will. Because I killed him. Whether I meant to or not, it doesn't matter. Accident or not, it doesn't matter. He was lost to me from that night on, no matter what happened."

He tried to pull his hand away but I kept it tight in mine. "When we were children, Jamie and I, we were led into a dark and scary place by the people in our lives who should have known better—and we were left there to fend for ourselves. Did they do it on purpose—lead us into that forest—and leave us there? Or were they just lost themselves? Because everything was upside down and backwards and inside out in that dark place and the birds ate the bread crumbs that we'd left as a trail and the gingerbread candy house was rotten inside and we were fed on deceit and lies. And all I knew was that I had to kill the witch, but in the end I wound up killing the thing she loved best. And wasn't that a sick, eye-for-an-eye rough justice?

"And you happened to wander into those woods and got caught up in the whole weird scene. Or maybe for you it was like a roadside wreck, all flashing lights and contorted metal and you just couldn't take your eyes off it, though you knew you should probably get the hell out of there."

He shook his head. "Wasn't like that at all—for me. It always felt like the right place to be—the best place. And Mrs. Sokol was always kind to me—your grandma, I mean."

"Kind, but blind."

"You got out, you escaped."

"I tried to. I couldn't go fast or far enough away. Told myself I wanted no ties to bind me to anyone ever again. Because I couldn't trust anyone, least of all myself. But there's a price to pay for living like that. For always insisting on being the first to leave. He travels fastest who travels alone. But where are you going and what does it matter? God, you are right about baggage."

"Claire, I didn't want your dad to hear—there's something Jamie said—and I know it was just the anger talking—and the shock—but he said he'd never forgive them."

Whatever crossed my face caused Kevin to shake his head quickly. "I'm sorry," he sputtered. "I just keep saying the wrong thing. Let me just shut up."

"Kev... Kev." I brushed his cheeks with my lips. "We all kill the things we love, sooner or later, with a sword or with... a kiss. And then we save the remnants."

I left him sitting there, shifting sand, furrowing his fingers into its gritty, yielding, soft body.

Strange word, forgive. Traces back to the Old English **'forgifan'** *from* **for** *and* **gifan***, 'to give.' And pardon, too, from the Latin* **perdonare**— **per** *meaning 'thoroughly' and* **donare***, 'to give.' It all comes down to that—the giving.*

Perhaps Jamie was right. There are some things that we *don't—can't—won't* forgive. Some things that are unforgiveable, in others and in ourselves.

When I joined my father on the weathered log, its surface smooth and gray as a bone, he took my hand.

"She never told me outright. But I suspected it. They'd been in town for Thanksgiving and... it just happened. Your mother was pregnant with you, just a couple months, sick and angry... I know, I know, you don't have to say it, Claire. Cuz I've said it to myself. You go along living your life and you think you know yourself, who you are and how you act, and you tell yourself you can accept the fact that your little brother outdid you in any number of ways, the most important thing being he got out of the neighborhood and the mill. And he's landed a beautiful woman, too, but, hey, they live out of town and you only have to see them once a year, maybe twice—and then one particular year she's there and all of sudden, you don't even know who's coming on to who..."

"Baby announcement came the following September. I had you slung across my shoulder for a burp when I read it. Surprised the hell out of all of us. They'd never even told anyone up here that she was pregnant. Took 'em so long we thought he might be sterile—he'd had a case of the mumps before he shipped out and sometimes that happens. Guess we thought wrong. But when they brought the baby up at Christmas, I just got the feeling in the pit of my stomach that I was looking at something that I made. To this day, I wonder why he brought her back up here after he left the service. Why didn't he just find work down there? Was he rubbin' our noses in it?"

He squeezed my hand as he brought it to his chest. "Yes, I know, that's no excuse. None of it's an excuse. We were just..."

"In love? Did it ever occur to you that maybe she had used you as a studhorse?"

In the past—just yesterday even—he might have flung my hand aside like trash and I would have been all too happy to have filled in the blank with a clever, biting adjective and to answer the question for him, to have ranted on, dishing up and force-feeding him the cruelty that he—they—deserved. But today—on this evening, with the sun and clouds in the west turning the sky into a palette of colors biblical, epic—peaches, pinks, day-glo orange, blues bright and faded, violets and a scarier shade, the color of bruised flesh—in the midst of that everyday miracle of the bending of light through a prism of atmosphere, it was enough to let the self-reproach bleed through the silence.

"Twice we talked about going off together. The first time, she was the one brought it up. You and Jamie weren't more than toddlers and they were still living down south and we only saw them a couple times a year. She wanted me to leave your mother and go off and start a new family with her. When I balked, she said I could bring you along because she could mold you, squeeze the Mary out of you." He shook his head. "Maybe you're right, maybe she was looking for a studhorse. That's not how I looked at it, though I know I should've cut it off then, but..."

Again the self-reproach filled the silence. "Second time we talked about it, I did the asking. It was after Joey and your mother... I asked her to divorce Jimmie and marry me and we'd be the family that should've been, with you and Jamie, cuz by then I was pretty sure he was my son... but she refused. I don't know why, she never really gave me an explanation. Maybe she didn't feel like dealing with what I was on a full-time basis. Maybe she just preferred it on her terms. I know at that point I shoulda given her an ultimatum or put a stop to it, cuz it would've been the right thing to do, but we just kept...doing the wrong thing. I kept doing it. Maybe because even when she saw me at my worst—and she did, she did—she never once looked at me like I was dirty, like I was a mistake."

And there it was, another toad squatting in the mellowing light, ugly and beautiful at once, with its warty skin and goggle eyes and frank, truthful stare.

"Did my feelings factor into any of this? Did you ever stop to think about how your decisions would have affected me—and Jamie?"

"At the time you worshipped the ground Peach walked on—seemed to prefer her to your own mother. And Jamie would've been your brother, and I think you wanted that since we lost Joey." He stared at me with dry, rock hard eyes. "Truth? Or is that another fiction I was telling myself?"

I shook my head, as I slowly let my eyes drift from his questioning gaze to the strutting gulls that had clustered around us, off to the side, a feathered Greek chorus hungrily watching the action with their fierce black eyes ringed in gold.

"No, you're right. Jamie and I—brother and sister, yeah, that's how it was... until it changed. And with Peach, yeah, there was a time when I felt that way, when I wished she was my mother and my real mother would just—be gone."

The last toad, perhaps the most loathsome one of all.

He squeezed my hand and brought it to his lips. "She didn't make it easy to love her."

"Some would say the same thing about me."

"On the other hand, I've always been the most lovable cuss this side of Mickey Mouse."

We sat without talking until the sun reached the horizon and began to sink below its watery edge and the colors it bled began to mute under the layer of blue twilight stretching over the sky from the east. Every so often he'd squeeze my hand, as if to remind me he was still there, or perhaps to remind himself. Kevin shuffled up and stood beside us, hands jammed in his pants pockets, then he headed down the beach to the pavilion, in search of a cold drink. The sun was just a sliver of hot orange when I started to rise. My father's firm grip held me down.

"Him dying—that's what finally ended it. In some ways, it was like Joey all over again—same feelings, arguments, blame—only the look of the woman was different. But it was worse, too, because of all the lies that had gone before. And knowing that I had been flat on my ass drunk while she took his body away. I didn't even get to see him before they..." He sucked in a big breath and let it slowly seep out again. "But I didn't know, I swear to you, I didn't know it had gone so far between the two of you until she called me to tell me he was dead. If I'd known, I wouldn't have let... I would have put a stop to it. I would have let it come out—brought it out myself, come what may."

That bitter taste, here it is again, so spit it out. "You should have known. You would have known, too, if you weren't blinded by your own... affairs. No, let me say it the way it needs to be said to a millworker from the south side of Chicago with his white trash slut. You would have known it if you weren't thinking with your own dick." *And that is the last knife I will ever twist in you, I promise, because there is only one weapon sharper than that—and that one I will never use, because even after all you have done, and how wrong you have been, it just wouldn't be true.*

The way his stomach contracted, he felt it, deep. "You're right, I know that, and I'll take whatever punches you throw at me, because I deserve them. Because I was putting the most precious thing I had left in danger. Thinking of my own needs, how hungry I was for the little scraps she threw me. I know I left you out there to fend for yourself, I know that now. All the deceit—our deceit. Claire…" He was almost choking on the backwash of emotion. "The guilt, Claire, and the shame. Don't think I've been free of it. The taste of it, the smell of it, it's in the food you eat, it hangs on the clothes you wear, it's there, all around, wrapping you up, distorting everything, like a camera lens or a funhouse mirror. For years I saw them, my boys—out the corner of my eye on the street, filling up their beaters at the gas station—and her, too. For years I'd follow dark-haired women down the sidewalk and around the corner, thinking, maybe, just maybe—but never walking fast enough to overtake them and look them full in the face—because I knew she was just ashes and dust."

Ashes and dust, cool like the sand, bluish-white under our feet in the purple gauze world we walk through where everything is muted—colors and sounds—and the edges bleed together in a liquid flow – because nothing seems quite solid but your hand in mine…

As we neared the pavilion, in the settling gloom, we could make out Kevin's tall form leaning against the cement barrier that fronted the walkway, his back to the lake. His shoulders were squared, his head high. We slowly worked our way toward him, gingerly stepping around and over the detritus of the beach's day: crumbling sand castles; stout little cairns fashioned from the flat rocks that lined the lakebed at the shoreline; fading messages written in the sand—Katie + Brian 4-ever; tiny plastic shovels forgotten by their dimple-fisted owners; a single blue flip-flop half-buried; a wide, deep hole, industriously excavated, now slowly filling in again, as grains of sand pulled loose from its walls and cascaded to its pit, shaken by the earthquakes from every footfall that skirted its rim. Yet these felt less like obstacles than guide posts, remnants laid down to show us the way back.

"She's dead. When your grandma passed, I called down there—don't even know why—maybe thinkin' she should know. Number was disconnected. Got ahold of one of her brothers and he said she'd died this past November. Cancer." He kicked a Coke can out of his way, thought the better of it and stooped to pick it up. "I couldn't even cry for her. I wanted to, but I couldn't. And now it's just too late to make some things right."

Before we left the beach to step onto the concrete walk, my father stopped and turned to face the water. His left hand still gripped mine, but his free hand slipped into his pants pocket and I heard the brief tinkle of keys and coins tumbling, before he eased it back out and dropped to his knees before the liquid purple shroud spread before him.

"I used to go to church with her, your mother, when Marjorie and Joey were little. Then I had to stop, after... it happened, because that was just too big a lie. Lying to God. How do you lie to God? You can't. When I had to sit through Joey's funeral mass, I thought the church would come crashing down around me. Then your mother... and I was glad, underneath it all, when the priest refused her the mass because that meant I wouldn't have to go through with it. And I would take my punishment like a man, because I deserved it, every blow. Mea culpa, mea culpa, mea maxima culpa." He struck his chest with a fisted hand. "So it's been a long time, but I think I still know the words."

He spoke the Confiteor slowly, a man feeling his way across a chasm on a swaying rope bridge, uncertain if it could hold his weight, unsure of his footing and his balance. He confessed to God and the Virgin and to the saints by name that he had sinned exceedingly in thought and word and deed.

"Through my fault, through my fault, through my most grievous fault," pounding again at his chest as if he could reach through to pummel the beating heart below. "May the Almighty God have mercy on me, forgive me my sins..."

He reached out his hand as if to touch an invisible cheek before him. "I'm sorry. Forgive me." He turned his head to look up at me, his skin drained of color in the twilight.

"I'm sorry. Forgive me."

The dying may cling to life to achieve a purpose. Like O. Henry's heroine Johnsy, they may be waiting for the last leaf on the vine outside their windows to fall. Or for their birthday to pass. Or for some blessed event to take place: a wedding, a birth, a reunion. Some are determined to see the dawn of a new year. They draw from some secret reserve the fluid will to endure. Is it to satisfy their need for one last moment of happiness? Or to give their loved ones a brief joyous respite on the long march into oblivion?

My father willed himself through all three. He sat in his easy chair and watched, enraptured, through his bedroom window, as the cherry tree in his backyard donned her gaudiest gown of flaming yellows and oranges, danced under the October blue sky, the color of hope, and then stripped herself bare. He looked triumphant in November, with a renewed tightness at his jaw and a sparkling intensity in his eyes, as he walked me down the short aisle of Graham Chapel. His arm under mine was firm and steady, as he'd slept the entire car ride down to St. Louis the day before. When he put my hand in Aaron's, he cracked a grin that flashed an image of himself in his days of glory, the stallion of old.

Defiance flared in his eyes, when, as the cold descended throughout December, his limbs gave up the fight and he lay in his bed as the light faded and the early night stretched out beside him. He saw the new year come in, toasted the turn of the century sipping champagne through a straw, but with a swagger; croaked his brag about having lived in two centuries and chuckled as the Y2K fear bubble burst in a flurry of fireworks and the continuation of life as we knew it on planet Earth.

"Fools," he muttered, and we laughed at the thought of twenty-first century fall-out shelters filled with cans of pork and beans and flashlight batteries and mattresses stuffed with hundreds and twenties. "Well, there's gas and electricity to last the first decade—and fuel for the fires," he quipped. We laughed until it hurt too much to laugh anymore and in the quiet after, he looked at peace, with a pleasant slackness at the jaw and a liquid softness at the eyes.

"Don't leave me, Dad."

"I'll never leave you."

But he did.

He passed sometime in the night, for, when I came in to check him in the morning, the skin of his hand was cold to the touch under his blanket. But satisfaction seemed to curve the corners of his pale lips and give ease to his black lashes resting in the hollows under his eyes.

He'd seen what he wanted to see.

The box is back in its drawer. It's full now, my father's copy of Gatsby nestled over Jamie's letters, his decrepit toiletry kit tucked beside the 45s, his Bronze Star and dog tags draped over the perfume bottle. Occasionally, when the angle of the sun is just so or when the clouds pass over its face at a certain time of day, I see him walking toward me on the street, his smile grinning from another man's face. And I grin back and make an old man's day.

This is what it means to be haunted.

ABOUT THE AUTHOR

Joanne Zienty grew up on the South Side of Chicago and vividly remembers the "glow of industry" that lit the night sky with an orange haze. She attended the University of Chicago and Roosevelt University, has a Master's in Library and Information Science from Dominican University and works as a library director for an elementary school district. She lives in Wheaton, Illinois with her husband, two daughters, 3 cats and an obnoxious parakeet. Visit her at www.joannezienty.com.

Made in the USA
Charleston, SC
26 June 2014